A.J. SHIRLEY

A SAGA OF SMOKE AND SACRIFICE

THE AEGIS SAGA

Cover design by Miblart

Map by Natalia Junqueira

ISBN 979-8-9897874-5-6 (paperback)

ISBN 979-8-9897874-4-9 (ebook)

LCCN 2024917289

https://ajshirleyauthor.com

To the one who has walked beside me on this journey and who I know will be with me until the very end, no matter what. This series is a lot of things, but underneath it all, it is a love letter to you—my husband, my protector, my best friend, and biggest supporter. This is our story.

The Kingdom of
Kōsaten

Highview
Beechmont
Duànzào
Portland
Butchertown
Shively
Smoketown
Hillview
Belknap
Valley Station
Clifton
Nulu
Park Hill
Russell
Buechel
Neuburg
Avondale
The Highlands
Springhurst
Shakes Run
Middletown
Crescent Hill
Bon Air
Klondike
Anchorage
Bowman
Hurstbourne
Okolona
Pleasure Ridge Park
Bardstown
Hazelwood
Audubon
Edgewood
Lyndon
Fern Creek
Auburndale
Prospect
Spring Mill
Shelby Park
Glenview
Fairdale
Clarksdale
Lake Forest
Bonnycastle
Park Duvalle
Wyandotte
Fisherville
Kosmodale
Prestonia
N E S W

CONTENT WARNINGS

This book includes explicit sexual content/open door spice, as well as fantasy violence, mythological monsters, and murder. You can find more detailed content warnings for all of A.J.'s books at https://ajshirleyauthor.com/content-warnings/ or by scanning the QR code below. (Content warnings webpage may include spoilers.)

• • •

https://ajshirleyauthor.com
/content-warnings/

<h1 style="text-align:center">A Saga of Smoke and Sacrifice Playlist</h1>

If you like how music sets the tone in your favorite movies and shows, follow along to a playlist cultivated by the author. Parenthetical numbers in the text indicate when to play each song. If the music is distracting to you, simply ignore the numbers and enjoy the story!

1. "Nightshade" by The Lumineers

2. "Set Me on Fire" by Estelle

3. "Running with the Wolves" by AURORA

4. "I Guess You Get What's Coming" by Cody Crump

5. "Dance with the Devil" by Katy Perry

6. "Queen" by Ne-Yo

7. "your guilty pleasure x love is a bitch" by BDSMs

8. "Black Magic Woman" by VCTRYS

9. "Nothing Even Matters" by Lauryn Hill ft. D'Angelo

10. "Yours" by SG Louis

11. "Cut for My Condition" by Various Artists

12. "Wolf at Your Door" by Chloe x Halle

13. "Natural" by Imagine Dragons

14. "Crazy In Love (Remix)" by Beyoncé

15. "Careful" by Lucky Daye

16. "Where You Belong" by The Weeknd

17. "Hit Me Baby One More Time (Epic Trailer Version)" by J2 ft. Blu Holliday

18. "Death Bed (Coffee for Your Head)" by Powfu

19. "Show Me" by Black Atlass

20. "Crown" by Camila Cabello & Grey

21. "Bottom of the Deep Blue Sea" by Missio

22. "Blood Upon the Snow" by Hozier

23. "Season of the Witch" by Lana Del Rey

44. "Waking Up" by MJ Cole

45. "Afterlife" by Evanescence

46. "Epiphany" by Taylor Swift

47. "Legendary" by Welshly Arms

48. "Mount Everest" by Labrinth

49. "Blue Dream by Jhené Aiko

PROLOGUE

THE AEGIS AND THE WANDERER

Macella

The Crown serves the people, at the people's will. Now the people prepare to employ a new monarch to shoulder the duty of securing Kōsaten with protection, peace, and prosperity. Lady Macella of Shively, the king's betrothed from the north, has already established herself as a champion of the commonfolk. Her relationships with sex workers, Aegises, and the poor challenge us all to reflect on the prejudices that infect the very bones of our society. Perhaps our new queen will usher in a new age in Kōsaten's illustrious history—one in which all of its citizens know what it is to be seen and safe. -Excerpt from Royal Bulletin, Harvest Season, Year of the Serpent

Macella couldn't sleep (1). Again. She'd lain staring at the bedcurtains for hours before finally giving up and slipping out of bed. Now she stared at the stars, her bare feet buried in the soft, cool grass of the little courtyard that opened off of their new parlor. More and more often, Macella found herself out in this little patch of night. She would awaken from unsettling dreams, feeling as if she was suffocating. Sometimes only the open air could calm her racing heart and force oxygen into her lungs, allowing her bad dreams to fade away in the night air.

She hadn't appreciated the amenities of their new quarters at first. It had seemed an unnecessary nuisance to relocate, but King Khari had insisted Macella and Aithan take a suite of finer rooms with nearby apartments for the members of her growing entourage. The king had joked that it was a wedding gift, and they hadn't dared resist, considering how well she'd taken the news that the two had married in secret. Since they'd wisely framed it as something long planned and only executed clandestinely so as not to distract from the king's courtship of Macella, she hadn't been able to find fault with their secrecy.

It took some clever rearranging and renovations to ensure that the Protector of the Crown still had adequate access to his charges, but in the end, Macella had to admit that their new accommodations suited the changes to their lifestyle. With her new role requiring she entertain guests more often, the large dining room and parlor garnered frequent use. When the suite was full of raucous laughter or heated conversation, it was nice to be able to open the glass doors that led to their pretty little courtyard and let in the fresh air. It was their own secret garden deep within the walls of the mighty keep.

Macella found herself in the courtyard almost as much as she did her new study. While the courtyard was a place to breathe and train and let herself be at ease, the study—with its walls of books and stacks of papers for her to pore over—was the room where she must be the future queen. There was so much to learn that might aid them in defeating Khari, help them understand their natures, or assist them in planning for a better future. She had to stay focused and alert. She had to study and to listen. Any bit of information she gleaned from her readings or during the endless meetings and engagements that now consumed her life might be the key to restoring balance to the realms and saving Kōsaten.

And so, night after night, Macella awoke from feverish dreams or vivid nightmares and wandered out to the courtyard where she'd read in the grass or drill under the guise of invisibility or simply stare into the night sky. It had been a nightmare this evening—a massive spider with Khari's face wrapping her in an inescapable web as the king vomited a crown of molten gold onto her head. The scalding liquid had dripped down her face, melting her skin and filling her nostrils with the stink of her own burning flesh. Macella had jerked awake and fled to the courtyard, where she was grateful that the harvest season was growing close. Clad only in a thin silk sleeping gown, she let the night breeze cool her flushed skin.

"Do you want to talk about it?" Aithan asked gently from behind her.

He stood on the threshold between the parlor and courtyard, regarding her with quiet concern. Macella knew he'd listen all night or give her space if that's what she wanted. There'd been many nights where he'd either shaken her awake or simply gathered her into his arms and spoken into her mind, pulling her from the confusion of her dreams.

"Just a jorōgumo," Macella sighed, her eyes still on the night sky as she mentally shared an image from her dream. "I'm sure Khari would be pleased by how deeply her little lesson affected me."

The king had revealed her unique gift to Macella before their engagement was made official. She'd had to ensure her intended bride understood the consequences of disloyalty. Macella had not forgotten the terrifying, immersive power of Khari's visions. She would never forget how it felt to be trapped in the jorōgumo's web, insects swarming over her skin, while Khari drove a sword through Aithan's gut.

Aithan silently closed the distance between them and wrapped his arms around her waist from behind. Macella leaned into his solid, comforting warmth. He pressed a kiss to her curls, inhaling deeply.

"It was only an illusion," he reminded her softly. "She can never tear us apart. You are mine and I am yours. For all of this life and every other, if the gods will it. And if they do not will it, I will still make it so."

"I am my beloved's, and my beloved is mine. Wherever you go, there go I," Macella agreed, exhaling a long breath. "She can never tear us apart."

"But she can, it seems, tear you from bed," Aithan grumbled, squeezing her waist. "You're not getting enough rest."

Macella turned to face him. She wrapped her arms around his neck and stared up into his troubled face. Always worrying about her, her Aegis.

"We've already been over this, Lord Protector," she sighed, rolling her eyes fondly. "Our bodies are efficient and adaptable. I don't need much rest."

Aithan pursed his lips. "Your body might not need it, but your beautiful mind does. You spend every waking moment studying and planning."

He was right, of course, but there was nothing she could do about it. Their very existence and the survival of their entire world was at stake. If she missed some crucial detail or made a misstep out of ignorance, she could doom them all. What could she do besides study and plan?

"You're doing it right now," Aithan said quietly, startling her back to the moment. "You're no good to the Fate of the world if you're exhausted and distracted."

Macella felt a pang of guilt. He was right again. She'd once made a promise to cherish every moment they had together and, no matter how this all ended, she intended to keep that promise. This was what she was fighting for after all—Aithan's strong arms around her waist, his beautiful amber eyes staring lovingly into her face, the way everything else faded away when they were close like this. This was her why. She could not forget it.

"Well, since you are so full of wisdom tonight, what should I do to clear my mind and tire myself out?" she asked, brushing her lips lightly over his and pressing closer to him.

(2) Aithan stiffened against her, and Macella was suddenly very aware that only the thin silk of her nightgown and his soft cotton undershorts separated them. The hands on her waist slipped lower and began to rub slow circles over her hips and the curve of her ass.

"I am always full of wisdom," he replied gruffly, leaning down to brush his lips against her ear. "And you know I'm always happy to tire you out."

Macella's nipples tightened, and she arched her back, pushing her breasts against the solid muscle of his chest. The brush of silk against her sensitive flesh and the steady movement of Aithan's strong hands over her rear awakened tendrils of arousal deep in her core.

"Let's see if we can't put you back to sleep," Aithan whispered, before claiming her mouth with his.

Macella opened to him, yielding completely as he slid his tongue into her mouth, awakening her taste buds with his smoky sweetness. His hands kneaded her ass, lifting her slightly, holding her against the hard bulge of his erection. She whimpered and he swallowed the sound, deepening the kiss and guiding her backward until she felt the press of one of the courtyard's ivy-covered stone walls against her back.

Aithan bent his knees, working himself between her legs so that hard swell of his erection lay against her quivering warmth. He slid his hands beneath her gown, greedily caressing her hips, her thighs, her ass, while his mouth teased at the tender spot where her neck and shoulder met. Macella gasped, leaning her head back into the ivy and arching into his touch.

Every nerve ending in her body came alive, heat spreading like wildfire over her skin. She ground against him, her insides clenching with desperate longing. He lifted her, and she wrapped her legs around his waist, the rub of cotton maddening against her swollen sex. Aithan leaned into her, pinning her to the wall, his grip on her hips forcing her into stillness. With agonizing slowness, he rocked his pelvis side to side, his throbbing thickness so close to where she wanted—*needed*—it to be. The pulsating ache inside her reached an almost painful pitch.

"Aithan, please," she moaned, her voice ragged.

In response, he only moved a hand from her hip to cup her breast. He trailed his thumb over her nipple, his callouses rasping over the silk. Macella cried out as both nipples stiffened even further, straining toward his touch. Obligingly, he lowered his head and took one into his mouth, the moist warmth through the silk sending a thousand sensations through her center. She cried out again, a sound between a sob and a moan.

"Let go," Aithan growled around a mouthful of flesh and fabric. "Let it all go. I want to taste your release on my tongue. I want to feel it on my cock."

Macella moaned, tangling a hand in his hair, clutching him to her breast as he flicked his tongue over her nipple, sucking and nibbling in turns. Frantically, she forced a hand between them, sliding it into the waistband of his shorts. The back of her hand grew slick with her own wetness as she fumbled for the delicious throbbing thickness she knew lay beneath that wretched cotton.

Aithan shifted to give her access, moving his mouth to her other nipple, and sending fresh lightning to her core. Her desire had become a pounding ache deep within her, threatening to consume her completely. She wrapped her hand around his cock, loving the satiny feel of it, like velvet over steel. She ran her hand over its length, eliciting a groan from Aithan that made her pussy clench with the longing to be wrapped tightly around him. Fire built beneath her skin, racing hotly through her veins.

Aithan ripped himself away, and Macella's cry of protest turned into something else entirely when he dropped to his knees before her. He pushed up her nightgown, the silk bunching around her waist as he buried his face between her thighs. He gripped her hips, using his thumbs to spread her open, giving him better access. His tongue kneaded her clit, circling lower to dip inside of her before returning to the bundle of nerves at her apex.

Macella whimpered at the stars, head thrown back against the ivy, both hands buried in his hair. Aithan took her clit into his mouth and sucked gently, steadily, filling her with fire. He lifted one of her legs, settling it over his shoulder so that he could truly feast. Macella was grateful that he held her hips in his strong hands as her legs began to shake and electricity spread through her torso.

"Let go," he growled, slipping a finger inside of her. "I want you to cum on my tongue and then I want you to cum on my cock. I want you to cum until you're too wrecked to do anything but collapse."

Macella's hips bucked. Aithan slid a second finger inside of her, curling them in a beckoning motion that prodded the place inside her where the buzz of electricity had reached an absolute frenzy. He licked her clit firmly, rhythmically, his mouth and hands working in tandem to blot out everything in existence but his fingers and tongue.

The stars exploded and Macella erupted, moaning, shuddering, and clutching Aithan's head. He didn't falter for a moment, his nimble fingers and agile tongue pushing her to higher vistas, even as she thought her orgasm couldn't intensify further. She came again, tears on her cheeks, the courtyard ringing with her cries of pleasure.

Her legs gave out completely, and Aithan let her fall onto him. He guided her to the ground, settling on his back in the grass, Macella on his chest. Even as she caught her breath, she was aware that his shorts had vanished, and she could feel every inch of his hard cock pressed against her.

Her skin heated once more as she pushed herself upright, hands braced on the firm muscles of his chest. She slid her fingers through the soft silver hair there and stared into his fiery eyes, darkened with desire. Carefully, she reached between them, positioning him against her and enjoying the way his eyes widened in anticipation.

She eased him inside of her, and the feeling was almost painfully perfect. He filled her, stretched her, touched every quivering, aching bit of her. She thought she might simply implode, so exquisite was the sensation of their joined bodies.

"That's it," Aithan purred. "Let go."

And so Macella let go. She let her hips roll and grind and buck as she rode him in the grass beneath the night sky. Their moans mingled with the singing of insects and screeching of owls, as she worked up and down his magnificent length. She felt his hands on her waist, her ass, her breasts, worshipping everything he could reach, coaxing arousal out of her every pore. Fire built at her center, and Macella couldn't stop it, did not *want* to stop it. She let it go, let it burn through her until it obliterated everything else.

"Fuck," Aithan choked out, thrusting his hips up to meet her at the moment she felt herself lose her grip on the world. "That's it. That's my hell goddess. Gods, you're perfect like this."

She came in a rush of flame and electricity and jagged sobs. Aithan came with her, driving himself deeper, hitting the place inside of her that was nothing but weightless bliss. Hips jerking violently, Macella rode the orgasm for what felt like forever, until she finally collapsed onto his chest once more.

When her body finally ceased its spasming and the sounds of their mingled breaths grew calmer, Aithan spoke. "Well, I'm glad we have this courtyard after all. I don't know how we'd explain burned bedclothes to the staff."

Macella felt so completely wrung out that she hardly managed to lift her head. When she did, her mouth dropped open in surprise. The grass around them was singed black, some of it smoking or glowing with fire.

"Did I actually ignite?" she asked incredulously, touching a burned patch of grass near her knee.

"You did." Aithan shrugged, grinning mischievously. "I suppose I did tell you to let go."

Macella lay down on his chest once more, unable to sustain the effort of being upright. She yawned. "I'm glad hellfire can't hurt you, but it's a shame about the grass."

"Fuck the grass," Aithan replied. "You came so hard you burst into flames. That's a win."

Macella huffed a quiet laugh that turned into another yawn. Aithan kissed the top of her head, before shifting upright and scooping her into his arms. He carried her to bed, then disappeared into the bathing chamber. Macella barely felt the rub of a warm towel against her thighs as she drifted into a deep and dreamless sleep.

***

Aithan

The tinkling of chimes dragged Aithan from bed well before first light. He'd grown to loathe that sound in these many months as Protector of the Crown, though he'd never show it. He made himself breathe slowly, stilling his mind, forcing down the rage that roared in his chest like a caged beast. He pictured his anger as crimson fire, racing through his veins. Meticulously, he chased that crimson fire with silver ice, freezing the rage, taming it, containing it. He felt the ice settling over his features, coaxing his body into perfect stillness, his expression stoic and unreadable.

He could not allow his rage to show, even for a moment. It was his duty, his Fate, to stand steady against the coming storm, protecting Macella from its onslaught while she saved them all. *A shield, a scribe, a sword, a pen. Against hell's fury. Against our end.* He knew beyond a shadow of a doubt that his role in this conflict was always going to be that of the shield. It would be Macella who defeated Khari and restored the balance. He might be the seasoned warrior, but she was the true fighter. He'd never challenged the status quo before he'd met her. He'd been content—or at least resigned—to do his duty, protecting the kingdom from monsters while ignoring the monstrous actions of those he served.

But Macella had changed that, had changed him. And she would change their world for the better just as she'd done for him. She was an absolute force of nature, his wife. He'd known it from the first night they'd met, even more when she stood against the lamia and the sheriff in Hurstbourne, but especially since the moment she'd crossed into Duànzào. She'd appeared before him, materializing from thin air, her onyx eyes alight with a fire that stole his breath. With those stunning silver streaks threading through her glossy black curls and her skin glowing with obsidian flames, she looked more goddess than woman—a beautiful, terrible goddess of death. He'd wanted to fall down and worship at her feet, and he'd known, known as sure as he knew the sun would rise, that he would stand between her and hell until the very end. She would change everything. His job was to make sure she got the chance.

He lingered at their bedside, knowing he should not keep Khari waiting but needing to look at his wife for another moment. She slept like a spoiled child. It was one of the only times she didn't look elegant and graceful, and he imagined her siblings had hated sharing a bed with her. He'd have to ask Lotta about it. Macella was twisted in the bedsheets, having rolled and tossed and stretched out in her sleep as she always did once he let her out of his arms. Her curls splayed across the satin pillowcase, the onyx and silver of her tresses like the night sky streaked with starlight. Her lips were parted, and she occasionally made a little snuffling sound, her nose crinkling endearingly. She was the most beautiful thing he'd ever laid eyes on. Every time he saw her, it struck him anew.

He was grateful to see her sleeping peacefully. Night after night, he'd awoken to her tossing in her sleep or waking suddenly and slipping from the bed. What he saw in her dreams made him sick. He felt impotent in his inability to protect her from her nightmares, just as he'd felt those months ago when the king had taken her into the forest. He'd stood helplessly by, commanded to remain with the convoy, while Khari had led his wife away, alone. He'd let the king take her into that forest and trap her in those ghastly visions. Though he'd hunted for her, followed her scent and those horrible heartbreaking screams, he hadn't been able to find her—couldn't even pinpoint her location until Khari allowed the illusion to lift.

Aithan realized his hands were shaking, his fury rising again at the memory. Deliberately, he loosened his fists, unfurling his fingers one by one. He unclenched his jaw, forcing a slow breath in through his nose, then out through his mouth. Macella's scent permeated the room, pure, undisturbed, and untainted by fear. She was safe, or as safe as they could be given the circumstances, and for once, was sleeping peacefully. It was enough for now. It had to be.

He couldn't help but smile as she rolled toward his side of the bed, her brow furrowing when she found it empty. Even in her sleep, she had the most expressive face he'd ever seen. Perhaps it was the storyteller in her, but her emotions were so loud, so pronounced. Even if he couldn't hear minds, he could have easily read her thoughts on her face. He'd learned the meaning of every twitch of her full mouth, of every shift in those bright black eyes, and every quirk of her brow, though she'd gotten much better at stoicism during their time at the keep.

He felt his rage attempting to surge again at the thought of what this place had taken from her, the way it forced her to play its wicked games. He knew that it wore on her, despite her faith in their cause and her willingness to suffer for it. He would make sure that she lived to see peaceful days. He would make sure she was once again free to wander and write and spread her light throughout the kingdom.

He stooped and brushed a kiss against her temple, inhaling her delicious scent—citrus and cinnamon and acacia flame. Her scent always brought to mind cool streams, crackling fires, evening breezes, and very, very good pussy. He swallowed against the thought, the smell of her and of their lovemaking still lingering in the air. He could still taste her on his tongue, could still see the way she'd looked as she came, bursting into those inexplicable onyx flames. He'd never seen anything like it. The sight of her riding him, her eyes wild and her body aglow with hellfire—it had pushed him immediately over the edge.

Even now, the craving, the need for her threatened to swell again. He pushed it down, allowing himself one more press of his lips to her skin, right at the hollow of her throat. Her skin was warm, but he could feel the chill of the star charm that she wore, now on a delicate chain of silver links and onyx stones. He'd had it made in Highview after her betrothal announcement, deciding the length of braided leather would no longer be suitable for daily wear now that she was to be royalty. His mother's old charm had been cold since Macella was publicly announced as the king's next spouse.

Aithan straightened, sobering once more at the thought of Macella in Khari's grasp, bound to her by law and magic. The ice in his veins threatened to crack, and he again suppressed the heat of anger. He would see her free of that bond, see her free to wander as she wished. He had promised her that, and he would die before he ever broke a promise to her.

Aithan gave her one last, long look before slipping from the room. Off to see the king. Off to serve his wife's betrothed.

And thus continued the *Epic of the Aegis and the Wanderer*.

Part 1

Against Hell's Fury

My Dear Macella,

What can I say to you that I have not already said so often that you probably grow weary of hearing it? If I have somehow neglected to make it clear how much I cherish you, then I have failed unforgivably. You, Macella, are my truest friend, my greatest glory, my most precious gift. Macella of Shively, Savior of Smoketown, crossbreed abomination, defier of gods and kings. Child of Hades, daughter of Matthias and Lenora, the Shield's Scribe, my Macella, my hell goddess, mi corazón, my love, my wife, my life.

I do not know if you will ever have to read this, my love, but I must write it. I would not risk parting from you without ensuring there are no words left unspoken between us, no declarations unmade. I have never had a single regret when it comes to you, and I will not begin to here at the end. No matter how this story concludes, I would not change a word of it. I would not alter one moment of my life with you.

Macella, I waited nearly seventy years for you, without knowing what it was I waited for. I thought that loneliness and solitude were destined to follow me all the days of my long life. I did not dare to dream—never even dared to consider—that there might be another possibility. Then I walked into that brothel and there you were, the most unexpected adventure of my existence.

It was your mind that first attracted me to you. Yes, I heard the other women teasing you and desperately wanted to prove to you I was not what they said, but it was more than that. You see, when I first touched your mind, it was unlike anything I'd ever experienced. I was so used to the monotony of human minds that they'd become little more than ambient noise. But your mind called to me. It was different than any I'd ever touched, wholly unique and utterly familiar. I knew then what I wouldn't admit to myself yet—I knew I'd found my home...

CHAPTER ONE

Macella

"For the love of all the gods, Nyx, are you trying to murder me?" Macella exclaimed, peering around an armload of books at the adorable obstacle in her path. "How did you even get in here, you little goblin?"

Completely unbothered, Nyx blinked her yellow eyes at Macella and yawned. Macella stepped carefully around the little nuisance and set the stack of books on her desk with a thump, before collapsing into her chair with a deep sigh. Nyx hopped into her lap, forcing her soft little head into Macella's palm. Macella gave in and scratched the cat beneath the chin, eliciting a scratchy purr that was one of only a few sounds Nyx ever made. She was as stealthy as a shadow, always lurking silently in the darkness.

"There you are, nwa chat," Charlotte said, entering the study carrying yet another pile of books. "Aisling is looking for you. It seems that a very lovely, very old tapestry was found suspiciously frayed and unraveling, and the Grand Mage is not pleased about it. Aisling is supposed to be confining you to her room as punishment."

Nyx stood and stretched, giving Charlotte a baleful glance. The sleek black cat had appeared one day, as if by magic, curled up on one of Aisling's pillows.

The novice mage had opened her eyes to discover a pair of yellow eyes gazing back at her. Despite her surprise, Aisling had quickly learned that there was no getting rid of the creature, and now Nyx roamed Kōsaten Keep as if she owned the place. There had always been cats slinking around the castle, keeping the vermin under control, and occasionally allowing themselves to be petted, but none of the others were like Nyx.

"Unlikely," Macella said, giving the cat another scratch behind the ears. "She's impossible to contain. I've told Lucy not to let her in when I'm not here to keep an eye on her, but she finds her way inside anyway. It's as if she can move through walls."

Nyx nipped Macella's hand before jumping lightly to the floor. She padded silently out of the study, winding herself through Charlotte's legs on her way out. Then she disappeared through the slightly open door to the courtyard.

"She might be able to," Charlotte replied, shifting her books to one arm, and pushing her glasses up her nose with her free hand. "I read that familiars often have their own magical gifts."

Charlotte crossed the room, organizing the armload of books onto one of Macella's empty shelves. Shaking her head, she took the haphazard pile from the desk and shelved them as well, arranging them by content and importance for Macella's perusal. When she turned back around, there was a gleam in her sister's eye that meant Macella was in for one of her passionate lectures.

"Did you know that some scholars claim cats can move between realms and are often the first thing you see when you cross into the Otherworlds?" Charlotte continued, clearly preparing to launch into a litany of facts. "Others believe they are actually djinn or shapeshifting sorcerers."

Charlotte's new spectacles drew attention to her eyes, which were large, dark, and intelligent, and now sparkling with excitement. Macella smiled as she listened to her sister's lesson on Nyx's potentially magical nature. Her little Lotta had come alive these past few months. The timid, pliable girl was gone, and the woman who'd emerged was incredible.

After she'd realized that she truly had both the freedom and means to live as she pleased, Charlotte had begun exploring her options. She'd trained with

Aithan, had dancing lessons with Finley, and even endured etiquette lessons with apparent delight. But she'd truly found her joy in two places: the castle's library and Lynn's workshop.

Macella wasn't at all surprised by the first interest, so aligned was it with her own nature and what she remembered of Lotta as a child. Her little sister had always loved to listen to her stories; however, Charlotte now far outstripped Macella's own bookishness. Demanding to earn her keep, she'd become Macella's secretary, happy to take notes, handle correspondence, and to search through the library's endless tomes for information. It turned out that Charlotte's eyesight had long hindered her desire to read more. Fitted with a fine new pair of thick-rimmed spectacles, Charlotte began indulging a voracious reading habit that often saw her spending hours in the library or pleasantly passing the time curled up with a book in one of Macella's armchairs. It was Charlotte who'd filled the shelves of Macella's new study, and who provided constant insights that might benefit the future queen.

Macella hadn't, however, expected Charlotte's aptitude for garment-making. They'd grown up with so little by way of fashion that Macella couldn't fathom where her sister had developed such an eye for style. After only a few interactions with Lynn and a couple of timid suggestions to the high tailor, Charlotte had been enfolded into Lynn's flock of assistants. She'd taken quickly to the older woman's straightforward, no-nonsense instruction and now enjoyed a quiet collegiality with the tailor's team.

Even her appearance had changed. Always pretty, Charlotte's newfound confidence had elevated her into an exceptional beauty. She'd taken to tying her curly afro away from her face with colorful scarves that complemented her dark brown skin, which glowed with the health gained from the castle's amenities—like plenty of food, regular medical attention, and comfortable sleeping quarters. Even with her family's recent good fortune, the years of want had still clung to her. It was a wonder how quickly she thrived once her biological needs were met, which was a reminder to Macella that there were many people in Kōsaten whose lives would be drastically altered with access to basic resources.

"That's not even mentioning the ancient civilizations that revered cats as vessels for the gods," Charlotte was saying. "But let's not mention that around Nyx. She already thinks pretty highly of herself as it is."

Macella laughed. "I won't tell her. But I sure hope that the Grand Mage doesn't get ahold of her today."

"Nyx can take care of herself," Charlotte replied confidently. "I saw that vicious snollygoster Queen Annika aim a kick at her the other day, and Nyx was gone so fast it was as if she'd vanished into thin air. The queen nearly fell on her fool face."

"Language, Lotta!" Macella scolded, snorting a laugh into her hand. "You've been spending too much time with Finley."

Charlotte gave her a sly grin, eyes glittering with mischief behind her spectacles. "Finley would say there's no such thing as too much time with them."

"True," Macella agreed. "Still, they've taught me a fair few words and sayings that would scandalize Maman."

Charlotte's grin widened. "I know. Isn't it wonderful?"

Macella couldn't help but laugh again. Their mother, Babette de Pointe, was a hard woman, who was relentless in her pursuit of a more prosperous life for her family. It was why she'd taken in the orphaned Macella, accepting the money Shamira had offered in exchange for their cooperation. Though they'd kept their promise to care for Macella, Babette and her husband Tomas had never learned to love their adopted child.

Babette had more affection for Lotta and the other children she'd borne, but that love manifested in rigid expectations and stern rebukes. She'd bullied Lotta into a meek, docile thing, who dutifully complied with her family's wishes, regardless of her own inclinations. Before Macella invited Lotta to live at court, her sister had been on the precipice of an arranged marriage to a horrible, though relatively wealthy, blacksmith.

Of course, Babette had been overjoyed about Charlotte's new prospects, believing her daughter would soon find a rich spouse at court. Instead, Lotta had focused on herself, and she seemed happier than ever. Macella regularly dodged pointed questions in her mother's letters, which were full of wonderings about how Lotta was progressing in finding a "suitable match."

Aside from one exception, Macella had seen no indication of a potential love interest for her younger sister, and Babette would not at all approve of that choice. Regardless, their mother would have to accept it, because Macella was determined that Lotta would be free to make her own decisions. Babette's endless ambition would have to be satisfied with having just one daughter marrying into wealth and rank.

"Well, at least we do not have to endure her this morning," Macella said. "Neither Maman *nor* Queen Annika."

"It is a relief," Charlotte agreed, settling into her favorite armchair. "Small council meetings are far less interesting than I expected."

Charlotte's role as Macella's secretary had led to her assisting with the duties of the Royal Scribe. Naturally, that often meant joining Macella at small council meetings. As her queenly responsibilities began to take more of Macella's time, Charlotte would take on more of the work of Royal Scribe and would eventually take the position, if she wished.

"Let's hope they stay dull," Macella answered dryly. "The last time King Khari decided to make things more interesting, we ended up betrothed. Besides, I'm sure we'll be very busy for a while, trying to deal with the rise in rifts."

Charlotte frowned. "I pray Finley and Aithan are alright."

"They're fine, cher," Macella replied, reflexively slipping into her familial vernacular, as she often did with her sister. "Dispatching demons is practically no more dangerous for them than sparring with us."

"Now I know you're just trying to soothe me," Charlotte said, rolling her eyes. "You are nearly as good a combatant as they are, while I couldn't fight my way out of a wet paper sack."

Macella laughed but didn't argue with the assessment. Charlotte had actually never seen Macella's full fighting prowess. She intentionally held back unless she was completely alone, invisible, or with just Aithan or Finley. Even restricted to her human abilities, however, Macella was an exceptional fighter. Charlotte, on the other hand, struggled to even hold a sword.

"You just need more practice," Macella lied. "My point is, Aithan and Finley will be perfectly fine and back in the keep shortly. You needn't worry so."

The two Aegises were out closing a rift in the city, King Khari accompanying them to observe. While Macella wasn't worried for their safety, she was concerned about the rifts. This was the third breach in Pleasure Ridge Park in the last fortnight. Rifts used to rarely occur repeatedly in any given region, least of all in the capital, and certainly nowhere near the keep.

Now they were appearing regularly and not just in the areas of town no one cared about. King Khari had been more amused than concerned when a rift had grown in The Bardo, but the latest had been just outside Hülya, the wealthiest area of the capital, aside from Kōsaten Keep. The nobility were growing anxious.

And so was Macella. Hades had warned her that the balance between the realms was in danger and that the mortal realm would suffer utter destruction unless it was restored. Unless *she* restored it. The uptick in rifts and their proximity to the Crown indicated that things were growing rapidly worse.

Macella had to stop King Khari. Soon.

"You're worried about something too," Charlotte said, her eyes shrewdly assessing her. "I know you carry a lot on your shoulders these days, Ella. You can talk to me if you wish. About anything."

Macella smiled. "I know. It's just...you know—"

"Queen things?" Charlotte suggested.

Macella nodded. That was partly true. Being betrothed to a tyrant king was certainly worrying. However, planning to depose said king and prevent the total obliteration of the living realm outweighed her other concerns.

Macella considered confiding in her sister. The two of them spent so much time together, often along with Aithan and Finley. Aisling and Nyx joined them whenever the young mage's training schedule allowed. They all grew closer each day, taking solace and pleasure in one another and creating their own bubble of peace in the den of serpents that was the castle. She was sure their little circle would grow even better once Zahra arrived at court. Macella wanted to be her truest self with her friends, her family. But with truth came danger, and Macella couldn't bear to put them any further into harm's way.

"Would you like to train with me for a bit?" Macella asked, deliberately changing the subject. "I could use the fresh air and a break from these books, and you could use the practice."

Charlotte rolled her eyes again. "How about I walk with you to the training grounds and read a book while you work off your stress?"

"Fair enough." Macella smiled. "Let's go."

The old Lotta would've done exactly what she was asked without the slightest objection. She'd grown more assertive, and Macella absolutely loved it. She grabbed her sword, Lotta hoisted her satchel of books, and together they headed to the Aegis training grounds. Sir Kamau trailed them at a respectful distance, attempting to be as unobtrusive as possible. Now that she was betrothed to the king, Macella was under constant guard.

(3) As she drilled in the cool morning air, she let her mind wander over her "queen things," as Lotta had called them. There was plenty to consider. The frequent rifts were indicative of the realm's imminent destruction. With luck, the cold season would arrive early and offer them a brief reprieve from hell's attacks.

Then they could focus on the task of dethroning King Khari, thereby restoring the balance and dealing with the root cause of the increase in rifts. And then, somehow, they'd rebuild Kōsaten's leadership with integrity and honor and help those leaders create a more just society. And, however they were to achieve that lofty goal, it would have to happen quickly. With each passing day, Khari grew closer to breeding her own Aegis offspring. Every day drew Macella nearer to her coronation as queen. After that, she would be bound by magic, unable to lift a hand against Khari or any of her spouses.

After she completed the Blessed Rite.

Macella thrust her sword into the target with a bit more than human force. Sand leaked from the gash she'd torn. Luckily, Charlotte was so lost in her books that she didn't even look up, and Sir Kamau was facing away, scanning the tree line. Macella quickly swapped out the target, tossing the ruined one into a pile of others similarly destroyed by other Aegises.

The Blessed Rite was the ritual during which she'd stand with King Khari before the gods of light to receive their binding and blessing. It would install her as a member of the Crown, linked to her spouses by the shared thread of King Khari's sovereign power. Of course, that was only if the gods of light found her worthy, and if her crossbreed nature could tolerate their gifts. She didn't know if she could survive it, especially not with the secret of her origin intact.

So, they just had to withstand the barrage of hellspawn until the cold season, when they would have mere months to enact some mad plan to depose the king. All while she played the part of the perfect northern rose, the center of attention throughout the busy cold season, when most of the kingdom's nobility would sojourn at court.

Macella spun, throwing her dagger at a straw man's chest, before beheading him with a sharp slash of her sword.

Macella paused to appreciate the weapon's craftsmanship. She had grown quite skilled with her sword since Aithan presented it to her on their wedding day. The Duànzào-forged steel seemed to maintain its deadly sharpness with little effort on her part. Maybe if a few of the visiting nobles saw her wield it, they'd decide to keep their distance and give her a little peace this cold season.

Last year, the Crown had invited dozens of noble families to join the Aegises, who also spent the season at court. It had been Macella's introduction to life among the elite. The scribe's tales had made the warriors so popular that it had been a coveted invitation and high entertainment for the wealthy guests.

This year, King Khari had invited even more nobles, in honor of her impending nuptials. Macella was to be the entertainment this time. She, the Crown, and their guests would spend the season in celebration and grand talks about their future plans. On the first day of the warm season, Macella would undergo the Blessed Rite, and then they would hold a lavish wedding and coronation ceremony.

Unless Macella and Aithan could somehow overthrow the king during the most auspicious event of the decade, while the castle was at its most crowded, and therefore most heavily protected.

If they failed and the warm season dawned with Khari still in power, hell would surely be waiting, and war would be upon them. Humanity would stand no chance against the Otherworldly onslaught.

And where would the other Aegises stand in all of this? Some of them had already plotted to raise a hellspawn army against the king, damning humanity in the process. Would Macella be able to convince them there was a better way?

She caught herself before she savaged another target. Training was obviously not distracting her from her queen things. Perhaps she should focus on something else for a while.

Sheathing her sword, she plopped down beside Charlotte in the grass. The younger woman jumped, fumbling with the book that lay across her lap. Macella saw the pages held a detailed illustration of a creature she'd seen during one terrifying adventure, when Aithan had been called upon to seal a rift.

"That drawing hardly does the brucha justice," Macella remarked, looking more closely at the page. "I met several of those up close. They are truly the stuff of nightmares."

"Yes," Lotta said, not meeting Macella's eyes as she closed the book. "I am learning about the kinds of beasts Aithan and Finley might be facing out there today."

"Oh, Lotta," Macella replied, giving her sister a one-armed hug. "You shouldn't look at this while you're already worried. When did you even have time to find such a book?"

Again, Charlotte didn't meet her gaze. "I borrowed a few books on the topic a while ago. I've been exchanging letters with a friend who is interested in the subject and doesn't have access to the kind of information we have here at the keep."

Macella hid a smile. She would bet a large sum of money that her sister's curious friend was a certain young Aegis who was new to patrolling the kingdom. Charlotte's cheeks took on a rosier tint, as if in confirmation of Macella's unspoken suspicions. She hadn't yet lost all of her shyness.

Macella took pity on her little sister and decided to change the subject. Lotta would confide in her when she was ready. Perhaps if Macella told her sister more of her own many secrets, then Lotta would've already felt comfortable sharing.

"What's the ghastliest creature you've discovered?" Macella asked.

Gratefully, Charlotte launched into a description of a horrid demon known as the Adze, which took the form of a firefly in order to gain access to people's homes so that it could suck their blood or possess them. Then Macella told Lotta about the lamia, a snake-like demon she'd found draining a child of its blood. They thus passed the morning, trying not to count the minutes Finley and Aithan had been gone.

Suddenly, a sharp pain ripped through Macella's chest. Her star charm turned icy against her skin. She turned her head quickly, hoping Lotta hadn't noticed her eyes shift into their hellform—deepest onyx from rim to rim. They'd responded to the tearing sensation inside of her, knowing it meant another rift was about to open.

Macella could feel the heaviness of the air, the prodding fire of the world rending in two. It was far too close. There had never been a rift this close to the castle before.

That's when the screaming began.

Chapter Two

Macella

Macella forced her eyes to clear and leapt to her feet, unsheathing her sword. Beside her, Lotta scrambled to stuff her pile of books into her satchel. Macella jerked her sister to her feet impatiently. Sir Kamau gestured for them to stay back, his sword drawn as he watched the castle.

"Follow me and stay close," Macella ordered. "I am going to put you into the nearest secret passageway. Stay there until I come back for you."

Macella didn't give her sister time to respond, turning and running toward the castle, her sword at the ready. She could hear Lotta hurrying along behind her, her breathing ragged—whether from fear or exertion, Macella didn't know. With a cry of protest, Sir Kamau chased behind them.

While the knight easily outpaced Charlotte, he couldn't catch Macella, who allowed herself to use just a touch more than human speed. She burst into the nearest entrance, pausing to let her eyes adjust to the relative dimness. She could feel the rift blazing, deeper inside the castle.

"Lady Macella, allow me to secure you—" panted Sir Kamau, catching up at last.

"Save your breath, Sir Kamau," Macella interrupted sharply. "I have no intention of being secured anywhere while the castle is under attack. Take Lady Charlotte to safety."

"With all due respect, my lady, if you will not be taken to safety, then I will not leave your side," the knight replied resolutely.

Charlotte appeared beside them, chest heaving. Macella and Sir Kamau stared each other down. Screams echoed through the corridors.

"Fine," Macella relented. "Lotta, stay close until I find a place for you to hide."

Charlotte's face was tight with fear. "What is happening?"

"Another rift," Macella replied grimly, starting toward the closest screams, toward the pull of hellfire. "In the keep."

Sir Kamau's eyes snapped to Macella, his face stricken. "That is impossible."

"That has never happened in recorded history," Charlotte agreed. "I've read everything I could find on the topic."

"Quiet," Macella hissed. "It is happening now. Watch and listen. Any manner of hellspawn might be lurking these corridors."

Her companions fell silent. Sir Kamau walked ahead of them, diligently surveying their surroundings. Charlotte stayed close to Macella, eyes wide behind her spectacles. The screams were much closer now. As they rounded a corner, they began to see why.

(4) The corridor opened into a wide foyer that branched off into several smaller hallways. Macella knew the mage's annex was nearby and, from the sound of it, its inhabitants were doing a fine job defending it. The halls to the library and infirmary seemed quiet. The latter would certainly prove useful in the coming hours.

Hhhhuuuuunnngggggrrrrryyyyyyyyy!

Macella felt a ravenous hunger invade her mind. She'd heard thoughts like these before. They were actually the first thoughts she'd ever heard. It was how she'd learned of her ability to hear the minds of Otherworldly beings.

A chill rippled down her spine, swiftly chased by a defiant rush of fire. She knew precisely what had come through the rift. And she knew the damage it could cause.

The foyer was in complete chaos. Near its center, the air shimmered with heat. Blazing brightly, an impossible slash of flame hovered a few feet above the ground. Servants and nobles alike were huddled against the walls, shielding themselves behind whatever cover they could find. Separated from the others, Macella saw Queen Annika barricaded in a corner near a narrow passageway, surrounded by knights of the Royal Guard. Captain Drudo and several others stood against a huge creature, roughly the size and shape of a wolf. It was hairless and covered in sharp quills as long as daggers.

"A brucha," Charlotte breathed. "You were right, Ella. The illustration in that book didn't do it justice."

The brucha suddenly curled into a ball of spikes and hurled itself at the knights. They dodged as best they could, slashing uselessly at its impenetrable exterior. The beast stood and shook itself, then turned toward a huddled mass of bystanders.

"Target its underbelly!" Macella cried. "Attack before it curls into itself again!"

The members of the Royal Guard looked toward her in surprise before snapping to attention when Drudo struck his fist against his chest in salute. The soldiers spread out to follow Macella's orders. When it noticed the guards surrounding it, the brucha lost interest in the innocent bystanders, snarling viciously at the knights instead.

"Go!" Macella commanded Sir Kamau. "Help them!"

"Stay here," Sir Kamau replied, though his resigned expression indicated he knew she'd do as she wished.

He ran to join his comrades, who were attempting to draw nearer to the growling beast. Macella turned her attention to the rift. Until it was closed, other hellspawn—both seen and unseen—might be escaping into their realm. She'd never learned to close one of these tears in the fabric of reality, and she certainly couldn't try while surrounded by all these people. Could she slip away and return in her invisible form, then attempt to close it? Surely Aithan and Finley were hastening toward the castle at this very moment, having sensed the rift as she had.

There was a gasp from the crowd of onlookers, along with the screech of metal and a human scream. Macella snapped her attention back to the battle, where a knight fought to free himself from the spike piercing his chest plate.

Drudo.

Macella gasped, noting how deeply the brucha's iron quill pierced the armor just beneath his ribcage. He cried out in pain but used the force of his weight to throw the brucha off balance, tipping the beast to one side. Sir Kamau and Sir Igor rushed forward to throw their weight behind the attack, and together they brought the brucha to the ground. The knights stabbed at the creature's exposed underbelly, eliciting a roar that shook the chandeliers.

"Ella, look!" Charlotte squeaked, pressing closer to Macella. "Something else is emerging."

She was right. As Macella watched, a humanoid figure pulled its head and torso from the fiery gash, twisting and contorting its gangly body as it forced itself through the rift inch by inch. It appeared as a woman—sort of—with long, dark hair hanging in a filthy curtain around its face. It clawed at the floor, pulling itself forward, its nails like talons as they scraped against the stone. Its skin was pale gray and leathery, stretched tight over its bony frame.

Every movement appeared painful as it labored into the realm. Macella could hear its bones cracking as its arms snapped, bent at impossible angles. And still it jerkily crawled forward, talons carving deep gouges into the stone floor.

Its mind was filled with but one thought.

Feed.

"Hide, Charlotte," Macella ordered. "I will find you after this is done."

Macella started forward. The guards were all engaged with the brucha and hadn't yet noticed this new horror.

Charlotte clutched her arm. "Do you even know what that is?" she whispered frantically, her grip almost painfully tight.

"It's a monster," Macella said gently, prying herself free. "And I must kill it before it hurts someone. Get out of here, Lotta."

"Of course you must!" Charlotte agreed, pushing her glasses up her nose. "But do you know how? Because I think I might, and if you'd just listen to me for a moment, I'll tell you."

Macella paused, surprised by the resolve in her sister's voice. She turned back to look into Lotta's frightened face. The younger woman looked petrified but determined. Macella had worn that look many times herself. She took a deep breath and nodded for Charlotte to continue.

"There are several possibilities, I'm afraid, so there's a bit of guesswork here," Lotta explained, slipping automatically back into her lecturing voice. "It might be an aswang or a krasue or even a penanggalan. With those bat-like wings, though, I think it's a manananggal."

"Wings!" Macella exclaimed, spinning back toward the creature.

(5) Sure enough, it was unfurling a set of large, membranous wings as it dragged its legs free of the rift, its body still twitching and cracking as it writhed into the realm. A long, forked tongue darted from its mouth, as if it were tasting the air as a serpent would.

"Okay, let's assume it's the manananggal, now tell me what that means," Macella pressed.

"Right, of course." Charlotte swallowed hard and dragged her gaze from the terrifying creature. "They feed on blood, preferably that of children. Most of all, they love to prey on pregnant people and—um—drink the fetus."

Muscles tensely coiled, Macella barely contained the urge to spring forward and kill the demon. This near a rift, her Aegis blood sang in her veins, compelling her to do what her kind were created to do. Her flames simmered insistently beneath her skin.

"How do I kill it, Lotta?" Macella hissed. "Hurry!"

Charlotte jumped a little at the sharpness, but it seemed to snap her out of her fear for a moment. "Right. When it feeds, it detaches its torso...l—l— Like that."

Muffled cries of alarm and a frisson of terror rippled through the foyer. People were beginning to notice the manananggal. It would've been difficult not to notice the winged abomination that was slowly stretching like bread dough, bloody entrails dangling as its torso cleaved from its lower half, which remained immobile as the top half detached. Retching sounds joined the general clamor of prayers, curses, and weeping echoing through the hall.

"Lotta!" Macella barked.

"It's vulnerable now," Charlotte blurted hurriedly. "We have to sprinkle its bottom half with salt or ash so that it cannot reassemble itself and flee. Then both halves must be thrown into the sunlight or the pyre."

"There must be an empty grate in some nearby room. Fetch some ashes," Macella commanded, and then she was running, trying to hold herself to human speed.

The manananggal had flown into the rafters of the high-ceilinged foyer, shrieking, and splattering the hall with its blood and viscera. Macella ignored the gore raining down upon her as she stalked it from below, prepared to defend wherever it struck. As the roars of the brucha grew pained and then silent, several knights came to flank Macella. She could smell the brimstone in the air and knew the brucha must be dissolving into inky black smoke, leaving only the manananggal to deal with.

"Spread out and protect these people," Macella commanded the knights. "When it attacks, we shall drive it back through that narrow passageway there. Sir Igor, scout ahead and make sure all the doors along that corridor are closed."

The knights moved quickly, Sir Kamau stubbornly moving only slightly away from Macella to guard the nearest cluster of innocents. Even as she instinctively barked orders, Macella spared a thought to hope that Captain Drudo was alive and with the medical mages. She couldn't risk a look away from the manananggal to check for herself.

The creature hissed and flapped its wings, that forked tongue darting out as it scanned the room. Macella watched it, waiting. She freed her iron dagger from its holster, shifting her sword from her dominant hand for the moment.

"Macella, I have the ashes!" Charlotte called from the edge of the hall.

Without turning, Macella ordered a nearby knight to retrieve the ashes and spread them on the manananggal's lower body. "Keep hold of that half. We've got to force it into the sunlight."

The air was taut, silent, aside from quiet sniffling, everyone waiting for the demon to strike. Macella felt the tension rolling off the knights around her, could sense the rift pulsing behind her, promising more bloodshed with every passing moment.

"Hold steady," Macella said, voice rich with quiet command. "On my strike, press forward and drive it back before it can rise again."

Almost as soon as she gave those orders, the manananggal let out an earsplitting shriek. Macella sensed a shift in the creature's thoughts and knew this was the moment she'd been waiting for. The manananggal dropped from the ceiling with surprising swiftness, swooping toward the corner where Queen Annika crouched behind her guards. Macella silently thanked the gods for this bit of luck—the monarch was huddled nearest the narrow passageway. Mouth wide, sharp teeth and talons bared, the creature barreled directly for the young queen.

When the manananggal was just above the reach of the queen's guard, Macella threw her dagger. It pierced one of the thing's membranous wings, ripping clean through and embedding in a painting on the wall beyond. The impact sent the monster careening off course, and it slammed into an ornate vase as it frantically attempted to right itself. The manananggal shrieked louder than ever, the chandeliers rattling as the screeching reverberated through the hall.

"Now!" Macella screamed, and the Royal Guard lunged forward.

They drove the manananggal away from the young queen and into the tight corridor. The creature screamed and attempted to dart free of the passageway, but it was too narrow for it to fully extend its wings, and the ceiling was too low for it to escape over their heads without being in range of their weapons.

Thus, the Royal Guard drove the beast back. Macella retrieved her dagger and trailed after them, behind the two knights carrying the manananggal's ash-covered, writhing lower body. A handful of onlookers dared to follow the procession in hopes of seeing the creature meet its end.

When Macella emerged into the sunlight, the manananggal was already dissolving into a writhing plume of brimstone, its screams splitting the stillness of the early afternoon. In the distance, Macella could see several riders galloping toward them from the direction of the nearest gate. King Khari and the Aegises.

An eerie chill crept over Macella's skin, settling deep inside her bones. She felt, rather than saw, the rift closing inside the castle, just as the riders halted at the edge of the small crowd. Aithan and Finley were off their mounts before the horses had fully stopped.

Aithan didn't hesitate for a moment. Macella could sense him gathering all the information he needed from the minds around him. He passed close by her, one hand brushing hers as he charged into the castle. Finley followed, their beautiful face uncharacteristically solemn.

The king was scowling and cursing as she dismounted, Sir Quirino and Sir Griselda beside her as she stalked into the keep. The members of the Royal Guard who'd dispatched the manananggal quickly busied themselves escorting stragglers to safety. Charlotte remained stubbornly close to Macella, who followed the king toward the other Aegises and the site of the rift.

When they reached the foyer, Macella found that it had all but cleared. The rift and onlookers were gone, leaving only the two Aegises, and three looming, robed figures. The air was frigid, and both Aegises were shivering noticeably, their eyes in hellform—Aithan's crimson and Finley's glowing emerald from rim to rim. Macella wondered how much Aithan was playacting—the Chosen didn't affect crossbreeds as intensely as typical Aegises. Macella felt the compulsion and cold, but she willed her eyes to remain normal. Just to be safe, she lingered in the shadows with Charlotte, far from the robed figures.

The Chosen were three beings of immense power, bound to King Khari by the gods of light, a counterbalance to the Thirteen. Macella had only seen them once before, when she'd watched them execute Shamira. She knew that they'd also executed her own father, these mysterious creatures who seemed crafted from light. They were incredibly tall and slender, completely shrouded in pristine white robes. They emitted a constant glow that obscured their features, aside from an occasional glimpse of their smooth, marble-like hands. The only variation between them was the color of their flawless skin—one had hands of amber, another porcelain, and the third onyx.

"So, you three are alive after all," King Khari spat. "I thought you must surely have suffered some grisly fate since my castle was breached by hellspawn. Lord Protector, have you a report of the damage?"

Macella wondered if the Chosen could speak or whether Aithan could read their minds. She certainly couldn't, but it was different than the mental silence she heard from humans. Instead, she could sense a cold, foreign hum where their thoughts should be.

"The Chosen have cleared all hellspawn and closed the rift," Aithan told King Khari through chattering teeth. "No deaths, but several injured. Captain Drudo's wounds are quite severe."

Finley's head snapped in Aithan's direction, eyes wide. Of course, they hadn't learned of Drudo's battle with the brucha yet. Though Finley was known for breaking hearts with their aloofness, Macella knew her sibling was unusually partial to the young captain.

"What happened here?" King Khari demanded. "Why is this hall covered in blood and the captain of my guard dying?"

Finley flinched, but Khari didn't notice. The king paced angrily as Aithan relayed the story as he'd gathered it from the minds around him. Macella noticed that he downplayed her role in the attack, not wanting to draw the king's attention to her. In his thoughts, though, Macella saw herself reflected again and again from the minds of the knights and onlookers. A lump swelled in her throat at the way they saw her—fierce and fearless. Aithan's thoughts were bright with pride.

"So, you're telling me that both my current and future queen were attacked in our home?" King Khari's voice had gone deadly quiet, her ochre eyes locked on the Chosen. "This has never happened in Kōsaten's history, and it happens to me when I am on the cusp of a second century on the blessed throne. If you cannot even protect my home, what good are you specters to me?"

The chill in the room grew sharper, so much so that Charlotte began shivering like the Aegises and drew nearer to Macella. The Chosen towered over the king, taller than her by another half her height. The cold white light they emitted flared brighter.

"We have always done our duty. You must do yours, Sovereign. Your kingdom is disrupting the balance of this realm. It will be restored. If not by you, then through annihilation and rebirth."

The words seemed to come from all three figures simultaneously, and as sound in both Macella's ears and mind simultaneously. Their voices were an eerie chorus, like a whisper of wind rustling through a field of corn. It made the hairs on the back of Macella's neck stand on end. Instinctively, she moved to place herself between Charlotte and those awful celestial terrors.

"I did not request your counsel," King Khari snapped. "All I ask of you is your service. I'll leave you to your business, and you leave me to mine. Lord Protector, assemble the small council immediately."

The Chosen swept silently from the foyer, taking their cold, austere light with them. Aithan and Finley visibly relaxed once they'd disappeared. Macella felt her own shoulders loosening, that creeping dread finally fading from her skin.

Unfortunately, another distasteful presence took the Chosen's place moments later. The Grand Vizier bustled into the foyer and hurried to the king's side, bowing and fussing over Her Majesty's well-being. The king barely acknowledged him, turning instead to the de Pointe sisters.

"Lady Macella, Lady Charlotte, I am glad to see you both unharmed," King Khari said, bowing deeply. "I am very sorry that you were ever in danger, here in our home, where I have promised you safety. Forgive me."

Surprised by the gallantry, Macella let the king kiss her hand. Charlotte did the same, blushing furiously.

Khari turned away, clapping her hands sharply as she strode from the hall. "Lord Anwir, have this mess cleaned up, and make sure that every guest in the keep remains confined to their quarters today," the king commanded. "But ensure they receive every possible comfort. Tell them their king has ordered a day of rest, recovery, and reflection, in light of this unprecedented tragedy."

Everyone made haste to obey the king as she departed, flanked by her knights. As Macella and Charlotte turned to follow, Aithan stepped into their path.

Before they'd managed to come to an abrupt halt, he'd pulled them into an embrace. He kissed the top of both of their heads.

"You're gross with monster guts," Charlotte complained, even as she hugged him tightly in return.

"And you've got manananggal blood on your blouse," Aithan replied. "As does your sister, who is apparently high commander of the Royal Guard when I'm away."

Macella shrugged. "I only did my duty. Don't believe the embellishments of traumatized bystanders."

Charlotte disentangled herself from Aithan's arms and gave Macella an incredulous look. "You were incredible, Ella. If it wasn't for you, so many more people would have gotten hurt today. You didn't hesitate to fight for your people, like some kind of warrior queen!"

"Macella of Shively, warrior queen of Kōsaten," Aithan murmured, pulling Macella tightly against him. "I saw you reflected in dozens of minds, and every one of them confirmed Lotta's assessment. I am so proud of you."

Macella leaned into his embrace, grateful for the steady beat of his heart, and the miracle of her loved ones surviving the day's horrors. She pulled back, preparing to hug Finley, but they had already slipped away. Macella knew where they'd gone.

She hugged Aithan again, more tightly this time. Drudo would survive. She wouldn't even entertain any other outcome. Her family was okay. They'd all faced death and walked away that day. Next time—for there would certainly be a next time—they might not be so fortunate.

Chapter Three

Macella

A long while later, their little family loosely followed the king's order by confining themselves to Macella and Aithan's quarters (6). They'd all spent the intervening hours in tense strategy meetings, issuing directives, redoubling the castle's defenses, or tending to the needs of the wounded and frightened.

"Gracious me, I'm positively knackered," Aisling exclaimed, plopping down on the plush rug in the center of the parlor. Nyx silently sat beside her and neatly curled her tail around herself, as if showing the novice how to properly behave. "I used more magic today than I ever have in my life!"

Everyone murmured their agreement. Macella could commiserate. She was exhausted and grateful to be clean, fed, and among friends. She had spent the day being the warrior queen. It had been easier to battle the manananggal than it had been to offer comfort and assurances to the castle's frightened inhabitants. But Macella had done it willingly, knowing it was her duty to be present for her people. It was strange to think like a ruler, to think of *her people*. But she had to get used to it. If it should prove her Fate to be queen, she would be the best queen she could.

So, even though King Khari only sent out messages via servants, and her spouses remained locked in their rooms, Macella had visited every guest, helped in the infirmary, and personally thanked the servants for their hard work under such extenuating circumstances. It had been a difficult day for the staff. She would have to find a way to do something special for them.

You don't have to solve it all today, your grace, Aithan thought at her, pulling her back to the present.

Macella appreciated the reminder, happy to focus on her friends instead of her people. Washed clean of monster blood and dressed comfortably in a loose tunic and leggings, she sat on one of their sofas, curled against Aithan's side.

"How is Drudo? He was unconscious when I visited," Macella said, gratefully accepting a glass of wine from Lucy. "We can fend for ourselves, Lucy. Please go and get some rest."

Draped across a plush chaise, Finley looked bored and beautiful, but Macella saw the way their mouth tightened. "He hasn't awoken, but the medical mages say he's stable."

"Is that where you went after the king released us?" Charlotte asked, brow pinched with concern. "I was worried sick about you all morning, and you didn't even let me get a good look at you to make sure you were okay."

"Don't fuss, Mother dear," Finley drawled, examining their nails, and suppressing a pleased grin. "That godawful hallelujah trio gives me the collywobbles. I had to get away from that freezing foyer immediately. The infirmary was nearby, so I decided to check in on Aithan's young captain. I had no notion you were fretting over me, darling."

From the looks on Aithan's, Aisling's, and Charlotte's faces, Finley's nonchalance wasn't fooling anyone. Even Nyx seemed aware. She left her spot at Aisling's side and rubbed her head against Finley's dangling hand. They absently scratched behind her ears, eliciting her scratchy purr.

"The medical mages here are the best I've ever seen," Aisling said brightly, propping herself up on her elbows. "I wish I'd been born with healing magic like theirs, instead of stupid foresight."

"Are you kidding?" Charlotte exclaimed, eyes wide with wonder. "You can see the future and do spellwork. You're incredible!"

Aisling's pale cheeks pinkened, and she busied herself by adjusting the elbow-length gloves she always wore these days. Lynn had fitted the novice with at least a dozen pairs, made of different styles and fabrics, perfect for a variety of weather conditions and activities. Stylish though they were, their real purpose was to allow her to interact with her friends without fear of their touch provoking a vision, as Macella had on two previous occasions.

"Me? No, I'm barely average." Aisling demurred, brushing off Charlotte's compliment. "Maybe that'll change when I'm a full mage and know how to better control my Sight. I'm still learning simple spells that I should've mastered as a child."

"That's not your fault," Macella interjected firmly. "It's unfair that so many born sorcerers never gain access to formal training."

"Ella is going to change that kind of thing when she becomes queen," Charlotte said, beaming at her.

Macella felt a stab of anxiety, even as her heart swelled at the love and confidence in Lotta's words. There was so much that her friends didn't know about the task that lay ahead of her. She hoped she wouldn't fail them.

"If there's going to be a kingdom for Macella to change, we have to survive this growing onslaught of hellspawn," Aithan said, shifting the subject.

"Please tell me the small council came up with a plan," Aisling begged. "I could happily live the rest of my life without ever seeing another monster."

Nyx padded silently back to the mage and nestled in Aisling's lap. She stared around the room with her lamplight eyes, and Macella wondered how many things the cat saw that people couldn't. Nyx locked eyes with Macella and blinked slowly, her yellow eyes full of mystery.

"For now, we're calling reinforcements to the capital," Aithan said. "We've sent word for Kai and Diya to come at once. Since Young Jacan worked so well with Finley and me, we've also sent for him. Together, we'll be more than capable of defending the capital and surrounding region. When the remaining Aegises arrive for the cold season, we'll devise more long-term strategies."

Finley cast a sidelong glance at Charlotte, who was suddenly very interested in the book she'd been idly perusing. Her cheeks had taken on a rosy glow. One corner of Finley's mouth quirked up in a smile, but they didn't say anything. Macella laughed inwardly. It seemed Charlotte wasn't fooling else anyone either.

"My goodness, I've never met so many Aegises," Aisling gulped. "Are they all like you two?"

"Darling, there is no one like me," Finley replied breezily. "They're mostly like Aithan of Auburndale, though."

Macella snagged a decorative pillow from the end of the sofa and hurled it at Finley. They caught it easily and launched it at Aithan, who batted it out of the air with a longsuffering sigh. Charlotte giggled, but Nyx jumped up and disappeared through the glass doors into the courtyard, out of the range of flying projectiles.

"We're all alike in our training and obviously some aspects of our appearance," Aithan told Aisling. "But our personalities are as varied as anyone else's."

Aisling blushed furiously, her pale skin an alarming shade of scarlet, even brighter than her hair. "Of course, I didn't mean—it's just, you know. You two aren't as scary as Aegises are supposed to be."

Finley laughed musically. "Oh, honey, you have no idea."

Aisling's eyes widened, and Charlotte leaned from her seat to pat the novice's shoulder. The two were close in age and experience, though Aisling was more worldly. They often allied themselves when the entourage gathered this way.

"Don't let them frighten you, cher," Charlotte said, the familiar patois of the endearment reminding Macella of home. "The Aegises are all just people. And they can't be much scarier than the king."

"Now I'm offended," Finley protested, but Aisling looked relieved. "And what does Lotta know about it anyhow? She's only met extraordinarily civilized types like Aithan and me. And Jacan."

"And you're all lovely," Macella replied, sparing Charlotte from having to respond. "You'll like Valen too. Most of the others keep to themselves, but it's only because they're used to solitary lives."

"And because they're pricks," Finley said dryly. "Especially Cassian and Cressida."

Macella snorted a laugh. "Let's not taint Charlotte's and Aisling's opinions before they even meet the others."

"Finley has a rivalry with the twins," Aithan explained. "So, you'll have to ignore their opinion and form your own."

"You don't like them either," Finley said accusingly.

"Perhaps, but it's not for such a shallow reason as yours," Aithan shot back.

Macella laughed again. This easy, teasing banter was one of her favorite things about her life with her chosen family. She'd never had this before, hadn't known what she was missing during all those years of being an outsider.

"Cassian and Cressida are uncommonly beautiful," Macella explained. "They often compete with Finley for suitors."

Finley scoffed. "My dear Macella, there is no competition. And as for my reasoning being shallow, I will have you know, I am very deep and contain multitudes. Besides, I was breaking hearts long before they were born. Their audacity to even presume to challenge me is unforgivable."

This time everyone laughed, Nyx creeping back into the room at the sound of it. Macella loved that sound. She wanted a life where she and her loved ones had the safety and freedom to laugh together as often as they wished.

"Will we still get together like this after all of the Aegises and fancy nobles are here?" Aisling asked timidly. "Or will you all be busy with your other friends?"

Everyone looked at Macella. Finley grinned with wry amusement, but Charlotte looked almost as anxious as Aisling. Even Nyx watched Macella, waiting for her answer.

"We will be busier than we are now, but we will always make time for each other," Macella promised. "You all are the most important people in the world to me."

Aisling smiled widely, sagging with relief. "This is the first time I've ever had friends. I'm still learning how it all works."

Everyone laughed, and Aisling blushed, laughing too. Aithan squeezed Macella to his side, his arm around her shoulders, and kissed the top of her head. Charlotte looked thoughtful.

"We should have a name," she said. "Like a guild or a family name."

"Yes!" Aisling exclaimed. "We need a name! Then we're our own little coven. Just the five of us." Nyx nudged Aisling's hand. The novice rubbed the cat's head apologetically. "Six, I mean."

"Seven," Macella amended. "Zahra will be here soon."

"Eight," Charlotte added quietly. "Jacan greatly admires Finley and would do anything for Ella and Aithan."

Macella smiled, looking at each of her friends in turn. "I have never had people who make me feel like this—like I am one of many. I've always been full of fire, but I was a solitary flame. Those closest to me tried to smother that fire and make me softer, safer, more palatable. But you feed the fire. You make me feel stronger. You give me something worth burning the world down for. I've always been willing to stand up for others, but you've given me something of my own to fight for."

"I never had anyone either," Aisling said. "I burned with rage and resentment, but then you lot showed me I could channel that fire and let it drive me to be more, to push back against the society that let me down."

My hell goddess, Aithan thought at Macella, eyes crinkling in a smile. Then he spoke aloud. "Aegises are forged in flame, but Macella ignited something new in me when we met, and that fire has only grown with the addition of each of you."

Charlotte pushed her glasses up her nose. "I had a lot of family around me, but I was still alone, suppressed by other people's expectations. I didn't know there was still fire within me. You all helped me find it."

"You do certainly have a knack for sparking something in others, Macella dear," Finley drawled lazily. "I personally had no intention of finding myself in league with you, and look at me now."

Aithan chuckled, shaking his head, before turning his adoring gaze on Macella. "You simply cannot be contained. You impact everyone you touch, spreading your fire everywhere you go.

"Well, that's it then!" Aisling declared. "From henceforth, Queen Macella's entourage will be known as the Wildfire Court."

Finley sat up, and Macella prepared herself for a witty retort or an aloof dismissal. Instead, they rose and refilled everyone's goblets, before lifting theirs in a toast. The corner of their mouth quirked up in a smile. "To the Wildfire Court," they proclaimed.

Grinning, everyone else lifted their goblets. The warm light of the setting sun shone through the courtyard's glass doors, illuminating the parlor. Macella smiled at her family, and the tension from the day melted away.

"To the Wildfire Court!" they chorused.

Eventually, Charlotte declared herself exhausted and, as a mage-in-training, Aisling had a curfew to adhere to. The two young women departed arm-in-arm, Nyx trailing silently at their heels. Not long after, Finley claimed they were ready for bed, as well, though Macella suspected they'd be returning to the infirmary.

"Alone at last," Aithan murmured into her hair, trailing a hand down her arm. "I love our family, but I must admit I have been waiting for this moment all day. I've craved you desperately since the moment I saw my warrior queen reflected in all those adoring minds."

(7) Macella shivered, though her skin heated at his touch. She lifted her head to look at him and grew even hotter. The lust in his eyes filled her stomach with butterflies.

"You've seen me fight before," she replied. "What's one little manananggal compared to crossing into Duànzào and fighting three Aegises to free you?"

Aithan's eyes dropped to her lips. When they lifted again, they'd darkened with desire. The arm he'd had draped around her shoulders all evening tightened, pulling her closer.

"I had the same reaction then," he growled, his gaze falling back to her lips. "Or do you not remember how vigorously we celebrated our victory after that battle?"

Macella flushed, remembering. It had been a terrible and exhilarating thing, using her newly unearthed Aegis gifts to fight at Aithan's side against their misguided siblings. Once they'd come to a tentative truce with Kai, Diya, and Finley, they'd been left alone after days of separation, danger, and fear. Their Aegis blood had been running hotly through their veins, still full of battle adrenaline, and they'd turned that passion on each other. Macella had learned then how her flames responded to her emotions—she'd had to be careful not to set their little cabin ablaze.

Aithan inhaled sharply, sensing and scenting her arousal. When he looked at her mouth again, Macella parted her lips in welcome, and that was all he needed. He kissed her, one hand tangling in her curls, cradling her head, as he slid his tongue into her mouth and filled her with his smoky sweetness.

Macella moaned against his lips, and he tugged her hair gently in response. She arched her back at the sensation, pressing her breasts against his side, nipples stiffening against the soft fabric of her blouse. She hadn't bothered with a corset or binder as they relaxed that evening, so the thin material did nothing to disguise her eagerness.

She slid a hand over his chest, marveling as always at the honed muscles beneath his shirt. His breath caught as she moved her hand lower, over the taut ridges of his abdominal muscles, and then lower still. She stroked his cock through his trousers, finding it hard and ready. Aithan moaned, his tongue stumbling in its exploration of her mouth. Macella took advantage of the moment, sucking on his tongue while she squeezed and rubbed at the throbbing bulge of his erection. A promise.

Aithan groaned, breaking away and letting his head fall against the sofa back. The desire emanating from his mind made Macella's own arousal skyrocket. She stared at his beautiful face as she unbuttoned his pants, reaching inside to free his cock from its confines. Aithan drew in a sharp breath as she wrapped a hand around his shaft and slid off the sofa to kneel between his legs.

"Macella," he choked out, orange eyes blazing. "I am too riled. I am not sure I can be gentle and patient."

She smirked up at him, tracing a lazy circle around the tip of his dick with her tongue. His hips spasmed at the contact, and he let out another long, low moan. She flicked her tongue over his tip, licking away the salty wetness.

"Then don't be gentle and patient," she replied. "I fought a demon today. Fuck me like a warrior. I want you raw, and reckless, and rough."

She took him into her mouth in one swift movement, forcing him as deep into her throat as she could manage. With her hand squeezing the rest of his considerable length, she lingered, taking him incrementally deeper into her mouth. He moaned as she finally gagged and then began to suck.

"Gods, Macella," Aithan gasped, his hand finding its way back into her curls. "Fuck, why does every part of you feel so incredible?"

Macella worked her mouth up and down his immaculate cock, her hand pumping him in time with her mouth. He moaned, leaning his head back again, looking absolutely beautiful in his bliss. Macella sucked harder, moved faster, wanting to wring every ounce of pleasure from him.

Both of his hands were in her hair now, his fingers convulsing against her scalp. She could tell he was fighting the urge to thrust his hips up and force himself deeper into her mouth. She did it for him, loving the way it felt and the sounds he made in response. She sucked and stroked him, not minding that her eyes teared up when she gagged. Macella loved being in control, making the stoic Lord Protector lose his composure.

"Enough," Aithan growled, pulling her head away from his lap. "I need to be inside you right now."

He didn't give Macella a chance to protest, standing and lifting her from the floor in a single, fluid motion. In another moment, he'd forced her leggings and panties down, nipping at her taut nipples as he helped her step out of her clothes. She whimpered, feeling wetness spreading to her thighs.

Aithan spun her around, urging her onto the sofa on her knees. She looked back at him over her shoulder as he stepped out of his pants, his cock rigid and glistening. Macella's pussy clenched, her need rising to match his.

Aithan positioned himself behind her, jerking her hips up roughly. She arched her back eagerly as he slid a hand up her spine, pressing her head down, then gathering a handful of her hair. Macella buried her face in a throw pillow, waiting, pussy quivering, wanting him inside of her, needing him so deep that their bodies became one.

"Do you still want it rough?" Aithan asked in a strained voice.

Macella could feel his need struggling against his restraint. He would be gentle, if she asked. She knew that. But that was not what she wanted.

She lifted her head from the pillow to look over her shoulder at him, and let her eyes slip into their glowing onyx hellform. "Fuck me, Aegis," she said.

Her words unleashed him. One hand gripping her ass, the other pulling her hair, Aithan shoved into her hard and fast. They both cried out as he buried himself completely, bottoming out in that way that made Macella's stomach flip deliciously. The feeling of finally connecting was so intense it was almost painful. Macella panted, heart racing.

Aithan didn't give her a moment to catch her breath, thrusting into her again and again, hard and fast and deep. Macella whimpered and moaned, tears wetting her cheeks, hands clutching desperately at the sofa frame. It felt so terribly, unbearably good. She thought she might explode.

Aithan did not relent, did not restrain himself. He released her hair so that he could grip her hips with both hands. His powerful thrusts drove her into the cushions, filling and stretching her and urging her toward a fiery precipice. Macella bit the pillow, letting it absorb her cries of ecstasy.

She came in a spasming, shuddering mess, hips bucking against Aithan's strong grip. She came crying and cursing and calling his name. She came again and again, and he kept fucking her, and it felt so good she thought she might die.

Finally, he shuddered and thrust hard, holding her hips, and pulling her tightly against him, lingering as deeply as he could. She felt him swell inside of her, and she quivered, the aftereffects of her orgasm lingering at the sensation. He came a moment later, groaning her name as he finally found his release.

They collapsed together, Aithan still inside her, both breathing raggedly. Macella loved the weight of him, the solid *realness* of him. There was nothing better than being with him this way, so intimately connected. She sighed happily.

"I wonder if crossbreeds need a mage's help to reproduce," Macella mused, idly tracing the veins on his arm as they lay together on their sides afterward. "We know that humans and Aegises can procreate, with magical assistance, but what of us? We're both Aegis and human. Maybe it works differently for us?"

Aithan went very still, and his voice was careful when he spoke. "Have you changed your mind about wanting children?"

"Gods, no!" Macella exclaimed with a horrified laugh. "I only thought about it because I am practically drenched in your seed right now. Don't worry—you know I take my contraceptive herbs faithfully."

"Perhaps I should start them as well," Aithan said thoughtfully. "Aegises have never needed to. But you're right that we don't know whether the same applies to Aegisborn."

"It's so frustrating how little we know about our capabilities and limitations," Macella sighed. "One day, we won't have to keep our origin a secret. We'll be able to proudly proclaim who and what we are."

Aithan hummed thoughtfully. "You know that, if you ever change your mind, we can find a way, right? I am not interested in parenthood, but I would happily and gratefully embark on that adventure with you, if it's what you wish."

"I know," Macella replied, extricating herself from his arms so she could stand. "Let's check in about it in, say, a few hundred years."

Aithan chuckled, standing, and stretching luxuriantly. "That sounds like a fine plan. Now, let us get you cleaned up. I can't have you getting into bed all drenched in my seed, as you so delicately put it."

They'd just gotten cleaned up and were climbing into bed when there was a soft rap on the outer door. Aithan left to answer it, returning after a few moments with a folded page and a gold box. He slid into bed beside Macella, handing her both items.

Macella unfolded the paper to find a hastily scribbled note of only four words:

Thank you.

Queen Annika

Macella lifted an eyebrow in surprise and handed it to Aithan to read. He gave a noncommittal hum. Macella was less surprised by the box, immediately recognizing the handwriting on the card. She'd seen it often lately, since Khari's idea of courtship involved lots of expensive gifts.

Allow me to apologize again for today's unfortunate incident. Nevertheless, I am pleased to hear that you conducted yourself bravely, my affianced. Please accept this small token as befitting a warrior queen.

Fondly, King Khari

A pair of cuff bracelets lay atop a fold of garnet satin inside the elegant gold box. The bracelets were made of intricately carved gold, inlaid with patterns of garnet gemstones and black diamonds. They were breathtakingly beautiful.

Macella hated them.

"Those will look nice on you," Aithan said quietly. "You can't deny she has excellent taste."

Macella grimaced, closing the box and tossing it onto her bedside table. Then she snuggled against Aithan, draping an arm across his chest. He stroked her curls.

"I cannot believe Annika actually thanked me," Macella marveled. "This day has been full of surprises."

"Hmm," Aithan murmured, heaving a sigh. "I have the sense that there are more surprises yet to come."

As usual, his instincts proved correct.

⚜

Aithan

This time, it was Aithan who lay awake, staring at the bedcurtains. Macella had fallen asleep in his arms and was dreaming peacefully, her mind awash in warm colors and gentle sensations, no trace of the day's horrors disturbing her rest. He could still see the image of her as it had been in the minds of the knights and onlookers, fearless and beautiful despite the blood and viscera streaking her skin and clothes.

She'd somehow contained herself enough to resist igniting her flames or letting her eyes shift into hellform, but she still looked every bit the warrior with her sword drawn and daggers at the ready. And she issued orders like a queen. She'd been cool and collected, had acted instinctively to protect those people. Her quick thinking had saved lives.

He knew that she was unique as a human-Aegis offspring, but it still surprised him how quickly she'd taken to her abilities and training. Her swift adaptability was a gift from the gods, given how little time they seemed to have at their disposal. It was hard to believe that he'd met her only seven seasons prior, after seventy years of solitude. He'd read that, in ancient times, years were much shorter, less than 400 days in some cultures. It felt like he'd crossed into such a place, his time with Macella truncated in comparison to the interminable years before she'd upended his life.

Now that he had his earliest memories back, he knew that the years before his mother's death had also passed too quickly. Time was strange that way, meandering during the worst experiences, and racing past the best days. He'd still been so young when Queen Rhiannon had taken him. Those happy times with his mothers were but the blink of an eye compared to the agonizing months of being studied and tormented in the bowels of Kōsaten Keep. He'd been relieved when they'd finally wiped his memories and sent him to Smoketown. Unfortunately, it had been but a temporary respite.

He'd spent the next decade training and enduring the soldiers' abuse and mages' experimentations. But all the while, he'd kept one secret to himself. He'd quickly realized that he had gifts the other children didn't. He could use those gifts to keep himself safe—reading minds and intentions so he knew when to speak and what those around him wanted to hear him say, when to fight and when to appear cowed and broken. He did not remember the mother from whom he'd inherited those gifts, or the mother who'd taught him to control them, but he'd instinctually remembered the skills they'd lovingly drilled into him. He excelled at every task put before him but remained an island unto himself. An outsider among outsiders.

He was the youngest to ever cross into Duànzào. Emerging with Lucifer's blessing had felt like finally being free of skin he'd outgrown. It was as if he'd been living blindfolded with weights on his limbs. He'd suddenly been able to stretch, to stop holding back. When he'd become a shield and began patrolling the kingdom, he'd thought that he'd reached the pinnacle of his existence. He was free to roam, and fight, and find his pleasure where he so chose. It had been enough.

Then he'd met Macella, and everything had changed again. He realized that there was another layer of skin to shed. It was as if he'd never fully expanded his lungs before she walked into his life. A missing piece of his identity had clicked into place, and not only could he see and stretch, but he could truly breathe.

Time, which had seemed an endless thing as he moved through decade after decade of single-minded existence, now seemed to be slipping through his fingers. Perhaps that is why he found himself awake, cherishing these quiet moments where he could hold her in his arms and listen to her steady breathing, smell her citrus and cinnamon scent, feel the warmth of flame simmering beneath her skin. They should have centuries of nights like this, endless evenings laughing with their family, millions of hours to spend loving and being loved.

But the sands of time were moving quickly now, rushing toward an inevitable apogee.

Aithan was troubled by how fast matters had escalated. Escaped hellspawn seemed to be launching coordinated attacks near the capital. They'd typically avoided it in the past, preferring to cross into the realm in areas where they might hunt and feed unnoticed. Now, however, they'd been emboldened to strike at the very seat of Kōsaten's power.

It should've gone against the demons' instincts, to gravitate toward a place marked by the gods of light and inhabited by creatures of that light. If they were purposely crossing into Pleasure Ridge Park, they were obviously prepared to wage war. If it came to that, Kōsaten would be reduced to the embattled wasteland it had been before Khalid's rule.

Aithan had dedicated his life to protecting the realm against just such a fate, but everything was different now. He was no longer defending a world that he lived on the outskirts of, shunned and alone. He had a best friend, a confidante, a wife. And, miracle of miracles, he had yet more to fight for.

He had a family. A strange, like-minded group of former outsiders—the Wildfire Court. And, together, they had a future.

He would fight for that future. Not only because he believed in the better world they were building, or because their civilization would perish otherwise, but for this family he'd found. And for the little boy who'd been knocked unconscious by his mother's pain, only to wake up beside her dead body. For his own wounded heart that had finally found its way home.

Chapter Four

Macella

The days following the brucha and manananggal attack were a flurry of activity. Macella spent most of her time visiting the injured, comforting the frightened, and assisting in repairs where she could. Aithan and the rest of the Wildfire Court were likewise occupied, helping as much as their own duties allowed.

It was nearly a week before the castle returned to some semblance of its normal routine and the king gathered her small council for a tense planning meeting. She was still angry about the breach of the castle's defenses and was clearly looking for someone to take her frustrations out on. Her ochre eyes were cold and hard as she smiled and exchanged pleasantries before calling the meeting to order. Macella felt a shiver of foreboding when those flat, adder's eyes met hers.

She looked away quickly, scanning the rest of the room. Seated at the king's left hand, Queen Annika was pale, and there were dark circles beneath her bright blue eyes. Rather than her usual false politeness or thinly veiled hostility, she gave Macella a small, shaky smile in greeting, before settling into an unusual silence.

Observing the young queen's odd behavior, Charlotte caught Macella's eye from the other side of the room where she sat at the desk of the Royal Scribe. She raised her eyebrows in surprise, cocking her head toward Annika. Macella lifted her shoulders in an almost imperceptible shrug.

The meeting soon began, the king's advisors settling into their spots to her right, while her spouses sat opposite them. King Khari brooded at the head of the table, her crown tilted forward to shadow her face. As Acting Captain of the Royal Guard, Sir Griselda held Captain Drudo's post behind the monarchs, while Aithan stood at attention behind the king.

Now that she was to join the Crown, Macella officially sat on the small council, seated beside Monarch Meztli in the place that had belonged to the late Queen Awa. Every time she sat down, Macella remembered that, after nearly a century at this table, Queen Awa had been accused of treason. The elder queen had sat in the very chair Macella now occupied, as King Khari passed a supposedly lenient punishment for her spouse's alleged crime.

However, after an elaborately staged amicable separation, King Khari had ruthlessly murdered the former queen. She hadn't shown the slightest hesitation or remorse. The blessed throne was a tenuous perch. Macella would never let herself forget it.

Monarch Meztli brushed a gentle hand over hers beneath the table, their face carefully blank as they attended to the conversation. Macella relaxed a fraction, grateful for their comforting presence. Thanks to their gift, Meztli likely felt her anxiety and anger.

They'd continued to be a friend to Macella after the Crown's convoy had returned from the king's centennial tour. Though Meztli had stayed behind to oversee matters at the keep, Macella was certain they suspected what had truly befallen Awa. Though they'd never discussed it, Macella knew Meztli grieved deeply for the former queen and blamed Khari for the loss. While they seldom showed much emotion, Macella knew them well enough to notice they'd been colder toward the king of late. She wondered if Khari noticed or cared.

"Lord Kasper, what of the harvest?" King Khari demanded suddenly, snapping Macella out of her reverie. "Our profit margins from the warm- and hot-season crops were unacceptable. Down fourteen percent from last year's yield."

Lord Anwir, who had been interrupted in his report by the king's abrupt shift, pursed his lips, evidently trying not to appear insulted by the slight. Across from Macella, Lord Kasper smiled affably, shuffling through the dossier of papers before him. King Khari did not return the Grand Treasurer's smile.

The former Grand Treasurer, Lord Theomund, had finally become too ill and infirm to serve. Macella imagined he was relieved to finally be free of the job, though he wouldn't have much time to enjoy his retirement. The medical mages gave him but a few weeks to live. The old man had been forced to work well into his advanced years, because the Crown couldn't agree on a replacement. When they could put the decision off no longer, Queen Annika had somehow managed to manipulate the council into giving the position to her cousin.

"I'm sure we're on track to improve those numbers," Lord Kasper said, still smiling, though it didn't reach his cold blue eyes that were so like the young queen's. "Lord Theomund, though a fine man, was unable to attend to matters as I can, given his advanced age and infirmity. I, however, meet regularly with our farm operators and can assure you all is in hand."

Macella stifled a sigh. So many words used to say nothing at all. She glanced to Aithan. His face remained stoic, but the slight quirk of his mouth when he felt her looking showed her that he was thinking the same thing. Macella knew that Lord Kasper was in for a rude awakening. He hadn't been in the role long enough to have King Khari's temper directed at him, but the king's steely expression indicated that was about to change.

"And what plans have you and the operators concocted to improve our numbers?" King Khari asked quietly.

Lord Kasper's smile faltered. He must have finally noticed the venom in the king's tone. Macella saw him glance toward Annika, but the young queen appeared preoccupied with her own thoughts. Her gaze was unfocused, fixed on a far window. She didn't seem to notice her cousin's distress.

"Well, ah, we've discussed more diligently monitoring the day workers to increase their production," Lord Kasper replied hesitantly. "We won't tolerate any slacking this season."

King Khari stared at him, letting the silence stretch for an uncomfortably long time before finally speaking in a voice as cold as her eyes. "Is that all?"

Lord Kasper swallowed and shuffled his papers. "I meet with the operators again in a few days. Our planning was interrupted by the attack. But this is a top priority, and I assure you it will be attended to."

King Khari sat back in her chair, watching Lord Kasper intently. A coiled snake. A bird of prey. Waiting.

Lord Anwir coughed delicately. "If the Grand Treasurer has nothing further, I could continue my report—"

King Khari held up a hand, silencing him. "Lord Kasper, I would very much like to hear what ideas you have for addressing my concerns. The success of the harvest is of utmost importance."

Lord Kasper shuffled through his papers again, as if expecting the right answer to suddenly appear. He glanced toward Queen Annika, who'd finally turned her attention back to the conversation. The young queen widened her eyes slightly. Macella didn't need to read her mind to recognize the warning. But it was too late.

"Lashings," Lord Kasper blurted. "Those who don't meet their quotas will not only have their pay docked but will also be whipped. As I said, we will not tolerate idleness."

King Khari cocked her head, considering. Macella clenched her jaw. She'd made it a point to visit the vast fields and orchards a few times over the past weeks. The workers were all poorer citizens of the capital, who relied on the seasonal harvests to feed their families. They toiled in all manner of weather, earning a meager daily wage. Meanwhile, the crops were used to feed the court, with the surplus being sold and shipped all over Kōsaten for a sizable profit. The idea of those exploited workers also being whipped made Macella's blood boil.

"Your grace, if I may," Macella said softly, drawing the king's gaze. "I'd like to offer the Grand Treasurer an alternate perspective."

Lord Kasper reddened slightly, but King Khari waved a permissive hand. "By all means, my lady. We welcome varied opinions in this chamber."

A pretty lie, but Macella went on, nonetheless. "Lord Kasper, how many acres of crops fall and rot in the far fields each season? How many acres of viable land aren't even planted? How many other resources grow naturally on the castle's vast estate, unnoticed and unused?"

Lord Kasper chuckled, though his cobalt eyes were hard. "An interesting question, but surely not one you expect to be answered. There aren't enough decent laborers in the capital to tend the orchards and fields we actively cultivate, let alone to scour the Crown's endless lands for whatever wild plants may or may not be useful to us."

"Perhaps you can give us a rough estimate," King Khari suggested, her voice deceptively calm.

Lord Kasper reddened further. "I could ask the operators, your grace, but I am sure such things are difficult to measure. I doubt anyone has even attempted to do so. Lady Macella is an exceptional woman but is new to nobility. I'm happy to teach her more about how these things are done, at a more appropriate moment. We needn't waste the council's precious time."

Macella felt another flash of anger, but she held on to her complacent smile. Lord Kasper was not the first, and certainly wouldn't be the last, to try and put her in what they considered to be her place. And he would fail. As would all who doubted her.

"Lady Charlotte," Macella said in the voice of the warrior queen. "How many acres of crops go unharvested each season?"

"According to the agricultural archives and the operators' calculations, in a typical warm or hot season, an average of fifty acres of crops go bad before they can be harvested," her sister responded immediately, pushing her glasses up her nose. "In a typical harvesting season, the number is twice that."

"And how many acres of fertile land go untilled?" Macella asked, her voice as smooth as her expression.

Charlotte replied promptly. "Without diminishing any of the property's natural beauty and biological diversity, there are approximately 200 acres of prime farmland unused on the Crown's estate."

King Khari's mouth twitched, a dangerous gleam in her eye. Lord Kasper squirmed, his smile growing strained. Queen Annika bit her lip.

"And what other natural resources of value grow wild on the estate?" Macella asked, holding Lord Kasper's furious gaze.

"Hundreds of grains, nuts, herbs, tubers, and fruits have been recorded," Charlotte answered, "but the findings suggest there are many yet to be discovered. Among those recorded, an example of the most valuable might be the vast networks of edible and medicinal fungi that thrive in the woods along the southwest border of the grounds."

"Thank you for that information, Lady Charlotte," Lord Kasper said through gritted teeth. "Be that as it may, we haven't enough laborers to tend the fields we already plant."

King Khari tilted her head at Macella. "How does the information you've gathered help resolve the issue of declining agricultural profits?"

Macella smiled pleasantly at the king. She'd discussed her ideas with the farm operators just a few weeks prior. She'd planned to present her proposals to the small council soon, but it had seemed unimportant in light of the attack on the keep. How surprising that one of King Khari's whims would work out in Macella's favor for a change.

"I've heard it said that you catch more kappas with cucumbers than pickled beets," she said. "Perhaps incentivizing hard work would motivate our employees more than fear of punishment. And it would cost us nothing, considering how many crops rot in the far fields.

"In addition to their daily swage, we give the laborers the equivalent of a tenth of their daily haul of crops. They can harvest it themselves from the untended fields after they've completed the day's work."

King Khari was nodding along, clearly connecting the pieces of Macella's plan more quickly than the latter could even explain it. To the side and behind the king, Charlotte scribbled away, head lowered to hide her smile. Aithan's eyes twinkled with pride.

"Our laborers work until nearly sunset," Lord Kasper rebuffed. "There won't be daylight enough for them to pick their own crops and get out before the gates are locked."

Macella smiled a bit wider. It was as if she'd planted these protests herself. She couldn't have written the scene better if it'd been in one of her stories.

"That is why we won't ask them to leave," Macella replied. "We will offer our laborers stability and shelter, rewarding their loyalty and dedication. We will take a few acres of land near the fields and dedicate them to worker housing—simple, safe homes for them and their families. They will have their own small plots of land to farm as they see fit in their own time and will be welcome to keep any livestock they can afford."

Lord Kasper scoffed. "That sounds like a costly plan, which does nothing for our profits."

"Hardly," Macella retorted. "We have the materials and manpower to construct the homes for mere coppers. With the workers and their families living on-site, we can extend the workday by an hour, which the farm operators calculated will easily cover any deficit incurred by sheltering the farmhands. Their continued employment and boarding will be contingent upon satisfactory daily production. They will be more invested in the success of the harvest and will be more loyal to the Crown than ever for elevating them from relative poverty. And we'll undoubtedly attract more high-quality workers when the word spreads of our generosity, meaning we'll have the capacity to harvest more of the estate's resources."

"You spoke to the farm operators about this?" Lord Kasper demanded, his face turning from red to purple with anger. "What right have you to interfere in the affairs of the treasury?"

"Careful, Grand Treasurer," King Khari drawled lazily, malice glinting in her icy ochre eyes. "You'd be wise to consider your tone when addressing my betrothed. My future queen is authorized to inquire into any matters concerning the well-being of her kingdom."

Instantly, Lord Kasper deflated. "Apologies, my lady. I was surprised and spoke out of turn. Please continue your enlightening proposal."

Macella almost felt bad for Lord Kasper. He was a pompous, entitled snob who had wanted a cushy position at court and hadn't expected to do any real work. He hadn't been malicious, just mediocre.

She went on more gently. "Additionally, the families of the farmhands will be permitted to harvest as much as they wish from the far fields or to forage the wild plants Lady Charlotte mentioned. The Crown will keep half their daily yield, while also gathering significantly more of the estate's resources.

"We will improve the lives of some of the capital's poorest citizens, attract more workers, and exponentially increase our profits in the long run." Macella paused before adding demurely, "And, if you'll excuse my impertinence at mentioning it, an announcement like this could not come at a better time. With the recent attacks, people could use a reminder that the Crown protects and cares for its people."

Macella finished her speech with a defiant lift of her chin. Lord Kasper had gone red again, while Queen Annika was alarmingly white.

Grinning darkly, King Khari gave a slow clap, eyes locked on Macella. "Brilliant, as always, Lady Macella," the king said, finishing her languorous applause. "Every day you remind me what a gift you are to Kōsaten, and to me. Lord Anwir, begin the arrangements immediately. You are to run every particular by Lady Macella for her approval. Lord Kasper, you will ensure she has any funding she requires. Lady Charlotte, prepare a statement for the Royal Bulletin. We will announce it as the future queen's first initiative. Make the headline 'Lady Macella of Shively, Champion of the Poor.'"

There was a general bustle as the small council members made notes, asked questions, and congratulated Macella. The mood in the room had lightened. It seemed the meeting would end much better than it had started. Macella was eager to return to her study with Charlotte to begin planning the details of her new initiative.

Lady Macella of Shively, Champion of the Poor, Aithan crooned in her thoughts, his mental voice taking on a teasing lilt. Macella winced. She and Charlotte would definitely have to come up with a better title for the article.

Amusement danced in Aithan's eyes. Macella mentally stuck out her tongue at him. Despite his teasing, she could practically feel the pride and affection radiating from his thoughts. She smothered a smile, maintaining her modest expression.

(8) "Before we wrap up, there is one more thing." King Khari's voice, quiet and deadly calm, sliced through the chamber. Conversation fell silent. "We must resolve the matter of how to reprimand Lord Kasper."

"Excuse me?" the Grand Treasurer sputtered, his face going from red to deathly pale in a matter of seconds. "Your grace, I assure you I would have developed a satisfactory plan if given more time—"

King Khari cut him off with a click of her tongue. "You said it yourself, Lord Kasper. We will not tolerate idleness. While you sat and did nothing, someone else took the initiative to do your job for you."

Lord Kasper began to tremble—with fear or anger, or both. "Your grace, the hellspawn caused costly damage to the keep during their rampage. Surely you understand that we have all been preoccupied with the more pressing matter of recovering from that traumatic attack. My own dear cousin was very nearly killed—"

"And Lady Macella saved her life!" King Khari snarled, all pretense at calm disappearing. "She fought against the hellspawn and, instead of using the attack as an excuse for indolence, she did her job and yours besides! She did more than half this fucking council combined!"

The king slammed a fist into the table, eliciting a loud crack from the ancient mahogany. Macella jumped at the sudden explosion, along with nearly everyone else in the room, excluding Aithan. Lord Kasper paled as King Khari shot to her feet, nearly toppling her chair. She stalked toward Lord Kasper like a lion approaching particularly succulent prey.

The air shimmered and Macella felt a wave of vertigo. The room darkened as the air grew cold. A palpable odor of fear filled the room. Macella gripped the arms of her chair, trying to calm her racing heart.

It is an illusion, Aithan thought at her soothingly. *Khari is manipulating our minds. Just breathe.*

Macella tried to do as he commanded, slowing her breathing. She could almost see the real room beyond Khari's vision—just as brightly lit and warmed by a roaring fire as it always was when the weather was cool. Then the darkness snapped back into place, the chill returning to the air.

King Khari stopped at the foot of the table, between Macella and Lord Kasper. She braced her hands against the heavy wood, leaning menacingly toward the Grand Treasurer. Despite his robust frame, Lord Kasper appeared to shrink in the king's shadow.

"Lady Macella seems to believe that reward is more motivating than fear of punishment," the king mused, her voice once again low and calm. "However, you and I are more cynical, are we not, Lord Kasper?"

The Grand Treasurer gulped loudly. "My king, I—"

"If I'm not mistaken, it was your idea that the punishment for unsatisfactory work should be a lashing," King Khari purred. "So be it. Guards!"

In another moment, two knights Macella had never seen appeared behind Lord Kasper. He squawked in surprise as they took him roughly by the arms and jerked him from his seat. King Khari moved to Macella's side as the guards shoved Lord Kasper to the foot of the table. They forced him forward, placing his palms flat against the wood, just as Khari had stood moments ago.

Macella felt sick. Lord Kasper's terror was palpable in the gleam of sweat now coating his skin. She could see the whites of his eyes, the twitching muscle in his cheek, the strain of his knuckles as he gripped the table. It was unbearable. She could not sit a handsbreadth from a person being beaten. All for no reason other than the king's bad mood and need for an outlet.

Macella had given her a perfect target. The Grand Treasurer might've come away from Khari's interrogation only mildly chastened, but she had given the king fuel. She'd humiliated Lord Kasper, made him appear incompetent. She was to blame for the trauma he was about to endure.

As if sensing her discomfort, King Khari laid a hand on Macella's shoulder. Macella fought against a shudder.

The king squeezed lightly. "Thank you, my lady, for revealing this weakness in our ranks," King Khari said solemnly. "Let this be a reminder to us all to not grow complacent in our duties. Five lashes."

Macella's stomach roiled as the guards ripped Lord Kasper's surcoat from his shoulders, then tore open his shirt to reveal his broad, pale back. Khari's grip tightened on her shoulder in silent command, warning her not to look away.

It isn't real, Macella, Aithan whispered in her mind. *Resist her. You've done it before.*

Macella tried. She clenched her fists, focusing on the sharp bite of her nails into her palms. She stared hard at the space beyond Lord Kasper, willing the familiar tapestry on the distant wall to materialize from the heavy darkness. But all she could see was the Grand Treasurer's frightened face, his trembling shoulders.

Look, love, Aithan whispered, reflecting the room as he saw it. The king's glamour seemed not to affect him at all. To Aithan, Lord Kasper stood alone, gripping the edge of the table, face white with terror. There were no guards. The man's clothing was fully intact.

How are you doing that? Macella marveled internally. It couldn't just be because he was a crossbreed. Though Macella could resist the king's gift, it was not so fully and with such apparent ease. Aithan had accidentally slipped into the king's mind once and had even defied the gods' magical bindings enough to strike the king in defense of Queen Awa. Now he seemed to be resisting the king's god gift with little effort. He was the strongest Aegis alive, but this was something more.

Macella didn't have time to think about it any further, because one of the guards had produced a wicked leather whip. He brought it down on Lord Kasper's bare back with brutal force. Macella flinched at the horrible crack of the whip and the hoarse, terrible scream that ripped from Kasper's throat.

Again, Aithan pushed images into her mind. In the bright morning light of the chamber, Lord Kasper's pained expression was even starker. And yet, nothing actually struck him. There were no guards, no whip. But the stricken faces of the other council members made it clear no one but Aithan could see past the king's influence.

As Macella concentrated, the room took on a doubled appearance. Lord Kasper stood alone one moment, the next he was flanked by guards. The room was bathed in darkness and daylight. Gooseflesh pricked her skin, but the fire's warmth blanketed her. A headache began to form behind her eyes.

Four more times the phantom guard brought down the whip, and each time Lord Kasper's screams were worse. Macella could see the blood on the whip, on the raw, red skin of the Grand Treasurer's back. She could almost smell the coppery tang of it in the air.

She could also see him jerking violently at nothing, flinching away from an invisible blow. Charlotte was sobbing quietly, while Queen Annika had gone from pale to a worrisome shade of green. King Khari kept her hand on Macella's shoulder, watching the proceedings with cold indifference.

Then, suddenly, it was over. Light and heat rushed back into the room. King Khari was lounging in her chair, crown perched at a rakish angle. When had she left Macella's side? Lord Kasper stood perfectly unharmed, though his face was drenched in sweat, his hair plastered to his head. His wet eyes were locked on Macella, nothing in them but unabashed loathing.

"Perhaps Lady Macella is right after all," King Khari mused, surveying her nails. "Rewards might be motivation enough. Your reward is that this was but a warning. Don't disappoint me again, Lord Kasper."

"Never, your grace," Lord Kasper choked out, his voice breaking in a sob.

"Meeting adjourned," King Khari announced, rising to depart.

As if on cue, Queen Annika promptly vomited on the table.

Aithan lunged toward the young queen just as her eyes rolled back into her head, and she slipped from her chair, fainting dead away.

Chapter Five

Macella

Aithan caught the queen before she hit the floor.

In the tumult that followed, Macella slipped from the room. If she'd remained much longer, she'd likely have followed the young queen's example. Her stomach churned, her head pounding from the effort of trying to see through Khari's trickery. She needed air. She could not get enough breath into her lungs, and the walls of the keep seemed to be drawing closer.

Sir Kamau snapped to attention as she emerged, preparing to fall into step behind her. The knight looked at her with a level of respect and devotion that made her stomach twist further. Many of the knights had been looking at her that way since the attack, even those who hadn't seen her lead the fight against the manananggal. She couldn't stand that look—not when, mere minutes ago, Lord Kasper had looked at her with such hatred. Hatred she so rightly deserved.

"I wish to take the air, Sir Kamau. Would you please send for Cinnamon?" Macella choked out, not looking at the knight trailing her.

"Right away, my lady." A brief salute and he was gone.

Mechanically, Macella returned to her rooms and dressed for her ride. The leather of her belt was a whip biting into pale skin. The tightening of her boot laces reminded her of a cold hand squeezing her shoulder. She was both in her dressing room and back in the dark, frigid small council chamber. It was like her mind existed in two places, as it had during Lord Kasper's flogging.

By the time she emerged into the open air, her head felt as if it might burst. Sir Kamau was waiting, holding Cinnamon's reins, along with those of a second mount. Macella felt a rising panic at the thought of him following her, *protecting her*, when all she wanted was to be away from watching eyes. She couldn't be the warrior queen right now, not when she needed to scream and cry and burn and burn and burn until the terrible image of the Grand Treasurer as the king's whipping boy was nothing but ash. Until her guilt and shame were swallowed up by hot onyx anger.

"I will accompany and protect Lady Macella, Sir Kamau." Finley's musical drawl held a note of authority. "You should have a break, perhaps visit your captain. He was awake when I left him a quarter of an hour ago."

With a bow and a murmur of thanks, Sir Kamau passed Finley the reins, and returned to the castle. Macella's shoulders loosened the slightest bit. She took a long, ragged breath as she climbed into the saddle.

Finley mounted the second horse and urged it into a trot. Automatically, Macella clucked for Cinnamon to match their pace. For a few minutes, they rode in silence. Macella thought only about breathing, forcing air into the tight, bitter places in her head and heart.

"Your heartbeat sounds almost right again. Take a few more deep breaths. Look at the trees and sky. Feel your mount beneath you. This is real," Finley said after a while. "Since he couldn't get away himself, your husband spoke to me in that unnerving mind speak the two of you seem to enjoy so much. He thought you might be in need of some fresh air and trusted company. And someone to remind you that the terrible things you're thinking about yourself are untrue. Whatever happened in that small council meeting was not your fault."

Macella barked a harsh, humorless laugh. "Tell that to the man who was just beaten and humiliated due to my interference."

Finley paused, then spoke more quietly. "The bit Aithan shared with me was dreadful. I am sorry that it happened, even to that pretentious peacock. But you are not to blame."

"I can't do this, Finley," Macella half-sobbed. "No matter what I do, Khari wins. Every time I attempt to do something good, someone gets hurt."

"That is the nature of war, dearest," her sibling replied, a little sadly. "No one comes out unscathed, least of all those with good intentions. Things will get worse. Innocents will be harmed. You must accept it or give up altogether. And, either way, innocents will still be harmed."

Macella angrily wiped away the tears that had escaped despite her efforts to stifle them. "How can you be so cavalier about it?"

Finley gave her a sidelong glance, before turning their orange eyes back to the horizon. "They moved Drudo back to his room yesterday. His vitals have improved, and he's even woken up a few times over the last few days, though never for long. The medical mages insisted he was well enough to leave the infirmary. They have a very organized schedule and check on him every few hours. A servant is with him at all times.

"Still, I found myself uneasy. I could not sleep. I was sure he would die in the night. The servant would fall asleep, and Drudo would take a turn for the worse and he'd die before the mage's next visit, and I would never have the chance to tell him—"

They broke off suddenly, shaking their head as if to clear it, their sleek silver tresses glimmering in the sunlight. Macella had rarely heard Finley so serious and never heard them come so close to admitting to a romantic attachment. It was enough to distract her from her own despair.

"I went to his chambers, sent the servant away, and watched him all night," Finley went on. "I realized something then. I realized I had allowed myself to want something. I had been daring to expect good in my life. After more than ninety years of carefully living in the moment, never risking a look ahead, I'd somehow begun to believe in a future. I believed that I would have plenty of time to flirt with the dashing young captain."

Macella's heart ached. She'd heard similar words from Aithan. She couldn't imagine being born into a life where it wasn't safe to want, to hope, to dream. Even at her family's poorest, darkest times, she'd felt free to dream of a better future.

"If you want to be blamed for something, that's what it should be," Finley declared, tossing their hair over their shoulder. "It's your fault I've come to expect a life. Being around you, learning to love you, and allowing you to love me—it has changed me."

Hot tears spilled down Macella's cheeks. She shook her head, but she wasn't even sure what she was denying. Her feelings were a jumbled mess.

"You are fighting for a world in which everyone is entitled to truly live, to expect that they will have time to love and learn and fuck and fail and hope. Everyone, not just the privileged few," Finley said fiercely. "If some people must be hurt in the process of creating that world, then it is a necessary sacrifice. I can live with that, even be cavalier about it, to mask how much it hurts. Can you?"

Macella didn't reply. They both knew her answer. She'd made this decision long ago. It seemed she would have to make it again and again. Every day she would intentionally decide to do whatever it took to restore the balance between realms, and to narrow the gap between the privileged and the unfortunate in this realm.

"Drudo was awake when you last saw him?" she asked finally. "Was he lucid?"

Finley smiled devilishly. "Not after I finished showing him how grateful I was that he'd woken up."

"Finley!" Macella exclaimed, letting out her first genuine laugh of the day.

"Just a kiss," Finley promised, raising their hand with mocking sincerity. "A very long, very gentle kiss. I wouldn't dream of setting back his recovery."

They rode for a long while, talking on less serious matters. Macella let the beautiful harvest day and the melodious comfort of her sibling's voice soothe the raw ache in her chest. Gradually, the gloom of the morning lightened. By the time they returned to the keep for midday meal, Macella felt more herself.

Finley headed to their chambers to freshen up before joining Macella in her parlor for lunch. Charlotte would most likely join them, and Aithan would be along if his duties allowed. Even with the pressure to entertain alongside King Khari, Macella had been delighted to find that the Crown nearly always opted to have their earlier meals with their respective entourages. She wasn't sure if the other monarchs found their chosen company as pleasurable, but for Macella, the hours passed with her friends helped her endure all the rest.

She reached her rooms in time to see Lucy struggling to squeeze out of the door without letting Nyx slip past her. It was a hopeless attempt, as the cat easily wound through her legs and vanished into the room before Lucy could stop her. Macella laughed, and Lucy blushed guiltily.

"She won't be unattended!" she exclaimed. "Lady Lotta and your other friends are already in the parlor. I was just trying to keep her away from your lunch. She's been sneaking into the kitchens trying to steal fish all day."

Macella laughed again. "It's alright, Lucy. Nyx is always impossible on sea-delivery days. We'll all pretend we're not feeding her under the table, and eventually, Aisling will have to carry her out of here like a stuffed goose."

Lucy grinned. "Aye. She'll eat herself sick. She's already had Miss Aisling's share. Since she doesn't eat flesh, I figure the cat can have her portions." She turned to go, but called back over her shoulder, "I'll be back in a tick with a few more pitchers. I can tell that you lot are going to need more wine."

As she entered her antechamber, it dawned on Macella that she hadn't asked Lucy what other friends waited with Charlotte in the parlor. Perhaps Aisling was here, and Finley would be along soon. But Lucy had plainly said Lotta and her other *friends*. Plural.

Just in case, Macella went first to her room to freshen up and change. Unexpected visitors might mean putting on the mask of the northern rose or the warrior queen.

But when Macella finally entered the parlor, all pretenses fell away.

Charlotte beamed, her cheeks stained with a blush. Beside her, sitting a respectful distance away, Jacan of Prestonia smiled widely at the sight of Macella. Aisling sat cross-legged on the rug, eating from a plate of fruit and cheese. The side table was laden with food, filling the room with an intoxicating mixture of smells.

And curled up in one of the plush armchairs as if she'd always been there, was Zahra Shelby.

Macella wasn't sure which of them squealed first, but then they were hugging and laughing, and everyone was talking at once. After exclaiming over Zahra's sudden arrival and fussing over Jacan's health like a mother hen, Macella officially introduced her friend to the young Aegis, her sister, and her mage. Of course, Zahra being Zahra, she had confidently barged into Macella and Aithan's apartments while Macella was riding with Finley and immediately engaged Aisling, Charlotte, and Jacan in easy conversation. She'd recognized each of them from Macella's letters, and they'd likewise heard enough about her to deduce her identity. They'd obviously become fast friends.

"Gods, you're even more beautiful than I remember!" Zahra gushed, the words coming out in a torrent. Macella had forgotten how quickly her friend talked, since it'd been a while since they'd spoken outside of letters. "That wasn't the first thing I intended to say to you after nearly a year apart, but when you walked into the room, my brain jammed. So, let's just pretend I said something witty and coy and now you're realizing just how much you missed me."

Macella let out a sound between a laugh and a sob. "I *have* missed you! So very much."

It was true. Sheriff Zahra Shelby had been the first friend Aithan and Macella had made. She'd been easy to like, with her wicked humor, mischievous mismatched eyes, and stunning beauty. She was petite but fearless, skilled with a bow, deadly with a knife, and even better at outsmarting opponents. Aithan and Macella had passed much of the previous year in her company, between their visit to her home in Shelby Park and when she joined her fellow nobles for the cold season at Kōsaten Keep. She'd become something between friend and lover, often sharing their bed. Macella couldn't help but wonder if that relationship would continue now that they were together again. Perhaps the sheriff wouldn't want to be romantically involved with a soon-to-be member of the Crown.

Macella didn't care, as long as Zahra was around. They'd figure everything else out. For now, it was more than enough that her friend had left the city where she'd passed her entire life, serving as both sheriff and vicereine, to join Macella's entourage at court.

"I can't believe you're here," she said, pulling Zahra to sit beside her on one of the room's lush couches, and greedily breathing in her lavender and honeysuckle scent. "How did you arrive so quickly? I thought it would take much longer to arrange matters. You are the very heart of Shelby Park."

Zahra waved a dismissive hand. "Hardly. More like its smartass motor-mouth."

Aisling cackled, nearly choking on a grape, her face turning almost as red as her hair. Nyx appeared at her side, watching her critically until she settled into a subdued giggle. Charlotte had also laughed, resting her hand lightly on Jacan's shoulder as she did so. Then, as if realizing what she'd done, she'd blushed and leapt abruptly to her feet. She covered her embarrassment by pouring wine for Macella and Zahra. Jacan watched Charlotte's every move.

"I'll have a glass as well, Lotta dear, if it's no trouble. Jacan of Prestonia, well met. I'm glad to see you again," Finley drawled, strolling into the room. They signed as they spoke, their hands moving as gracefully as the rest of their svelte frame. "And Zahra of Shelby Park is here as well! I should've known you'd arrive today, totally unexpectedly. I've never met anyone so obviously born beneath an Isis moon. Come and hug me, you teacup temptress."

Finley and Zahra embraced warmly. They were a striking pair—Finley, lithe and graceful with fair skin and silver hair, Zahra with her small stature, long, dark braid, and olive skin. They'd spent enough time together last cold season to have developed a begrudging respect for one another that eventually be-came friendship. Both quick-witted, charming, unfiltered, and gorgeous, they couldn't help but like each other—the only alternative was to become sworn enemies.

"How do you always smell so good?" Zahra demanded when Finley released her. "It's like you bathe in honey and orgasms."

This time, Aisling completely collapsed in a fit of giggles. Charlotte covered her face with her hands, shoulders shaking with laughter. Zahra's eyes—one brown and one green—danced with humor. Jacan frowned, looking between them all.

Macella caught his attention, falling easily back into accompanying her words with fairly proficient sign language. She'd practiced quite a bit since meeting the young Aegis, who she'd always liked on his own merit and now liked even more for his obvious love of Charlotte. "I know. She talks fast. But trust me, you don't want to catch everything she says. She's got an even bawdier sense of humor than Finley."

"She does not!" Finley retorted, signing animatedly. "Don't start comparing us. You'll make me jealous, and then I'll have to kill her, and you'll be so mad at me."

Zahra grinned, plopping back onto the couch beside Macella. She tried a few clumsy hand signs as she spoke. "I'm sorry, Jacan. Macella told me you read lips, so I practiced speaking slower, but I sucked at it, so instead, I started learning hand signing. I kind of suck at that, too, but I'll get it eventually! I'm nothing if not determined."

"I'm still learning too. We can learn together," Charlotte offered, shyly attempting a few signs as well.

Jacan smiled an endearing boyish grin, catching enough of what they'd said to look a bit bashful. He signed smoothly but carefully as he spoke, obviously mindful that many of them were still learning a language in which he was fluent. "That's thoughtful of you both. We'll figure it out. It seems like we'll see a lot of each other. I mean, I hope so." Jacan's blush deepened, the entirety of his bald head taking on a rosy tint. The jade tattoos encircling his scalp gleamed, the ink's faint magical glow enhanced by the blush. "I mean, I guess it's different now, and Lady Macella is busier with her new queenly duties, and might not want—or, um, have time, for people like me. I mean, I know all of you have more important ways to spend your time."

Macella gave the young Aegis a sympathetic smile. When he'd last been at the castle, he'd spent most of his time with Macella, Aithan, and Finley. Now, she had an entourage, a busier social calendar, and new duties. He wasn't sure where he fit anymore.

(9) "Hasn't Charlotte told you about the Wildfire Court?" Macella asked, gesturing around the room. "You're one of us. We're a family."

"And father is home!" Finley exclaimed jovially, sparing Jacan from having to reply. The young Aegis was blinking rapidly, as if fighting tears. "Aithan of Auburndale, have you brought us more wine?"

Aithan ignored Finley as he entered, slipping off his sword belt and setting it aside. Zahra squealed and bounded across the room to hug him, and he lifted her easily from the ground in a fond embrace. Jacan rose to shake his hand, but Aithan pulled the young Aegis into a hug as well. Macella pretended not to notice Jacan again blinking against tears. He was so unused to kindness. No wonder he'd been so uncertain about his place.

She couldn't imagine what life had been like for him. He'd surely received little to no affection growing up in Smoketown. Furthermore, after losing his hearing when he was very young due to a vicious beating at the hands of one of the soldiers, he'd had to navigate the horrors of Smoketown without being able to hear its many dangers. If only the exceptionally gifted few survived Aegis training, trials, and transformations, then Jacan was truly remarkable. Another remarkable member of their remarkable little family of outsiders.

Eventually, they'd all embraced, found comfortable seats, and resettled with goblets of wine. Macella felt a warm fuzziness enveloping her. She wasn't sure if it was from the wine or the company. Probably both. She leaned into the crook of Aithan's arm, her legs stretched across Zahra's. Zahra lounged against the couch's other end, absently tracing shapes on Macella's shins.

"Who's running Shelby Park while you serve at court?" Aithan asked, draining his goblet in a few gulps.

"That's what I said!" Macella cried. "She's the heart of that town."

"She said she's the motormouth," Aisling corrected.

"Well, I've missed her quick tongue," Macella declared, taking another long drink.

It wasn't until Finley said, "I'll bet you have," that Macella realized the double entendre. Finley, Macella, and Zahra dissolved into laughter, and Aithan just shook his head. They laughed harder when Charlotte innocently asked what was so funny. Soon everyone was laughing, and the terrible weight that had been in Macella's gut since the small council meeting lifted at last.

"We're well on our way to being drunk, and we have so much more to discuss," Finley declared, crossing the room to the side table, Nyx following in hopes of catching more dropped fish. "Zahra, explain how you managed to come to court without your city falling into ruin. Eat, everyone."

Finley filled several plates with food and began to pass them out. Moments later, Lucy appeared and shooed them away from the table. She'd brought a half dozen pitchers of wine and another tray of food, which she occupied herself with doling out. Macella made a mental note to get Lucy a gift. She wasn't quite a member of the Wildfire Court, but she was near enough, and she understood them. Perhaps she'd heard about the small council meeting and wanted to cheer Macella up, or perhaps she did it for no particular reason, but she made sure they had plenty of food and drink to last the many hours they spent talking that afternoon, cocooned in their bubble of peace and laughter.

***

Aithan

If only he could stop time.

Aithan would give anything to see Macella as happy as she'd been all afternoon. After King Khari's disgusting display in the small council meeting, it had taken every bit of his carefully honed discipline to remain at his post, to resist the urge to pull Macella into his arms and not let her out until he'd wiped away that devastatingly forlorn expression and chased away her guilt and self-loathing. The utter despair emanating from her mind had threatened to shred his resolve, awakening a primal rage, a need to destroy the source of her pain. Instead, he'd had to remain with the Crown, tending to their needs and comfort, while the love of his life faced her heartache alone.

Yes, he'd sent Finley after her, but it hardly seemed enough. Though he wished he'd been with her himself, he was unendingly grateful for Finley's presence in the capital and their lives. Aithan had always liked and respected his elder sibling, but he'd learned to truly love them through Macella's eyes. Watching the two of them become friends had shown him a different side of Finley—or rather, it had shown him more of the truly good person he'd always suspected lurked beneath their detached demeanor. The love for Macella that he felt in Finley's mind was enough to guarantee Aithan's undying loyalty and affection.

He'd easily found the familiar melody of their mind, exactly where he'd expected it to be, at Drudo's bedside. Aithan had noticed that his telepathic reach had gradually expanded, especially when reaching for familiar minds. Speaking to Finley across the castle had been as easy as if they'd been beside him in the small council chamber.

Love leads wanderers to their truth. Unknown power now unloosed.

It seemed Aisling's prophecy proved truer each day. The love of their little family seemed to be changing them all. Finley was softening, feeling safe enough to remove their mask. Charlotte was learning to trust herself, to see the capable young woman she really was. Aisling and Jacan, too, were growing more confident, more hopeful for the future. Macella was showing them all another way, another world.

He'd thought that his and Macella's new powers had fully manifested when she'd crossed the veil to rescue him from Duànzào. Apparently, that had only been the beginning. Since then, they'd each continued to grow in strength, speed, power, and skill.

Aithan had surprised himself that morning. It had been almost too easy to see through Khari's illusion. He could smell the magic in the air, could watch as the king wove it into a tapestry of alternate reality. All Aithan had to do was pull a single thread, and the vision unraveled, revealing the true scene beneath.

Though it had been easy, he knew that it had not been without effort. He'd actually been honing the ability for months. After Khari had taken Macella into the woods and Aithan hadn't been able to see through the king's magic to save her, he'd been determined not to be caught unawares again. So, he'd begun to practice.

He'd watched the king carefully, observing her every interaction. Whenever she showed the slightest sign of using her magical gifts, Aithan scrutinized her methods. Slowly, he'd begun to sense the very structure of her magic. It was like perceiving another layer of the realm.

Initially, the effort gave him a headache, but eventually, he found it became more natural. Soon enough, he hardly had to concentrate. He was surprised to discover how often King Khari used her gift. She constantly manipulated people's perceptions, making herself appear more threatening, more beautiful, more desirable. People never saw her true face.

That morning, he'd felt how difficult it was for Macella to penetrate the king's illusion. Perhaps he could train her as he'd trained himself. She was a crossbreed, as he was. This could be another of their natural gifts. He made a mental note to discuss it with Macella.

Later.

Because, right now, all he wanted to do was listen to the music of her laughter and watch her ebony eyes sparkle with delight, and bathe in the scent and sensation of her joy.

He knew his wife didn't quite realize how much they all loved her. Somewhere deep inside, he knew she still saw herself as the outsider she'd once been, the woman who even now only earned her parents' affection because of her newfound wealth and rank. She didn't know how she impacted people. How her selflessness and goodness drew people to her. How everyone in this room, and many outside of it, would die for her without hesitation. How they would fight beside her, protect her, give all of themselves for her cause.

They were doing it now, the whole family. They were all loving her. He'd seen the threads of Aisling's magic crisscrossing the outer door in a protective spell to deter listening ears and unwanted interruptions. Finley was ensuring that everyone ate and drank enough, but drinking less themself, staying alert and lounging nearest the door, ready to act at the first sign of danger. Even Lucy, who surely had other duties to tend to, returned again and again to check on their comfort, and keep them plied with refreshments.

How had he gotten here? How had he gone from being content with his solitary existence, to this miraculous place on the precipice of a new world? When had he started to love all the people in this room?

Finley, he understood. And Zahra had wriggled her way into his heart during their stay in Shelby Park. But he loved the others too. He loved his little sister Lotta, with her big bright eyes and shy smile. So like and so different from his Macella and growing more into her own each day. He loved Aisling with her unpolished manners and jolly personality. He even loved Nyx, with her intelligent gaze and knack for appearing wherever she wished.

And Jacan. The Aegis who was little more than a child—as much as an Aegis was ever allowed to be a child. He reminded Aithan so much of himself at that age. He'd survived the same horrors Aithan had but was starting his duties under entirely new circumstances. Because of Macella, Jacan would never know the profound loneliness of being a shield. He had a tether, an anchor, a family. Furthermore, if Aithan's instincts were correct, as they usually were, the young Aegis was already experiencing something Aithan had waited so many decades for. The surreptitious glances the kid constantly snuck at Lotta spoke volumes. Despite the slight pang he felt for his younger self, Aithan was genuinely happy for Jacan. Seeing the boy thrive seemed to nourish the lonely young man inside himself.

So, no, he wouldn't worry about training or Khari's illusions or the dangers that lay ahead. Not right now.

For now, they were happy. For now, they were safe. And that was enough. For now.

For now, he would enjoy the love and laughter of his friends. His family. Their love was truth. Their love was power. Their love was prophecy.

Love leads wanderers to their truth. Unknown power now unloosed.

Who knew how powerful they would become? What they could withstand, what they could accomplish? Together.

Macella leaned into him, her curls tickling his face, as she dissolved into a fit of giggles at something Zahra had said. Aithan kissed his wife's wild curls and smiled to himself. He inhaled her scent—sweet burning acacia, citrus, and cinnamon—and the pleasant scents of their family—honeysuckle and lavender, cinnamon and cherry blossoms, heather and baked bread, honey and hazelnut, saffron and sandalwood.

It smelled like home.

Chapter Six

Macella

Zahra attended dinner with the Crown and their respective entourages. Macella's cheerfulness dulled a bit when she saw that Queen Annika and her cousin, Lord Kasper, were conspicuously absent. It seemed neither of them had recovered from the morning's trauma. Macella winced internally. She'd already begun to dread their next encounter.

She didn't have too much time to dwell on her guilt, as the dinner was loud and boisterous. The king was in a merry mood and seemed intent on charming everyone, especially Macella and her pretty friend, the vicereine. Though Zahra had been coming to court since she was a child, she'd never been in such a favored position. Macella watched her captivate King Khari with her quick wit and dazzling beauty. She wouldn't be surprised if the king decided to pursue Zahra—after all, Khari's rakish reputation was well-earned.

Zahra is way too smart to fall into that trap, Aithan thought at her from his position behind the king. As if in confirmation, when Khari's attention was elsewhere, Zahra turned to Macella and rolled her eyes, her pouty lips curled in disgust. Macella stifled a giggle.

After the meal, Macella led Zahra to her new quarters. The staff hadn't been expecting her that afternoon, so her rooms hadn't been ready when she'd arrived. Zahra had washed and dressed for dinner in Aithan and Macella's chambers, but now Macella was eager to show her to her new home. She'd taken special care to ensure Zahra's comfort, deciding every detail down to the color and fabric of the bedcurtains—a light, breezy silk of deepest violet. She pulled Zahra from room to room, pointing out amenities and special features.

Finally, Macella showed her the best part—a private, screened lanai, hung with delicate silks and overlooking a lush garden, ringed by lavender bushes. Honeysuckle vines climbed its wooden posts. The day they'd met, she and Zahra had spent hours talking and flirting while lounging in a lanai much like this one. By the end of that night, both Macella and Aithan were smitten with the brash, beautiful sheriff.

"Though you joke about it, I know it couldn't have been easy to leave Shelby Park, your father, and your work," Macella said, anxiously studying Zahra's face. "I tried to make this place feel a little more like home. The lanai is enchanted to remain warm year-round so that the lavender and honeysuckle will always be in bloom."

Zahra was silent, her eyes wide and glittering. Macella had never known her to be speechless. Just when she was about to ask if everything was okay, Zahra flung her arms around Macella's neck, standing on tiptoe to kiss her on the lips.

Macella laughed. "Do you like it?"

"Do I like it?" Zahra exclaimed, spinning in a circle with her arms outstretched. "Look at this place! It's perfect! This is the nicest thing anyone has ever done for me!"

Macella heaved a sigh of relief. "It's the least I could do. I want you to be happy here."

Zahra looked out over the lanai and shook her head. "Actually, there is one problem."

Macella tried to follow her friend's gaze but saw nothing amiss. "What is it? Whatever it is, we can have it fixed right away."

Zahra turned to Macella and grinned, mismatched eyes sparkling with mischief. "I was hoping my rooms wouldn't be ready tonight. Then I'd have an excuse to share your bed. But I wouldn't want to cause any drama with your royal fiancée. I don't know how her grace would like hearing that I staggered out of your room in the dead of night looking well-fucked."

Macella's blood warmed as she held Zahra's smoldering gaze. "That is very considerate of you. While Khari and I do not have a romantic relationship, we do try to be discreet in our private affairs."

She took Zahra's hand and led her back through the apartment to her new bedchamber. A large wardrobe sat against the wall near the foot of the bed. Macella opened the doors and pushed aside the dresses that hung there.

"The Lord Protector uses these passageways to reach the Crown in times of danger, but he also ensured that we'd have access to all our family in case of an emergency," she explained, guiding Zahra's hand along the back wall of the wardrobe. "The passages can also be useful in non-emergency situations."

Macella pressed Zahra's fingers against a hidden latch and showed her how to slide the false panel aside. Closing the wardrobe doors and the panel behind them, she led Zahra into the hidden passageway between their apartments. The former sheriff caught on quickly to the pattern of grooves and notches in the walls, navigating the dark corridors on catlike feet. When they slid open the panel into Macella and Aithan's bedchamber, Zahra immediately recited the path they'd taken, having already managed to memorize the directions.

"You are a marvel," Macella told her. "I am sorry to have robbed Shelby Park of your brilliance, but I'm so glad to have your cunning intellect in my court."

Zahra gave a slow smile as she pulled her thick, dark hair free of the elegant chignon she'd worn for dinner with the Crown. It fell to frame her face, a few glossy locks falling over one eye. Her uncovered green eye twinkled as she gave Macella a sly look.

"If I remember correctly, you like my cunning intellect, but you *love* my cunnilingus," she quipped.

(10) Macella laughed, closing the remaining distance between them, and pulling Zahra into her arms. Then they were kissing, Macella running her hands

through Zahra's heavy, silky hair, breathing in her lavender and honeysuckle scent. She tasted like honeyed wine, and Macella was immediately intoxicated. They stumbled toward the bed, kissing, laughing, and shimmying out of their clothes.

She'd forgotten how stunning Zahra was, how utterly bewitching. The smaller woman climbed into bed, stretching herself like a cat, before rolling onto her back and propping herself up on her elbows to give Macella a sultry look. Those mischievous, mismatched eyes were the biggest thing about her, aside from her personality—wide and bright and framed by long, dark lashes. Otherwise, she was petite, with a slender, muscular frame. Her hair shone against her olive skin, pooling around her shoulders to fall over her small, pert breasts. Macella ran her eyes from Zahra's flushed face, over her breasts and the flat plane of her stomach, to her narrow hips and the dark thatch of hair at the apex of her slim thighs.

Zahra lay back and spread her legs, smiling lazily. Her cupid's bow lips were rosy and swollen from their feverish kissing, somehow making them even more inviting. Macella crawled onto the bed, eyes on those deliciously plump lips. She slid between Zahra's legs, claiming her mouth again, and pushing her onto her back.

Zahra moaned, lifting her hips, and reaching up to bury her hands in Macella's curls. She pulled her closer and slid her tongue into Macella's mouth. Macella shivered and melted into the kiss, reveling in the press of Zahra's sharp angles against her soft curves. She rolled her hips, grinding against Zahra's wet heat. With one hand, she gathered both of Zahra's wrists, pinning them above her head. Zahra shuddered as Macella shifted her weight to slip her other hand between them.

They both moaned when Macella found the wetness waiting for her. Deepening the kiss, she slid two fingers inside that waiting warmth, loving the way Zahra clenched around her. Moving her own hips in tandem, Macella coaxed Zahra into a rhythmic rocking, as she worked her fingers while massaging Zahra's clit with her thumb.

Macella broke the kiss and trailed her tongue over the tender skin of Zahra's neck, savoring the taste of lavender and salt, and the way Zahra shuddered and moaned. She felt Zahra's vaginal muscles spasming, tightening around her fingers, and her own pussy clenched in response, her hips convulsing reflexively, as she ground against her hand moving between them. Her pleasure and Zahra's pleasure were one, a symphony of sensation nearing a magnificent crescendo.

"Fuck, fuck, fuck, *fuck!*" Zahra cried out throatily, her hips bucking, her small frame racked with tremors.

Macella flicked her tongue over a peaked nipple before taking it into her mouth and sucking gently. Zahra let out a series of expletives, shuddering and straining against Macella's grip on her wrists. She contracted around Macella's fingers, arching her back. Macella pumped her fingers faster, pressing against the spot she knew would drive Zahra over the edge. She trailed her tongue to Zahra's other nipple, teasing it with her teeth before sucking it into her mouth. Macella worked her tongue and hand steadily until Zahra's orgasm subsided and she lay spent.

Macella rolled onto her back, gazing up at the bedcurtains, and panting for breath. Her heart was racing, her skin buzzing with electricity. Her pussy throbbed, and she pressed her thighs together, reveling in the feeling of anticipation, the thrill of teetering on the precipice of climax. It was deliciously maddening.

"By the gods, you sure know how to make a lady feel welcome!" Zahra sighed out in her rapid-fire way, the huskiness in her voice softening the edges so that the words ran together. She rolled toward Macella. "Now let me show my appreciation."

Zahra grinned impishly and slid down the bed. She looked up with wicked, dancing eyes as she lowered her plump lips to Macella's clit. Macella shivered as Zahra exhaled a warm breath. She watched, heart racing, as Zahra's lips parted, and her pretty pink tongue darted out to flick against Macella's clit. Macella gasped and arched her back as Zahra ran her tongue down her center, sending jolts of electricity through Macella's veins.

Then Zahra sucked Macella's clit into her mouth, and coherent thought faded. The throbbing, shimmery excitement that buzzed through her core suddenly narrowed to a single point of agonizing sensation, focused on the apex Zahra was kneading with her tongue. It was too much. Macella was going to explode.

The sensation abruptly disappeared, and Macella huffed a frustrated, ragged breath. "Wh—"

"Daddy's home," Zahra cooed throatily.

Macella opened her eyes to see Aithan leaning against the bedroom door, a smirk playing around his lips and a noticeable bulge in his trousers. Already so close to the edge, Macella whimpered at the thought of his hard cock.

"By all means, continue. Don't let me interrupt," he said as he removed his boots and surcoat. "Would you like some privacy, or am I welcome to observe the festivities?"

Zahra slid her tongue along Macella's inner thigh, making her shudder. "I welcome your participation. Don't you agree, Lady Macella?"

Zahra flicked her tongue over Macella's clit, eliciting a loud moan. The throbbing in her pussy had grown unbearable. She was so close to her release.

Macella squirmed, watching through lowered lashes as Aithan moved toward the bed, slipping his shirt over his head. His eyes raked over her body, sending a rush of heat through her core. He stopped at the foot of the bed and let his pants fall to the floor, stepping out of them and freeing his massive erection.

Eyes on Macella, Aithan lifted Zahra by the hips, forcing her onto her hands and knees. Then he leaned down, and Macella could almost feel the moment his tongue found Zahra's clit from behind. Zahra moaned and lowered her mouth back to Macella. When she felt Zahra's tongue prodding, then massaging, Macella gasped, her head filling with stars.

Then she was falling over the precipice, finally releasing a bit of the tempest that had been building since her lips met Zahra's. And still, somehow, there was another level, a further peak to reach. If Zahra just stayed *right there*—

Zahra suddenly threw her head back, crying out. Clearly, Aithan had found the right spot as well. Macella tried to catch her breath as she watched Zahra cum again. The sight of her—skin flushed, dark hair falling over her eyes in a sexy mess, full lips open in an expression of ecstasy—made Macella ache with desire.

Zahra collapsed, rolling onto her side. Propping her chin on Macella's hip, she gave a sheepish grin. "Sorry, love. You were close, weren't you? Blame that damn Aegis of yours and his relentless tongue."

Macella chuckled. "I forgive you. I've fallen prey to that tongue many times. I know its powers."

Aithan smirked at them from the foot of the bed. He wiped his mouth and winked. Macella shivered, heart racing. The throbbing ache in her core heightened another notch.

"Apologies," Aithan said, rounding the bed and slipping in beside Macella. "Allow me to make amends."

He nudged Macella on to her side, positioning himself behind her. Macella's breath quickened at the feel of his body against hers, the press of his steely cock against her rear. He ran a hand down her side, spreading heat everywhere he touched. Zahra slid higher on the bed so she could take one of Macella's nipples between her lips, making her gasp and her hips buck. Then Zahra slid a hand between Macella's thighs, rubbing over her quivering warmth, and spreading her open as Aithan sheathed his cock inside of her.

Macella almost came from that first thrust, so taut were her nerves. She whimpered, throwing her head back, and arching her back, pressing her breasts into Zahra's face and her ass against Aithan, driving him deeper. It seemed both were determined to give her a release worthy of the anticipation. Zahra's tongue circled her nipple, while her fingers found Macella's clit and mirrored the movement. Aithan pressed kisses against the nape of her neck as he slid in and out of her slowly, clutching her hip and thrusting deep, filling her aching, throbbing core.

Her orgasm took her suddenly and completely, and still they pushed her higher. She was completely overwhelmed, drowning in sensation. Zahra's tongue. Aithan's cock. Zahra's fingers. Aithan's lips. They were everywhere, coaxing pleasure from her every pore. Macella let wave after wave of ecstasy wash over her, coming again and again, crying out their names until she was hoarse.

Finally, she lay utterly exhausted between them, sore and satisfied.

"You are welcome to sleep here," she murmured sleepily to Zahra after they'd lain in companionable silence for a long while. "Neither the king nor anyone else in the keep will bat an eye about it."

Zahra yawned loudly. "Another time. After being on the road for so long, everything about luxuriating in my new quarters sounds just heavenly. I am going to sleep sideways in that massive bed. Good night, loves."

Zahra sat up and leaned to kiss Aithan, then Macella. Then she rolled out of the bed, gathered her clothes from the floor, and trudged, naked, to the hidden panel in the wall. She blew them another kiss before she stepped into the darkness and closed the panel behind herself.

"It is good to have her here with us," Aithan said quietly, stroking Macella's curls. "She has a gift for making things lighter and brighter somehow. And she makes you happy."

Macella snuggled closer to him. "You all do. Our little family brings me so much joy."

"Me too," Aithan replied, wrapping her in his arms. "Me too."

⚜

After they'd broken their fast the following morning, Aithan handed Macella an apple. She raised an eyebrow at him, then inspected the fruit. They'd just eaten, so she wasn't at all hungry. She looked at Aithan quizzically.

"What do you see?" he asked, gesturing for her to look at the apple again.

Macella studied it. "It's a green apple, fairly ripe, as they are in season, of course. Is there something special about it?"

Aithan frowned. "Concentrate. Are you certain it's an apple?"

Macella huffed and stared harder at the fruit in her palm. She squinted, turning it this way and that. It looked completely ordinary. She gave Aithan an exasperated look.

"It's not an apple," he sighed, sitting back, and crossing his arms. "I asked Aisling to glamour an object for me to use in a training exercise. Of course, I didn't explain that it was for training *you*. I want you to practice resisting Khari's visions. I've trained myself to see through her illusions, and I believe you can too. I suspect our crossbreed nature allows us some greater awareness of, and natural resistance to, most magic."

Macella scrutinized the object in her hand, considering his words. It stubbornly remained an apple.

She shook her head doubtfully. "I'm not sure about that," she countered. "I couldn't see through Khari's illusion yesterday, even after you showed me the truth as you saw it. It is as if her magic didn't impact you at all."

"I've practiced," Aithan insisted. "You will find it grows easier over time. Look at the apple closely. Search for the threads of Aisling's magic. I thought, perhaps, since her magic is so familiar to us, it might be easier for you to detect."

Macella furrowed her brow. "What do you mean by familiar? I've never noticed any *threads* when Aisling does magic."

Now it was Aithan's turn to look confused. "You can't sense it? Every sorcerer's magic has a certain...smell. That isn't the right word, but it's the closest I can offer. We're around Aisling so much that the scent of her magic has grown familiar."

"Have you always been aware of magic in this way?" Macella asked. There was something about this ability that struck her—an idea slowly forming in the recesses of her mind.

Aithan frowned again. "I believe so, but not to this extent. It's grown stronger, clearer recently. Actually, since..."

"Since we found each other," Macella finished for him. "Both of us have discovered new or enhanced abilities since we met."

"Hmm." Aithan hummed thoughtfully. "Unknown powers now unloosed."

"There is something about *you* that allows you to detect magic. It's an inherent gift that has grown, just as your other abilities have of late. But it might not be because you're a crossbreed, since it doesn't appear that I have the same ability." Macella said each word carefully, still trying to see the full picture. "I don't know enough about magic, and no one knows enough about Aegis-human offspring, to explain these variations. Lotta would know how to search the library's tomes for helpful information but there's no way to ask her for help without revealing our secrets."

"Would that be so terrible?" Aithan asked quietly. "We have a lot to learn before the Blessed Rite. We could use the assistance of a book moth like Lotta."

Macella shook her head vehemently. "It's too dangerous. I can't risk her coming to harm."

Her voice broke a little and Aithan took both her hands in his, cradling the apple. "Of course. Anyway, I'm sure you just need more practice." He fixed her with a serious look. "Macella, I *need* you to be able to resist her. I hate that she can torment you at will, as she did during the small council meeting."

"Me too," Macella whispered. She stared at the apple in their cupped palms, straining her eyes, trying desperately to detect the threads of Aisling's glamour. But all she saw was the fruit's thin, green skin.

"We'll try something else," Aithan said, standing at the sound of a knock on their chamber door. "It's a ball of yarn."

Macella glared at the ball of yarn, which still appeared to be an apple. A servant stepped into the room, bowing politely at them both.

"I apologize for interrupting your morning, but her grace, King Khari, has summoned all of the castle's inhabitants to the throne room for an important announcement," the servant told them apologetically. "She asked that we assemble everyone immediately."

The now-familiar, heavy weight of dread settled in Macella's stomach. What new game was this? She couldn't help but think about Lord Kasper and the king's horrible display of power. Perhaps Khari wanted to make a public example now. Or maybe she'd decided to replace him and was going to announce the appointment of a new Grand Treasurer.

Aithan stepped to her side, placing a comforting hand on the small of her back. "Thank you, Bailey. We'll be there at once."

The servant bowed again before exiting. Aithan wrapped an arm around Macella's waist and kissed her temple. She exhaled slowly, leaning into his solid warmth.

"Perhaps the king is going to announce your new initiative," he said teasingly. "Lady Macella of Shively, champion of the poor."

Macella laughed shakily and gave Aithan a playful shove. She appreciated the effort to make her laugh, and even his attempt to train her against magical attacks. She knew how much it wore on him, watching her navigate her new role, unable to protect her from Khari's machinations.

"If she says that in front of the whole castle, I will burst into flames," she retorted, taking his arm. "Let's hurry before she grows impatient."

Macella would soon wish Khari's announcement *was* about a poorly named new initiative.

Unfortunately, it was much, much worse.

Chapter Seven

Macella

When they reached the throne room, Macella joined the small council members positioned below the dais, while Aithan took up his post with Sir Griselda behind the Crown. Macella avoided Lord Kasper's stealthy glares, knowing he wouldn't dare openly show hostility—not after King Khari had made it so clear she would defend Macella's honor. Still, she could feel the icy loathing emanating from the Grand Treasurer. Steadfastly ignoring him, she surveyed the impromptu gathering, occupying herself with idle musings about the purpose of this assembly.

The room was quickly filling with the various nobles currently residing at court, along with higher-ranking servants and other workers who slipped in quietly to line the back wall. Macella saw Charlotte greet Lynn, the high tailor, before taking a seat at the Royal Scribe's desk. Aisling stood with the castle's other mages and novices, while Jacan, Finley, and Zahra stood together on the edge of the crowd nearest the Royal Scribe. The throne room was about a quarter full by the time everyone arrived. Macella couldn't help but feel a stab of anxiety at the thought of how soon this room would be overflowing, the castle filled with guests for the cold season, all gawking at her, jostling for her favor, hoping to draw her into their power games. And then, after being shown off like a prize mare all season, she'd ascend to the throne and take a seat on the dais above her.

If you survive the Blessed Rite, a nasty voice whispered in her mind. *If you stop Khari. If you hold back hell.*

(11) "Their graces, King Khari, Queen Annika, and Monarch Meztli!"

Macella's bleak thoughts were interrupted by a herald announcing the Crown's arrival. Everyone in the hall dropped to one knee as the royals entered and ascended the dais. Head lowered, Macella watched them take their seats. The king draped herself languorously across her huge throne, the intricate vines threading through its iron and wood matching the gold of her crown, her surcoat, and even her glowing skin. A grin played around the corners of her mouth—what Macella thought of as her cat-that-caught-the-canary look. That look never meant anything good.

Beside her, and in stark contrast, Queen Annika sat upon her throne of driftwood and sapphires, her porcelain skin paler than usual. With her long flaxen hair and vibrant blue gown accentuating her wide cobalt eyes, she looked like a princess from a child's storybook. On Khari's other side, Monarch Meztli looked regal and inscrutable, their black eyes fixed on a point beyond the watching crowd. They sat rigidly on their stone throne, their stiff posture and solemn countenance contrasting the liveliness of the inlaid gold, turquoise, and amethysts adorning their throne's intricately carved patterns of geometric designs and animals. Macella wondered what emotions they were sensing that made them look so grave.

Not long ago, there'd been a fourth throne—one of pristine ivory, inlaid with obsidian gems. Soon, there would be a new seat in its vacated place. Macella had been agonizing for weeks over its design. The artisans were growing anxious, worried they wouldn't have time to complete their work satisfactorily before her coronation. She pushed the thought away.

"You may rise," King Khari announced, lazily waving a hand.

Macella stood, along with the rest of the crowd. For a long moment, the room was silent, waiting for King Khari to begin, to explain why she'd gathered everyone together. Slowly, the king stood. She looked thoughtfully over the crowd, letting the silence stretch for an uncomfortable length of time.

Finley caught Macella's attention with a delicate toss of their lovely head. When she met their gaze, they rolled their eyes, then tapped their temple as they tucked a strand of hair behind one ear. It was an invitation. Macella reached for their mind.

She is milking the moment excessively, they thought at her. *It's so tacky. Have you any idea what this is about?*

Macella shook her head slightly and saw Finley sigh in response. They both turned their attention back to the king, who finally appeared ready to speak.

"Thank you all for joining us on such short notice," King Khari began, her voice rich and sonorous, filling the cavernous space. "I know that it has been a difficult time, with the attacks on the capital and this sacred castle."

An uneasy murmur passed through the crowd. Macella felt the shift in the air, smelled the spike of fear many in the room experienced at the memory. Behind the king, Queen Annika grew paler still. Macella saw Aithan shift closer to the young queen, preparing to catch her if she fainted again.

"The safety of Kōsaten and its people is the Crown's top priority," King Khari continued. "As such, please know that we are taking immediate action to protect the keep, and the entire kingdom. Among other precautions, we have summoned several additional Aegises to the capital so that we can increase patrols in the city, while simultaneously retaining skilled protectors within the castle walls at all times. I assure you that we will find a more permanent solution when the kingdom's best minds and all of its Aegises convene here at Kōsaten Keep for the cold season."

Again, the crowd murmured, but the discomfort in the sound had lessened. Macella had to admit that King Khari could turn on the charisma when needed. She seemed sincere and caring, but firm—the picture of a ruler concerned for her people, but fearlessly determined to fight for their well-being. Macella relaxed a bit. Of course, King Khari would want to reassure the castle's inhabitants that she was still in control. It was a perfectly sound reason to gather everyone together.

"However, that is not why I have gathered you here today," King Khari said.

Macella deflated immediately, her anxiety rising once more as the king continued.

"Well, not entirely. I believe, given the recent tribulations, it is particularly fortunate to have a reason for celebration."

At that cue, a team of servers entered the room, and began distributing goblets of sparkling wine. Khari smiled benevolently at them all as she watched her cupbearer taste her wine. Then she lifted her goblet, its ornate gold and garnet design glinting in the candlelight.

"My heart is so full," King Khari exclaimed warmly, lowering her goblet, and positively beaming at her audience. Macella would almost believe she was being genuine, were it not for her cold ochre eyes. "Already, we have much to celebrate with my impending nuptials to the brave, brilliant, and beautiful Lady Macella."

The king lifted her goblet again, smiling that false, adoring smile she liked to put on whenever they were in company together. The crowd lifted their cups, whispering as they scrutinized Macella. She wondered how many of them had heard of her actions during the demon attack. Most likely they all had, considering gossip was the currency of the keep. She inclined her head graciously, accepting the king's praise as she was expected to.

"The gods have seen fit to bless me further—to bless our kingdom during this time of turmoil," King Khari declared, turning her attention back to the crowd. "Your king is truly favored above all other rulers, my legacy still growing after a century of achievement."

The king swelled with pride, her smile so wide it had become wolfish. Macella shivered, a wave of nausea passing over her. The truth struck her suddenly, just a breath before Khari confirmed her fears.

King Khari lifted her goblet high, sweeping her arms wide in an all-encompassing gesture. "It seems I am to have not only a new wife, but also my first offspring. Her grace, Queen Annika, is with child!"

Macella's blood froze, her eyes snapping to meet Aithan's. His eyes reflected her distress for a moment before he smoothed his expression. Macella tried to do the same. The room filled with enthusiastic applause as the king turned and extended a hand to her young queen. Queen Annika rose shakily and took the king's hand, stepping to her side.

"A toast to Queen Annika and the blessed babe she bears!" Lord Anwir proclaimed.

Macella didn't taste the sweet sparkling wine as she mechanically sipped from her goblet. She hardly heard the king's gushing words or the subsequent prayers led by the Grand Mage. *Her grace, Queen Annika, is with child.* She should've known. Annika had been so quiet, so pale of late. She'd been sick during the last small council meeting. And...there'd been something else, hadn't there?

Most of all, they love to prey on pregnant people and—um—drink the fetus. Charlotte's voice echoed in Macella's memory, taking her back to the day of the attack on the castle. Her sister had been spouting facts about the manananggal, helping Macella devise a plan to defeat the creature. Moments later, the demon had gone straight for the young queen, targeting her specifically, despite the fact that she was the most heavily guarded person in the foyer. The manananggal had known.

Macella wondered what King Khari had told Queen Annika. Did the young queen know the true nature of the child she carried? Was she aware of her wife's nefarious plans for it? She didn't seem as smugly pleased as Macella would've expected. Instead, Annika accepted the king's praise with a subdued smile, looking like she'd rather be elsewhere.

The dark gods would see this as a further affront, another example of King Khari pursuing power and threatening the balance between realms. Would they guess the king had learned to breed Aegisborn as a first step in her plan to create a loyal Aegis army? If the gods took it as an act of war, the realm might not make it to the cold season.

A shield. A scribe. A sword. A pen. Against hell's fury. Against our end.

Macella could've cried with relief by the time she returned to her chambers for midday meal with her friends. The morning had been full of insipid talk and celebration. Queen Annika had finally excused herself, apologetically explaining that the pregnancy made her tire easily, and the impromptu party had waned from there. King Khari and her entourage had taken their revelries to the king's chambers and, thus, Macella had been free to make her escape.

At least she wouldn't have to feign excitement among her family. Though only Finley knew the true horror of the news, none of the Wildfire Court cared much for King Khari or Queen Annika. As they sat in the parlor enjoying their meal, Zahra summed up everyone's thoughts in a few quick words, accompanied by her clumsy hand signing.

"Poor kid," she said, shaking her head. "I cannot think of two people less suited to be parents."

"Maybe they'll surprise us," Charlotte offered hopefully, signing simply but more smoothly. "Queen Annika has been a lot less annoying lately. Maybe the prospect of parenthood is maturing her."

Finley laughed and pinched Charlotte's cheek. Charlotte batted their hand away, making them laugh their musical laugh again. "Dear Lotta, your optimism is utterly adorable. Maybe they'll be good parents, and maybe we'll actually use Macella's lovely dining room for midday meal instead of lounging in the parlor while we eat, like a pack of heathens."

Charlotte stuck out her tongue. They went on, teasing and talking, everyone speaking and signing with the familiarity of people who'd learned to communicate easily with one another through frequent practice. All around her, Macella's family ate and laughed, while she and Aithan exchanged worried thoughts.

Poor kid, indeed. They'll be a pawn in their mothers' games.

And a coveted bargaining chip for any enemy who could capture them. Macella shuddered at the thought of the dangers this child would face on all sides.

"Are you two going to tell us what's really going on, or are we going to keep fucking around?" Zahra demanded suddenly in her blunt way, cutting into their mental conversation, and looking from Macella to Aithan impatiently.

Macella opened her mouth to respond, but Finley's melodious laugh interrupted her. She closed her mouth and turned helplessly to Aithan. He shrugged.

"I like you more and more each day," Finley told Zahra, before fixing Macella with a shrewd look. "She's not wrong. We're all here because you trust us. But you've not been completely open with everyone."

"It's not a matter of trust," Macella replied carefully. "It is a matter of safety. You are the dearest people in the world to us. We've already endangered you enough by inviting you to live here with us. We don't want to risk you any further."

Unbidden, Khari's pre-betrothal threat sprang to Macella's mind. *I would simply request that you remember, it is not only you who will suffer my displeasure if ever you should cease to be an asset. Finley, Charlotte, Zahra, Aithan—even people you hardly care for or only briefly knew, like the madame at that shitty brothel, the blacksmith's daughter, your servant Lucy, or our dear high tailor—they are all at my mercy. And even once we are wed and the magical bindings preclude me from harming you, it will not protect your friends. You are well aware of the sights I can show them.*

Macella shuddered at the memory. She bit her lip and exchanged an anxious glance with Aithan. He only tilted his head slightly, indicating that the choice was hers to make. He would support her decision either way.

Zahra made an exasperated sound. She flapped an impatient hand at Aisling. "Mage, can you give us some privacy?"

Aisling reddened but gave Zahra a defiant glare. "I'm an ember in the Wildfire Court. I might be the newest to this merry little family, but I am as loyal as Argos. I owe Macella of Shively and Aithan of Auburndale my life. They can trust me."

Macella felt a rush of affection for the novice mage that surprised her. She'd known that she could count Aisling among her friends but had sometimes worried the young woman might fear more than like her. Now, seeing the glint in the novice's eye, Macella knew she'd underestimated her courage.

"Do you know what happens to sorcerers who never become mages?" Aisling asked quietly, not giving Zahra a chance to respond before continuing. "We're all born the same, you know. But if we can't afford to go to a school to be properly trained on how to control our powers, the magic will consume us—burn through us until there's nothing left. Eventually, it will drive us mad or kill us. Death is the far better option. The way the magic twists a sorcerer over time—"

Aisling broke off for a moment, swallowing hard. As if summoned by her distress, Nyx materialized from the shadows and hopped into her lap, turning in a circle before curling up against the young mage's soft stomach. Gratefully, the novice planted a kiss on the cat's head. Then she regained her composure and continued.

"I have no idea why the gods spared me so long. By my age, it is usually far too late to learn control," Aisling said. "I was already descending into madness when I met Lady Macella and Lord Aithan. I had begun to hurt people, even while I justified it to myself, and lied to myself about being in control. They pulled me back from that precipice and put me on the path to getting the training I needed to heal."

Zahra smiled, her face softening as she took Aisling's hand. "I believe you are to be trusted. And that bit about being an *ember* instead of a *member* of the Wildfire Court was a pretty delightful play on words. But I meant, could you actually give us privacy. Like, do some of your magical gobbledygook to protect us from any prying ears."

Aisling's blush deepened. "Oh, yes. I've already done that. I usually do when we're together. I hope that's okay."

Her gray eyes fixed anxiously on Macella. Nyx purred scratchily, her yellow eyes following Aisling's gaze.

Macella took a deep breath, smiling at them both. "Of course, that's okay. I chose you to be my personal mage because I trust your instincts," Macella assured her. Then she looked at each of her friends in turn. "I do trust all of you unequivocally, and that will not change if you decide right now that you would like to take your leave. There are some outside of this room that we respect and trust but cannot risk sharing our secrets with because of their positions. People like Meztli and Lynn and Drudo. You will have to keep this from them." Macella looked at Charlotte, then Finley, before continuing. "If you stay for this conversation, you will become privy to information that could get you—and us—killed."

Macella paused, letting her words hang in the air. Aithan took her hand, reassuring her that he trusted her decision and, as always, would support her. Nyx wrapped her tail around herself and laid her head on her paws, blinking lazily at Macella. No one else moved. The silence stretched for a long moment.

"Well, this is all very dramatic, but can we get on with it? King Khari provided enough theatrics for one day," Finley drawled, studying their nails. "Everyone here would die or kill for you, you honorable fools. We would not have joined your entourage otherwise. We all knew we were walking into the viper's nest."

"I didn't," Charlotte interjected. "But even if I had, I still would've come. I was drowning and you threw me a line. I've spent years being carried on a current of everyone else's decisions, but you gave me a choice. And I...I have come alive in these past few months. I would certainly give my life for your cause. I owe it to you."

Macella swallowed the lump rising in her throat. Lotta beamed at her, tears glistening on her cheeks. Jacan hesitantly placed a hand on Charlotte's shoulder, and Macella's little sister smiled up at the young Aegis, covering his hand with hers.

It's about time those two got on with it, Aithan thought at Macella wryly.

"You are the Saviors of Smoketown," Jacan said simply. "You will always have my loyalty."

"You saved my town," Zahra said. "And I love you. Why else would I have given up my badge and hauled ass to Pleasure Ridge Park without hesitation? Gods, you two *are* dramatic."

"Thank you," Finley huffed, throwing up a hand. "So, to recap: we all love you and are committed to your brave little cause, whatever it may be exactly. Now you can stop with all the noble efforts to protect us and tell us precisely what we're getting into."

Macella's heart swelled. Aithan squeezed her hand. She looked into the faces of her entourage—her most trusted advisors and friends. Finley, Zahra, Charlotte, Jacan, Aisling, Nyx, and, of course, Aithan. The Wildfire Court. Her family.

As if reading her thoughts, Aisling repeated the advice Aithan had given her when they'd first met. "Find an honorable way to live this life, and the right people will find you."

Macella nodded, swallowing against another wave of emotion. She sighed, refilled her goblet, and then settled herself on the plush sofa. Aithan sat beside her, putting an arm around her shoulders.

And then she told them everything.

Aithan chimed in occasionally, offering additional details, helping her with the sign language, or explaining some relevant aspect of Aegis ways. But mostly, he let Macella be the storyteller, let her weave the tale as she saw fit.

She told them about the way she and Aithan had both changed as they spent more time together, ultimately discovering the truth of their crossbreed natures and the gifts that came with their heritages, and how she'd become her full self after surviving Hades's trials. She told them about meeting her father beyond the veil, and about how, later, the Grand Mage had helped recover the memories of Aithan's mothers in exchange for any knowledge that might help breed Aegisborn children for the king. She told them about her ability to touch Otherworldly minds and see the dead, about her temporary healing ability, and the about the unique abilities of each member of the Crown. Finally, she told them about the imminent war they were facing, from Kiho's ill-fated coup attempt to Hades's demand that Macella and Aithan defeat King Khari to restore the balance between the realms.

When she had finally finished speaking, the room was utterly silent aside from Nyx's low purring. Macella's throat was dry and her heart hammering with all she had revealed. She took a moment to compose herself and drank deeply from a glass of water Aithan poured. Then, hesitantly, she looked around at the faces of her friends.

Charlotte's cheeks were wet with tears, her eyes wide behind her spectacles. Jacan had an arm around Charlotte's shoulders, his expression solemn. Aisling had gone very pale, while Nyx looked as unfazed as always, aside from her swishing tail. Zahra had leaned forward, chin propped on a fist, her mismatched gaze intensely focused. She opened her mouth to speak.

Before she could say a word, Finley held up an imperious hand. Expression inscrutable, they slowly crossed the room to the side table, where they refilled their goblet of wine and drained it in one long sip. Then, they filled the goblet again before making their way around the room, handing out fresh helpings of wine for everyone. At last, they settled back on the chaise and exhaled a heavy sigh.

"Let us play a game," they suggested, a half-smile tugging at the corner of their mouth. "Everyone gets a single, uninterrupted reaction sentence before we truly begin this conversation. Zahra, you're first."

"Fuck," Zahra replied.

Everyone waited, allowing her to think. Several long moments passed. Finley lifted an eyebrow.

Zahra looked around at their expectant faces and laughed. "That was my entire sentence. Fuck." She shrugged. "Your turn, fancy fox."

Finley grinned. "I'm going last, because it's my game. Aisling?"

Aisling jumped a little, but her voice was surprisingly steady. "I knew there was more to you two. I could feel it from the first time we met."

Macella reached for Aithan, who took her hand and intertwined their fingers. She remembered what Aisling had said after their first encounter. *I want to know nothing of this. Your Fate is not a safe one.* Macella wondered if the Seer had known even then that she'd eventually encounter them and their dangerous Fate again.

"That sounded like two sentences, but I'll allow it," Finley drawled. "Your penalty is that you have to finish your wine and refill your cup. Get some color back into those delicious, chubby cheeks."

Aisling blushed as scarlet as her hair. She obeyed, draining and then moving to refill her goblet. Nyx watched her with round yellow eyes until the mage had resettled on the rug. Then she turned her lamp-like gaze on Finley.

"Your turn, Nyx," Finley told the cat.

Nyx looked to Macella, as if considering. Then she crossed the room and hopped gracefully into Macella's lap. She kneaded Macella's thighs with her little paws, turned in a circle, and then lay down, purring contentedly.

"Well said, you little imp," Finley proclaimed. "Jacan?"

Jacan looked straight into Macella's eyes as he spoke. "I'm all in."

She felt a surge of love for the young Aegis, hardly more than a boy. He'd seen so little of life, and mostly only the worst parts of it. There was so much time and possibility before him. But he hadn't even hesitated.

"Lotta," Finley said quietly.

Macella's stomach dropped. Charlotte had known little of what Macella had just shared—much less than any of the others, really. Even Jacan had already known or suspected about the Crown's powers and wouldn't be as surprised by things like visions and conversations with gods. He'd been in Smoketown when Macella visited and had seen so much growing up there. Charlotte was younger and less experienced than anyone else in the room but had also known Macella the longest. Macella couldn't imagine what her sister might be thinking, couldn't help but fear she might be reconsidering their entire relationship through the lens of this new knowledge.

Charlotte's eyes were still glistening with tears as she said, "I guess this explains why you're the only family member I've ever really liked."

Macella choked out a relieved laugh that sounded more like a sob. She sagged against Aithan. He disentangled their hands and wrapped his arms around her, pulling her closer.

"Finley?" he said expectantly. "Intentionally last but not least for maximum theatrical effect."

Finley smiled a smile so feline it rivaled Nyx's predatory grace. "The thing about wildfire is, it is not easily contained or controlled. It spreads. It's time Khari learned the consequences of playing with fire. Let's burn her empire to the fucking ground."

Chapter Eight

Macella

Macella hadn't realized the weight of the secrets she'd been carrying. In the weeks following her confession to the Wildfire Court, she found herself filled with a lightness she hadn't felt since she and Aithan had moved to Kōsaten Keep. Of course, she'd always been able to be her true self when alone with him, but it was different having an entire family of people who knew her fully and loved her wholly. Even with the insurmountable obstacles ahead, she felt freer and more hopeful than ever.

One morning, Macella, Aisling, and Zahra, with Nyx racing silently through the grass behind them, rode out to assess the progress of Macella's new initiative. She had insisted the preparations begin immediately, determined that the workers would be able to move into their new homes before the cold season set in. Though she'd framed it to the small council as a smart public relations decision and a way to secure a workforce that would be ready to go as soon as the warm season dawned, her real reasoning was much less mercenary.

She knew the homes being built on the castle's grounds would be substantially warmer and safer than those the workers currently occupied in the city. The field laborers typically came from the poorest areas of the capital—places like The Bardo. No matter how decent and hardworking they were, there were few opportunities for most of Pleasure Ridge Park's lower classes to earn a comfortable living. The housing the Crown would provide was worth far more to the laborers than any other aspect of Macella's plan.

In fact, most of the workers had eagerly accepted the invitation to camp on the grounds until their quarters were complete. Already, clusters of tents and lean-tos dotted the edge of the acreage cleared for construction. The little encampment was always abuzz with activity. The hammering and sawing sounds from the builders mingled with laughter, lively conversation, and singing, as the workers' families went about their days.

Macella loved the comfortable, cheerful bustle. She knew what it was to be poor and how an opportunity such as this would've drastically improved her family's lives. She knew how worry became a stone around your neck when you didn't know how you'd be able to afford your next meal, or life-saving medicine, or a pair of boots that weren't too-big or too-small, battered hand-me-downs. The atmosphere in the laborers' camp was that of people learning what it was to know that their basic needs would be met.

Before Macella had even dismounted, a handful of children eagerly raced forward to take Cinnamon's reins. Most of the laborers' partners and children spent their days helping in whatever way they could with the construction, harvesting from the far fields, foraging wild plants, and getting to know one another. Already, they were forming routines, norms, relationships. Becoming a community.

Plus, Macella and Charlotte's calculations had proven correct. Yields were higher than they'd been last harvest. Even with a tenth of the crops and half of the foraged plants supplementing the workers' meager daily wage, there was still more than enough left to feed the castle's inhabitants *and* to continue to sell and trade as usual. It might have been a small victory in the grand scheme of things, but Macella still felt damn good about it.

"Don't give him too many apples, he's getting quite spoiled," Macella told the children as she dismounted.

The laborers and their families had quickly become somewhat accustomed to Macella's presence. They'd been told that they owed their good fortune to the future queen but had certainly not expected her attention as well. After all, average citizens only ever saw the Crown on rare, formal occasions, and usually from afar. But if she must be queen, Macella had no intention of being that kind of ruler. She made a point of visiting the fields and the encampment several times a week, often accompanied by one or two embers of the Wildfire Court, and always with Sir Kamau trailing behind.

"Yes, my lady," the children chorused, bowing, and stifling giggles.

Macella crossed her eyes and made a silly face, and they burst into laughter. "I don't believe you for one moment," she said, shaking her head. "You're all as incorrigible as Cinnamon."

The children laughed again, the bravest among them chattering and vying for Macella's attention. Most were still a bit intimidated by the future queen and didn't dare come too close, but they watched her every move. They reminded Macella of her siblings and niblings back home. She greeted each of them by name, asking after their families, and listening to the bits of news they wished to share. Several of them wanted to show her how they'd practiced rolling a coin across their knuckles, an old trick Macella had taught them during her last visit—one her father had taught her during the early childhood years she couldn't remember.

"Don't you go spoiling that one either," Aisling interjected as Nyx appeared, and several children ran to pet her sleek black fur.

The cat was another favorite in the encampment, happily joining Aisling on these visits. She would follow their horses for a while when they left the keep, then wander off to stalk small animals and investigate interesting smells. She always met them at the encampment eventually. Tired from her hunt, Nyx would lie in the sun and allow the children to rub her head and scratch her chin while she dozed. When it was time to return to the keep, she'd curl up in one of their saddlebags and nap until they got home.

Of all her entourage, Aisling was the one who most often accompanied Macella on these visits. The Grand Mage was thrilled by the discovery of various magical herbs on the grounds, thanks to the laborers' families and their foraging. She sent Aisling to catalog their findings and acquire samples, but Macella was pretty sure Aisling would've found a way to tag along even if the Grand Mage hadn't tasked her with the duty. The young mage seemed at home among the laborers. She, too, had known what it was like to work for every scrap of food. These people were hers as much as Macella's.

Macella, Aisling, and Zahra made their way through the camp at a leisurely pace, exchanging pleasantries and assisting with minor tasks wherever they could. Lagging behind them, Sir Kamau tried to keep up with his charge while simultaneously entertaining a horde of children. They adored Macella's knight almost as much as they did her furry companions. He let them touch his armor and wear his helmet and even taught them a bit of swordplay. At least half the children had declared they'd be joining the Royal Guard when they came of age.

"Those kids would shit a shisa if Aithan or one of the other Aegises came through here," Zahra mused. "Sir Kamau is impressive and all, but he can't hold a candle to our darlings. I guarantee those cute little fuckers would immediately disavow the Royal Guard in favor of joining the Thirteen. The gods have truly blessed the harvest, haven't they?"

Macella hid her laughter as they passed a woman scrubbing clothes in a metal basin, and Zahra switched from the quick, low voice she'd been using with her friends to an elegant tone befitting her noble birth. The woman bowed and smiled, her expression warm and open. Macella offered a silent prayer of thanks for Zahra's presence. She was learning much from her friend about how to be both genteel and approachable.

"If they knew how impressive Lady Macella is, they'd all want to be warrior queens," Aisling said proudly as they moved on. "She's the best Aegis of all."

Macella gave Aisling's arm an affectionate squeeze. "Finley would be devastated to hear that. I'm certain they believe *they're* everyone's favorite Aegis." She sighed heavily, a pang of worry tightening her chest. "I know the others would love to see how well things are going. If only as a reprieve from their duties."

Aithan, Finley, and Jacan were on near-constant patrol, the former always remaining near the keep, while the latter two guarded the city. They slept in shifts when they slept at all. Macella had sensed a rift long before dawn that very morning, around the hour of Mên. Of course, Finley and Jacan had been on watch and had likely long since closed it, but they would still be diligently hunting for any demons that may have crossed before they reached the rift.

Their enemy was relentless. Rifts routinely appeared within and around the capital. Surprisingly, however, the Aegises shielding the rest of the kingdom reported a *decrease* in rifts. Again, it seemed the attacks were purposely targeting the seat of Kōsaten's power—or perhaps targeting the person hoarding that power.

"Kai and Diya should be here any day," Zahra said soothingly, taking Macella's arm. "They'll lighten the load. And then it will be the cold season, and we'll have a chance to figure everything out."

The Wildfire Court had hardly had time to discuss the plethora of problems before them in the fortnight since Macella had told them everything. Nonetheless, everyone was working toward solutions in their own ways. Charlotte practically lived in the library, Jacan assisting her during his rare free time, and Aisling joining her between lessons to offer a magical perspective and help search for any tidbit of information about Aegiskind, the Blessed Rite, resisting god gifts, or a million other tangential topics. Meanwhile, Zahra moved among the nobility, ingratiating herself to the wealthy and powerful, stealthily charming them out of their secrets, and gaining allies for the future queen. In spare moments, Aisling patiently helped Macella practice her magical resistance, despite how little progress she seemed to be making. Aithan and Finley—whether in company with the Crown, nobles, soldiers, or citizens—listened and watched, gathering whatever information they could, and comparing it to all they'd heard and seen over their long lives. Though none of them had yet come up with many answers, it felt nice to have allies.

"Nyx has been voraciously hunting mice lately! There must be hordes of rodents trying to nest in the keep," Aisling added cheerfully. "You know that means the cold season is drawing near."

Macella smiled. With all the trouble before them, it was odd how content she felt. She talked with her friends and her people, enjoying the cool bite of the morning air. It caressed her skin as she checked on the progress of the construction, helped dig a well, and gathered wild mushrooms, falling into the natural role of storyteller as she worked. There always seemed to be a loose crowd around her, straining to catch her words over the noise of their own chores.

(12) Just before the hour of Helios, when Macella was thinking it was time to return to the castle for a hardy midday meal, she felt a sudden chill. Her star charm grew colder against the hollow of her throat. Her skin prickled with gooseflesh even before she heard the gasps and exclamations behind her. She turned to see several people approaching Aisling, who stood stock still, skin starkly pale, eyes empty white pools. The pail of water in her hand swung wildly, as if she'd stopped moving rather abruptly.

"Don't touch her!" Macella commanded, and everyone obediently froze. "Give her space. We do not want to impede her Sight."

Ignoring Macella's order, Nyx materialized from wherever she'd been napping and rubbed against Aisling's leg. Macella drew nearer to the young mage, watching her face for any signs of distress. Slowly, Aisling's head turned toward Macella, fixing her with that eerie, empty gaze. An icy finger trailed along Macella's spine.

Instinctively, she slid her hands into the pockets of her wide-legged trousers—toward the daggers in her thigh holsters. She would forever be indebted to the high tailor for the practical alterations to her wardrobe.

In another moment, Aisling's eyes cleared, pale gray irises returning. She inhaled a shuddering breath, eyes darting around in surprise. Nyx circled her, rubbing against the mage's legs insistently. Aisling took another breath, her shoulders relaxing when she looked down and saw the cat. Then she seemed to recognize her surroundings and panic filled her face.

"It slipped through. It's coming. We have to get away from here right now!" she exclaimed, grabbing Macella's hands. Aisling's hands were ice cold despite her customary elbow-length gloves. "It comes from the south in a ball of flame!"

Macella pulled her daggers free and pointed one west toward the fields, where there would be laborers with tools that might be used as weapons if needed, and there would be stalks and other plant cover. It wasn't perfect, but it would have to do, since the workers' housing was still just wooden frames.

"Everyone take cover in the fields immediately! Danger approaches!" Macella ordered. "Sir Kamau, we must evacuate the encampment. Get these people out of here now!"

Dazedly at first, then more frantically, people began to move, calling for loved ones, and scooping up small children. Macella watched Zahra shift easily from the fine lady to the no-nonsense sheriff. She expertly herded the crowd, all-business in the face of the looming threat.

"How much time do we have?" Macella asked, eyes scanning the trees to the south of the encampment. The area had been cleared to build the houses, but the woods beyond were thick, even with most trees bare of leaves this late in the season. She wasn't sure she'd be able to see the beast coming.

"Minutes," Aisling replied, wringing her hands. "A quarter of an hour if we're lucky."

Sir Kamau approached. "They're headed to the fields, and the workers have been released to guard their families. The Grand Treasurer happened to be visiting, and he was none too happy about the interruption to the workday."

"He'll be plenty happy when we save the fields from being burnt to ash," Macella grunted dismissively. She didn't have time to worry about Lord Kasper's feelings right now.

"Lady Macella, we should get you to safety," Sir Kamau said hesitantly. He sounded halfhearted, as if he already knew his attempt was in vain.

Macella didn't take her eyes off the tree line. "A demon will emerge from those trees in a few minutes. We are all that will stand between it and those good, defenseless people. We, who have the good fortune of a Seer's warning to prepare us for its arrival. Shall we seek safety rather than serve our purpose and protect our people, Sir Kamau?"

"No, my lady," Sir Kamau replied. He turned away, muttering something that sounded suspiciously like "why do I bother?", but he drew his sword and scanned the forest.

Zahra appeared on Macella's other side, bow drawn, arrow loosely nocked. "What's coming for us, mage?"

Aisling shrugged miserably. She scooped Nyx up in her arms, cradling the cat to her chest. "I don't know. I only saw a great ball of flame barreling from the trees, flying toward the houses."

"The houses!" Macella hissed, snapping her head toward the abandoned construction.

A fire there would destroy the progress they'd made. The setback might make it impossible to complete the structures before the cold season, leaving several hundred laborers and their families unhoused during the long, brutally bitter months. She couldn't let that happen.

(13) Macella turned, preparing to make a run for the unfinished houses. She suddenly felt it—the presence of a dark, unfamiliar mind. It was approaching from the south, moving quickly. With nothing but destruction in its thoughts, it was inexorably drawn toward the abundance of human flesh gathered in one place. Perversely, the people's happiness drew it as much as their presence. It wanted to burn that happiness away, to snuff it out.

Macella broke into a sprint.

She heard the others behind her, but none of them would reach the site before she did. She cursed the necessity of holding back her true speed. She knew she wasn't going to make it. She could see a reddish glow in the trees, growing larger by the moment. If it emerged where she sensed it would, it would be on the perfect trajectory to reach the nearest house before she could.

Even in their early stage of construction, it was clear the homes would be simple and cozy. They sat in dozens of long, neat rows. Most were family homes, each with its own plot of land large enough for modest gardens or a few livestock. There were also larger structures more suitable for individuals or small families, with four sets of private rooms that all shared a single kitchen, common area, and plot of land. These homes were going to change so many lives.

Macella clutched her daggers in shaking fists, allowing herself to move just a little faster. She could sense the others behind her—Zahra a dozen or so paces behind, Sir Kamau close on her heels.

Too quickly, the fiery glow in the forest resolved into a huge ball of flame several cubits across, just as Aisling had described it. It burst from the trees, leaving branches burning in its wake, barreling straight for the houses.

Macella heard a surprised curse behind her but couldn't spare a look back. If she could get close enough, perhaps she could throw a dagger and knock the demon off course. She just needed to slow it down, and see what it was, so she could determine the best way to kill it.

It was going to beat her to the houses. She was still too far away to accurately throw her dagger, and the fireball was seconds from colliding with the nearest house. Why hadn't she sent for water and sand? They would salvage what they could once they subdued this beast.

Something whizzed past Macella's head, whistling in the wind as it narrowly missed her ear. Moments later, it hit the ball of flame. The flame careened wildly, emitting a chorus of earsplitting shrieks.

Macella glanced over her shoulder to see Zahra crouched on one knee, a second arrow nocked and at the ready. Sir Kamau was recovering from what appeared to be a fall that occurred when Zahra unexpectedly stopped to take that shot.

Macella turned her attention back to the demon, tracking it as it struggled to right itself. It was still shrieking angrily, but its flames seemed to be sputtering and dying. Macella eyed it as she moved to place herself between the creature and the half-built homes.

For a moment, the flames nearly flickered out completely, revealing the monster beneath. Macella's mouth went dry. She knew what this was.

A horrible, humanoid face grinned at her. It had no skin, only exposed, bloody tissue and ropey muscle. Milky, sunken eyes fixed on her, and its lipless grin widened.

This wasn't a creature she'd met with Aithan. No, this was a creature from her childhood nightmares. This was the thing that her mother's sister, Matant Dorotea, said would come and drink her blood if she was naughty.

The loogaroo was said to be a woman by day but able to shed its skin and fly around as a fireball at night. Maybe the stories got it wrong, because it was midday, and this was definitely a loogaroo. But no. Macella unconsciously prodded the thing's mind. It shouldn't be out, but it had no choice. It had slipped away as soon as the rift opened in the wee hours of the morning, shedding its skin, and escaping before the Aegises arrived to close the rift. It'd managed to evade them but had thus been unable to return to its skin for fear of discovery. Jacan and Finley had probably destroyed its skin by now.

So, it came here, an inhabited area away from the Aegis-patrolled city, to feed and take a new body. Macella swallowed. She would have to stop it before it could succeed.

Suddenly, the loogaroo burst back into flame. It shot straight for Macella. Instinctively, she threw up her arms, crossing her daggers defensively and widening her stance to brace for the impact. She had only a moment to try something she never had before.

Focusing her energy, she ignited her onyx flames, isolating them to her crossed arms and the daggers she held.

The loogaroo slammed into her, driving her backward several steps, her feet leaving furrows in the dirt. But it didn't hurt. The creature's flames couldn't penetrate her hellfire.

She surged forward, forcing the monster back enough to give her space to plunge her daggers into the core of the ball of flame.

It shrieked, flames guttering as it fought to free itself from Macella's blades. Its lipless maw gaped wide, revealing rotting, oozing gums, and a withered black tongue. The sulfurous stench of its breath made Macella's eyes water as she thrust her daggers forward, trying to drive them deeper.

She fell forward onto her knees, driving the loogaroo into the ground, and pinning it with her silver dagger. She extinguished her flames immediately, hoping no one but her friends were near enough to notice.

Her blouse caught fire, the loogaroo's dying flames licking at the fabric. Quickly, she drew back, just in time to get knocked to the ground again by Sir Kamau. Frantically, he rolled her in the grass, slapping at the flames until they were extinguished.

"I'm fine, Sir Kamau," Macella insisted, letting him help her to her feet as Aisling, Nyx, and Zahra joined them. "But we need to salt and burn the loogaroo and send a message to alert the Aegises that they must find and destroy its skin."

Everyone looked at the remnants of the loogaroo where it lay writhing in the dirt. It looked like some massive, unholy infant, curled in on itself and mewling as it died. Earth clung to its exposed flesh and viscera. Macella jerked her daggers free, wiping black blood from her blades before she stood.

Solemnly, Aisling stepped forward, releasing Nyx, and producing a small bottle of salt and a match from her satchel. She sprinkled the salt over the loogaroo, then struck the match, and let it fall. With a final shriek, the creature erupted in black flames that quickly dissolved into wisps of brimstone.

"You are truly favored by the gods, Lady Macella!" Sir Kamau exclaimed. "I saw it coming for you, and I tried to reach you, hoping to push you to the ground, but I just wasn't fast enough. You could've been burned alive!"

"Well, I thank the gods for my good fortune," Macella said, laughing shakily to hide the lie.

"Thank the gods for all of our good fortune. The entire kingdom would despair if Lady Macella were to come to harm."

Macella's star charm, which had returned to its normal cool temperature after she'd subdued the loogaroo, had grown icy again. Nyx hissed, her fur standing on end, her tail stiff and puffy.

Everyone's attention snapped to the owner of the voice. Lord Kasper stepped from the cover of a nearby structure perpendicular to the one Macella had defended—a spot where he would've had a very different vantage point of the battle than Sir Kamau.

An oily grin spread slowly across his sallow face as he drew nearer, cold cobalt eyes locked on Macella. That look told her everything she needed to know.

The Grand Treasurer had seen her hellfire.

CHAPTER NINE

Macella

"Are you *sure* he saw you?" Charlotte asked, brow furrowed in concern.

Macella sighed. She'd answered this question multiple times already, despite everyone knowing the answer. He had definitely seen her.

Macella hadn't spoken to the Grand Treasurer after his sudden appearance in the workers' encampment. The Aegises had arrived almost immediately after Aisling burned the loogaroo, bringing several knights with them. The laborers and their families had followed, and in all the commotion, Lord Kasper had slipped away—no doubt to ponder how best to use his new knowledge against Macella.

"I am absolutely certain," she replied, dropping into the chair behind her desk. A moment later, she stood and began pacing again.

They'd gathered in her study, all of them grim and restless. Curled in Aisling's lap, Nyx's bright yellow eyes tracked Macella as she walked up and down the floor. Aisling sat cross-legged on the rug, anxiously chewing her bottom lip, and absently petting the cat. Zahra looked just as rattled, one leg bouncing incessantly as she slouched in her chair. Charlotte was the only other ember who'd been able to join them so far and, despite her typical optimism, she was visibly upset by this new problem.

Macella, Zahra, and Aisling had returned to the keep in tense silence, retiring to their individual chambers to wash up and change after the morning's exertions. Though they should've been ravenous, they only picked at their midday meal, soon abandoning the comfortable parlor for the more businesslike study. Unfortunately, they'd yet to do much besides worry.

"My charm had just warmed back up after the loogaroo attack—well, as warm as it ever gets these days," Macella said, fingering the eight-pointed star at her throat. "Then it went cold again, and there he was."

"That is old magic," Aisling mused, tilting her head quizzically and staring at the necklace. "With all you've told us recently, I never even thought much about that charm, but it's quite remarkable. Who enchanted it?"

"I'm not sure," Macella responded, pausing her frenetic pacing. "Aithan's mother gave it to him. She said it had been a gift from her grandmother."

"And his mother was a mage?" Aisling asked.

Macella sat down again. "Yes, but not the mother who gave him the charm. His other mother, Maia, was the mage."

"Maia!" Aisling exclaimed, sitting up straighter in a movement so sudden she startled Nyx, who jumped from her lap with a reproachful glare. The young mage didn't seem to notice. "Of Kosmosdale? Are you telling me Maia of Kosmosdale was Aithan's mother?"

"She was really powerful and well respected," Charlotte interjected, eyes wide. "I've read about her quite a bit in my research, but I didn't realize she was Aithan's mother."

Macella looked between the two young women before giving a slightly sheepish shrug. "Did we not mention her name?"

Zahra, who'd been unusually quiet, finally spoke up. "You might well have, but considering the number of jaw-droppers we absorbed during that conversation, we easily could've missed it. What are you getting at, Red? Why does it matter that Aithan's mum was, like, the queen of magic?"

Aisling laughed, shaking her head. "I don't know that it does—oh gods, I'm an idiot!"

She slapped her forehead so hard that they all jumped. When she dropped her hand, it had left a bright red mark. She dissolved into giggles, her face reddening to match the spot above her brows.

"I think you broke your mage, Lady Macella," Zahra quipped, one eyebrow raised, the twinkle back in her mismatched eyes.

Aisling's laughter seemed to lighten the mood in the room. Macella relaxed in her chair, noticing that Charlotte and Zahra had done the same. Even Nyx crept back into view from wherever she'd hidden after Aisling's initial outburst.

"We've been giving ourselves headaches trying to figure out why it's so much easier for Lord Aithan to detect magic than you, even though you're both crossbreeds," Aisling managed to get out finally, between giggles. "Frankly, Lady Macella, you're pretty shite at it, but I thought maybe it was because you didn't go through the magical transformations in Smoketown as he did."

Macella started to laugh, unable to believe they hadn't figured this out already. "Oh, gods, *I'm* an idiot! He's *half mage*!"

Charlotte's eyes lit up. "Your birth mother was one of us humdrum humans, while Aithan's was the most revered mage in recent memory. And, if that star charm is any indication, there might have been magic on his other mother's side as well."

Zahra shook her head. "We are not humdrum, Lotta, but gods, how does Aithan keep getting more interesting? He's already a fucking dream and now this!"

Macella laughed harder, suppressing a snort. She shared Zahra's sentiments. She'd known almost immediately that Aithan was special, but he continued to surprise her. Even if he hadn't been half Aegis, he almost certainly would've had magical abilities. Who knew what all he was capable of?

"Well, my prophecy is a lot less impressive now," Aisling joked. "Anybody with a little bit of information could've predicted you two were marked for something. Finding each other like you did and then learning the connections between your families and your natures. And now knowing he's twice, perhaps thrice, blessed by the gods."

Macella tilted her head. "What do you mean? He has Lucifer's blessing, the same as his Aegis mother."

"And at least one of his mothers, perhaps both, were blessed by one of the gods of magic. Hekate or Oya, I'd say for Maia, based on how powerful she was," Aisling explained. She looked around at their confused faces and covered her mouth with her hands, eyes wide. "Oh gods, I talk too bloody much! That's a mage secret. Our gifts come from the gods, much like the Aegises do—some ancient pact with our foremothers. I've only learned about it since I began formal training."

"You know you can trust us." Macella soothed. "Another secret the Wildfire Court will guard with our lives."

Aisling looked relieved, but before she could speak, Charlotte clapped her hands together, clearly struck by an idea. "You know what this means, right? We have a real shot at defeating the king. No matter what kind of power King Khari has, she isn't a thrice blessed Aegis-mage crossbreed! With Aithan and Ella together, she doesn't stand a chance!"

Her words drew Macella up short. She wasn't the only one. Both Zahra and Aisling looked just as stunned.

"Neither does that sniveling little milksop Kasper," Zahra declared, grinning savagely. "When the rest of the Aegises join us, we'll figure out how to deal with him."

The arrival of Diya and Kai soon after precluded the Wildfire Court from gathering that afternoon. King Khari had called a brief strategy meeting with the small council, after which everyone dispersed to tend to their own duties. The Grand Treasurer had smiled broadly at Macella every time their eyes met, banishing any lingering hope that he hadn't seen her hellfire. Still, she felt a great deal better after the tête-a-tête with the other women of her court. They'd reminded her how truly formidable a force they were together. What were kings and lords to mages and Aegises—to hope and love and family?

Macella hoped that the Wildfire Court might get to take their evening meal together for the first time in nearly a fortnight, since the arrival of the additional Aegises would lessen their time on patrol. She soon learned, however, that Diya and Kai had rode hard overnight, sensing the rift that released the loogaroo. Since Jacan, Finley, and Macella had apparently dispatched all the escaped demons, the new arrivals were given the remainder of the afternoon and evening to recover from their travels. They'd take first patrol that night.

It seemed the problem of Lord Kasper would have to wait. Macella left notes inviting each member of her entourage to join her for a late-night drink, then shut herself up in her study. She had a fair bit of correspondence and other matters to attend to, so an afternoon to herself and a solitary dinner wasn't unwelcome.

Unfortunately, she would have no such luck.

Macella had just finished responding to a lengthy letter from Laird Parul when there was a light knock at her outer door. She heard Lucy's quick, light footsteps, then her speaking to whoever had knocked. Her expression was apologetic when she appeared in the doorway of the study.

"Begging your pardon, Lady Macella, but her grace, King Khari, requests that you join her for a private dinner," Lucy said, wringing her hands. "She asks if dining in a half hour would suit you. What shall I tell the messenger?"

Macella forced a smile, attempting to set the girl at ease. Lucy, always a loyal servant, seemed to grow more protective as Macella neared her coronation. She could tell the young woman worried about her, especially whenever she was in company with the king. Macella's scalp prickled with dread. The keep's servants must see a great deal of disturbing behavior as they cooked and cleaned and waited on the nobles and royals. Surely, they talked amongst themselves. What did Lucy know about Khari that made her so afraid for Macella?

Macella decided she didn't want to know the answer to that question. She'd already seen enough of the king's depravity and cruelty. No need to stoke further fear.

"A half an hour is just fine," Macella said firmly, ignoring the pounding of her heart. "Please convey my gratitude for the invitation."

(14) Thus, she soon found herself at the door of King Khari's chambers. She'd dressed in a simple bronze sheath dress suitable for the cooler evenings of the late harvest season, the soft knit fabric clinging to her curves before pooling around her feet. The bodice laced up the back with a thick scarlet ribbon that matched the one securing her curls atop her head in an elegant disarray. As a final touch, she'd donned the cuffs Khari had gifted her after the manananggal attack. The intricately carved gold bracelets with their inlaid garnet gemstones and black diamonds felt heavy on her wrists.

Like shackles.

A servant led Macella through the foyer into the king's private dining room. The king was waiting for her, standing behind the seat at the foot of the table. Aithan stood behind King Khari's seat at the head.

"Lady Macella, you look unbearably attractive this evening," the king said, taking Macella's hand and pressing a kiss to her knuckles. Khari's lips were soft and cool against her skin. "Allow me to get your chair."

Macella let the king help her into her seat, noticing the way Khari's chilly hands lingered on her shoulders as she adjusted the chair. She smelled of pomegranate and musky vanilla, heady and not entirely unpleasant. Macella shivered.

"Thank you for agreeing to join me on such short notice." King Khari smiled and poured Macella a goblet of wine. "I simply couldn't wait."

Macella's stomach dropped. What urgent need could the king have of her? Had Lord Kasper acted so quickly? Was the dinner invitation a pretense meant to lure her into a trap? She locked eyes with Aithan as the king made her way to the head of the table. He gave the slightest shake of his head, his jaw tight.

Macella relaxed slightly. No serious danger, but still, something Aithan didn't like. Macella smiled at King Khari, watching her take her seat.

"It's my pleasure, your grace, but to what do I owe this honor?" she asked, lowering her head demurely. "What urgent matter may I assist you with?"

King Khari leaned back in her chair. Her cold ochre eyes assessed Macella over the rim of her goblet as she took a long drink. She had decided to forgo her crown that evening, choosing more casual, intimate attire. Her skin seemed to glow in the candlelight—golden and warm—and there was a great deal of it on display that evening. She wore a loose silk shirt over fine, fitted trousers and dark leather boots that showed off her powerful legs. The king never wore corsets, but it was clear that she hadn't bothered with any of the binders she typically favored. Her blouse's plunging neckline stopped just above her navel, revealing the subtle swell of her small breasts. Somehow, the thin fabric stayed put over her nipples, but just barely. Macella tried not to think about it.

The king ran a hand over her shorn blond head and smiled, her lips stained red with wine. "I want only your company, Lady Macella. The arrival of those Aegises reminded me how near we are to the cold season and the influx of guests it will bring. Soon, I'll have to share your attention with even more people. Tonight, I wanted you to myself for once."

Macella shivered again, feeling the king's gaze raking over her possessively. Khari's cold, cruel beauty seemed to intensify with her words. Macella was finding it difficult to think clearly. She was spared the necessity of a response by the arrival of the meal. The king remained silent, watching Macella over the rim of her goblet as the servants laid out trays of food, filling their plates with helpings of everything on offer. Macella took a generous drink from her own goblet, letting the wine spread warmth over skin that felt chilled by Khari's gaze.

"You're all dismissed. We will serve ourselves for the remainder of the meal," the king said, once the table had been prepared. A smirk played around her mouth, but she didn't look away from Macella as she continued. "And, if it doesn't displease my lady, you may be excused as well, Lord Protector. Surely you can't begrudge me a few hours alone with my betrothed when you get so much of her time."

Macella and Aithan locked eyes again, and this time she gave a slight nod.

A muscle in Aithan's jaw twitched, but he only bowed. "Of course not, your grace. Shall I return tonight?"

"No, no. You've worked tirelessly of late. Now that reinforcements have arrived, you may take some respite," King Khari replied, waving a hand at Aithan, though her eyes remained on Macella. "I'll summon you when I'm ready in the morning. I don't yet know what time. It depends on how my night proceeds."

The king held Macella's gaze until the door clicked quietly shut behind Aithan. Macella could feel the tension rolling off his skin as he passed her. She stroked his mind wordlessly, offering what little reassurance she could.

I am but a thought away if you want me, he replied, his mental voice tight.

King Khari made idle conversation as they ate, asking Macella about the progress on the laborers' housing and a few similar business items. Macella tensed when she asked about the loogaroo attack that morning but relaxed again when she realized the king only asked out of her typical fascination with rifts and hellspawn. She still enjoyed accompanying the Aegises on hunts, despite her frustration with their increased frequency.

"Have you heard from your mother lately? How is the mages' academy coming along?" King Khari asked next, and soon she'd managed to get Macella talking about her family and telling stories from her childhood.

The king laughed her throaty laugh at Macella's unflattering descriptions of some of her family and peppered her with probing questions. Before Macella had even realized it, they'd finished the meal and followed it with several additional goblets of wine. Her head felt pleasantly fuzzy, and she was surprised to find that she was actually enjoying the king's company.

King Khari seemed to be thinking the same thing. "I am glad you joined me this evening. I haven't had such a pleasant dinner in a long time."

"Thank you for inviting me. I've had a lovely time," Macella responded truthfully. She realized it was nearing the hour of Tõlze and she should be going. If she hurried, she could have perhaps an hour alone with Aithan before the Wildfire Court arrived for their nightcap.

"If I am being perfectly honest, I have been rather lonely of late," King Khari said, pulling Macella from her thoughts. "Meztli has been a bit cold since Awa left us, no longer seeming eager to share quiet evenings together. And Annika is so tired all the time. I can't blame her, of course, with the pregnancy. But she's been my most frequent bedfellow since she joined the Crown, and her vigor is sorely missed. And with the attacks, the preparation for the cold season and your coronation, and all the festivities, I haven't had much time to spend on pleasure."

The king fixed Macella with a sudden, hungry gaze. Macella drew in a sharp intake of breath as all the air seemed to rush out of the room. She didn't know she could be so simultaneously attracted to and repelled by a person. Anxiety cut through the fuzzy warmth in her mind.

She knew that Meztli was furious with Khari over Awa's death. Though the monarch didn't partake in carnal pleasures, they could be quite affectionate. Macella had been on the receiving end of one of their incredible scalp massages and could easily understand how Khari must miss their touch. And, if the lust in the king's eyes was any indication, she missed the sexual ministrations of Queen Annika and the workers at Wildfell Hall even more.

"Your grace, I—" Macella began, but the king held up her hand.

"Hear me out," King Khari said coaxingly, leaning forward, and taking a halved pomegranate from a platter near her end of the table. "We've never fully discussed these particulars of our marriage. We owe it to ourselves to consider our options."

Macella watched the king pop a pomegranate seed into her mouth. She didn't speak until she'd sucked the fruit from the seed, a glimpse of pink tongue flashing between her full, wine-stained lips as she plucked the seed from her mouth and dropped it into a small silver bowl. She kept her eyes on Macella the entire time.

"Pomegranate is easily my favorite fruit," King Khari went on. "It takes a lot of work to eat, but it's worth it when you feel the delicious burst of juice on your tongue."

Macella swallowed hard. The room had grown a bit too warm, making her regret the weight of her woolen dress. King Khari looked cool and comfortable in her thin silk blouse with its plunging neckline.

"Since Lady Zahra arrived at the keep, I've learned that you and the Lord Protector aren't entirely sexually monogamous—not that you ever claimed to be. I shouldn't have assumed." The king popped another pomegranate seed into her mouth, savoring it silently as she had done the last. "That said, I am very open to exploring the physical possibilities of our arrangement."

They were on very dangerous terrain now. Macella felt a bead of sweat trickle down her spine, but she shivered. What would be the consequences of refusing the king's advances? What would be the consequences of accepting them?

(15) "Let me show you," King Khari cooed, slouching back in her chair, and sucking another pomegranate seed into her mouth. "Relax and watch."

Macella felt the air in the room grow colder, the glow of the candlelight dimming slightly. King Khari seemed far away at the other end of the long table. Then, they were no longer alone. Two other people stood beside the table.

Macella and King Khari.

Macella gasped, watching as King Khari's double stepped closer to the Macella doppelgänger. She tensed, her breath catching as the false king wrapped a hand around her double's throat. Slowly, the king's double pulled the other Macella's face to hers, their mouths hovering a hair's breadth apart. The fake king nipped at fake Macella's lower lip, before claiming her mouth with a low moan.

Macella shivered, watching the false Khari tangle her other hand into the double's curls, forcing her tongue deeper into the other Macella's mouth. The faux king pulled her double's head back, exposing the throat she still held tightly.

"I am a woman who knows what I want," the real King Khari said, briefly drawing Macella's attention away from the display. "I am a woman who takes what I want."

The false king broke the kiss, spinning false Macella around so that her back was pressed to the false king's front. The fake king's fingers gripped the other Macella's throat as she grazed her teeth over the exposed skin of her neck. Both Macellas shivered.

The faux king released her double, and Macella pressed her thighs together tightly as she watched herself lean over to brace her hands against the table. King Khari's double stepped closer to the false Macella and ran a slow hand down the laces of her bodice, pausing to press her palm to the small of Macella's back. Macella's double arched her back, exaggerating the tilt of her hips so that her ass was more pronounced. The Khari double smacked her rear approvingly.

"You'll learn that I am a highly visual lover. I want you on display for me, offering yourself up to do with as I see fit," explained the true King Khari from her seat at the head of the table.

At least, Macella *thought* the seated king was the true one. She was growing increasingly disoriented, the surreal nature of Khari's vision confusing her senses. Aisling's magic lessons were no match for the king's gift. Macella knew the vision wasn't real, but it *felt* real. Both kings gazed at her as the false Khari rubbed slow circles over the false Macella's ass. Macella felt a very real clenching deep in her belly as she watched. She couldn't decide how angry to be, not when her traitorous body was responding to the sight of Khari slowly untying the laces of the other Macella's dress.

"I would take my time removing that gown," King Khari went on.

The king's double brushed her fingers down the other Macella's spine, palming her ass again before rubbing the back of her thighs, lingering at the point where they met. False Macella whimpered and arched into the touch, lifting her ass higher. The king cupped her sex through the dress, then ran her hand up Macella's seam to resume the slow unlacing of her dress.

"But I would leave the bracelets on. They look so good on you," Khari purred, a wicked smile tugging at her lips. "They'd look even better once you were naked and kneeling before me with your arms bound by that lovely scarlet ribbon."

The false king pulled the other Macella to a standing position, having completely removed the ribbon from her bodice, and used it to quickly tie a few intricate knots just above the cuffs on her arms. Unlike the real Macella, her double wasn't wearing a corset beneath. She held the dress in place with her bound hands as it tried to fall from her shoulders to reveal her breasts. The fake king gave her a swift, hard smack on her ass.

"Hands down," both kings said in unison, and the false Macella obeyed. Her dress slipped from her shoulders.

Macella bolted to her feet, unable to watch any longer. "Your grace, I'm very tired and would like to return to my chambers, if it pleases the king."

Their doubles vanished. The room was warm and bright once more. The king spat a pomegranate seed onto the floor.

"It does not please the king. It seems the king is not to be pleased tonight," King Khari snapped, before taking a deep breath and regaining her composure. "Forgive me. I am a bit...tense. Please just think about my offer. Enjoy your night."

Macella practically ran from the room. As she escaped into the corridor, she heard the king calling for a messenger. Macella didn't want to know who she would send for now.

It was quiet back in her chambers. She found Aithan sitting alone in the parlor, drinking deeply from a goblet. His hair hung damp around his bare shoulders, as if he hadn't long been out of the bath. He hadn't bothered with a shirt or shoes, and Macella paused to enjoy the sight of him in just a pair of soft gray cotton pants.

"I should've warned you that I invited the Wildfire Court for drinks tonight," Macella said, crossing the room to stand beside his chair. "I absolutely hate the idea of you putting on a shirt."

Aithan looked up at her and his eyes softened. Macella put a hand on his shoulder, and he pulled her close, pressing his face against her stomach. He'd obviously been worried, while she'd been having a good time.

"She didn't hurt you," Aithan stated, rather than asked. He would've known if she had.

"Not exactly," Macella hedged guiltily.

(16) Aithan lifted his head from her stomach to study her face. He took a slow breath, and Macella could almost see the change in his eyes as he scented her arousal. Snippets of Khari's vision sprung, unbidden, into her mind. One corner of Aithan's mouth lifted in a knowing smile.

"Oh, I see," he murmured, running his hands over her hips and down her legs. "Well, I can't say that I blame her for taking her shot."

He slid his hands beneath her gown and up her calves to rest on the backs of her thighs, dragging her dress up her legs. Macella shuddered, her stomach tightening. Aithan pressed his face against her again, lower this time, and took another deep breath.

"How wet are you, my little hell goddess?" he murmured, voice husky. "How wet did the king make my wife's good pussy?"

Macella gasped, a thrill shooting through her belly, nipples tightening against the confines of her corset. "Aithan, I—"

He cut her off before she could try to explain. "Shh, love. Let me see how wet you are."

Macella's pussy clenched. She let him bunch her dress up around her waist and pull her down to straddle him. She could feel him growing hard beneath her. Almost involuntarily, she rolled her hips, grinding against him.

"None of that," he chided, sliding a hand between them, and slipping his fingers into her panties. "We haven't the time—we have company coming and I need to put on a shirt. Besides, that isn't what you wanted tonight."

Before she could argue with his pronouncement, he slid two fingers inside of her, making her cry out. She clenched around him immediately, a spasm racking her body. He curled his fingers, and she rocked her hips in tandem.

"Oh, you are very, very wet, wife," Aithan purred, pumping his fingers in and out of her throbbing warmth, eliciting liquid sounds that gave credence to his words.

Macella moaned, clutching his shoulders for support.

"Is all of this for Khari or is some of this for me?"

Macella rode the thrust of his fingers, panting, as the sensation in her core began to build. "For you, always for you," she gasped.

"Is that so?" Aithan murmured, trailing his tongue down the side of her neck, and moving his hand faster, pressing that spot inside her that made her want to explode, while simultaneously brushing his thumb over her clit. "Show me. Who are you about to cum for? Khari or me?"

Macella moaned, her head falling back, all her energy seeming to coalesce in the tightening of her pussy muscles around Aithan's fingers. "For you, Aithan," she gasped, nails digging into his skin.

"Cum for me, then," he commanded, his voice low and rough against her ear.

He scraped his teeth across her skin, the sensation making her insides quiver. Macella's blood roared in her veins. She was so close to shattering completely.

Aithan licked and bit his way down her neck, before locking his mouth over the spot where her neck and shoulder met, sucking hard on her flesh, as he dexterously worked his fingers. Macella knew there'd be a bruise on the spot tomorrow, but she didn't care. The thought of him marking her, claiming her, was oddly exhilarating. It sent an electric thrill straight to her core.

Then every muscle in her body tightened at once and she cried out, stars exploding behind her eyes. Finally, she collapsed onto his chest, panting. Aithan slid his fingers out of her and into his mouth, humming quietly as she caught her breath. Macella wanted to apologize, to explain what had happened with the king, but she seemed to have momentarily lost the ability to speak.

"You need not apologize. I'm not angry," Aithan murmured quietly. "I'm embarrassed to admit I'm a little jealous, but not angry. Well, not at you. I think Khari's behavior pushed the boundaries of consent, and I kind of want to rip her throat out with my teeth, but instead, I'll put on a shirt and pour some drinks. I'm sure the others will be here soon."

He kissed her on the top of her head, holding her a little longer before lifting them both out of the chair. Macella wrapped her arms around his waist and hugged him tightly, grateful for the steady beat of his heart and his comforting smoky-scented warmth. He smelled like home.

Chapter Ten

Macella can take care of herself. Macella can take care of herself.

Aithan had thought the words over and over like a mantra as the hours passed and his wife did not return from King Khari's quarters.

The absolute truth of the words didn't make him feel any better. He knew beyond a doubt that Macella was smart and capable and strong. She *could* take care of herself. But he wanted to take care of her. She was his and he was hers and they were supposed to take care of each other. It tormented him, knowing he couldn't protect her—hadn't been able to since the day they were sentenced to life in this gods-forsaken castle.

He'd poured another drink and forced himself to sip it slowly, while trying not to count the minutes until it would be reasonable to return to the king's quarters and check on his wife. He'd already reached out for her mind a few times and, finding no signs of distress, had withdrawn to give her privacy.

Aithan had known what Khari's intentions were, of course, and he hadn't been happy about it. Not that he wasn't used to people lusting after Macella. It usually didn't bother him. How could he blame them when he was still as insatiable for her as the day they'd met? He'd had her every way and at every opportunity since their introduction at that brothel, and his need hadn't cooled one bit. So, when he caught fragments of lewd daydreams or longing glances, he usually felt only an amused kinship with her admirers.

But Khari was different. Her desires came with dangerous strings and secret motivations. More and more frequently, he found himself catching glimpses of the king's mind. As useful as it might be to read the king's thoughts, he almost wished he couldn't. King Khari's mind was a dark and hungry place.

He didn't want Macella anywhere near her. But there was nothing he could do about it.

He couldn't protect Macella.

He had to protect Macella.

Even if it cost him everything, he would give it. For her. His wife, his hell goddess, his warrior queen. His only true and real thing in this savage world. She was worth his last breath, his very last drop of blood.

If Khari's thoughts were any indication, it might just come to that. And now there was this mess with the Grand Treasurer. Aithan had known it was only a matter of time before the many watching eyes at court saw something they shouldn't. It was dumb, rotten luck that it had to be someone they'd already made an enemy of—someone who would relish the chance to harm Macella, rather than use the information for leverage with the future queen. Kasper wouldn't want favors; he would want revenge. He would want to see Macella suffer.

Aithan wouldn't let that happen. He could and would protect her from this. Even if he had to kill the Grand Treasurer.

⁕

Macella

"We should just kill him," Finley said, looking bored as they swirled the wine in their goblet. "There are endless ways to make it look accidental. And several I've been wanting to try."

"Don't tempt me," Macella sighed. Both her hand signing and her voice were weary after the day she'd had. Was it just this morning that she'd slain the loogaroo? She could hardly believe it, despite feeling the exhaustion deep in her bones. "You know I've considered it, but I'm not sure the risk is worth the reward. With everything we're facing right now, we can't afford to draw any undue scrutiny."

"This place is a powder keg, and upsetting the balance of the small council might be enough to light the fuse," Zahra agreed. "There are whispers among the nobility about the nature of Queen Awa's death, concerns over the viability of Queen Annika's pregnancy, and even hints that a growing faction would back Macella in a bid to replace the king entirely."

Zahra's words hung heavy in the air. Macella had long known that there were only two possible routes to defeating King Khari: deposal or assassination. Deposing her would mean Macella must survive the Blessed Rite and become queen, then lead a successful coup, which would require more than the cadre of allies Zahra was carefully cultivating. An assassination attempt would have to happen soon and prior to the Rite—before the gods' magic bound her to Khari and prevented her from inflicting harm upon any member of the Crown. Both options tied her stomach in knots, despite her resolution to do what was required. The safety of their world depended on her steadfast commitment to restoring balance.

In her heart, Macella knew that Khari would never go quietly. Even a successful coup wouldn't stop her—not forever. She would never stop fighting to regain her crown. Macella and Aithan had glimpsed the king's dark hunger time and again. They would have to pry her power from her cold, dead hands.

Macella forced herself to inhale slowly, willing the knot it her stomach to loosen with her exhale. One battle at a time. First, they would deal with the Grand Treasurer.

"You people never want to do things my way," Finley pouted, flopping dramatically back against the chaise. "Aren't friends supposed to take an interest in each other's ideas?"

Zahra bounded lightly across the room and dove onto the chaise, wrapping her small frame around Finley's long, lithe form. "Don't worry, precious. We'll let you kill someone soon."

Macella joined in the laughter that followed Zahra's proclamation, though she felt the sad truth of the promise. This would end in bloodshed one way or another. Finley wouldn't be the only among them who'd be forced to kill if all went badly.

A pillow landed in Macella's lap, drawing her attention to Jacan, who sat beside Charlotte on one of the parlor's plush couches. When he spoke, he signed one-handed, his other arm slung around Charlotte's shoulders. Charlotte watched him with rapt attention, a blush staining her cheeks.

"Stop fretting, big sister," Jacan ordered, his big boyish grin spreading across his face. "*We* will figure this out. You're not alone anymore, Savior of Smoketown. Remember? None of us are."

"You tell her, pup!" Zahra seconded, taking Finley's goblet of wine and raising it in Jacan's direction.

Aithan planted a kiss in her curls, agreement rumbling in his chest. Aisling grinned up at her from where she sat cross-legged on the rug. Nyx, curled up in Aisling's lap, blinked slowly at Macella. Finley gave an exaggerated eye roll, reclaimed their goblet, and draped an arm around Zahra, resting their chin on top of her head. Everyone watched Macella expectantly.

"Alright," she huffed, feeling better despite herself. "What ideas have we got that don't involve murder?"

Ultimately, the Wildfire Court decided it was best to keep a close watch on Lord Kasper and await his next move. If he didn't act before the next day's small council meeting, Aithan would have the opportunity to search the Grand Treasurer's mind for answers when they convened. Surely when he saw Macella again, his thoughts would betray his plans.

But the Grand Treasurer moved more quickly than they'd expected.

The following morning before the small council meeting, Macella sat alone in her study, poring over a history of Kōsaten's monarchy in hopes of learning more about the Blessed Rite, when Lucy appeared in the doorway.

"Her grace, Queen Annika, requests an audience," Lucy announced, wringing her hands anxiously. "I showed her into the courtyard at her behest."

Macella's heart raced, but she hid her alarm. She didn't want to worry Lucy any more than the queen's visit already had. Her favorite servant was a smart woman—she knew that Macella and the young queen were not friends.

"Thank you, Lucy. Would you mind going to the kitchens to brew me a pot of tensyon tea? I imagine I'll need it after this visit." Macella smiled and stood, patting the other woman's arm as she made her way out of the study.

"Aye, I suspect you will."

Lucy hurried to do as Macella asked. The young woman had learned from Lotta how to make the headache- and tension-relieving brew that Macella remembered from her childhood—something Macella greatly appreciated and took advantage of more and more often. Casting a last, anxious glance over her shoulder, Lucy slipped from the apartments, leaving Macella to face the queen.

Macella took a steadying breath. She couldn't let Annika rattle her. She lifted her chin and strode toward the courtyard to greet her uninvited guest.

(17) Queen Annika stood in the morning sunlight, her ivory skin almost crystalline in its pale glow. She wore a simple cornflower blue gown, its high waistline indicating Lynn had made it expressly for the young queen's current condition. Though she was naturally very plump, the pregnancy was beginning to show itself in the high, rounded swell of her growing belly.

"This is a lovely space," Queen Annika said, surveying the area with her bright blue eyes. "The king certainly made enough fuss about fixing it up for you."

Her gaze darted around the little courtyard, taking in the ivy-covered walls and the now-covered garden beds, before resting on its new centerpiece—a low fountain carved from stone and filled with an assortment of brightly colored fish, which Lucy and the Wildfire Court kept fat and contented and probably a little overfed. Aithan had somehow found the time to install the fountain as a surprise for Macella, claiming the water would prove useful the next time she accidentally ignited the grass. Macella suspected it was as much a gift for Nyx as it was for her, considering how much the cat loved perching on the stone edge to watch the fish flit about.

"Thank you, your grace," Macella replied with a tight smile. "Though I found our previous apartments more than satisfactory, I've grown quite attached to these. King Khari is wise and anticipated my needs better than I could have."

The young queen made a noncommittal sound and moved to sit on a cushioned bench near the fountain. She lowered herself gingerly, keeping a protective hand on her belly. Once she was settled, she patted the bench and looked at Macella expectantly. Macella sighed and joined her, careful to leave as much space between them as possible.

"I assume your mage has warded your chambers against listening ears. Does that magic extend to include this courtyard?" Queen Annika asked bluntly.

So, they'd be getting straight to the point, then. That was fine with Macella. She'd rather not pretend this was a social call. Still, she would let Annika lead the conversation. It was better that she let the young queen reveal her hand before admitting anything herself.

"The warding extends throughout our rooms, including this courtyard," Macella conceded.

"Good," Queen Annika said. "I'm sure you don't wish for others to hear the tale Lord Kasper shared with me yesterday."

Macella's stomach dropped. She'd wanted to dispense with the preambles but had expected the young queen to toy with her a bit. After all, there were few things Annika seemed to enjoy more than goading her.

"Yesterday was a frightening and chaotic day," Macella hedged, trying to keep her voice even. "I am sure the Grand Treasurer saw much excitement and confusion. The loogaroo's attack was so sudden, I can hardly make sense of what actually happened."

Queen Annika fixed Macella with her icy blue gaze. "I think we both know exactly what happened. I've taken precautions to ensure Kasper will keep it to himself and let me handle matters. This conversation will determine what I do with the interesting information he's given me."

Macella bristled at the threat. She returned the queen's stare, certain that the fury burning in her eyes outmatched Annika's icy glower. "Your grace, why don't you tell me what this is about? I have several tasks I'd like to finish before the small council meeting, and no time for idle chatter."

Annika's plump cheeks reddened. She narrowed her eyes and leaned toward Macella, closing the space between them. Macella glared at the young queen, refusing to budge.

"This is about you catching fire, but remaining unburnt," Queen Annika hissed. "This is about you showing up here, weaving your stories like spells and seeming to know things you shouldn't. It's about your annoyingly plucky determination to *help* and *protect* people, as if you have some gods-given sense of duty. It's about your uncommon beauty and the silver streaks in your hair and the way you and the Lord Protector seem to have some resistance to the Crown's gifts. It's about you being at the center of two demon attacks and emerging unscathed and victorious."

Macella couldn't help her sharp intake of breath. Her lip curled in a snarl as she leaned toward the queen. She opened her mouth without knowing what it was she planned to say. It didn't matter, because Annika cut her off, silencing her with a final statement.

"This is about you *not being human*."

This was it. The moment Macella and Aithan had feared since their arrival in Pleasure Ridge Park. The moment that could change everything.

Macella stood, fixing Annika with a defiant scowl. She poured every bit of frustration, fear, and anger into the venom lacing her words. "I don't care what you think you know. Tell me what you want and get out."

The young queen looked up at her, indignant rage dancing across her pretty features. A long moment passed as the two women appraised each other, neither giving an inch. Finally, Annika's mask slipped, revealing something different beneath. Suddenly, she looked very young and very afraid.

"I am not threatening you, Macella. Or, at least, I didn't plan to. It's just a force of habit," Annika said quietly. Her wide blue eyes shimmered as she held Macella's gaze. When she spoke again, her voice wavered. "You saved my life once. I'm hoping you might be willing to do it again. I am trying to ask you for your help."

It took Macella a moment to register the young queen's words. She snapped her mouth shut so abruptly she heard her teeth click, cutting off the defensive retort forming on her tongue. She eyed the queen warily.

"I know you do not trust me," Annika sighed, turning her attention back to the fountain. "You don't even like me, and I can't blame you. In fact, I have spent most of your time here making sure you hate me as much as I hate you."

"It worked," Macella said dryly, annoyance helping her to recover from her surprise at the queen's request. "You do not like or trust me, and the feeling is mutual, so why would you ever come to me for help?"

Still not meeting her gaze, Queen Annika replied hesitantly. "Because...I need you. You are the only person I can turn to right now."

Macella lifted her eyebrows, shocked by the admission. Queen Annika needed *her*? Every logical part of Macella's brain screamed that this had to be a trap—yet another game of the wealthy, powerful, and bored. But another, softer part of her heard the catch in the young queen's voice and wondered if she might be telling her something real for a change.

"I have no illusions about the nature of the child I'm carrying. Khari practically told me as much herself, going on and on about how special and strong our child will be, and I had no trouble getting the remaining details out of the Grand Mage. I mean, it was obvious there was more to all the so-called *magical blessings* I had to endure. I've seen pregnancies before, and I know they don't typically require so much spellwork," Annika went on, her attention fixed on the fountain, as if she couldn't bear to meet Macella's gaze. "But I went along with it anyway. Maybe I thought it would keep her attention on me and off of you. Or maybe I thought it would finally make her love me—not for the influence my father has in the west, but for who I am. I know she'd loved Awa once. Why not me?"

Annika was silent a moment, several emotions clouding her features as she appeared to wrestle with her next words. A rustle of ivy caught Macella's attention. Nyx slunk quietly out of the shadows and hopped onto the edge of the fountain across from the young queen. Her big yellow eyes watched the woman with unblinking intensity.

"Hello, demon," Queen Annika greeted the cat. "I don't know how you got into my chambers, but I do not appreciate the little gift you left in my slippers. It wasn't even properly dead. I should have you skinned and stuffed."

Unperturbed, Nyx lifted a paw and licked it, before proceeding to clean her sleek little black head. Macella made a mental note to give the cat an extra treat later. Amused, she lifted an eyebrow at the queen.

"Nyx is an excellent judge of character. I'm sure she meant it as a gift," Macella said, smirking, before growing somber again. "You can't truly believe Khari loves me any more than she loves you. She cannot love anyone but herself."

Queen Annika shrugged. "It was a childish fancy. I was not raised to be loved; I was raised to be acquired. I was taught to be whatever the powerful desired, to cloud their better judgment with my wiles. And did I ever deliver. My father never deigned to notice me, but when I caught the attention of the king, that all changed. I finally served my purpose and proved my worth. And still he wants more. They always want more."

"And what do you want, Annika?" Macella sighed. "What do you want from me?"

The young queen looked at her steadily, determination replacing her hesitance to meet Macella's gaze. "We know little about Aegisborn. We know even less about their human parents. Aithan's mother was a mage. Was yours? Or was she just a human? And...did she survive?"

Unbidden, images of her mother sprung to her mind. They were hazy—a memory of a memory, as she'd seen them in her dead father's mind when she'd crossed the veil between worlds during her Aegis trials. Lenora, her very human mother, was a ghost with a sweet smile and purple flowers in her hair.

Annika paused and took a ragged breath. "Will *I* survive?"

Macella stood completely still. She couldn't begin to answer. There was too much at stake, too much hinging on navigating this deadly conversation. Her mouth felt painfully dry.

"Let the Grand Mage study you," Queen Annika pleaded. "I can promise you her silence—we'll do a blood bind as I did with Kasper. Tell me what you know and help us find out more. My life could depend on it."

Unbidden, the secondhand memory of her own mother's death sprang to her mind. As an ordinary human, Lenora hadn't been able to survive bringing her crossbreed child into the world. Would the young queen share Macella's mother's fate?

Macella still didn't move or speak. If she trusted Queen Annika, she would be handing her enemy the tools to destroy her. Conversely, if she didn't help, the young queen might not survive her pregnancy, and that blood would be on her hands. But then she'd be out of the way...

"If I die, the magic binding Kasper to secrecy will die with me," Annika warned, as if reading Macella's thoughts. "He will relish your destruction."

"I thought you didn't come to threaten me," Macella snapped, tangling a frustrated hand in her curls.

"I didn't!" Annika snapped back. "But I will if I have to, because this isn't only about me. It's about my baby. If I die, they will have nothing standing between them and whatever nefarious plans Khari has for them."

The young queen struggled to her feet, bracing a hand against the bench to push herself up, her other hand over her stomach. Macella fought the urge to help her up, preferring to keep distance between them.

Annika managed to stand and stepped toward Macella with a look of stalwart resolve. "My child will not be a pawn," the queen promised, cobalt eyes hard. "They will not be raised to believe their worth is measured by what they can gain, or by their proximity to power. They will not waste their lives trying to earn the love of an unfeeling parent. I cannot die—I will not die—because I must live to protect them!"

The queen's pale face was red when she finished speaking, chest heaving as she caught her breath. She was trembling slightly, and Macella wondered if she should make the pregnant woman sit back down. There was something wild in the queen's gaze, behind the icy rage and cold determination. It struck Macella again that she might be speaking to the true Annika for the first time.

The queen yelped and nearly leapt into Macella's arms. Recovering from her surprise quickly, Macella saw that Nyx had decided to weave through the queen's legs and now rubbed against Macella's calves. Annika glared at the cat, but the air seemed to lighten a bit, and her frantic gaze softened.

"Just think about it," the young queen implored quietly. "I'm appealing to that annoyingly plucky honor and sense of altruism that makes you so unbearable. You helped all those kids in Smoketown. I'm begging you to help one more."

Impulsively, Annika grabbed Macella's wrist and pressed her hand against her belly. It was firm and tight. Macella thought she felt movement.

Then the slightest whisper of consciousness brushed against Macella's mind.

She jumped, jerking her hand away and nearly tripping over Nyx in her hurry to put space between herself and the queen. She knew exactly what that had been. She'd sensed the fetus's undeveloped mind. Macella couldn't sense human minds. Any doubt of the child's Aegisborn nature vanished with that glimpse of thought.

"You know something," Annika insisted, studying Macella's face. "Something that can help my baby. You can help in a way no one else can."

It was true. Aside from Aithan, she wasn't sure of anyone else who could touch minds, including that of the fetus the queen carried. That might make it easier to help both mother and child survive the pregnancy and delivery. And if she let Grand Mage Kiama unearth whatever facts hid in her genes, it could teach them more about their kind—information she desperately craved.

But that meant trusting her earliest enemy at court. The woman whose petty vindictiveness led to her friend's death. The woman who tried on multiple occasions to have Aithan killed in battle.

"Just think about it," Queen Annika said again. "Talk to your little band of outcasts about it if you must. We'll speak again soon."

The queen turned on her heel and marched back through Macella's apartments. A moment later, the outer door clicked. Lucy appeared, carrying the requested tray of soothing tensyon tea.

Macella definitely needed it.

CHAPTER ELEVEN

Macella

Macella's body seemed to be entirely composed of jagged nerves by the time the small council met that afternoon. Even after smoking some calming herbs Aisling had prepared for moments like these, her anxiety was barely contained. Could she trust the blood bind would keep Lord Kasper quiet? Could she trust Queen Annika to keep her mouth shut until she and the Wildfire Court decided what to do with the queen's plea for help?

The way Kasper looked at Macella as she took her seat was not at all reassuring. While his gaze still held loathing, there was also a self-satisfied smirk playing around his pink lips. What had Annika told him she planned to do with the information he'd shared? It'd made him willing enough to enter an unbreakable magical vow of silence on the matter, which had to be something that would benefit him and punish Macella. Did he want her dead or just to put in her place? Would Annika keep her word to him, whatever it was, or would she truly protect Macella's secret in exchange for help with her pregnancy?

Too many questions and too few answers, and none within her control. She didn't even know how close the queen and her cousin really were. Annika was

Kasper's golden goose, so she had his loyalty to an extent, but did they trust one another? Macella doubted it. Trust was in short supply in Kōsaten Keep.

The rest of the council filled in around her as Macella pondered this latest catastrophe. Charlotte smiled absently at her sister as she settled at her desk, and Aithan tossed her a wink from his position behind the king's place. She was not alone. Macella's chest loosened. She was so unbelievably grateful for the Wildfire Court. Without them around her, holding her up, she was certain she would've collapsed under the pressure by now.

King Khari entered, and the meeting began with updates from the Grand Vizier. Macella caught Kasper watching her again with that vengeful gleam in his eyes. This time, buoyed by Aithan's and Lotta's presence, she returned the look with a fierce grin. Kasper's anger gave way to uncertainty, followed by a distinct flash of fear. Perhaps he recalled what had happened the last time he challenged her. Or maybe he'd realized that a woman who fire couldn't burn wasn't to be trifled with.

Good, Aithan thought, his voice in her head cold and hard. *He* should *be afraid of you.*

"How are the preparations for the cold season?" King Khari asked when Lord Anwir concluded his report. "There's been a distinct chill in the air. I expect guests to begin joining us as early as the next fortnight."

Lord Anwir, usually skilled at keeping an ingratiating expression at all times, looked suddenly uncomfortable. "Preparations are nearly complete. We've had a few cancellations, which have allowed our staff to get ahead on their work."

The false cheer in his voice didn't mask his trepidation. Macella was surprised to see the wizened politician so rattled. Perhaps Lord Anwir was also thinking of the last time someone on the council disappointed the king.

"Cancellations?" Khari asked with a cold smile. "How many *cancellations*?"

Lord Anwir flinched as though he'd been struck. "I will have to inquire as to the exact number, your grace."

"Estimate." The king's voice and eyes had gone flat, all pretense at congeniality vanishing in a single word.

"Perhaps a dozen, give or take a few," Lord Anwir replied quickly. "We'll hardly miss a few lily-livered lords."

King Khari steepled her fingers contemplatively, a familiar predatory edge hardening her expression. "Lily-livered? What on earth could these wayward guests be more afraid of than their king's displeasure? What could persuade them to reject my invitation to join me for the biggest celebration of my life?"

A muscle twitched in Lord Anwir's jaw. The small council chamber was completely silent, everyone watching the Grand Vizier with expressions ranging from pity to amusement. The latter could only be attributed to Lord Kasper, who seemed to be finding glee in not being the whipping boy of the day.

"They're obviously not thinking clearly, your grace," Lord Anwir said, finding the courage that must've helped him survive in his position as long as he had. "Too much faith in exaggerated rumors and nonsense. They've heard that the capital is being attacked more frequently than the regions and are fearful of encountering hellspawn during their stay."

Queen Annika let out a derisive snort, perhaps deciding it best to come to the assistance of her frequent ally. "That is ridiculous and insulting. The Crown can guarantee their safety, which should not be a concern as hell slumbers during the cold season. That is how it has always been."

"I concur, your grace, but they seem to take a few unprecedented attacks as evidence that anything may happen in these uncertain times." Lord Anwir shrugged dismissively. "As I said, we will not mourn the absence of such craven fools."

"Remind them how the world works," King Khari commanded, managing to look both bored and irritated at once. "Remind them how disappointed I will be should they miss the celebration of my new child and the coronation of my new bride. And assure them that we will have the problem sorted by the dawn of the warm season. Because we *will* have it solved."

King Khari let her predator's gaze drift over each member of her small council, her tone making it clear that each of them would bear the brunt of her displeasure should they fail to make her assertions true. Macella shivered. There was so much at stake this cold season. What would be left of them by first thaw of the new year?

The remainder of the meeting was relatively brief and uneventful. King Khari was pleased by Lord Kasper's announcement that the field workers' housing was all but complete, and harvest yields were at a record high. Macella ignored the look of vitriol the Grand Treasurer gave her when the king praised the success of her first initiative. She was proud of the accomplishment and determined to find joy wherever she could.

"We should commemorate the occasion with a celebration," King Khari suggested, idly swirling her wine. "We'll show our fine guests the settlement, boast of my lady's brilliant initiative, and provide for a little party at the settlement's meeting house. It will be the perfect start to their holiday season and first cold season in their new homes."

Macella thought that the people would likely prefer throwing their own party to having a bunch of peacocking nobles gawk at them, but she knew it was a small price to pay for all the workers had gained. She'd make sure the visit was brief and the refreshments plentiful, so that they could have a real party after the Crown and their guests returned to the castle. The thought made her smile.

"Hopefully, they've planned wisely for the season," Lord Kasper sneered. "They won't be receiving handouts just because they now live and work on the grounds."

Macella fought the urge to roll her eyes. The poor always had to think about preparing for the cold season, when work and game were scarce and the climate unforgiving. Between their improved housing, increased wages, foraging and harvesting from the far fields, and their personal gardens and livestock, the field workers would be better equipped for the off season than ever before.

"You are too conscientious, my lord. They are well aware of all the Crown has done for them and wouldn't dream of asking for more." Macella smiled complacently at the Grand Treasurer before turning her attention to King Khari. "However, Lord Kasper does raise a good point, your grace. We have a dedicated and loyal workforce right at our fingertips. We should hire from the settlement for any additional staff needed for the cold season."

Lord Anwir sniffed delicately. "We never have trouble finding seasonal staff, but I'll pass the suggestion on to the house manager. Lady Macella has such a creative mind for business matters. Her grace, the king, has made another excellent choice in matrimony."

If Macella kept having to hold back eyerolls, she was going to give herself a headache. She couldn't be sure whether the Grand Vizier cared for her or not, but she was sure he wouldn't trouble himself with staffing concerns. It was no matter; she'd speak to Evangeline herself. The house manager was smart and fair and would understand what a position in the castle would do for any of the field worker families. And with so many of the city's poor now employed by the monarchy, there were more resources and opportunities to go around for the remaining inhabitants. Eventually, the good fortune would spread, allowing the poor of Pleasure Ridge Park to escape the shackles of poverty. It would take years, perhaps even decades, but the capital could finally become a place of peace and prosperity rather than decadence and despair.

When I told you how terrible a place the capital was, I wasn't suggesting you should fix it yourself. You are a shameless showboat. Aithan's thoughts were full of teasing amusement.

Macella remembered how he'd shared his memories, trying to prepare her for what she'd witness in the city, but she still hadn't been ready. It'd been sickening watching the castle's inhabitants waste seven-course meals while people died of starvation in the streets just beyond the gates. But now, she was doing something about it.

And this was only the beginning.

Despite her concern over Annika and Kasper, Macella was feeling surprisingly cheerful as she left the small council chamber, arm-in-arm with Charlotte. She thought she'd wait to tell her sister about Annika's visit until the Wildfire Court could gather to discuss. In the meantime, maybe Lotta would want to eat with her in the Aegis dining hall. Now that Kai and Diya were settled in for the season, the rest of the Aegises dined with them from time-to-time, knowing that, soon, the hall would be filled with all their siblings. Macella wanted to spend more time around them, to build trust with and among them. They would need each other if they were going to topple Khari and rebuild the kingdom.

Macella was about to ask Charlotte about the meal when she realized she'd already been absently guiding them toward the dining hall and her sister hadn't protested. Macella had been so lost in her thoughts that she hadn't noticed Charlotte's silence. She took one look at her sister's face and brought them both to an abrupt halt.

"What is it, Lotta?" Macella caught her sister by the arms and forced her to meet her gaze. "Something is bothering you. Spill."

Charlotte's pretty brown skin took on a pink cast. She bit her lip and stepped closer to Macella. When she spoke, her voice was a hushed rush of words.

"I think Jacan wants to physically consummate our relationship and I have never attempted carnal delights and I do not know what I'm doing and the library books on the topic are quite informative but not necessarily instructive and I don't know what to do!"

Charlotte grew even pinker as she snapped her mouth shut as though forcefully stifling the torrent of words. Her eyes were huge and round with worry behind her spectacles. Macella resisted the urge to laugh, smiling softly instead. She wasn't surprised that her shy little sister was sexually inexperienced. Macella was glad she'd gotten Charlotte away from Gaspar before he'd condemned her to an inevitably unfulfilling sex life. That jobbernowl was too selfish to be a good lover.

"What do *you* want, petite?" she asked gently, the familiar endearment slipping easily from her tongue as it sometimes did around her sister. Charlotte was a constant reminder of Macella's past, but in the best possible way. She would never forget where she'd come from, but she knew she'd brought the best piece of her past into her new life. She loved that Charlotte was here, making her own decisions, and living freely as she deserved. "I know that you and Jacan care deeply for one another, but that doesn't mean you have to have sex—of any kind. Romantic relationships can take many forms, and what matters is that you feel safe. Jacan will respect your wishes."

Charlotte's expression softened. "I know he will. It isn't that I don't want to. He is such a big lovable puppy of a man! And when he signs or plays his lute, his hands are so incredibly graceful and strong and capable, that I can imagine those hands on me and—"

Charlotte broke off, clapping a hand over her mouth and reddening further. This time, Macella had to chuckle. If Charlotte got any more embarrassed, there was no telling what colors she might turn.

"That's perfectly healthy and reasonable, cher," Macella assured her. "It sounds like your concern is more about being inexperienced than about the act itself. What sorts of books have you been reading?"

Charlotte pushed her glasses up her nose, her brow wrinkling in confusion. "Well, there are many medical and philosophical treatises on sexual intimacy, as well as very detailed anatomical renderings. I've consulted all the most respected scholarly works. Why are you laughing?"

Macella had nearly doubled over with laughter, holding onto her sister's arms for support. "Lotta, you are so adorably charming. I need you to look in the library's collection of novels and literature. Find the romance section and pick out a half dozen books. I'll make you a list of authors to read. I assure you, you'll find art more instructive than academia in this instance."

Charlotte smiled. Her blush faded with her embarrassment. "Thanks, Ella."

Macella tilted her head, sensing her sister still wasn't completely at ease. "What else is worrying you?"

Charlotte shifted her weight anxiously, lowering her gaze to her wringing hands. Macella released her sister's arms and took her hands, forcing her to stop fidgeting. She ducked her head to meet the younger woman's eyes.

"What if he's making a mistake?" Lotta whispered. "He's only recently escaped a terrible life and has seen so little of the world. Does he love me because I'm the first romantically available woman to show him kindness? What happens when he sees more of the world and realizes I'm a dullard who knows even less of life?"

Macella gathered her sister into her arms. Charlotte melted gratefully against her, as though releasing the words had sapped her energy.

Macella squeezed her tightly. "Marie Charlotte de Pointe, you are no dullard, and neither is Jacan," she stated firmly. "He knows that Fate blessed him with finding you so soon. After all he's been through, he's due a bit of Fate's favor. Besides, before he met you, he'd been at court for months. The resident nobles were quite aware of his lovable puppy man appeal. He never showed the slightest interest in anyone until you joined us on the centennial tour."

Charlotte sniffled and squeezed Macella tightly.

Macella held her for a long moment before pulling away and fixing her with a stern look. "Jacan loves you, Lotta," she asserted. "It's okay to let yourself love him back."

Charlotte flung her arms around Macella again, hugging her fiercely. "I'm so glad you're my sister! Now I have to go to the library!"

Charlotte released her, whirling away in a flurry of cheerful activity. Macella shook her head fondly as Lotta scurried off toward the library.

When she turned back toward the Aegis dining hall, Macella found Diya watching her, her expression softer than Macella had ever seen it. A warm feeling washed over her, followed by a pang of bittersweet longing.

(18) A sweet laugh, followed by a fit of coughing. She was holding a tiny, dark-haired child of about five or six years old. Pooja. When the coughing began, she hurried to set the child down, but Pooja clung to her arms, dark eyes wide and excited.

"No, Diya! One more time, pleeeease! I want to be an eagle now!" Pooja pleaded between coughs. "I'm alright."

Diya could never say no to Pooja. She flew her sibling around the room, even though her arms had grown tired from their games. Pooja loved to test Diya's strength, always so proud of the way Diya could best the other children in physical activity. Diya wondered if Pooja idolized her strength because the child had so little of their own.

As if on cue, Amma appeared in the doorway and scolded Diya for overexciting her sibling. Amma tucked Pooja into bed with a mug of barley water, left Nani to mind the child, and headed off to the market with Diya in tow. Before they left, Diya kissed Pooja's forehead, finding it clammy and sweaty. Her sibling looked so small and frail, obviously worn out from their games, but their dark eyes danced with delight, and Diya couldn't manage to feel bad about overindulging them.

Diya hated the market. She didn't like the onslaught of sensation—the noise, myriad of smells, chaos of colors, and the press of bodies. But most of all, she hated listening to her mother haggle and plead for the things they needed. Pooja's medicine took most of Amma and Appa's meager earnings, and it was difficult to stretch the scraps of leftover coin far enough to feed and house them all. And Amma was growing rounder every day, meaning there would soon be another person to care for. What if the new baby was sickly like Pooja? Would it die like the other babies that had come during the sad, lonely years between Diya's and Pooja's births?

Diya tried not to think about it all, but the market always overwhelmed her, weakening the stone wall she built around her fear. At ten years old, Diya was the eldest child. She was strong and healthy. She couldn't be afraid. She had to help Amma and Appa take care of Nani, Pooja, and the new baby. She had to be brave. She could not be afraid.

But Diya was afraid. She was afraid of so many things. Most of all, she was afraid that, one day, there wouldn't be enough money for Pooja's medicine and Pooja would die and there would be a gaping hole in their family that would destroy them all. She couldn't let that happen.

Diya was thinking these impossible thoughts, tuning out the wheedling tones of Amma's voice negotiating the price of tamarind, when she noticed an unusual bit of space in the bustling crowd. She wandered toward the spot, drawn by the promise of a whiff of fresher air and a few moments without someone else's scratchy clothing or sweaty skin brushing against her. She stepped out of the crowd and froze.

A horse and cart sat near a brick wall. A handful of children were in the cart, some sleeping, others listlessly watching the crowd. A few had climbed down, apparently to stretch their legs, but they didn't wander far from the cart. They all moved lethargically, as if in a daze.

A tall, broad-shouldered man stood beside the cart, watching Diya with orange eyes that glittered dangerously. Or perhaps they were simply reflecting the glint of the coin he was rolling across his knuckles. His curly silver hair was tipped in onyx, his skin a dark brown. Though his posture indicated boredom, his gaze was alert.

Diya knew immediately what he was. Park Hill was in the same region as Smoketown, farther east, but bordering the same mountain range. She'd seen Aegises passing through before. They always left the poor city with a full cart.

Diya watched the coin flowing smoothly across the Aegis's hand. It was gold. Had she ever seen Amma or Appa with gold? That single coin could buy Pooja's medicine for...well, Diya didn't know how long, but she knew it would be long enough to help her parents save a little money, maybe enough to cover for the weeks Amma wouldn't be able to work when the baby came.

"You're too old," the Aegis said flatly, startling Diya out of her thoughts. "You're more likely to survive the transformations if you start them young."

"I'm strong," Diya replied, surprising herself. She didn't usually talk to people willingly. "I can survive it."

The coin sparkled in the sunlight, rolling first one direction, then reversing seamlessly.

The Aegis watched her watching it, his face impassive. "Perhaps," he said. "Perhaps not. I don't suppose we'll ever know."

Diya saw his gaze shift up slightly before she felt Amma's hand on her shoulder. Her mother shoved a parcel into her arms, then ran a protective hand over Diya's hair. The Aegis smirked as her mother hustled her away.

"You know not to wonder off that way, beta! And not to talk to those wretched creatures!"

Amma scolded her all the way home. Diya nodded and murmured apologies at the appropriate spots, but she wasn't listening. She was thinking about that gold coin.

When Diya slipped out that night, her mother was asleep in a chair beside Pooja's bed. It had been a bad night, and Pooja had finally fallen into a fitful sleep after coughing so much they'd vomited a terrifyingly reddish phlegm. Appa had decided to sleep on a mat on the floor of Pooja's room rather than in bed, too worried about Pooja to sleep comfortably, though he should really rest for the few hours before he had to return to the mines.

That had made it easier for Diya to sneak out, since Pooja's room was at the back of the house, and their parents slept nearest the door. She'd had no concerns about waking Nani when she slipped out of the cot they shared in the home's main room. Nani slept like the dead.

Nani had still been snoring when Diya returned to leave the pouch of coins on the table for her mother to find in the morning. She didn't risk another peek into Pooja's room, in case anyone had awoken. The cart waited for her just down the road—too close for her to be caught and foiled now.

She allowed herself one moment to pray for her family—for Amma and Appa and Nani and the new baby, and, most of all, for Pooja. For them, she could be strong and brave.

Even though it meant she'd never see them again.

Abruptly, Macella was jolted back to the present. Diya glared at her, her orange eyes blazing with anger. Before Macella could choke out an apology, Diya spun on her heels and stalked away.

CHAPTER TWELVE

Macella

Though the following days afforded Macella no opportunity to talk to Diya about the memory they'd shared, she thought about it often. She couldn't imagine the fortitude it must've taken for a ten-year-old child to willingly leave behind everything and everyone she knew and condemn herself to brutal conditions and a life of service. Macella wondered if Diya had ever seen her family again, and if little Pooja had gotten better thanks to their big sister's sacrifice. She liked to believe they had, and that the family had lived an easier life thanks to Diya's efforts.

She also wondered if Diya had ever noticed the resemblance between Macella and the Aegis who'd carted her away from her home. Macella had only one memory of him, and it was from long after his death, but she'd recognized Matthias immediately. His onyx-tipped silver curls and the deep dimples that appeared when he'd smirked were just like her own. With their long lives and small number, it was likely most Aegises would cross paths at some point, but Macella still hadn't expected to find out that her father had recruited Diya.

Depending on how long Diya trained in Smoketown before she crossed into Duànzào and became an Aegis, there was a chance she'd met Matthias during the last quarter of his life. Soon after that stolen memory, Matthias would've fallen in love with a human, lost her during childbirth, and spent ten years raising their daughter alone before being forced to give her up. When he'd sacrificed his happiness to keep Macella safe, had he remembered the brave little girl who'd sold herself to save her family? What would Diya think if she knew Macella's Aegis parent had been her erstwhile captor?

As intriguing as those questions were, Macella didn't have long to dwell on them. King Khari's prediction proved correct, as they so often did. Within a fortnight, nobles and Aegises began streaming into the castle—the Aegises arriving alone and on horseback while the wealthy guests arrived in carriages and caravans, loaded with trunks and servants. Once more, the castle bustled with activity, and Macella was more entrenched in it than ever. As the king's betrothed, she was expected to greet these guests as they were presented to the Crown. Often, they were invited to dine with one or all of the monarchs, and Macella's duties included socializing alongside her future spouses.

Private dinners with the full Wildfire Court were rarer than ever, but they still made time for each other over early breakfasts or late-night drinks, or whatever other moments they could spare. Macella intended to keep her promise to Jacan—to all of them—so she refused to allow more than a few days to pass without gathering the family together, however briefly.

The rest of the Wildfire Court was just as busy as Macella, all playing their expected roles, while continuing to gather information that might serve them during the coming confrontation. Lotta flitted about the castle with Lynn and her assistants, fitting folks for new finery and mending all manner of garments thrust upon them by the visiting nobles. Aisling alternated between her mage lessons and practicing her new learning at the workers' settlement, where she and Macella had agreed she should serve whenever she could, healing simple injuries and supplying various potions and tinctures. Meanwhile, Zahra continued charming the nobility, courting allies and currying favor for the future queen. Between them, the three women brought the most useful bits of information to the group's discussions.

Aithan, Finley, and Jacan were, of course, busy defending against rifts. Thankfully, with the extra Aegises around, it was a much less time-consuming task. Even better, after the incident with the loogaroo, the attacks seemed to stagnate. As each day grew cooler than the last, the appearance of rifts began to taper off, giving the small council hope that their problem would resolve itself.

Of course, Macella knew it was only a matter of time before all hell broke loose. Hades's words haunted her dreams.

"Your king believes herself a god. She blasphemes, believing she can create life. She believes she can evade death. She threatens the balance... The blasphemer must be stopped. Child of both worlds, you and the son of Lucifer must stop her. Only you can."

"What if I cannot?" Macella had asked, and the god of the underworld had spoken the words that accompanied her worst nightmares.

"Your realm will burn. Everyone you know will have the flesh carved from their bones and their entrails devoured. The screams of the dying will serenade you at night, and the lamentations of the damned will haunt your days. Ammit will grow fat on human hearts, and the air will ring with an exquisite symphony of suffering. Your world will collapse into meat and viscera, and the gods will start again."

If King Khari remained in power when the final snow of the season thawed, the realms would be at war. And the king would do anything it took to hold on to that power, no matter how reprehensible and depraved her actions might be.

So, while Khari fixated on finding a way to reassure the nobility that she was in control of the situation, the Wildfire Court deliberated over a plan to wrest that control from her grasp.

Which was part of the reason Macella ultimately agreed to help Queen Anni-ka. Another ally in the monarchy could prove useful. Plus, anything they learned about Aegisborn might help her prepare for the Blessed Rite. Risky though it was, the partnership was just too beneficial to pass up. The rest of the Wildfire Court had reluctantly agreed.

"I reserve the right to kill the queen and her cousin should they decide to betray us," Finley had said, sounding a bit too gleeful about the possibility.

Macella had been in company with Annika enough lately to see that her pregnancy continued to plague her. She was paler than ever and tired quickly—often excusing herself from events early and returning to her chambers to rest. That very evening, she'd vomited after dinner, and the king had ended their little party so that she and the Grand Mage could attend to the young queen.

Macella was less concerned for Queen Annika than she was pleased by the evening's abrupt conclusion. She'd returned to her room to find Aithan in the bath and had been just about to join him when Lucy announced the arrival of the high tailor. Macella sighed and trudged to the dressing chamber.

"You're not eating enough," Lynn asserted, hands on her hips as she stepped back and scrutinized Macella's waistline. Charlotte and another assistant were positioned behind Macella, helping fit her for a new gown. "Nip it in a quarter of an inch."

"You'd better make it a half," Charlotte suggested firmly. "She trains more when she's anxious. She'll be slimmer still by the opening ball."

"She can hear you," Macella sighed, rolling her eyes. "I haven't got time to train as much as I'd like, and I eat all day long. The Crown so loves to entertain."

"You nibble," Charlotte corrected. "You're too busy captivating and impressing everyone to get a proper meal down."

"My king enjoys showing off her future bride," Macella replied, keeping her voice light. She knew both Charlotte and Lynn would understand her true sentiments. "It is my honor to impress on her behalf."

Lynn eyed Macella shrewdly. "Well, Lucy has been worried sick about you, haven't you, Lucy?"

Lucy who'd been passing by with an arm full of linens, gave the high tailor a wide-eyed look. "Beg pardon, miss?"

"Never mind. Go and fetch Lady Macella some vittles," Lynn said, waving the young woman away.

Lucy scurried off quickly, as frightened by the high tailor as most everyone else.

"She told you she was worried about me?" Macella asked, a pang of affection and guilt aching in her chest.

"There's not much goes on below stairs that I don't know about," Lynn replied, circling Macella to take in the gown from every angle. "Sofia, go and find that crimson brocade we set aside. We may need to add a belt."

The other assistant hurried to follow the high tailor's orders. Macella stared at her reflection. King Khari insisted she get a brand-new gown for the opening ball of the cold season. It would be the first in a long line of celebrations of their pending nuptials, and Lynn had designed accordingly. The gown featured an overlay of fabric that appeared to be embroidered with patterns of rose petals—black at the hem and fading slowly into shades of crimson.

"The northern rose." Macella sighed again, wrinkling her nose. "It's becoming my least favorite flower."

Lynn scoffed. "Not just roses."

Without further explanation, Lynn scooped up the large windup lantern she kept with her and carried it into the hall. The dressing chamber dimmed, lit only by candlelight. Macella gasped. Among the crimson petals were amber jewels that had been invisible in the brightness of the lantern. In the low light, similar to the way the ballroom would be lit, her dress was no longer made of rose petals.

It was made of flames.

"Wildfire," Charlotte whispered.

"It spreads," Lynn said quietly. "Faster and farther than you can possibly imagine. My assistants all love the new settlement. Their families have gotten work in the fields and are living in comfortable homes in the encampment. Same for the families of many other servants on staff. And someone must've talked to Evangeline, because she hired most of the cold-season help from the settlement, meaning even more opportunities for those families. They're happy. They get to spend more time together and have more time to enjoy their lives now that there's this safe, thriving community only a short walk from the castle. No more spending half the day walking to and from homes in the city on holidays. Now, they don't have to walk at all if it doesn't suit them. Sofia's siblings are earning tips shuttling carts of folks between the settlement and the castle three times a day."

Macella understood what a gift it must be for the servants to be able to spend time with the families they worked so tirelessly to provide for. How wonderful it must be to go home each night rather than living in the servants' quarters. Many of the servants could now have real lives outside of the castle, beyond a few days off every month.

"Some of the other tailors and I are going to sell our work at their monthly market. And they're building a school next season," Charlotte added. "Right now, the children have half-day classes in the meeting house—littles in the morning and older children in the afternoon after their chores or shifts in the fields. But the community is growing so fast, the school needs its own space and more than a few volunteer parents to run it. I'm going to teach a few days a week. It's something I really wanted to do, but once I got engaged to Gaspar, he wouldn't hear of it. He said I'd be too busy with *his* children to babysit anyone else's. But now, I can do as I like."

"I don't know when you'll find the time," Lynn harumphed, though her eyes twinkled with pride. "You have Royal Scribe duties, and I'm certainly not giving you any extra days off."

Charlotte muttered something about unpaid internships, and Lynn barked a laugh. Macella swallowed against a lump in her throat. There was so much good happening, even in the midst of her overwhelming anxieties. She had the sudden, terrifying realization that they could really build this new world she'd dreamed of.

"I told you before that the gods have marked you for something," the high tailor stated. "Anyone with sense can see how brightly you burn. Nothing and nobody can hide that fire. It's going to keep spreading."

Macella remembered how Lynn had held her, comforting her after King Khari had decided on Macella to be her new bride. She'd been devastated and distraught at the prospect of a life sentence in the capital, a pawn in the Crown's games. That had been before the destruction of the kingdom had hung in the balance. The high tailor had already believed in her then, and that clearly hadn't changed. Knowing she had the faith of such a smart, strong woman, as well as that of the community, reminded Macella that she was far from alone.

Lynn bustled away, as if she hadn't noticed Macella's shining eyes. She brought the large lantern back into the room as Lucy returned with a tray of bread, cheese, cold meat, and fruit that was far too large for Macella to finish alone.

"This doesn't need a belt," Charlotte said, frowning at the dress, and breaking the silence.

"Of course not. It's perfect," Lynn replied matter-of-factly. "Just needs to be taken in half an inch."

They were helping Macella out of the dress when Sofia returned with the unwanted brocade. In a few moments, they'd cleaned up behind themselves and were headed to their next assignment, leaving Macella to her massive snack.

"Eat," Lynn said sternly before she left. "Your people need you."

Macella pulled on a robe and sat down to her meal. She couldn't let her people down. She wouldn't.

⚜

Aithan

(19) When Aithan emerged from the bath, he was surprised to find a simple wooden chair placed before the fireplace in their bedchambers. Macella stood beside it, wearing only a silk robe, her eyes filled with a familiar fierce heat that made his blood boil. Her fire always called to his, reckless and rough and wild. She might be forced to hide parts of herself during the day, but when they were alone together, she let him see the real her—his hell goddess.

"I want to try something," Macella said, full lips curling into a sexy smirk that sent his boiling blood rushing straight to his cock. "Drop the towel and sit down."

Aithan suppressed a grin. He loved it when she took charge, like the warrior queen she was. He would take Macella any time, any way, but there was something about seeing her uninhibited and demanding, taking what she wanted in a world determined to give her less than she deserved.

"As you wish," he replied, letting his towel fall to the floor and enjoying the way Macella's gaze burned hotter as she stared at his stiffening cock.

He crossed the room and sat in the chair, unsurprised when Macella immediately untied her robe, pulled his arms behind him, and began to wind the silk belt around his wrists. She was trying to shield her thoughts, but Aithan knew her so well that she couldn't manage to hide much, especially not when she was this excited. He could smell her arousal, could imagine the sweet slickness of her pussy beginning to drip down her thighs. Gods, he loved that smell. He could almost taste it.

Aithan flexed his hands involuntarily and found the bindings strong. Of course, he could escape if he wanted to. But why the fuck would he want to?

"Ready to play?" Macella asked, rounding the chair to stand in front of him. "Let's see how long you can last before shredding those restraints. If it's less than ten minutes, you're on curl-wrangling duty. I like it better when you wash my hair and oil my scalp than any of the servants."

She gave him another saucy grin, and Aithan knew that, if his hands were free, he would've already grabbed her and she'd be straddling his lap, enveloping his now fully erect cock in her wet heat. Her robe hung loose, the silk barely clinging to her breasts and gaping open to reveal the thatch of dark hair at the apex of her thighs. Aithan was an expert in discipline, but his wife was always the exception to his carefully cultivated self-control. He might lose this little wager, but if the reward was burying himself deep in her exquisite pussy, it felt like a win. Besides, they both knew full well he would happily wash and oil any part of her whenever she asked.

"If I don't last ten minutes, I'm going to fuck you until you cannot walk a straight line," Aithan promised, raking his eyes down her body—lingering on her taut nipples and thick thighs. "If I last more than ten minutes, I'm going to fuck you until *I* cannot walk a straight line."

Macella's lips parted in a sexy little gasp, before she smirked again, arching an eyebrow at him. Aithan's cock twitched. He loved that look.

"Deal," she said, shimmying her robe off her shoulders and letting it fall to the floor.

Aithan had only a moment to take in her beautiful bare body before onyx flames whispered across her skin, and she vanished completely.

He huffed out an impatient sigh, but held still, his cock twitching restlessly against his thigh. He could sense Macella circling him, her scent and warmth heavy in the air around him. She was intentionally muddying his senses, trying to disorient him so that he couldn't pinpoint her position.

"How long has it been?" he growled, glancing toward the ornate mechanical clock in the corner.

Macella laughed musically, her breath warm against his ear. "Not even a minute, Lord Protector."

Aithan shivered, though his veins were full of fire. He wanted to rip the fabric from his wrists and fuck her on the floor, but he also enjoyed the anticipation. It was a wonderful paradox.

He obviously wasn't the only one enjoying the anticipation. The scent of Macella's arousal enveloped him, making his mouth water and cock pulse. She seemed to be everywhere, teasing him. A hand trailing over his bicep. A whisper of lips against his neck. The brush of breasts against his bound hands.

"I think the monarchy is a bad influence on you," he groaned when her tongue flicked over his cockhead all too briefly. "You're obviously learning extremely effective torture techniques."

"I've barely begun, my lord," Macella purred in his ear.

When had she gotten behind him again? She pressed her perfect breasts against his shoulder blades as she ran her nails down his chest and abs. He hissed out a sharp breath as his stomach muscles clenched, his cock throbbing almost painfully, desperate for her touch.

Macella obliged him, wrapping an invisible hand around his cock and stroking lightly. Aithan's hips bucked, his forearms flexing, straining against the silk. Then she was gone again, the warmth of her embrace lingering alongside the delicious scent of her wet pussy.

His only preparation for her next move was the sudden appearance of a glob of saliva on the head of his cock. Aithan shuddered as his wife's invisible hand wrapped around him once more and began to stroke. A moment later, the wet warmth of her mouth enveloped his cock, ripping a low, ragged moan from his throat.

"Fuuuuuuuuuuuuuck, Macella," he gasped, unable to form anything more coherent as she swallowed him deep. "Fuck, fuck, *fuck*, Macella!"

Her mouth felt incredible, but the sight of his glistening cock appearing and disappearing was surreal. His brain couldn't make sense of feeling, smelling, and hearing her, without being able to see her at all. His cock, however, didn't need it to make sense. Already, his body was tingling, heat building in his core.

"Fuck it, you win," Aithan growled, ripping free of the bindings and reaching for her. Even without being able to see her, he easily pulled her to her feet and onto his lap.

Macella giggled, reappearing in a flash of onyx flames. "Oh, you were so close!"

"Yes, I was," he replied, before slamming his mouth to hers in a hungry kiss. She tasted tart and sweet, her cinnamon and citrus mixed with his salty tang. Aithan wanted to devour her completely, wanted to bury himself in her so deep he'd never find his way out.

He rose from the chair, lifting her into his arms as he moved toward the bed. Macella wrapped her legs around his waist, rubbing her wet heat against him in a way that pushed him dangerously close to exploding. Somehow, he managed not to cum as he collapsed onto the bed and thrust into her all in one movement. Her pussy gripped him greedily, feeling like home.

Aithan eased out, thinking of the most disgusting monsters he knew—bunyips, nuckelavee, squonks. It worked, but barely, distracting him just enough to pull himself back from the edge. He'd promised he was going to fuck her until she couldn't walk a straight line, and he intended to keep his word.

Aithan climbed out of bed, dragging Macella with him until her luscious ass hung off the edge of the mattress. Draping her legs across his arms, he lined his cock up with her entrance and thrust hard, sheathing himself once more. He set a punishing rhythm, slamming into her again and again, relishing the slap of his skin against hers as it mingled with her gasps and moans in a sexy symphony. Aithan loved the way her beautiful breasts bounced with each thrust. He leaned down to take one tight nipple into his mouth, sucking hard and making her cry out, her pussy clamping down on him in a way that made him see stars.

He bent his knees and focused on the burn in his thighs, letting it distract from the pleasure just enough to stop him from giving in to his orgasm. Instead, he focused on seeing how many he could coax out of his wife. The way her inner walls squeezed him made it clear she was well on her way to her first.

Aithan pressed the pad of his thumb to her bottom lip, and she opened to him, sucking his thumb into her mouth and swirling her tongue over it. He groaned, his cock throbbing insistently. Quickly, he pulled his hand free and slid it between them to circle her clit with his wet thumb. Macella arched off the bed, screaming his name as her orgasm ripped through her.

She looked so perfect like this—wild and joyful and free. As always, the sight threatened to undo him. But he wouldn't let it.

He had promises to keep.

Chapter Thirteen

Macella

"That's like the third time you've bumped into me. Why are you so off balance today?" Zahra demanded. Macella giggled and Zahra's mismatched eyes widened dramatically. "Did the future queen of Kōsaten just *giggle*? Oh gods, did you get fucked so well you can't walk?"

Macella shushed her, laughing harder at Zahra's exaggerated eyebrow wiggle. They'd nearly reached the Aegis dining hall, and Macella had, indeed, inadvertently veered into Zahra multiple times as they walked arm-in-arm through the corridors. Her Aegis always kept his promises.

"Don't get me distracted, I need to focus," Macella scolded. "This is important."

Zahra squeezed her arm. "It's cute that you're nervous, even after all the time you spent with this lot last cold season."

"I was nervous then too. I felt myself an outsider. Now it's even worse. I'm about to become a member of an administration implicit in their oppression." Macella sighed. "How am I to earn their trust, let alone their loyalty?"

"By being yourself," Zahra replied confidently. "Your actions speak for you, and the Aegises have undoubtedly heard much about you already, given your growing reputation. If they treated you as an outsider last year, it is because you are exceptional, my love. You'd just forced the Crown to change Smoketown, something none of these other Aegises have ever tried to do. Not one of them can claim to have done more for Aegiskind than you have, Warrior Queen."

Zahra pulled to a halt and stood on tiptoes to plant a kiss on Macella's mouth. Macella sighed against Zahra's soft, plush lips. She hadn't considered that the other Aegises were probably processing understandably complex emotions when they'd met the so-called Savior of Smoketown last year. It wasn't surprising they didn't know what to make of her while she was busily bucking tradition at every opportunity.

"Well, I will be even stranger now that I have gone from radical reformist to future queen in a year's time," Macella said wryly.

She tried to shake off her nerves by taking a few more deep breaths. She'd dined among the Aegises a few times already this season, but that was before the rest of the group had arrived. This meal would be the first time the entire Thirteen would be gathered. Would they sense that she was one of them or, worse, that she wasn't entirely Aegis nor human? And how many of them shared Kiho's more dangerous ideas about how best to reform the kingdom? Where did the Aegises' allegiances lie?

"Not even Kai and Diya can say you haven't overdelivered on your promises to improve the lives of Aegises. As well as the lives of the child recruits, the capital's poor, sorcerers in your home region, all of Shively, and gods know who else." Zahra held Macella's gaze with unblinking intensity. "Seriously, dearest, if you haven't already earned their respect, you never will. So just be your lovable, feisty, intelligent self. And help me choose an Aegis to have an affair with this season. If we're on the verge of a possibly world-ending war, I want to be walking as crooked as you until the curtains close. I'm going to need a few lovers with less busy schedules than you and the Lord Protector to keep me company this season."

They were still laughing as they strolled into the dining hall. Macella was delighted that the rest of the Wildfire Court had already arrived, though she was less pleased to see that Finley had secured them seats at the very center of the room's intimate arrangement of long, rectangular tables. Captain Drudo, now healed enough to be up and about a bit, sat beside Finley, grinning widely while watching them coax everyone into lively conversation. Charlotte was on Finley's other side, whispering with Aisling and smiling sweetly at Jacan, who sat across from her, pretending to be attending to the conversation but really staring at Charlotte the entire time. Aithan observed it all with quiet amusement, exchanging a few words here and there with the rest of the Aegises seated around him.

Macella took them all in quickly, these great warriors who'd survived impossible odds to be in their positions—positions that had only recently gained the respect they deserved. The scribe's writings had made Aegiskind more visible and swayed public opinion in their favor. Of course, the public was a fickle beast and very different from those the Aegises had been taught to slay. They'd gone from being reviled and ignored to revered and sometimes fetishized. Though fame was a double-edged sword, some had begun to adapt from solitary soldiers to more amicable protectors of a society suddenly willing to include them.

Cassian and Cressida, always beautiful and favored, had long been comfortable in a crowd. Their guild mate Valen, a jovial giant, had always been friendly as well. Kenji, Loi, and Vespera—Meng Po Aegises with silver hair tipped in violet—all seemed more open than Macella remembered, listening to whatever Finley was saying and contributing an occasional comment. Even Bellona, one of only two Aegises from the notoriously fierce guild of Kali, seemed to be enjoying the conversation. Macella had grown used to seeing Aithan, Finley, and Jacan being sociable, but seeing the others lowering their guard gave her a pang of bittersweet pride.

Then there were Kai and Diya, doing their best to remain aloof and apart despite their obvious partiality for Finley. Macella knew that the three of them had spent decades together, mostly confined to Duànzào and Smoketown, training the young recruits and new Aegises. Outside of the cold season pilgrimages to Kōsaten Keep, the three seldom escaped the bleak training grounds where they'd been raised. It was no wonder they'd been ready to join Kiho in a war against humanity. After all, Macella had been so enraged by what she saw in Smoketown that she slit a man's throat just to prove a point.

As if sensing her attention, Kai and Diya turned their heads toward her in near-perfect unison, their matching scowls deepening at the sight of her. Clearly, she was never going to be their favorite person. Considering she'd bested them in battle on their first meeting, she should probably be grateful they'd come to a reluctant truce. What would they say if they knew she was now plotting to overthrow the king?

The room fell quiet as the rest of the diners noticed her arrival. The sudden silence was disconcerting, but Macella didn't let her steps falter. That was, until a massive beast bounded toward her, its mouth open and tongue lolling. She had only a moment to brace herself before its paws hit her shoulders and its wet nose was pressed to her cheek, sniffing eagerly.

"Down, Váli! That's the future queen you're fondling, you fool frunti!" Valen pulled the beast away, giving Macella an apologetic grin. "Apologies, my lady. There's no training or getting rid of him. We fought over a deer once, and he's refused to leave my side since. Váli, show the lady your manners."

Macella was already petting the beast, well before Valen had finished his explanation. The massive animal sat at her feet, its tail thumping loudly against the floor as she scratched its thick white and gray fur. It looked like a wolf of some kind, though far bigger than any wolf she'd ever seen. Leave it to the biggest man alive to find a companion befitting his stature. Even sitting, the creature was nearly as tall as Macella. Despite its intimidating size, Váli had a sweet face and bright, intelligent blue eyes. Macella loved him immediately.

"Well met, Valen of Valley Station! Well met, Váli," she laughed, shaking hands with the big Aegis. "Well met, everyone."

She smiled, gestured for those who'd half-stood out of formality to sit, and slid onto the bench beside Aithan. Her husband slung an arm around her shoulders, Zahra squeezed in on her other side, and Finley winked before resuming the undoubtedly hyperbolic tale they'd been sharing. Váli flopped down on the floor beside his Aegis, watching eagerly for dropped food.

The conversation more or less continued as it had, and Macella was beginning to think that perhaps she'd been anxious for nothing, when, in the lull following Finley's tale, Cressida turned her big, bright eyes Macella's way.

"*Lady* Macella of Shively, we're so honored you've joined us!" the Mictlāntēcutli Aegis's voice was sugary sweet, while dripping with scorn. "We enjoyed your company last year, but now that you're to be well married, we never expected to find you in this part of the castle again."

Before Macella had a chance to formulate a reply, Finley laughed musically, tossing their hair. "Dear Macella is already well married to our brother Aithan of Auburndale. I performed the ceremony myself."

A shocked silence followed Finley's proclamation, which was undoubtedly what they'd intended. Macella couldn't read the collection of orange eyes now fixed on her. Feeling a little guilty about doing so, she let herself reach for their minds. She found mostly wonder and disbelief.

"Does the king know?" Diya demanded, her thick brows furrowed.

"Of course," Macella replied. "But it was supposed to be a secret from everyone else for the time being, because we didn't want to distract from her grace's celebration."

"Apologies, dearest," Finley said, not sounding sorry in the least. "But don't worry. Aegises are excellent at keeping secrets. Mum's the word, everyone."

Macella rolled her eyes, still listening to the minds around her. The consensus seemed mostly positive, though wary. She supposed that was a start.

She is to marry the king and yet still chose to wed an Aegis?

An Aegis is openly married...and with the Crown's blessing?

What manner of woman is this?

"Oh." Cressida sounded genuinely sincere when she spoke again. "Well, congratulations, both of you."

"Thank you," Macella replied. In the silence that followed, she took a moment to look around at the expectant faces of the Aegises and the Wildfire Court. Everyone was waiting for her to say more. She exhaled a breath and spoke as honestly as she could. "It has been an eventful year, full of unexpected developments. Still, I am happy to be among you again. Aithan, Finley, and

Jacan are my family, and you are theirs, so I consider you to be my family as well. I hope we can become better acquainted this season."

Aithan found her hand beneath the table and squeezed. Macella squeezed back.

"As if you'll be slumming it with us once you're queen," Kai scoffed, glaring at her from beneath his bangs, his orange eyes narrowed to angry slits. "You've gotten everything you ever dreamed of now—fame, fortune, and still, you get to keep your Aegis lover. You've obviously curried favor with the king, which means you're a good politician. Why should we trust you?"

Aithan tensed, but Macella only smiled. After months and months of the carefully chosen words and veiled threats that were the language of Kōsaten Keep, it was nice to have a frank conversation for a change. And it was better that they got it out of the way now, before the season began in earnest.

She took a moment to allow Kai's version of her story to unfold in her mind. King Khari had made her a beautiful northern rose, who she'd had the wisdom to pluck from obscurity and claim as her own. Now, Kai was painting her, not as a passive damsel, but a cunning temptress who'd leveraged her relationship with an Aegis into an introduction to the Crown, had used her wiles to gain wealth and proximity to power. It was a more entertaining story than Khari's, but it was every bit as false.

"I never dreamed of fame and fortune," Macella countered, gesturing around at the grandeur of the room dismissively. "I never dreamed of love, though I am grateful to the gods that I found it with Aithan of Auburndale. I never dreamed I'd have a loving family, though I am grateful the gods saw fit to bless me with my Wildfire Court. I did dream of one thing, however, and that dream was of a better world."

Macella paused, making intentional eye contact with Kai, then Diya, then every remaining Aegis in the room. She didn't need to look at her family to know that they were with her, ready to speak or act at the slightest hint that she needed them.

"I dreamed of a world where everyone could be safe, free of hunger and abuse. One where survival didn't depend on being born into the right family or working yourself to the bone," Macella went on. "Fate has seen fit to put me in a position where I can change things, can work to make those dreams a reality. Though I wouldn't have chosen fame and fortune, it has been thrust upon me, and all I can do is use it for good. All I can do is my duty. So, while you may not trust the Crown and, by extension, me—and with good reason—I will still fight for a better world for all of us. And perhaps I'll earn your trust along the way."

There were a few nods and murmurs of agreement, but Kai laughed bitterly. "You do have a way with words, but pretty speeches don't make you any different from those who've come before you."

"But her actions do."

Everyone's attention was caught by the small voice of a servant who'd been refilling their goblets. Macella recognized most of the castle staff by face and many by name. The sepia-skinned young man who'd spoken was called Omar. He seemed surprised by his own voice and shrank beneath the attention of the entire room but didn't back down.

"My family has a home and good jobs thanks to Lady Macella," Omar said, holding a pitcher of wine in front of him like a shield. "All the families of Ellasburg owe her our very lives. The settlement was her idea, and she's visited us many times since it was established. When a demon threatened to destroy our homes, it was Lady Macella who got us to safety and stood against the monster. As much as we love the stories she tells when she visits us, it is not her words that have earned our love and loyalty. It's her deeds."

Macella blinked. "Ellasburg?"

Omar flushed. "Beg pardon, m'lady. That's what we call it among ourselves. The *fieldworkers' settlement* is an unwieldy mouthful, and we're so much more than a settlement now. We're a community."

"And a right fine one at that." Aisling gave Omar a reassuring smile. "Full of happy, hardworking folks."

"Ella dreamed that place up, then made it a reality," Charlotte agreed. "That's what she does. It's who she is."

"You were there for what she did in Smoketown." Jacan lifted his chin at Kai and Diya. "You've witnessed firsthand the changes she and Lord Aithan set in motion. Her actions changed my life. I can clearly remember the first time I ever had a full stomach, because it was during Lady Macella's visit. I spent nearly two decades in that hell, and the night she slit Grizzle's throat was the first night in my life hunger pains didn't keep me awake. I still didn't sleep, though I was warm and clean for the first time, because I was afraid if I closed my eyes, it would all disappear. Lady Macella made that happen."

"Young Jacan speaks true," Valen boomed approvingly, and Váli woofed in agreement. "We've all heard the tales, and I've seen it with my own eyes. Things are different in Smoketown. Nobody else has ever cared what those bastards did to us. I'd say the lady has earned a bit of faith."

The room went silent again. Macella held her breath. Aithan held her hand tightly.

"We shall see," Diya replied finally.

Kai scowled at his plate. "I'm not going to start calling Smoketown *Macellaville* or any such shit. Can we eat now?"

Finley laughed loudly and soon everyone joined in. Diya's pursed lips had a decidedly upward tilt and even Kai was trying and failing to suppress a smirk. The air felt lighter as the servants bustled in with platters of food, and the meal passed pleasantly and unremarkably.

Unfortunately, Macella wasn't able to dine among the Aegises as much as she would've liked over the following days. The castle was buzzing with anticipation of the opening ball of the season, and Macella spent the days preceding it being introduced to what seemed to be every noble in Kōsaten. She fell into bed exhausted each night from all the socializing and dreamed of the months when she and Aithan had wandered the kingdom, killing monsters, and often speaking to no one but each other for days on end.

She gave a silent prayer of thanks to the gods that Khari had only extended invitations to the most prominent dignitaries from each region so, though they were technically invited, it had been easy to convince her parents that they would be too busy governing Shively to spend their first cold season as nobility away from their post. As much as Babette de Pointe wanted to continue her upward scheming, she was smart enough to recognize that her husband might need more time polishing his manners before he'd be ready to spend a season at court.

Besides, she *did* have much to do in her new role. Shively had never had more than an indifferent warden to oversee its affairs, so Babette was busy bullying the community into peace and prosperity. Her daughters were especially grateful to hear that, worst case scenario, Tomas and Babette might brave the last of the cold season weather to travel to Pleasure Ridge Park in time for a brief visit after Macella's coronation. It was a relief to know she wouldn't have to manage her parents on top of everything else right now.

Soon enough, the night of the opening ball arrived and Macella found herself plucked and fluffed and stuffed into her wildfire rose gown. Unlike last cold season, Macella would enter with the Crown and open the dance. She'd managed to nudge King Khari into escorting Queen Annika by demurely suggesting that the news of her pregnancy was fresher than that of her betrothal, and that the people would want to see the proud parents together. That meant Macella would have the relative relief of Monarch Meztli's company for their entrance and first dance.

She stood in the foyer just beyond the doors of the grand ballroom, watching the servants fuss over the king and queen. Queen Annika looked pale, as she so often did lately, and the man attempting to coax some color into her cheeks seemed a bit distraught by the futility of his efforts. For her part, King Khari seemed unbothered, lost in her own thoughts. Macella wondered if the king cared at all for the woman carrying her child. She doubted it.

"You dazzle me, my northern rose," Khari said, jolting Macella from her thoughts.

She realized she'd been staring at the king absently, and the king had noticed.

One corner of Khari's mouth curved in a smile, as she let her gaze travel across Macella's exposed shoulders and collarbones, before drifting to where her breasts swelled over her gown's scalloped neckline. "We've been so busy of late that I haven't had the opportunity to invite you for another private dinner, but I haven't forgotten how much I enjoyed our last evening. I hope you've thought about it as well."

Macella's cheeks warmed as the memory of that evening forced its way to the forefront of her mind. She'd tried to forget Khari's charming flirtation and that awful sexy vision of the two of them together. Despite her disdain, her body and her mind couldn't seem to agree on the effects of the king's seductive powers.

Luckily, Macella was spared from answering by the parting of the grand doors. Instantly, the king was perfectly poised—emanating beauty and strength as she guided her queen through the parted crowd. She was concerned and attentive, carefully supporting Annika with a gentle hand on her back, an affectionate rub of her stomach, a soft kiss on the temple. If Macella hadn't known better, she would've believed Khari was totally devoted to her wife and unborn child.

"If there is one piece of advice I'd give a future spouse, it is to trust your instincts, not your eyes," Monarch Meztli murmured. They squeezed Macella's arm as they led her onto the parquet. "But I suspect you already understand that."

Macella met their steady gaze, reading in it all that her friend wished to say but couldn't. The stoic monarch had gradually grown on her and, though they seldom spoke explicitly about the dangerous game they'd played for decades, Macella trusted them. She often wondered how much they knew or suspected about her true nature, especially at moments like this when they seemed so attuned to her thoughts. She would find out soon enough. Soon, everything would be laid bare, and everyone's true allegiances would be tested.

"You are very wise," Macella replied as they took their position on the dance floor. "It is a relief and a comfort to have friends I can trust...to give me such sound advice."

Monarch Meztli inclined their head, their depthless black eyes glittering in the candlelight. Macella was sure they took her meaning and hoped she was right in her instincts about them. They would be a useful ally in the end. And, hopefully, they'd be a friend for life.

(20) The mechanical lights dimmed, and whispers rippled through the crowd. The jewels hidden in the petals of Macella's gown caught the low light, setting the roses ablaze with flickering flames. Macella, however, was distracted by a glimmer of flame just beyond the dance floor.

Lynn has done it again, Aithan whispered in her mind. Macella met his warm gaze before taking in his dress uniform, which had clearly been recently updated. A burst of flame now flickered in his lapel.

More flames glittered in Charlotte's hemline and Zahra's bustle. On Finley's collar and the cuffs of Jacan's sleeves. Macella was sure Aisling and Nyx must also be wearing flames in Ellasburg, where many of the off-duty servants and apprentices had gone for their own party. The embers of her Wildfire Court, burning bright for all to see.

Lynn had, indeed, done it again.

"The king is going to be furious that she let me escort you tonight," Monarch Meztli said with an uncharacteristic hint of glee in their voice. "Everyone is watching the wrong pair."

They were right, of course. Eyes followed their every move, the Crown's wealthy guests murmuring to one another as they watched Monarch Meztli lead Macella gracefully around the dance floor. Even King Khari couldn't help but sneak glances, though she maintained her façade of loving devotion to Queen Annika.

"You do look beautiful tonight," Macella said, smiling warmly at Monarch Meztli as they touched palms and circled one another. "But then, you always do."

Monarch Meztli laughed throatily. "You don't have to have my gifts to sense how completely enamored the entire room is with you. I must say, I'm a little jealous that I didn't get any flames added to my ensemble."

The dance reached an interlude requiring them to switch partners, and Macella didn't have a chance to reply before she was palm to palm with King Khari. The king's adder eyes were cold, despite the approving smile she gave Macella.

"I admire your humility in yielding your place to Annika, and yet you still command the spotlight." The king's voice gave nothing of her true feelings away, leaving Macella to parse her words for hidden meanings and threats. "You are becoming quite popular among the nobility and commonfolk alike."

Macella lowered her gaze, both in false bashfulness and because she couldn't trust herself not to show Khari her true feelings. "I only wish to serve the Crown and her people, your grace. And popularity is no use without your favor. I pray you are pleased with how I have strived to be worthy of the great honor you've bestowed upon me with your affection."

King Khari seemed to soften a bit, though one could never be sure. The king was exceptionally skilled at making others see what she wanted them to see.

"Your next two dances are mine," the king replied, before the dance sent them back to their original partners.

King Khari was all chivalry and charm during her two dances, which were then followed by an endless blur of partners, occasionally broken up by more pleasurable dances with her friends. She took a turn with each member of the Wildfire Court—two with Zahra and three with Finley, who'd been determined to claim more dances than the king—and even a turn with Captain Drudo, who was recovered enough to dance a few slower numbers. Lady Seondeok and Laird Parul were among the bright spots as well. The leaders of Nulu had kept up a friendly correspondence with Macella and seemed genuinely delighted to see her again.

Most of her other partners were happy to talk about themselves or how much they were enjoying the season so far, but there were quite a few who were interested in her first initiative and her goals for the kingdom. They talked to her about the needs of their regions and their hopes for the future. Macella was happy to listen—these were the representatives of the people she was intended to rule. She would be their voice in the small council chamber.

Between the dancing and her "queen things," Macella found herself completely engaged all night. When she finally managed to sit out a dance and grab a drink, she did her best to find an inconspicuous spot where she might have a moment to herself. She stepped into a shadowy alcove, downing a mug of ale in one long, uninterrupted gulp. She belched and tossed the mug aside before taking a much slower sip from the goblet of wine in her other hand.

"I must admit that I might've been wrong about you."

Macella started, nearly spilling her wine as she spun toward the voice and simultaneously reached for a dagger with her free hand. Kai scowled at her from where he leaned in the alcove's darkest corner. Macella returned his glare with one of her own before turning her attention back to the ballroom.

"You nearly scared me to death," she groused, taking another sip of wine to steady her nerves. "What are you doing back there?"

"Same thing you are," Kai retorted, and Macella didn't have to look at him to know that he was rolling his eyes. "I'm not used to being around so many people. It's exhausting."

"Utterly," Macella agreed. "So, what were you wrong about?"

"I called you a lapdog once, a coward, someone who would stand idly by," Kai said matter-of-factly. "You've proven yourself none of those things. I don't like you, but I respect what you've done. Of course, it could all be a long con, and you may turn on us when you become queen, and I will tell everyone I suspected you all along. I hope you keep proving me wrong though."

Macella smiled into her goblet. "That is the nicest thing you've ever said to me."

"Don't grow accustomed to it," Kai retorted. "You'll have to settle for having two Apophis Aegises in your fan club. I'm not as easily befriended as Jacan and Finley."

Macella didn't bother pointing out the tremendous understatement. She decided she might as well push a little. "Nonetheless, you should join us for lunch tomorrow. It'll be cozy and casual, as everyone will be recovering from tonight's revelries."

Kai snorted. "Go away, Lady Macella, before your admirers notice you and flock over here and I'm forced to listen to your insipid conversations."

Macella laughed, finished her wine, and headed back into the fray.

Chapter Fourteen

Macella

More and more often, in the days following the ball, Macella caught King Khari watching her. Meetings, meals, and other social engagements continued to preclude any private evening invitations, but the king seemed determined to have Macella with her as often as possible. Her scrutiny began to feel like a physical weight, like insects crawling over Macella's skin (like a memory of huge, hairy spiders; wriggling, writhing centipedes; and fat, slimy maggots, all over her body and her helplessly trapped in a web). Still, she did her best to remain regal and unbothered, while carefully straddling the line between useful ally and possible threat.

Whenever Macella could escape the king's engagements, she hosted her own evening parties and afternoon teas, inviting those she most wished to cultivate relationships with. At first, the Aegises had been reluctant to accept her invitations, joining with stiff politeness, but Macella refused to give up. She carefully planned her guest lists so that there were nobles, knights, Aegises, and even off-duty staff present, and made sure to give everyone assembled equal respect and attention. The Wildfire Court helped to give these events a warm, family atmosphere. Soon enough, her little parties had become comfortable, lively conversations that taught her much about the spectrum of people she would serve as queen.

A few weeks after the opening ball, King Khari decided it was time to take a tour of Ellasburg. Macella found herself staring out of the window of a carriage, surrounded by the Grand Mage, Grand Treasurer, Monarch Meztli, and Zahra. The king, Aithan, and the Grand Vizier rode alongside them on horseback. Behind them was a procession of carriages carrying many of the king's noble guests, and at the rear of the cavalcade were all of the Aegises on their own mounts, Váli the wolf beast trotting along beside Valen. Knights of the Royal Guard flanked the convoy, their polished armor glinting in the bright sunlight.

It seemed a lot of pomp and circumstance just to show off a new initiative. Macella hoped the people of Ellasburg were prepared to have their day completely disrupted. They'd no more enjoy being gawked at than she did, but it should be quick and relatively painless for the citizens and would be followed by a special lunch provided by the Crown.

Macella, on the other hand, would never escape Khari's watchful eyes. She was relieved that Zahra had come along, at least, and that Annika had stayed behind. Unfortunately, Lord Kasper was there, glaring daggers at Macella at every opportunity.

The first snow of the season had fallen the previous night, and the horses' hooves crunched on the frozen ground. The air had grown cold enough to make Macella grateful for her fleece-lined finery and fur cloak. There hadn't been a rift in nearly a fortnight, indicating that hell was finally slumbering for the cold season. Lord Anwir had been visibly relieved by the peace, going as far as to mock the nobles who'd tried to refuse the king's invitation out of fear of demon attacks. King Khari had made sure to invite those very nobles on this promenade.

Still, whispers and rumors about the attacks on the capital persisted, and the king continued to press the small council for solutions. She would allow nothing to mar her celebrations, to distract from her glory. Yet, she was also uncharacteristically restless, as if she sensed the coming storm. She'd responded by redoubling her efforts to make this cold season the grandest in memory, determined to ensure the story of her centennial season would be told and sung for all time. Perhaps today was her attempt to make a lasting impression on the commonfolk.

As they neared the newly constructed homes and community buildings, it was impossible not to think about the loogaroo barreling toward their wooden frames, threatening to burn it all to ash. Macella hadn't been to the settlement in a few weeks, so she was surprised and a little chagrined to discover a beautifully hand-painted wooden sign that read "Welcome to Ellasburg" in large, ornate red letters beside the already well-worn path into the little village. She didn't have to look the king's way to know that her adder's eyes were watching as the other nobles exclaimed over the sign and settlement looming ahead.

"I'd heard that the natives were calling it Ellasburg among themselves, but I didn't realize the name had stuck." Lord Kasper sniffed peevishly. "Of course, the settlement was entirely Lady Macella's idea. It only makes sense that the inhabitants would demonstrate such gratitude and *loyalty* to their future queen."

There was a nasty edge to the Grand Treasurer's voice that had become all too familiar. Macella easily caught his insinuation. He was stoking the king's paranoia, which was already mounting without any such encouragement. The Grand Treasurer had probably noticed the king's budding suspicions and relished the opportunity to make matters more difficult for Macella. Kasper might be bound to keep the secret of the loogaroo attack, but he obviously hadn't given up on his quest for vengeance.

Macella had kept up her end of the bargain with Annika, though they'd had to come to an agreement about how much to tell the Grand Mage. For now, the story was that a friend of the queen's had procured what she believed to be the blood of an Aegisborn woman. Kiama was learning what she could from it, but it wouldn't be long before she'd need more tests or more information, if she was going to ensure the survival of Annika and her child.

Macella wasn't sure what she would do at that point. The Grand Mage did the king's bidding but had also been in cahoots with Annika and Lord Anwir. There was no way of knowing her true intentions or motivations. And, with her immense power, she would prove a formidable adversary should they find themselves on opposite sides.

That was a problem for another day. Regardless of what the coming months brought, Macella knew the last thing she needed was for Khari to think the castle's workers were more loyal to her than to king and crown. It was too early in the game for her enemy to grow suspicious.

For once, I think the king might be wise to be a bit paranoid, Aithan whispered in her mind. *Look closely at the bottom corner of the sign.*

Macella looked again, examining the intricate border the artist had painted. It took a moment, but she found what Aithan meant. Etched among vines and roses was something that hadn't been painted but carved into the wood itself.

A tiny flame.

Macella hardly listened to Lord Anwir's magically amplified voice providing endless commentary on the settlement's creation and management, though she maintained a polite smile. Beneath that smile, she was thinking of that tiny flame and wondering what it might mean. And how far it might spread.

Even with homes shuttered and gardens covered in preparation for the cold season, Ellasburg was a neat, attractive community. The people had made the homes their own, planting flowers and hanging banners, painting their exteriors, and adding personal touches that made each house unique. It was clear that the people loved it here and, from what she understood, there was so much talent in the community that its inhabitants rarely had to go into Pleasure Ridge Park proper if they didn't wish to.

The field where the families had originally camped during construction had been converted to a marketplace, the empty stands and carts now covered until the next market day. Though they had yet to build any shops, several folks ran businesses from their homes or barns, including a baker, tailor, blacksmith, and even a tavern. They traded and bartered and bought from one another, went to school and worship and parties in the meeting house. They raised children and livestock and didn't worry about how they would survive the cold days ahead.

We're so much more than a settlement now. We're a community.

Macella felt like she might burst into tears. Despite the fear and heartache she'd had to endure to be here, she'd survived and made it matter. She'd changed lives for the better.

If she didn't live through the coming conflict, she'd die knowing that much.

"Lord Anwir, as we're amongst friends, share the latest financials of my lady's first initiative," King Khari said, turning an adoring smile in Macella's direction. "I want our friends to know the brilliance the kingdom will be gaining in its new queen."

"You always flatter me, your grace," Macella said, returning the king's smile warmly. "The success of the settlement is the result of much hard work from a great many people."

"So modest, Lady Macella," Lord Kasper drawled in a voice dripping with sarcasm. "*Ellasburg* is entirely your doing. We have the highest yields in decades and have more than made up for the deficits of the spring harvest. If this level of productivity continues, the kingdom will be its most prosperous since the days of Khalid."

"Let's not put the cart before the horse, my lord," Macella exclaimed with a laugh. "We must give it much more time before we can even begin to make such claims. All we can say with certainty right now is that we've improved the lives of hundreds of families, and, in turn, those families have worked hard for the Crown. When the people are well, the kingdom prospers. The Crown has invested in their people and shown that King Khari's next hundred years will be even better than her last."

The words were sour on her tongue, but King Khari puffed up a bit, and Macella knew she'd managed to soothe her—for the moment, at least. Remaining in the king's good graces would doubtless prove more and more difficult with each passing day.

The Grand Treasurer seemed ready to speak again, but Grand Mage Kiama cut him off. "The settlement's foragers have unearthed plants and fungi that are so rare we haven't used them for decades, and even a few we thought extinct. We're discovering new magical and medical advancements every day. My apprentices are learning so much; they may prove to be the most accomplished group of mages I've mentored yet. Of course, you'll see for yourselves at the next Matching."

The Grand Vizier conveyed this information to the rest of the convoy, and the guests' appreciative murmurs filled the air. They peppered the Grand Vizier with questions, effectively taking the attention off of Macella. She breathed a sigh of relief. She thought she caught the Grand Mage watching her with a sly smile, but she could've been mistaken. Perhaps King Khari wasn't the only one who was paranoid.

Lord Anwir continued to elucidate the guests on the particulars of the settlement as their procession plodded slowly along. The people of Ellasburg stood before their houses, bowing as the cavalcade passed, and eventually falling into step behind it. Here and there, Macella noticed what might be flames etched into fenceposts or hidden in patterns adorning window frames. She also noticed that the people of Ellasburg all seemed to look for her when the procession passed.

Soon, they reached the de facto town square, where servants hurried to arrange everyone into orderly rows to kneel before the king. The meeting house windows glowed with firelight, looking warm and inviting, while the people shivered on their knees in the snow. Macella knew servants were waiting inside to serve a hearty lunch and good ale. She'd heard the citizens planned to have a real revel when the nobles departed.

Unfortunately, it appeared they would all have to wait. The procession of nobles was being arranged so that they had a clear view of the proceedings, without having to leave the relative comfort of their carriages. Along with the rest of the small council, Macella stepped into the cold and was escorted to stand beside a platform King Khari had mounted. It looked as though it might've been built specifically for this occasion. A frisson of unease ran down Macella's spine.

(21) The king studied the kneeling crowd for a long moment, before passing her gaze over the carriages of noble guests, the Aegises standing beside their horses, and finally, her small council. Her eyes lingered on Macella the longest. Macella felt like she couldn't breathe until the king turned back to the crowd. Monarch Meztli discreetly drew closer to Macella, and her heart calmed a bit.

"You may all rise. I must say it warms the heart of your king to see you thriving," King Khari began, spreading her arms magnanimously. "I had no intention of making a grand speech, and yet I feel compelled to commend you on what you've built here. You have done much with what your king has given you. I pray you have learned the benefits of loyalty, hard work, and dedication to the Crown."

Someone cheered, and then the rest of the crowd began to applaud. Khari beamed, soaking up their veneration. Or, perhaps, sucking it up. Feeding on it. Like a leech.

Macella shivered at the morbid thought. What had gotten into her? The king was simply currying favor, and soon they'd be headed back to the keep for their own lunches. She and the Wildfire Court would joke about the day's absurdities and laugh at the king for being overdramatic.

"I also commend you on choosing a fine name for your community," King Khari continued, smiling widely. "I completely understand your being enamored with my future queen, Lady Macella. I certainly am."

The crowd absolutely roared. Macella inclined her head toward the people of Ellasburg, then bowed low to the king. It was overkill, but she would take any opportunity to publicly stroke Khari's ego.

"I am very blessed in my choice of bride. A loyal queen is a rare gift," King Khari went on once the cheers had quieted. "Sadly, your king has learned that personally. I would hate to speak ill of the dead, but I'm afraid the actions of my former spouse, the late Lady Awa, have consequences that have outlived her. As I look around at all you have built, I can't help but recall how close all of this came to being burned to the ground before it was even properly begun. All because of an unprecedented demon attack caused by a traitorous queen and her accomplices."

Gasps and murmurs ran through the crowd. Macella's heart plummeted. She'd known the king was up to something, and still she hadn't prepared herself for whatever this was. She met Aithan's eyes and the look of horror in them was so unsettling that Macella shrank from his mind. She didn't want to know what he might've glimpsed in the king's thoughts.

"It is quite shocking, but you, of all people, deserve to know the truth," King Khari said sorrowfully. "The demon attacks on Kōsaten Keep, Pleasure Ridge Park, and Ellasburg were retaliation for my former queen's over-reach. She hoped to use hellspawn to help her take my throne. And she was assisted by persons uniquely skilled with hell's minions. Were it not for the tireless work of our Grand Mage in uncovering their identities, these accomplices might have gone unpunished, able to continue their efforts to upset the natural order and destroy all we have built together. Your king will *never* let that happen."

Macella's lungs constricted, her vision narrowing to a pinprick. She thought she might actually faint. It would be a relief to escape what she now saw so clearly. Far too late, she'd realized the truth. This wasn't a celebration.

It was an execution.

"Her co-conspirators were Aegises!" King Khari spat angrily, pointing to where the Aegises stood, already stiffening, shifting subtly into fighting stances. Váli's ears lay flat against his head, his teeth bared. King Khari pounded a fist against her palm. "Aegises! The sworn protectors of our kingdom, bound to uphold our way of life and to keep hell at bay, instead colluded with Lady Awa to release those horrors onto the capital. One of them met their end at the hands of their own hubris, just as they deserved. However, their accomplices remain in my service. That ends here and now. Such cowardice will not be tolerated, nor will such treachery amongst my most trusted soldiers go unpunished any longer!"

The king's words boomed through the square, her rage palpable in the air. She gestured to Captain Drudo, and, at his signal, the Royal Guard moved to surround the Aegises. When King Khari spoke again, her voice was icy cold.

"The only mercy I will grant you is a quick death."

Macella's knees gave out. She would've fallen to the ground if Monarch Meztli hadn't quickly wrapped an arm around her waist. Finley and Jacan stood with the other Aegises, surrounded by knights with hands on their sword hilts. King Khari's next words could condemn any of them, all of them.

No. Please no.

Not Jacan.

Please, gods, not Finley.

Macella looked frantically to the Grand Mage. She might've caught a glimpse of panic on Kiama's face before the Grand Mage managed to smooth her expression into an acceptably solemn mask. What did she know? What had she told the king? Did they know which Aegises had truly conspired against the Crown? Did she know it had been Kai? And Diya?

And Finley.

"My late wife had three additional accomplices. *Three,*" King Khari hissed. "How did such treachery spread so far through the ranks of my most elite warriors? Nearly a third of them, conspiring against me and the good, decent people of my kingdom."

King Khari paused again, and this time she looked right at Macella. Macella met her gaze, but she had no idea what expression might be on her own face. Khari looked away first, turning to glare at the Aegises again.

"Please, Meztli," Macella whispered. "I don't want her to see me cry."

Monarch Meztli squeezed her gently. A calm haze settled over Macella, pulling her back from the brink of a breakdown. She managed to look at the Aegises again, finding Jacan and Finley where they stood beside Kai and Diya. Not good.

"Bring me Diya of Park Hill—"

Even with Meztli's influence, Macella's heart was racing in her chest.

"Kai of Clarksdale—"

Bile rose in Macella's throat. She was going to be sick right here in front of everyone. She was going to vomit her heart onto the snow.

"And—"

She wouldn't allow it. She shifted her weight, reaching for a dagger. With her other hand, she began to unbutton her cloak. The heavy fabric would only slow her down.

Macella, wait.

"Bellona of Glenview."

Her knees nearly gave out again. She felt a relief so intense it hurt, followed by a rush of guilt. She shouldn't be happy. Kai, Diya, and Bellona were going to die.

The three Aegises stepped forward of their own accord, staring down the knights as they did so. None of the Royal Guard seemed eager to attempt to apprehend them. Instead, half of the soldiers broke away from the circle around the Aegises to flank Kai, Diya, and Bellona. None of the accused Aegises looked back as they marched toward their end.

An anguished cry drew Macella's attention back to the other Aegises. Finley drooped between Valen and Jacan, who seemed to be both supporting and restraining them, while Váli circled the trio, whining anxiously. The look of grief on Finley's face tore a hole in Macella's chest.

Diya, Kai, and Finley spent decades confined to Duànzào together, leaving only to offer advanced training for the most promising recruits in Smoketown or to visit the capital for the cold season. Macella didn't know exactly how old they were, but she knew the three had lived together for well over half a century. She couldn't imagine all they'd shared, the bond they'd formed. Of course, Finley was devastated.

Macella had no doubt that King Khari had her suspicions regarding Finley's involvement but had most likely spared them as a subtle warning to her bride-to-be. The king was reminding Macella of the consequences of disloyalty. She was burning too brightly, and King Khari didn't stand in anyone else's shadow. Khari wanted Macella to remember how much she stood to lose, and just how easily it could be taken away.

Kai, Diya, and Bellona stopped before the platform. King Khari glowered down at them, appearing somehow larger and even more intimidating than usual. It filled Macella with a fierce pride to see that none of the Aegises showed a hint of fear. They stood tall, returning the king's gaze or looking right through her. Kai and Diya wore matching expressions of barely contained rage, while Bellona's beautiful face was a mask of perfect indifference.

"Bring the pillories," King Khari commanded, and servants hurried to obey. "You three are not worthy of an honorable death by the Chosen. You shall die as common criminals."

Macella's stomach turned. They were to be beheaded. Macella had only seen one Aegis execution, and it had been terrible, but the uncanny brightness of the Chosen had somewhat obscured its full horror from most onlookers. Now, however, King Khari was going to make these families watch her chop off the heads of three of the mighty warriors Kōsaten's people had grown to revere.

The servants returned and quickly arranged the pillories in a row on the platform where all could see. The traditional structure had been modified so that each was basically a simple stand with a groove carved out for a neck. Macella fought down another wave of nausea. The king had intentionally made and brought these devices along, had always planned on turning this lovely celebration into a disgusting display of power. When had she decided on it? Was it when Macella became the center of attention at the opening ball or when the workers named their home Ellasburg or at some other perceived slight? And what would be the next trigger to set her off? Who would she hurt then?

"Join me," King Khari commanded, smiling coldly at the three Aegises standing before the platform.

Aithan moved quickly to position himself in front of the king, with Sir Griselda and Captain Drudo at her sides. Diya, Kai, and Bellona mounted the steps with the same fearlessness they'd shown thus far. Even arranged behind the devices that would hold their heads for removal, the Aegises didn't flinch.

"Have you got anything to say before you depart this realm?" King Khari demanded carelessly.

Macella's fear and helplessness was becoming cold fury as she watched the king callously sacrifice people for power. The crowd was completely silent, awaiting the final words of the warriors. It was so quiet that Macella could hear the sniffles and low shushing of parents and children. She stepped forward, dropping to one knee before the platform.

"Your grace, may I please have a word?" She made her entreaty as sweet and gentle as she could, though she was burning with rage on the inside. "Please allow your betrothed one request."

Macella kept her head bowed, awaiting the king's response. She counted her breaths, trying to keep herself calm enough to do what little she could.

"Rise and request, my lady," King Khari said, once she'd let Macella kneel in the snow for several long moments.

Macella stood, clasping her hands before her and looking up at King Khari with her most submissive expression. "Please, my king, grant your softhearted bride this small wish. The children have been promised a grand party today, and we've kept them waiting in the cold for quite a while. Could not they go inside and have warm drinks while the adults conduct business?"

She could see that the king hadn't expected the request. Maybe she'd thought Macella was going to beg for mercy for the Aegises or ask to be excused herself. The thought made Macella even angrier. There was no way she would give the king the satisfaction of seeing her turn away from this.

"You have a mother's tender heart, my bride," King Khari replied. "It's another of your endearing qualities that makes me eager for our future together. You, there! Get the children inside and tell the staff to give them hot cider and cake while they wait."

Several servants hurried to herd the children into the meeting hall. Hopefully, the sweets would distract the poor little things from the horrors unfolding outside. It was the best Macella could do. She caught grateful expressions from many of the adults in the crowd but was careful not to acknowledge anyone. She'd drawn as much attention to herself as she dared at present.

(22) When the door closed behind the last child, King Khari clapped her hands once. "There now, shall we get on with it? Last words?"

"I have served my kingdom for four decades alongside some of the greatest warriors in Kōsaten's history." Bellona, usually a woman of very few words, was the first to speak. She didn't look at the king, instead keeping her gaze on the tense line of Aegises. "I die with honor, regardless."

King Khari's lips curled in a sneer. "Impudent beast. My patience grows thin. Have you others anything worthwhile to say?"

Diya squared her shoulders. She looked from the people of Ellasburg to her fellow Aegises to the nobles in their carriages. When she spoke, her voice was strong and sure. "We do not fear death, and ours will not be in vain. Though we perish, our deeds remain; our impact lives on. We three acted completely alone, but our truth will find its way to others who will carry on the work of freeing our kind from tyranny. Revolution cannot be killed. *It spreads.*"

Diya glanced toward Macella then back to the Aegises. "There has been plenty of speechifying today, but we cannot put our faith in words. It is not words that should earn our love and loyalty. It is deeds. Remember that."

Macella swallowed hard, struggling to keep her face passive. She caught Diya's meaning, the endorsement beneath her words. And she'd bet the other Aegises, most of Ellasburg, and some of the nobles understood as well. Even through the haze of anger and fear, Macella marveled at the magnitude of having earned Diya's faith. That woman had once been a child who'd told an Aegis that she was strong and then proven it by leaving her family behind and becoming an Aegis herself. Diya had seen the worst of the world, had suffered its greatest injustices from a very young age, and had tried to find a way to make it better, safer, fairer. She was about to die for those efforts but had used her last words to back Macella.

Macella would prove herself worthy of that loyalty. The fight would not die with Diya, Kai, and Bellona. It would spread.

Impulsively, Macella reached for Diya's mind, her thoughts on that brief memory they'd accidentally shared. She lingered on the image of Diya's sibling looking up at her with adoration and reverence. On the platform, Diya's lip twitched slightly, the only acknowledgment that she received the message.

Pooja would be so proud of you, Macella thought.

Diya exhaled, her gaze lifting to the sky.

Khari looked like she wanted to throttle Diya with her bare hands. "Wise words from a traitor. You, boy? Say your piece."

"Just fucking get on with it," Kai replied, tossing his bangs out of his eyes, and bending to put his head on the pillory, scowling the whole while.

If Macella hadn't been so overwhelmed with emotion she might've laughed. It was such a very Kai thing to do. She was going to miss him. She was going to miss them all.

But she would avenge them.

We will avenge them. Macella pushed the thought toward Finley, who had regained their composure enough to stand without support. Their beautiful face was pale and hard. Macella's heart ripped further at the expression of hopelessness behind their orange eyes. *We will make her pay.*

Finley didn't look her way, but she thought she saw them exhale heavily. She turned her attention back to the platform. All three Aegises were secured in the pillories, and someone had placed baskets below them. Macella swallowed down more bile.

King Khari grinned humorlessly. "I agree. Let's fucking get on with it then. Lord Protector, relieve them of their traitorous heads."

Macella's attention snapped to Aithan, who looked grim and resigned. Is this what he'd seen in the king's thoughts? Macella thought she really might vomit this time. Khari could've had any of her Royal Guard deliver the killing blows or done it herself, as a proper king would. Forcing it upon Aithan was just another calculated cruelty.

Aithan drew his sword. The world went suddenly blurry. Macella realized she was crying.

"Don't watch," Monarch Meztli murmured.

"I must," Macella answered.

And so, she watched through her tears as her husband beheaded his siblings. She watched the moment of their deaths, when their eyes slipped into their hell-form for the last time: pupils changed and expanded, whites vanished. Bellona and Diya's glowed cerulean, while Kai's were the same intense emerald Jacan or Finley's would've been. Macella fought back the sob clawing its way up her throat.

She would remember three things about that moment for the rest of her life: the *thunk* of their heads tumbling into those baskets, the horrible pain that racked her body at the moment of their deaths, and the bright crimson of their blood seeping into the freshly fallen snow.

Part 2

Against Our End

...From the very first moment until this one, you have never stopped surprising me. Every day has been a new miracle. You have utterly enchanted me in every possible way. You have become more than my partner, friend, and wife. You are my anchor, my compass, my breath, and my heartbeat. I am completely, unapologetically, hopelessly yours.

My love, my light, my life. If the day comes that I am no longer at your side, know this: I am happy, healthy, and whole because of you. However long our time together is, know that it has been perfect. You have been perfect. I have held my paradise and can face whatever follows without fear. I have lived and I have loved. I am satisfied.

Do not mourn me long, my beloved. Just live. Live fully and freely and, when you are done, I will be waiting for you in the next realm.

Our Fates are intertwined, Macella of Shively. I was meant to wander into that brothel and to bring you on my journey. I was meant to stand at your side, to learn from and with you. I am yours, as I always have been and always will be.

I love you.

Aithan of Auburndale

Chapter Fifteen

Macella

"A ball of yarn?" Macella guessed half-heartedly, glaring at the shiny red apple in her husband's hand.

Aithan sighed and turned to the others. "Can any of you see through the spell?"

"Not even a little bit," Zahra replied cheerfully.

Charlotte and Jacan shook their heads in agreement.

Finley shrugged, flopping back on the chaise. "I don't know why we keep doing this. You're the only one who can resist her."

The Wildfire Court had assembled for a strategy session, something they did almost every night. It had become a routine. The execution of Kai, Diya, and Bellona had intensified the sense of urgency they'd all been feeling since the start of the cold season. No one had expected Khari to use the Aegises as scapegoats to explain the rise in rifts. The move had reminded them what a formidable adversary she would be.

So, they gathered nightly to make impossible plans and share bits of information that didn't yet fit into a cohesive picture. Charlotte and Aisling were still finding out what they could about the Blessed Rite, while Aithan and

Finley focused more on how to defeat the king in battle. Jacan and Zahra helped with both tasks whenever they could, while also doing what Charlotte called "diplomatic missions." Zahra continued to curry favor for Macella among the nobility, while Jacan did the same among the Aegises.

According to Jacan, his job was easy. The other Aegises had already begun to respect and even like Macella. After Diya's last words, anyone who'd been unsure seemed to trust the soon-to-be queen more. Thus, Jacan instead used most of his free time to linger wherever people of interest gathered.

"You'd be surprised by what people will say around a deaf person," Jacan had told Macella. "I just sit there pretending to tune my lute or polish my sword, and the nobles speak as if I am not there. They don't even notice me watching their lips."

Tonight, the Wildfire Court was trying in vain to see through one of Aisling's transfiguration spells. The novice mage was getting quite good at it. They'd all agreed that it was worthwhile to train against Khari's gift, but soon everyone else was as frustrated as Macella. No matter what type of test Aithan and Aisling concocted, they all failed.

"This is hopeless," Finley complained, draping an arm over their face dejectedly. Váli huffed out a heavy breath from his spot on the floor near their feet. Valen was on patrol and Finley had kindly volunteered Macella as wolf-sitter. He laid his head on his massive paws and huffed again. "See? Even the beast agrees."

Macella and Zahra exchanged a worried glance. Finley had been listless in the wake of Diya and Kai's deaths. They were grieving, of course, but it made Macella's heart ache to see their light so dulled. She'd grown accustomed to their boisterous stories and carefree laughter and she hated King Khari for taking that away.

"It is not *hopeless*," Macella insisted, even though she'd been thinking the same thing only moments ago. "We just have to try a different approach. We're not all half mage like my vaunt of a husband. We have to use what skills we have."

Nyx padded across the room, stood on her back paws, and stretched up Aithan's leg. Flames glimmered in the sleek black fur around the cat's throat. Lynn had made her a soft collar embroidered with fiery roses that appeared to be cut from Macella's wildfire ball gown. According to Aisling, since the high tailor had gifted her the collar, Nyx preferred to remove it at night but refused to leave their room each morning until the mage fastened it back on.

Váli lifted his head with interest. The white wolf had decided that he and Nyx were best friends, but the cat had yet to accept that reality. Váli watched raptly as Aithan lowered the apple for Nyx to inspect. She sniffed at it briefly, before trotting away and hopping onto the chaise with Finley.

"Don't you dare tell them, young miss!" Aisling warned the cat. "They have to figure it out for themself!"

"Just whisper it in my ear when she's not looking," Finley told Nyx in a low voice. "It'll be our secret."

Everyone laughed and the mood in the room lifted a bit. Váli woofed happily and scooted closer to where Nyx lay on the chaise, then laid his big head on the cushion just outside of swiping distance. The cat let out a warning growl, then curled against Finley's side, closing her eyes when they lazily stroked her little head. Macella smiled. Nyx always knew who needed her most.

"Ella, you're the only one here who has ever been fully immersed in one of the king's visions," Charlotte said, shuddering at the memory of Macella's harrowing tale of the jorōgumo in the woods. "Were there any weaknesses in it? Anything that gave it a sense of deception?"

Macella started to shake her head when Finley suddenly sat bolt upright, startling the cat who'd been falling asleep beside them. "That's it, Lotta! Well done! Nyx tried to show us how to use our other senses. Macella, when you told us about that horrid vision, you described the things you saw and felt and heard, but did you smell anything?"

Macella thought about it. She couldn't recall any scents. Even during Lord Kasper's faux whipping, she'd consciously noted that she could *almost* smell the tang of blood. The vision had just been so realistic that her brain had tried to fill in the gaps.

Macella grinned. She took the object out of Aithan's hand and sniffed it. "It's a candle."

"You win, Lady Macella!" Aisling exclaimed. "This is good news!"

Finley abruptly deflated again. "What good does it do us? We can't smell our way out of her visions."

"Probably not us humans, but you lot can smell things we can't, and from a greater distance," Zahra corrected. "When everything goes to hell, you can use your noses to discern what is real and what is an illusion. It might not break the vision, but it still gives us an edge. The king won't know that we know it's not real, and we can use that to our advantage."

Finley grinned despite themself. "That almost made sense, Teacup. Excellent work everyone. Can we move on to something less boring?"

Macella rolled her eyes, unconsciously touching the star charm at her throat. It was so cold all the time now that it no longer provided much of a warning. Danger was always imminent. At least now they could smell it coming. Or, more accurately, *not* smell it coming.

"That is a useful advantage. What else have we learned?" she asked the room in general.

"Well, we've finally learned some details of the Blessed Rite," Charlotte began hesitantly. She glanced at Macella then quickly looked away, turning a beseeching gaze toward Aisling.

"It won't be like the Aegis trials," Aisling began, though she didn't sound as relieved as she should by the prospect. "It's Khari's choice to share her power with her spouses, so you don't have to prove your worthiness. You just have to receive the gift."

"Okay," Macella replied slowly, waiting for the bad news. "What do I have to do?"

Charlotte and Aisling exchanged a nervous glance before the novice mage continued. "Nothing, really. The Chosen will act on behalf of the gods of light and bestow their blessing. It's a ceremony where you pledge your allegiance to the Crown, not unlike the one the Aegises undergo."

When Aisling paused uncertainly, Macella felt her patience snap. "Enough, you two! Just say it and stop trying to spare my feelings! I already know I may not survive!"

Charlotte's eyes filled with tears and Macella instantly regretted the outburst. Váli trotted over to the sofa, sat on his haunches, and lowered his big head into her sister's lap. Charlotte patted him gratefully, and Macella felt even worse. She knew that everyone was trying to be optimistic, but they were all feeling the strain of what lay ahead. Each day that passed reminded them how little time they had left.

"The magic is meant for humans," Aisling said, placing a gentle hand on Charlotte's shoulder. "With your Aegis blood and Hades's blessing already upon you, the magic might not take, and your secret will be evident. More likely, though, is that when the Chosen touch you with their light, it will destroy you. The light and darkness cannot exist within one soul."

A flash of memory. Shamira, shivering before the Chosen. Their inhuman hands reaching toward her. Blinding, freezing white light.

Shamira was on her knees, her head lifted, and her eyes glowing cerulean. A network of veins surfaced on her skin, crisscrossing her face and neck with jagged blue lines. She began to cough and gag, her body contorting painfully as she choked. Her back arched so sharply that Macella heard the crack of her spine...Shamira spat an inky black goo that dripped down her chin before taking on a smoky form and disappearing into the light of the Chosen's hands.

Soon, the same liquid smoke began to drip from Shamira's eyes, tracing black tears down her cheeks. It seeped from her ears and her nose as her veins blackened. The cerulean glow faded from her eyes, leaving them entirely blank—no iris, no pupil, only white nothingness.

The Chosen had sucked Kali's dark gifts out of Shamira, leaving nothing behind. Her death had been horrifying and most likely painful. Is that what was in store for Macella?

"So, we find a way to kill the king before the rite," Aithan asserted.

"Yes!" Finley nodded in enthusiastic agreement.

"Maybe," Charlotte answered dubiously, still sniffling a bit. Jacan wrapped an arm around her shoulders, and she leaned into him. "But the rite is also our best opportunity of defeating her. King Khari will be at her weakest as the

Chosen redistribute her power. If we strike at the right moment, we could end things quickly and with minimal bloodshed."

Macella sighed, the weight on her shoulders feeling heavier than ever. "So, I must attempt the rite to enable our best chance of victory."

"No." Aithan's voice was flat and unyielding.

Macella lifted a brow at him. "Have you got a better plan?"

"Yes," he shot back, his eyes flashing crimson with anger. "Anything that doesn't get you killed."

Before Macella could retort, Zahra interrupted. "We don't have to make any decisions today. We have some useful information, now we keep searching. We'll find another way."

The rest of the Wildfire Court murmured their agreement, and they spent a few more minutes talking about this and that before going their separate ways. Macella listened but didn't offer any further comments. She knew what she had to do.

Macella found the Grand Mage in the castle's massive conservatory. It was a maze of greenery, magically temperature-controlled and featuring plants of all kinds, from all over the kingdom. Each section of the greenhouse was tailored to mimic the unique conditions the flora needed to thrive, and servants and novices alike tended to them, ensuring that the castle's inhabitants had access to any food, medicine, or magical ingredient that could be grown in Kōsaten.

It was an extremely popular location during the cold season. The Crown's guests couldn't spend all their time cavorting and playing power games. So, when they felt the urge to promenade, they came to stroll the conservatory's paths and enjoy the warmth while gazing out at the frozen world beyond the glass enclosure.

The workers in the conservatory greeted Macella cheerfully and were happy to direct her to the Grand Mage. It was clear Macella's popularity was continuing to spread amongst the castle's employees. The knowledge encouraged and weighed on her in equal measure. She was glad that Kōsaten's people recognized her efforts to improve their lives, but she also felt increasingly responsible for their well-being. Of course, she'd known that it was her duty to defeat the king and restore the balance as Fate had decided. But it was another thing entirely to have so many people actively counting on her. The way they looked at her, those tiny flames that seemed to be appearing more and more if you knew where to look, the name of the settlement—it all meant these people believed in her cause, even if they didn't know the extent of it. She couldn't let them down.

(23) "I wondered when I might see you," the Grand Mage said without turning around. "I had a feeling you would turn up today."

Kiama was kneeling in a quiet corner behind a row of fruit trees, tending to some magical plants. How she'd recognized Macella without even turning around was a mystery and a warning. The Grand Mage was an extremely powerful woman. Macella needed to tread carefully.

"I had no idea you desired my company, or I would've visited sooner," she replied pleasantly. "Is this a bad time? I'd be happy to host you for lunch or tea in my chambers at your convenience."

Kiama straightened and turned her gray mage eyes on Macella, giving her a long, searching look that made her anxious. The air around them crackled with energy. Finally, the Grand Mage gestured to an extra pair of gloves and shears.

"This is a fine time for a visit, if you don't mind helping me prune this mugwort," Kiama said, still studying Macella carefully. "Excuse my impertinence if this is not a task you deem appropriate for Kōsaten's future queen."

Macella smiled despite her anxiety. It would be nice to do something as simple and therapeutic as gardening. She took the shears and knelt, pushing her hands into the sandy soil. She immediately felt more grounded.

The two of them worked in silence for a few minutes, focused on the plants. The Grand Mage already had a basket half full of the severed leaves, which she would undoubtedly use for some magical purpose or another—Macella wasn't sure what. As much as she'd learned about the world, she still knew so little about magic. Its practitioners guarded their secrets well.

"You are unlike any ruler I have ever met," Grand Mage Kiama remarked after a while. It wasn't an insult or a compliment. She just sounded interested.

"Probably because I am not yet a ruler," Macella replied with a shrug. "I imagine others were like me before the burdens of the crown took their toll."

The Grand Mage gave her a sidelong glance. "I highly doubt that. As a matter of fact, I am sure there have only ever been a very few people like you."

Macella's heart stuttered in her chest. The tone of the other woman's voice implied the words held a double meaning. Macella was suddenly reconsidering her decision to seek the Grand Mage out.

"You are weighing the risk of asking me what you came here to ask me, but you already know that you must, Lady Macella," Kiama stated matter-of-factly. "You need my help."

Macella's body tensed, preparing for battle or escape, she wasn't sure which. She forced her muscles to relax and steadied her breathing. She needed to think carefully about her next move.

"I am not sure I know what you mean," she stalled.

Grand Mage Kiama turned her silvery gaze on Macella once more, full lips curling into a knowing smirk. "Let us speak frankly, my lady. I warded this grove against prying ears as you approached. Anyone who wanders too close will have a sudden and overwhelming urge to visit the privy."

Macella looked around as if she could see the engulfment spell in the air. She couldn't, of course. Aithan would've sensed it, would've known for sure if the mage was telling the truth. Macella, however, would have to take her word for it. It did appear that they were quite alone in their little corner of the garden. She'd come here to get answers and there was no sense in backing out now.

"I am apprehensive about the Blessed Rite," Macella began hesitatingly. "Can you tell me more about what it entails?" She kept her eyes on the plants as she spoke, though she could still feel Kiama watching her.

There was a hint of amusement in the Grand Mage's voice when she replied. "It is quite simple, really. Not terribly unlike the ceremony you witnessed when

Jacan of Prestonia pledged himself to the Crown. We pray to the gods of light, I supply the necessary potions and speak the incantations, and the Chosen do the rest," Kiama explained. In her periphery, Macella could see the other woman turn her attention back to the mugwort. "They disseminate the Sovereign's power between you and your three spouses. There is a lot of light, a bit of cold, perhaps some nausea, and then you are queen. It won't hurt—not a human, anyway."

Macella froze, an icy finger tracing along her spine. Though the Grand Mage's voice was light, her words hit like stones. Macella once again weighed her own words, unsure if she should proceed.

"I imagine it would be fine for a mage as well," Kiama went on as though she hadn't noticed Macella's discomfort. "Though an Aegis would most likely be killed instantly. The war between light and darkness would tear their soul apart. Now, an Aegis-mage crossbreed like your Aithan would present an interesting conundrum. I will have to think on that more. As for you? Well, I guess that depends."

Macella swallowed hard, finally turning her gaze back to the Grand Mage. "Depends on what?"

Kiama cocked her head, lifting an eyebrow. "On whether I am wrong about you. If I am, you will be just fine. It will be interesting to see which of your many talents the gods will decide to enhance with their gifts."

Macella couldn't bother to speculate about something she might not live to see. She had to make a choice. It was now or never. The Grand Mage had given her an opportunity to steer the conversation in a new direction, or to stay on this more dangerous path. Macella took a calming breath. It was time to get what she'd come for. There was war on the horizon; the first skirmishes were already being fought. If she was willing to forfeit her life for victory, she couldn't shy away from every danger along the way.

"And if you are right about me?" Macella asked, lifting her chin and returning the Grand Mage's stare. "As we both know you are."

Kiama smiled, and Macella was struck by how beautiful the Grand Mage was. With her lustrous dark brown skin, enigmatic eyes, and the regal way she carried her full figure, she was truly a wonder to behold. She radiated raw power but, unlike King Khari, hers was subtle and refined.

But could she be trusted?

Kiama pursed her lips and shrugged. "I cannot be sure how the rite will affect you, since there have been so few Aegis-human crossbreeds, and none in known history have ever ascended the blessed throne. The human in you could perhaps withstand it, but it is possible you'd be stripped of your dark god's blessing in the process. More likely, you would die in the attempt."

Macella's heart sank. She was surprised by how much stronger she felt about the prospect of losing Hades's blessing than she did about dying. She'd felt like her full self for the first time when she crossed into Duànzào. Of course, she'd always be a crossbreed—they couldn't take away her Aegis blood—but she had earned that blessing, had fought for it like her father before her. It was a part of herself that she wasn't willing to give up.

"Is there anything you can do to keep that from happening?" Macella probed. "Some way to keep me both alive and fully intact?"

The Grand Mage regarded her for a long moment before responding, and when she did, her reply was completely unexpected. "Do you want to be queen, Lady Macella?"

"No."

Macella didn't even have to think about her answer. She'd already begun to formulate a strategy for renouncing the throne once the kingdom was safe. Meztli and Annika could rule, or someone else entirely, and Macella could be free of the burden of the crown.

"All this effort for a crown you do not want," the Grand Mage mused. "You've garnered quite the following and certainly demonstrated a gift for strategy with Ellasburg. You could easily be a token bride, like Queen Annika, or maintain the peace, like Monarch Meztli, but you're actively leading initiatives and collecting allies. For what purpose, I wonder, if you do not care about the crown?"

"I care about the people!" Macella exclaimed with a frustrated huff. "I care about the kingdom. I care about my family. Are you going to help me or not?"

"Of course," Kiama responded, as if it was the most obvious thing in the world. "You've confirmed everything I already knew. The people need you on the throne. I am going to make sure you live to take it. Just as I have been doing all I can to protect you since you arrived, I will do everything in my power to help you survive the rite."

Macella's mouth popped open. This was the most she'd ever spoken to the Grand Mage. The woman's intentions and desires had always been a complete mystery, and still were, despite this unexpected alliance.

"And you are not going to tell the king that I'm a crossbreed?" Macella demanded. "Why would you risk keeping such a secret from her?"

"Who do you think put the silencing spell on Lord Kasper?" Kiama answered, surprising Macella again with the seeming shift of subject. "Again, the Grand Treasurer only confirmed what I already knew. I've suspected your true nature since I first learned of Aithan of Auburndale's parentage. I always sensed a uniqueness about him, and you have a similar aura. I have had every opportunity to share my suspicions with King Khari over the last year and yet, I have not."

Macella pressed her lips together, trying to find a flaw in the Grand Mage's rationale. Her reasoning seemed solid. Even if it wasn't, what good would it do for Macella to turn back now? She'd confessed her secret already, so the biggest risk was taken.

And she needed the Grand Mage's help.

"I delayed the king for as long as I dared when she asked me to help her breed her own army," Kiama went on matter-of-factly. "You helped by destroying my samples—I'm still not sure how you managed that, by the way—but I understood the magic as soon as the king asked. I protected Awa, Kiho, and their accomplices for as long as I could. I helped your husband recover his memories, in case there was something in them that might aid your cause, not because I needed the information. I am perhaps the most powerful mage in Kōsaten's history, and I am offering you my allegiance and my assistance. You are going to have to trust me."

"Why?" Macella blurted, giving up on politeness. "It cannot just be that you believe I will be a good queen. Why are you so willing to risk your safety to aid me?"

The Grand Mage looked at her with fathomless sadness in her pale eyes. "I have done many things I am not proud of. We all do what we must to survive, but my choices have hurt others. There is blood on my hands. You are my opportunity to make amends. And I do truly believe in your potential to lead Kōsaten out of darkness."

Macella stared into Kiama's solemn face, searching for the truth. The Grand Mage gazed back silently, waiting. Finally, Macella exhaled a heavy breath and nodded. She would have to have faith in Fate and her own intuition.

"Thank you," she said finally.

Kiama smirked again. "Don't thank me just yet. I do not know for sure how to keep you alive, but I am certain I can figure it out. And in the process, I might learn how to save our young queen. Thank you, by the way, for being the mysterious friend supplying crossbreed blood."

Macella snorted a laugh, and the Grand Mage joined in. The tension in the air eased a bit.

Macella turned back to the mugwort. "Well, let's get to work, shall we?" she declared.

The two women worked for nearly an hour, talking the whole while. When Macella left the conservatory, she felt considerably better—hopeful even.

There was still a chance she could save everyone, including herself.

CHAPTER SIXTEEN

Aithan

Aithan took his midday meal alone—a rare luxury these days. The king had taken a new lover among the aristocracy and had dismissed him so that she could spend the afternoon enjoying her paramour's company. He could've gone to the Aegis dining hall or sought out the Wildfire Court for company, but his mood was much more suited for solitude.

Aithan sat in their parlor, brooding over his meal. He'd been brooding almost continuously since his family discussed Macella's potential death the previous night. The very idea infuriated and terrified him beyond his capacity to process. He was on edge, his instincts preparing in vain to protect his wife from forces he could never defeat.

Aithan poured himself a mug of ale. He drained it, refilled it, and sat down, only to get back up to pace the floor. His anger was a tangible thing, smothering him, filling him with restless energy without any appealing outlet. He didn't feel like training—he wouldn't be satisfied with plunging his sword into anything other than flesh, which was obviously not an option—and sparring would only put someone in grave danger. Aithan had honed his self-control over more than a half-century of service, and Macella had effortlessly and completely unraveled it.

So, I must attempt the rite to enable our best chance of victory, she'd said, as if she'd been discussing the weather. The acceptance in her voice had confirmed that she'd probably been considering her death an inevitability for some time. She was resigned to it, determined to sacrifice herself if that's what it took. How hadn't he noticed sooner?

Aithan clenched his fists. He was livid. He had the good sense to know that what he really felt was fear and helplessness, but he wasn't listening to his rational mind at the moment.

Thus, when Macella returned from her ill-advised visit to the Grand Mage, his anger was primed to boil over. She hadn't tried to hide her thoughts from him, but she hadn't discussed her plans with him either. There was an unusual silence between them, the air heavy with tension.

"Using your afternoon off to brood, I see," Macella said dryly when she entered the parlor. She'd donned leggings and a tunic and freed her curls, looking more like herself than the warrior queen or the northern rose for a change. She gave him a tired look, which somehow made him angrier. "You know it had to be done."

"We do not know if she can be trusted," Aithan replied stubbornly. He knew he was being unreasonable, but he couldn't stop himself. He couldn't think clearly when his wife insisted on putting herself in danger.

"We do not know if anyone can be trusted!" Macella retorted, throwing her hands up in exasperation. "Time is short, Aithan. Risks must be taken. The Grand Mage is the only person in the kingdom who could help me survive the Blessed Rite. Is that not what you want?"

Aithan ran his hands through his hair, trying to rein in his frustration. Of course, he would do anything that would help her survive that fucking ritual. Except she wasn't going to have to go through the ritual. It was too risky, no matter what the Grand Mage might say. He wouldn't allow it.

"I want you safe, Macella," Aithan said slowly, keeping his voice as even as he could manage. "I don't want you attempting the rite at all."

Macella glared at him, her black eyes full of fire. Here was his hell goddess, ready to burn down an empire to save the world, even if it meant burning herself to ash in the process. Just this once, he wanted her to put herself first.

"The king will be at her weakest during the rite. It's our best opportunity to take her down," Macella insisted, a challenge in her tone. "I will take that risk if it means saving the kingdom."

"Fuck the kingdom!" Aithan snapped, his voice coming out a bit louder than he intended. Macella flinched and he instantly regretted the outburst. He managed to keep his voice level when he spoke again. "I won't let you sacrifice yourself."

Macella lifted her chin, that familiar glint of defiance in her eyes. "I will do what I must. You will not stand in my way."

Anger and sorrow and guilt and a million other emotions ripped through Aithan's chest. How could the things he loved most about her also be the things that made her so willing to walk into the belly of the beast without hesitation? She was so maddeningly brave and fierce and unerringly altruistic.

He had promised to never stand in the way of her Fate, but the thought of losing her was too much for him to bear. His brain couldn't even fathom a life without her. She would take every true and perfect thing with her into the Otherworlds, and he would be left a husk. How would he survive without his heart? How would he breathe without his air?

"Macella..." he began, but it came out as a plea. Her name was a prayer, a supplication. She was his hell goddess, and he was begging for her mercy. He would prostrate himself before her if he had to.

Her face softened. "Love, we have been fighting for our lives for quite a while now. This time, everyone else's lives are on the line as well."

"I don't give a fuck about everyone else," Aithan growled. "I only care about you."

Macella shook her head. "You know that's not true."

"It's true enough."

Macella huffed out a breath, rubbing her temples. Aithan ran his hands through his hair again. They stared at each other, neither speaking, at an impasse.

Finally, Macella's shoulders sagged. "I don't want to die. I am terrified of what's to come. Every day, I am afraid I'll make some misstep, commit some tiny faux pas that causes ripples until there's another execution or forced battle to the death or a thousand other horrors. I don't want to lose you or Lotta or any of the Wildfire Court. I don't want to lose me."

Macella stepped closer, reaching out to lay a tentative hand on his forearm. Aithan shuddered at her touch. His anger shifted into something more difficult to name—something that hurt more.

"I am terrified," she said again, forcing him to hold her gaze. "I do not know if I can do this, but I know one thing for sure: I cannot do it without you."

Aithan's heart broke a little, as did his voice when he spoke. "You won't have to. You'll never have to."

Then he was pulling her into his arms and breathing in her scent of citrus and cinnamon and fire. Macella responded immediately, catching his mouth in a desperate kiss. Her face was wet, or perhaps it was his, the salty taste of tears trickling into their mouths. Aithan pulled her tighter against him, running his hands over her hair, her neck, her back. He needed to touch her, to feel every part of her and remind himself that she was alive and here and his.

(24) Matching his energy, Macella molded her body to his. She wrapped her arms around his neck and buried her fingers in his hair. Aithan groaned against her mouth, his cock already hardening. It was always like this with her; the craving never went away. One look or touch or thought from her and he was rabid with need.

He walked them backward until Macella's back hit a wall, then pulled her shirt off over her head, and raked his eyes over her perfect breasts. Her peaked nipples made his mouth water. He lowered his head to suck one into his mouth, cupping her other breast and brushing his thumb over the stiff bud.

Macella moaned, her hands tugging at his hair making him growl. "Clothes off. Now."

The way she panted the command, voice raw with desire, nearly undid him.

Between their combined efforts, they were soon completely naked. Aithan reveled in the feel of her skin against his. He kissed and licked her neck, relishing the taste of her. Everything about her was right—her smell, her taste, the sounds she made when he ran his tongue along her collarbone.

She was alive. She was here. She was his.

"Aithan, please," she begged, arching her back and pressing her breasts against his chest.

The last of his patience snapped with that needy little whimper. He scooped her up easily and laid her on the dining table, sweeping the place settings out of his way. He barely registered the crash of ceramic and glass. Nothing mattered at that moment but Macella. *His* Macella. His hell goddess. His wife.

He bent and buried his face between her thighs, earning a surprised yelp. The taste of her made his cock impossibly harder. He shoved his tongue into her pussy, gathering more of her exquisite taste and another of those desperate whimpers.

He could feast on his wife for hours. But not right now. Right now, he needed to be buried deep in the only place that felt like home.

Aithan licked his way up her torso, lingering on her stiff nipples as he notched himself at her entrance. Then he thrusted into her, finding her soaking wet and impossibly tight. Her warm heat engulfed him, squeezing his cock greedily, threatening to unravel him when they'd only barely begun.

"Gods, Macella. Do you have any idea how fucking perfect you are?" He hissed through clenched teeth as he pulled almost all the way out of her, only to slam back in. "Do you know how perfect you feel?"

Macella cried out, gripping his forearms and rocking her hips to meet his thrusts. He lost himself then, driving into her again and again, wanting to be as deep inside of her as humanly possible. He watched the way her full breasts bounced in time with his strokes and how her face contorted with pleasure—lips parted, brow furrowed, and burning onyx eyes fixed on his.

"Oh, gods, Aithan! *Fuck!*" she cried, her nails digging into his forearms as her back bowed off the table. "Oh, *gods!*"

Aithan hooked his elbows beneath her knees, lifting her hips off the table and plunging deeper, pulling her toward him with each long, hard thrust. Macella cried out, his name a song on her lips. He moaned, a telltale tingling starting at the base of his spine. Luckily, Macella had already reached her climax. He could coax out another, get her pussy to clench around him while he filled her with cum.

"Aithan, fuck!" Macella cried, trembling beneath him.

She was close and so was he. He shifted so that he could reach between them and find her clit with his thumb. Gathering her wetness, he swirled the pad of his thumb over the swollen bud, applying just a bit of pressure.

Macella's pussy constricted and that was it. His moans joined her chorus of pants and expletives as he came. She milked him for every drop, her perfect pussy squeezing him like a vice.

When he could move again, he propped himself up on elbows to stare down into her face. Her eyes were hooded, but bright, that tired look gone for now. Gently, he brushed her curls out of her face.

"It's going to be okay," she whispered. "You'll protect me, and I'll protect you. And when this is all over, we're going to explore the many parts of the kingdom I've yet to see."

Aithan's chest ached. He wanted that for her, for them. If the gods were just and Fate true, they'd get to live that dream.

If not, he would tear hell and earth to shreds to get her back.

⚬

Macella

It was odd seeing the Grand Mage at the next small council meeting, knowing that she knew Macella's deepest secrets. For her part, Kiama seemed the same as always, showing no sign that anything had changed between them. Still, the small council chamber was tense. It'd been that way since the Aegises' execution.

The king had tasked the council with solving the issue of the rifts, then had very publicly presented her own conclusion. Thus, the members of the council had only two choices: agree with the king's assertion or risk taking her wrath and blame themselves.

King Khari seemed to enjoy the tension, as usual. "Isn't it nice that we can focus on the joys of the season rather than worrying about demon attacks? What would we do without our Grand Mage?"

Kiama's face remained placid, but Macella thought she could sense discomfort in the mage's posture. Macella hadn't had an opportunity to learn exactly what information Kiama had provided the king and when. It was just as likely that Kai and Diya had been implicated as long ago as Kiho and Queen Awa, and Khari had saved the information until it could be of most use to her.

And as for Bellona...well, she was just an unfortunate casualty of the king's power games. Either Khari had no real idea who the other conspirator was, or she was using the fact of Finley's involvement to keep Macella in line.

The catlike smile on King Khari's face every time she looked at her bride-to-be suggested the latter.

"We all admire Grand Mage Kiama. The king is wise in her council selection." Lord Anwir was the first person to manage a response. "I encourage each of you to keep me abreast of such developments, so that I can best advise her grace, the king. It is imperative that we work as a team during these challenging times."

Macella resisted the urge to roll her eyes. Three warriors had been senselessly executed for the king's own crimes, and the Grand Vizier was more worried about being left out of the king's confidence than about the callous loss of life.

Anger burned beneath Macella's skin. This small council was a farce. This entire monarchy was a farce. Nobody at this table represented the people or even cared about them. They were all here to advance their own interests.

Perhaps it wasn't only King Khari who needed to be replaced. The system was broken. The Crown needed to create something new—something that actually served the people of Kōsaten.

"Yes, do keep the Grand Vizier and I informed of any relevant information," King Khari rejoined, her ochre eyes dancing with amusement. "We believe we've punished the culprits, but we must be diligent in maintaining the balance so as not to invoke further wrath from the gods. If you have the slightest suspicion of any treachery, I want to hear of it immediately. We cannot be too careful. Treason has a tendency to spread."

There was no mistaking the implied threat beneath King Khari's words, but Macella wasn't sure how pointed the threat might be. Had she chosen her phrasing to intentionally allude to the Wildfire Court, or was Macella reading too much into her word choice?

Either way, Macella was relieved the small council meeting adjourned soon after. She lingered after the others had departed, reviewing (and irritably editing) a financial report the Grand Treasurer had prepared about her initiative. It was riddled with a litany of silly errors that could only be intentional.

After a while, Macella shivered. The fire had gone out and she was late for lunch. She should take the offensive paperwork back to her study to pore over later, but she was perversely determined to find every mistake right away so that she could be as annoyed as possible. She was mumbling a string of colorful curses under her breath, when a soft voice interrupted.

"Ella?"

The worry in that voice pulled Macella from her thoughts. She tried to smile reassuringly at her sister, who hovered in the doorway looking uncharacteristically pensive. Macella hoped Lotta hadn't heard her little tirade. Finley had already taught the young woman enough new curse words.

"Were you waiting on me for lunch, Lotta?" Macella stood and began to gather her things. "I'm sorry for keeping you. I'm ready now."

Charlotte stepped farther into the room, wringing her hands and looking over her shoulder nervously. "It's not that. I—I need to talk to you about something."

Macella frowned, watching her sister frantically scan the room to ensure they were alone before easing the door shut. Something was obviously bothering her. Even after she'd closed the door, she didn't move any closer, and seemed unable to look at Macella, focusing instead on her own feet.

"What is it, cher?" Macella asked gently, taking a careful step forward. "Should we talk about it in my chambers?"

Charlotte's head snapped up, her eyes wide and frightened behind her glasses. "No! The others are there, and I wanted to tell you first. Alone."

Macella lifted an eyebrow. Now she was really concerned. What could Charlotte have to say that she wouldn't want the rest of the Wildfire Court to hear?

"I'm listening. Whatever it is, we can figure it out," Macella promised. "Sit down and tell me what's going on."

Hesitantly, Charlotte took the seat across from Macella. She clasped her hands on the table, keeping her gaze fixed on them as she spoke. "King Khari requested a private audience with me right after the small council meeting."

Icy dread slid down Macella's spine, followed by white hot rage. "Did she threaten you? Are you hurt?"

"No!" Charlotte blurted quickly. "Nothing like that. She just asked me some questions. But, Ella, she's so frightening. I don't know what happened. I couldn't help but tell her the truth."

The flames of Macella's anger were quickly extinguished by another flood of cold dread. "The truth about what, Lotta?"

Charlotte covered her face with both hands, her muffled voice full of tears. "Everything."

Her little sister began to cry, and Macella rounded the table to comfort her as best she could. Her mind raced, wondering what the king could've possibly asked about. What could Charlotte mean by *everything*? Finley's involvement with Kiho? Macella's true nature?

"I'm so sorry," Charlotte sobbed. "What are we going to do now?"

Macella rested a hand on her sister's trembling shoulder. Charlotte didn't look up at her, but she calmed a little under the touch. "First, you're going to take a deep breath, and then you're going to tell me exactly what happened."

Lotta did as she was told, sniffling and taking a few deep breaths before speaking again. "It was all so fast. She told me she knew what we were hiding from her and that if I would just talk to her about it, we could find a way forward. So, I thought I should tell her something—just enough to appease her paranoia."

Macella frowned. Charlotte was speaking in riddles, which was very un-Charlotte behavior. Her sister was a natural teacher and a very thorough explainer. Even distressed, like when they'd battled the manananggal, she'd managed to provide way more detail than necessary. Now, when she'd sought Macella out intentionally to tell her something important and private, she was being maddeningly vague.

"Well, Maman did teach us to be honest," Macella murmured. "She always said lies were a luxury we couldn't afford."

Charlotte exhaled a little laugh. "She was right. But what should I have told the king, Ella?"

(25) Macella's heart pounded, even as she maintained a bland smile for her alleged sister. Babette de Pointe had taught her children many things, often through the repetition of wise or witty sayings. She had not, though, ever uttered the phrase Macella had just made up. Babette taught her children that lies were a ladder—dangerous but useful. She'd often said the wealthy used them to climb above the rest of us. There'd been begrudging respect in her tone.

Macella placed a kiss on the top of her sister's head. There was no scent of cinnamon and cherry blossoms, a scent as familiar to Macella as her own. In fact, there was no scent at all.

It might not break the vision, but it still gives us an edge. The king won't know that we know it's not real, and we can use that to our advantage.

Macella smiled inwardly. "I'm sure you did right, Lotta."

What was King Khari fishing for? She'd gone through great pains to make Macella believe one of the people she trusted most had given up a crucial secret. Was there something in particular she suspected, or was this just a shot in the dark? What could Macella offer that would ultimately benefit their purpose?

Macella thought quickly, knowing that the king was waiting for her response. She wouldn't tell her anything she didn't already know, but she *could* reveal that they knew one of the king's own secrets. Perhaps she could give her a distracting thread to follow.

"King Khari is a smart woman, she knew we'd figure it out eventually." Macella gave the fake Charlotte's shoulder a reassuring squeeze. "I'm sure you didn't tell her anything she didn't already know. Everyone is whispering about the pregnancy, and with how much time we spend with the Aegises, it isn't a huge leap for us to think there might be something different about the queen's baby. It didn't take much to connect the stories about Aegisborn to the special interest the Grand Mage has taken in Aithan."

Charlotte looked up at her, and Macella shivered. How could she have believed for a moment that this abomination was her Lotta? The eyes were all wrong. Even in Lotta's dark brown hue, they were unmistakably Khari's eyes.

"Even if she suspected we knew about Aithan and the queen's child being crossbreeds, I still confirmed it for her." Fake Charlotte sniffed mournfully. "I've betrayed you."

Macella fought back a sneer. She was so tired of playing a part for this woman. For the first time, the ticking clock hanging over her head seemed more friend than foe. Soon, she would be able to show King Khari who she was truly up against, and she was going to relish the revelation. Because this bitch had absolutely no idea who she was fucking with.

But she was going to find out very, very soon.

"Don't even think such a thing," Macella told her supposed sister through a smile that felt more like a grimace. "Maybe now that the king knows that we know, I can help. You know what a good midwife I am. I've been wanting to offer my services to the queen and the Grand Mage. Now that we all know the truth about the baby, we can work together to ensure they get here safely."

Maybe now, when Macella started spending more time with the Grand Mage and Queen Annika, King Khari would have no need to be suspicious of their activities. It would've been risky otherwise, considering the king was already watching her and her alliances so closely, and now the king herself had provided the perfect excuse. A spider trapping herself in her own web of deception.

"I didn't think you liked Queen Annika that well," Fake Charlotte said, eyeing her dubiously.

Macella knew she had to be truthful about some things if she was going to sell this performance. She laughed and ruffled her fake sister's hair. She had to resist a strong urge to wipe her hand on her trousers afterward. "You know I don't care for her at all, but I *do* care about the king's child," Macella said, moving back around the table to gather her things and, more importantly, put some distance between herself and the sickening illusion. "Besides, I need her pregnancy to go well...in case the king asks me to carry her next crossbreed child."

Even as a vision, the false Charlotte couldn't hide the fierce hunger in her eyes. Macella had thought King Khari would like the sound of that. As sickening as it was, she felt no qualms about teasing the possibility to further distract the king. They would never see that dream through. One of them would be dead long before that could happen.

"You didn't do anything wrong, Lotta, and we never need speak of this again," Macella said cheerfully. "Now run along to the parlor. I'll be there momentarily. I just want to finish reviewing the last few pages of this gods-awful report."

"You're the best, Ella!" False Charlotte smiled sweetly at Macella as she made her way to the door. "Hurry and come and eat. You work too hard."

Macella smiled vaguely, already flipping through the papers once more. She waited until Charlotte left, then counted to ten before exhaling the breath she'd been holding. The room felt noticeably warmer, a low fire still glowing in the hearth. Macella shivered, nonetheless. They were all going to have to be more careful than ever.

They could trust nothing in this place—not even their own eyes.

Chapter Seventeen

Macella

"Are you certain you're not an asanbosam?" Macella grumbled, watching the Grand Mage cork yet another vial of her blood. "Surely you can learn something without draining me dry."

Having grown used to Macella's sense of humor lately, Kiama only laughed. "I have always been fascinated by the Otherworldly creatures who thrive on blood. There are so many of them."

The two women had begun spending more time together in preparation for the Blessed Rite, and Macella found she enjoyed their short visits more than she'd expected. Grand Mage Kiama was a fount of knowledge, and she was willing to share everything she knew about Aegiskind, as well as the relatively little she knew about crossbreeds.

"You two are so strange," Queen Annika interjected, rolling her eyes. "How can you be fascinated by such dull, morbid tales?"

"They're more than tales to us, your grace. Aegises fight those monsters to protect you," Macella replied, quirking an eyebrow at the young queen. "I myself put down a bloodsucking loogaroo and a manananggal, only to now give my blood freely to aid in your survival."

"At least she's the only person draining you. I have a little warrior parasite feeding off of me all day long." Queen Annika sniffed indignantly, even as she rubbed her belly affectionately. "Between the vomiting, the peeing, and the Grand Mage's tests, I'm surprised I have any fluids left."

Kiama maintained a polite expression, but Macella snorted a laugh, earning a glare from the young queen that was halfhearted at best. Annika had actually been bearable in their increased interactions over recent weeks, and when they were in private, she was almost likable at times. The king had been delighted to see Macella taking an interest in Annika's pregnancy, obviously believing the lie she'd been fed during the conversation in which she'd masqueraded as Charlotte. Every time she saw her brides together, Macella could practically see the king imagining them both with prams full of her crossbreed offspring. Khari would use her queens to breed her own shields and then dispose of any Aegises she suspected of disloyalty.

Did King Khari truly believe Macella would willingly participate in such a scheme? That she would give up her own children and see her friends murdered in the pursuit of more power and control? It was a sickening idea, but it was convenient to have Khari's approval.

"At least it's only coming out of two holes. It could be worse," Macella offered with a shrug.

"I wish it would!" Annika exclaimed. "I haven't had a proper shit since this pregnancy began. I am going to celebrate this child's nameday with a strong cup of senna tea and my chamber pot."

This time, the Grand Mage laughed with Macella. Queen Annika looked a little surprised and pleased to have amused them. Macella realized the young queen might not have many friends. The assorted nobles of her entourage were mostly sycophants and social climbers. She'd thought Annika was just like them, but she was beginning to wonder if she'd been wrong.

"That settles it. I never want to be pregnant," Macella declared. "I may even sew my womb shut."

"Thank the gods. I couldn't handle more of you," Queen Annika replied, her tone more teasing than mean. It softened further when she spoke again, cradling her belly. "It's not all bad. And in the end, you get to meet an innocent little person who needs you, and you'll know you put something good in the world."

The queen's words hung in the air for a moment, their vulnerability shocking them all into silence. Realizing she'd perhaps said too much, Annika tossed her hair over her shoulder and struggled to her feet, gathering her purse and finishing her water in a few gulps.

"Then again, you're just as likely to end up with a little terror who sasses you and looks too much like their other parent." Annika shrugged nonchalantly, her mask of cold haughtiness sliding back into place. "I have other appointments and have gossiped enough for today. Send for me, Kiama, if you learn anything of use from these latest tests. I'm disappointed by our progress thus far. I am beginning to wonder if allying myself with Lady Macella was worthwhile. She's taught us nothing of consequence."

Grand Mage Kiama inclined her head deferentially, the picture of polite contrition. "Apologies, your grace. I will not disappoint you when it counts. I'm certain Lady Macella's heredity holds the key to a healthy birth for both you and the child. Please allow me a bit more time to prepare the answers you seek."

Queen Annika made a dismissive sound, nodded at Macella, and left. The other women remained silent until they heard the doors close behind her.

"I should be going as well," Macella said finally. "But I, for one, am fascinated by what we've discovered so far. Even if you are secretly drinking my blood."

Kiama laughed, shaking her head and shooing Macella toward the exit. "Though it doesn't serve the queen's purposes, I did learn something that may interest you. It actually explains the strong connection you have with your mage. Young Aisling is from the line of Cerridwen, and Samhain is one of her worshippers' most important holy days. It is a time when the veil between the living realm and the Otherworlds is thin, and we can commune with the spirits of our ancestors. As a Hades Aegis, with his gifts flowing through your veins, Samhain is a holy day for you, as well, as it is for all Aegises, as blessed by the gods of death. And it is less than a week away, the midpoint between the harvest equinox and cold solstice. You should celebrate it this season, I think."

Macella frowned, trying to follow the Grand Mage's logic. "That is interesting, but I don't think you needed my blood to learn it."

"No, certainly not," Kiama agreed. Her face lit up, her bright smile and dark skin contrasting appealingly, and again Macella was struck by her beauty. The Grand Mage shook her hand in farewell, squeezing it affectionately before releasing her and opening the door. "But I did need your blood to learn that you were born on Samhain forty-one years ago, meaning this Samhain will mark your forty-second year of life. Forty-two is a very prophetic and fortuitous number. It seems you were destined to be exactly who you are. Have a good afternoon, my lady."

Macella pondered this new information as she made her way back to her chambers, where she knew her Wildfire Court awaited news of the Grand Mage's progress. It was an odd thing to learn so much about herself so late in life. Before she'd met Aithan, Macella had no idea she had been adopted, let alone that she was Aegisborn. She hadn't even known her true age, since Tomas and Babette believed she was a human child, and her slowed aging made her appear younger to them. Now, in just two short years, she'd gone from an outsider with dreams of more, to a warrior queen with a rich history and a remarkable family.

"What did the Grand Mage teach you today that has you looking so thoughtful?" Lotta asked, as Macella wandered into the parlor and settled at Aithan's side on the sofa. He immediately wrapped his arm around her shoulders and pulled her closer.

"Did she figure out how to save the queen?" Jacan asked, his boyish face hopeful and his hand signs quick and choppy with excitement. Lotta smiled and leaned her head on his shoulder.

"Gods, I hope not," Finley said, stretching themself languidly, before lying across the chaise and putting their head in Zahra's lap.

Zahra ran her fingers through Finley's long silver hair, her big, mismatched eyes fixed on Macella. "They don't mean that. We've all we decided we want her to live at least long enough to be useful to us."

Macella shook her head. "You're both incorrigible. And no, dear Jacan, we did not learn anything that might aid Queen Annika in this pregnancy."

"But you did learn something interesting," Aisling pressed, her light gray mage's eyes seeing through Macella's evasion. "Something about yourself."

Aisling sat cross-legged on Charlotte's other side with Nyx curled up in her lap, watching Macella with the same unblinking intensity as her mistress. It was striking how obviously magical the pair were: the pale, plump, redheaded mage absently stroking her sleek, yellow-eyed, black cat. If Macella wasn't mistaken, they were both growing more powerful by the day. She'd always known Aisling had potential, but it was becoming increasingly obvious that the young mage was destined for great things.

Macella sighed, slipping her feet from her slippers and tucking her legs beneath her on the sofa. She loved her family and had no reason not to share this with them, but it still felt odd to discuss. She pulled a coin from her pocket, concentrating on rolling it smoothly across her knuckles instead of meeting Aisling's gaze.

"The Grand Mage was able to pinpoint the day of my birth," she said quietly. "I will be two and forty in a week's time. During Samhain."

Macella noticed how Aisling's eyes widened, even as she was distracted by squeals of excitement from Zahra and Charlotte. Jacan grinned widely and Finley sat up, clapping their hands, orange eyes sparkling with excitement. Aithan's arm tightened around her in a reassuring squeeze.

"That's wonderful news! We must have a party!" Finley exclaimed, to enthusiastic agreement from the others. "I do not observe Samhain, but I know of it. We can celebrate both events at once. Lotta can research more about the traditions so that we do it right."

"She doesn't have to," Aisling said, still watching Macella thoughtfully. "It is one of my most sacred holy days as a mage from the line of Cerridwen. I can help with the preparations."

"My mother, Gabriela, observed a similar holy day around this time of year. I used to love helping her decorate skulls made of sugar and prepare altars to honor her abuela and other ancestors," Aithan added slowly, as if the memory was only just returning to him. "She told me wonderful stories of boisterous celebrations remembering those they'd lost. They called it Día de los Muertos. I always thought it sounded like something I'd like to see."

"Perfect!" Finley proclaimed, looking more animated than they had in a long while—since before the execution. "We are going to make your wedding reception look like an afternoon tea. This time, I will not be reined in!"

Macella sighed, though she knew that she'd do anything that made Finley's eyes sparkle like that. "Please control yourself. If it is too big, the king will expect an invitation, and then it will not be much of a party."

Finley declared that they would personally oversee the guest list, and Khari would certainly not be on it. Jacan promised to learn to play all of Macella's favorite songs on his lute. Charlotte and Zahra eagerly chimed in with game and costume ideas that immediately got out of control.

"You do realize that this is the only time during the cold season the living can commune with the dead and the only time of year the dead can move so freely?" Aithan queried when they'd all calmed a bit. "It might be...a lot for Macella. As a Hades Aegis, I mean."

The others fell quiet, until Aisling broke the silence. "I will keep close to Lady Macella on Samhain. I'll make sure you don't become overwhelmed by the spirits."

Zahra gave Macella a concerned look. "Fuck, I forgot you can see dead people. It's pretty extraordinary that you were born on the day of the dead *and* you're blessed by Hades."

Aisling gave Macella a small, sad smile. "You were always meant to balance the two worlds."

Child of both worlds, life and death in your blood. My gifts already flow through your veins.

It was one of the first things Hades had ever said to her. Even then, she'd been marked for this. The puzzle pieces had always been there.

The blasphemer must be stopped. Child of both worlds, you and the son of Lucifer must stop her. Only you can.

"Well, now we're definitely having a party," Finley declared resolutely. "We have to."

It could be their last real revelry—their last chance to ever celebrate together in this realm. No matter whether they succeeded or not, it was possible they would not survive with the family fully intact.

No one said it aloud. They didn't have to. The truth hung heavy in the air.

"I've never had a proper nameday party. The wedding reception was the first event anyone had ever thrown in my honor, and the guests didn't even know what we were celebrating." Macella looked around at her favorite people in the world, a familiar pang filling her chest. She loved them all so much. "And some of you weren't here yet, so part of my heart was missing. I would love to celebrate life and love with all of you. Let's have a party."

---

(26) Thus, a week later, Macella found herself in the Aegis dining hall, which had been decorated for the occasion. Along one wall, tables had been lain with white tablecloths and covered in fresh flowers of all kinds from the conservatory. The Wildfire Court had spent all week painting skulls sculpted from sugar, which now nestled among the flowers and candles, alongside offerings of food for lost loved ones.

The rest of the tables had been arranged around the room, leaving an open space for dancing, and for the huge bonfire in the room's center. It was contained within a massive metal tub, smoke curling toward the high ceiling and through a partially open grate. The Wildfire Court had assembled early, and Aisling had prayed and lit the massive wheel of fire. Afterward, they'd each lit a candle in the bonfire and used them to light the candles for the dead.

Macella thought of Matthias and Lenora, the Aegis and human who had fallen in love and brought her into existence, and of Maia and Gabriela, the mage and Aegis who'd done the same to create her husband. She thought of Bellona and Kiho, Kai and Diya and Shamira, Aegises who had lost their lives to

King Khari's schemes. She thought of Anwansi and Tuwile and the many others who'd died in Smoketown and all the other ravaged areas of the kingdom.

She could feel them all in the flames of the candles she lit in their honor and in the bonfire of burnt offerings at the room's center and in the fire simmering beneath her skin. They were with her, even without Hades's gift, and had all lived so that she could too. They'd fed the fire of who she was now. They gave her the strength to do what she would do next, what she must do.

"Dance with me." Aithan's voice was right behind her, pulling her from her meditations.

She turned to face him, taking his proffered hand and noticing that the room had filled and the musically gifted among them had begun to play. Aithan led her closer to the fire, where several pairs of her friends were already moving to the lively music. Macella let her husband sweep her across the floor, laughing breathily as they fell into step with the others.

Soon, all of the Aegises, a fair few knights, and even a few nobles had joined the festivities. As promised, King Khari was not in attendance. It seems the Grand Mage had convinced the king and queen that this holy day was a vital opportunity to seek the blessings of the gods of the Otherworlds on their unborn crossbreed child. The pair would be confined to their chambers to pray and commune together all night. Though Macella felt a little sorry for Annika, she still appreciated the diversion.

Macella had insisted on Monarch Meztli receiving an invitation and she was pleased to see them sitting comfortably, watching the revelry with a serene expression on their lovely face. Ever since Macella had learned more about how their gift worked, she'd taken every possible opportunity to surround them with pleasant emotions, hoping to counter the tension they absorbed every day in the keep. It certainly seemed to be working at the moment, especially since Váli had managed to worm his way closer and closer to the monarch until his big head was in their lap. They smiled and scratched his head, and the wolf's tongue lolled out of his mouth, the picture of canine bliss.

After several additional dances, Macella collapsed onto the bench beside them with a goblet of chilled wine. Meztli smiled warmly at her, their dark eyes full of a peacefulness that had been far too absent since Queen Awa's death. Váli stood, turned in an excited circle, and shoved his wet snout into Macella's palm, his tail whipping madly and likely bruising every shin in the vicinity before he resettled with his head in her lap and much of the rest of his big body pressed against the monarch's legs.

"I see you've met Váli. He's very shy," Macella joked, ruffling the wolf's ears. "You're a very good boy, aren't you, Váli? Never met a stranger in your life."

"He is a wonderful host. I was already thrilled to receive an invitation to this celebration, but the furry welcome was a nice touch." Meztli laid a hand on her arm, giving it a gentle squeeze. "Happy nameday, Lady Macella. I've never met anyone so full of life, and yet this day suits you well. My people observe Día de los Muertos. It is always a time of joy, creativity, and community. And storytelling. So, it fits you quite perfectly."

(27) Macella pressed her shoulder against Meztli's, warmth blooming in her chest. She hadn't initially known how to feel about all of this, but she was realizing what an amazing gift it was to be able to share this day with her loved ones—both living and dead.

"I am not sure of the schedule of the event, so I am risking invoking your Finley's wrath, but I am royalty and am not used to being made to wait," Monarch Meztli declared with an exaggerated pompousness as they placed a small parcel in Macella's hands. "Open your gift. And don't bother saying you can't accept it or that I shouldn't have. It is silly and it will make you smile and that will make me happy. So, really it is as though I'm giving myself a gift."

Macella laughed at the circuitous logic and resisted the urge to argue. Somehow, she hadn't anticipated anyone bringing presents. She should have known her friends wouldn't be able to resist doting on her.

When she managed to untie her parcel and see what was inside, she threw back her head and laughed. It was a silver bracelet with a clasp made of aquamarine jewels. It was shaped like a toad.

"I knew that first day we spent together on the grounds that we were going to be great friends. The burst of pleasure you felt over something as inconsequential as a toad told me so much about who you are. It has been a comfort and a delight having you here, my lady."

Disregarding all rules of politeness, Macella threw her arms around Monarch Meztli. They hugged her back, and Macella was awash in peace and contentment. She held on for a long moment.

"Now that our lovely monarch has had their turn, it's time for everyone else to present their gifts, before we resume the revels!" Finley announced, clapping their hands for attention, as the musicians ended another song. "As you all know, in addition to observing various remembrances of the dead, we are celebrating the birth and life of your future queen, my sister, Lady Macella of Shively!"

Somehow, despite being constantly in the spotlight lately, Macella still felt herself blush when everyone turned her way. It was a pleasant feeling, but she wasn't used to being popular and praised. Growing up, everyone in Shively had found her strange, and she'd been a constant disappointment to her parents. Now, here was a room full of people who admired and loved her well enough to give her a party. Life was so unpredictable.

"Thank you all for being here." Macella stood, smiling at her guests, and pressing her hands to her heart. "It means so much to me to share this day with you. Your presence here is gift enough—"

"Booooooooooo!" Zahra yelled, startling everyone. "You do not get to be all self-deprecating today. Open your presents!"

The sound of laughter filled the room, drowning out any further protests. Macella threw up her hands in surrender. She took her seat, nodding at Finley, which was all the permission they needed to proceed with their elaborate program for the evening.

There were too many presents. Some that made her laugh and others that made her eyes prick with tears. With Lynn's help, Lotta had translated her first original design into a stylish jacket with hidden weapons holsters and a train that made Finley drool with envy. Aisling and Grand Mage Kiama had made a red rose and patchouli candle and enchanted it into an everflame, promising Macella that it would burn indefinitely and attract love and abundance. (It also boasted a familiar pawprint embedded in the wax.) Zahra and Aithan—with contributions from many others—had put together a keepsake book for her with clippings of her writings, society paper articles about her, handwritten notes, and other memorabilia all arranged alongside drawings and pressed flowers and other pretty bits and baubles.

There were sweet offerings like the song Jacan composed just for the occasion, Finley crooning along to lyrics they'd written to accompany the tune. There were total surprises, like a canvas covered in drawings of Macella and her friends, drawn and signed by the children of Ellasburg, and a collection of sweet-smelling massage oils sent by Brontë, the proprietor of the king's favorite brothel. Then there were silly gifts like Valen publicly declaring her as Váli's godmother, which the wolf endorsed with a hearty woof, and a series of naughty limericks about her composed and performed by Captain Drudo, Lady Griselda, and even Sir Kamau, who blushed furiously the entire time.

After gifts, there was far too much food, including all of her favorites, and more sweets than they could possibly consume. The knights sang a bawdy rendition of a local nameday song, and Macella laughed until her stomach ached. Once they'd filled their bellies, the musicians began to play again, and Macella found herself back on the dance floor, swaying happily in Aithan's strong arms.

She closed her eyes and exhaled, thanking her ancestors for this moment. She thought again of Lenora and Matthias, Maia and Gabriela, Shamira and Diya and Bellona and Kai. All those who'd come before, contributing their energy to this perfect moment in time. Macella thought of each of them, hoping that wherever they were in the Otherworlds, they could still feel love.

When she opened her eyes again, the room was full of dead people.

CHAPTER EIGHTEEN

Macella

They were everywhere, filling the hall with bodies. So many faces. Some familiar, some strange.

(28) It wasn't like the other times Macella had encountered the dead. Usually, she couldn't tell the dead from the living, unless she was already aware of their death or if she tried to touch them. The dead she'd met spoke and behaved as other people did and seemed to be fully aware of the present.

Those surrounding her now were more like the spirits of the old tales—ethereal and translucent. They were eerily silent and watchful. Though they seemed wholly unaware of the other spirits around them, they appeared enraptured by the living. It seemed they'd come to observe, to glimpse life again, however briefly. Their eyes were dark and empty. She'd never feared the dead before, but all of those unmoving, blank faces were a bit unnerving.

Though they stood disconcertingly still, there was a fluidity to their presence. They faded and appeared constantly, the faces changing as different spirits came and went. Macella wondered if they were flickering between other Samhain and Día de los Muertos observances around the kingdom, perhaps searching each celebration for familiar faces.

As though the thought had summoned her, a woman appeared on the opposite side of the dance floor, her attention locked on Macella. Her dark hair was piled atop her head in a coif of intricate braids and her almond-shaped eyes crinkled merrily at the corners when she caught Macella's attention. Even muted and diaphanous, her skin was a deep, rich brown. She smiled, revealing a slight gap between her front teeth. Macella recognized the woman immediately, though she'd only ever seen a memory of her reflected in a dead man's mind.

It was her mother.

Lenora disappeared and Macella's stomach dropped. She pulled away from Aithan, spinning and frantically scanning the dead faces. To her immense relief, she spotted her mother among the specters grouped near the dining hall doors.

"Are you alright, love?" Aithan asked, following her gaze.

Even without checking his mind, Macella knew that her husband couldn't see any of the hazy figures scattered among the living revelers. It was her gift from Hades to commune with the dead, and today, on Samhain, it seemed she was able to see them all. But she only had eyes for one.

Lenora disappeared again.

"I'm fine," she lied, giving him a tight smile. "I just need a breath of fresh air. I'll be right back."

Before he could ask anything more, Macella hurried across the room, weaving through her friends and well-wishers quickly. She burst into the corridor, looking in every direction for a glimpse of her mother. Like the dining hall, the corridors were full of incorporeal figures, appearing and disappearing, drawn toward the celebration, drawn toward the spark of life.

Macella ignored them, glimpsing Lenora further along the corridor. She followed her mother without hesitation, noticing only distantly how the other revenants' heads turned to watch her as she passed. The skin on her neck prickled, but she plowed on.

When Lenora disappeared again, Macella pushed through an outer door and stepped into the frigid night air. The ground was covered in snow, and Macella was reminded of the day Diya, Kai, and Bellona's blood had stained it red. Were they here somewhere, watching their siblings dance and drink? Would they, too, come to her before the night ended?

Macella could not think on it when her mother was only a few feet away, wreathed in silvery moonlight. There were others standing among the courtyard's bare trees and stone statues. The snow sparkled beneath feet that left no prints and were unaffected by the cold. Macella's mother smiled, even as gossamer tears rolled down her cheeks.

"Lenora?" Macella whispered. Her breath fogged the air, and her skin prickled with gooseflesh, but she hardly noticed. "Mother?"

Lenora nodded, pressing her hands to her heart in a gesture that was a perfect mirror of the one Macella had made earlier that night when expressing her gratitude to her guests. A sob clawed its way up Macella's throat. That brief bit of recognition, that tiny confirmation that she'd inherited traits from the mother she never knew, made her ravenous for more. There was a gaping maw inside of her that wanted to gobble up every detail about her mother.

"I love you," Lenora said in a voice as insubstantial as her form. It was barely a whisper, and yet it reverberated through Macella's entire being. She'd never heard her mother's voice, never heard her say those three devastating words. "It is hard for me to speak...to hold on to this realm. But that is the most important thing. I love you, Macella."

Macella's feet carried her closer to Lenora of their own accord, pausing only once they were as close as they could be without touching. She studied her mother's face hungrily, her own face wet with tears that cooled on her cheeks, making her shiver.

"Is that why you've never come to me before? It is too hard for you?" Macella asked in a hushed voice, afraid of speaking too loudly lest she pop the delicate bubble of this moment.

Lenora shook her head. "Difficult to have a...form...a body. But I come. I watch over you. Always."

Macella laughed and it sounded like crying. Her arms ached to wrap around her mother, but she knew it would be futile. Lenora already seemed to be growing fainter, her vaporous form flickering in the moonlight.

"I miss you," Macella blurted through her tears. "It doesn't make sense because I do not even know you, but I miss you so much. And I'm afraid. I do not want to die yet. And I do not want to lose anyone else."

Lenora smiled sadly, reaching out as if to touch Macella's cheek. Her hand hovered in the air between them. Macella fought the urge to lean into it.

"You never truly lose the ones you love," Lenora murmured, her voice far away. "We remain. We live. In you."

Macella couldn't feel her own numb fingers as she dashed away the tears attempting to freeze on her cheeks. She risked looking away from Lenora for an instant—just long enough to ensure they were still unobserved by any living souls. When she was satisfied, she let her hellfire rise to coat her skin. Their warmth was enough to stop her teeth from beginning to chatter and interfering with the precious time she had left with her mother.

"I'm still afraid," Macella replied honestly, her chest aching with the magnitude of her fear.

"Good." Lenora's eyes were full of fierce pride. "That is smart. Be afraid and do it anyway, my brave girl."

"Lady Macella?"

Macella spun toward the voice, extinguishing her hellfire as quickly as she could. She cursed herself for taking such a stupid risk. Her Aegisborn nature would've protected her from any real harm from the cold for quite a while. She'd been so intent on her mother that she'd let it cloud her judgment.

Luckily, only Aisling stood behind her, holding out a cloak. "I promised to watch out for you, remember? Are you alright? Were there too many spirits inside?"

"No, it's not that. I was talking to—" Macella cut herself off abruptly. She whirled back toward her mother, only to find the space empty. She swiveled her head, searching the courtyard desperately, trudging forward through the thick snow. "No, no, no, no, no! Lenora? Mother? Mother!"

There was no sign of her mother among the lingering spirits in the courtyard. Macella started toward the far gate. Perhaps Lenora would reappear further away, out on the grounds. She had to find her. She couldn't lose her again so soon.

Aisling caught her, wrapping the cloak around her shoulders and forcing Macella to stop. The look in the mage's eyes made it clear that Lenora was gone. Macella's knees buckled, and Aisling grabbed her arms, slowing her descent toward the ground. Both women fell to their knees in the snow.

"You cannot follow them," Aisling told her quietly. "No matter how much you miss them, or how weary you may be of this realm. It is not your time. But you can remember them, and that is what they truly want. More than they want to be seen and heard, they want to be remembered."

Macella covered her face with her hands, choking out words between her sobs. "Can you see them? The dead all around us?"

"Not with my eyes, but I can feel them," Aisling replied gently. "They feel peaceful. They are well. You needn't weep for them."

"These tears are for me," Macella admitted, still crying openly. "And all the love I missed out on as a child."

Instead of speaking, Aisling gathered Macella into her arms. Without thinking, Macella buried her face against the other woman's shoulder. Aisling's heather and baked bread scent was soothing, and Macella clung to her for several minutes, trying to regain her composure.

Everything was fine until Macella pulled away. Aisling tried to help her to her feet, but they'd sank deeper into the snow and their legs got tangled. Somehow, one of Aisling's gloves slipped down her arm, and Macella's fingers brushed against her wrist. The Seer went rigid, her eyes going white. A current sparked between them, holding Macella in place, her hand a frozen claw around Aisling's wrist.

All around them, the spirits grew thicker. Their heads turned in unison, watching the Seer with their dark, empty eyes. Macella could feel the weight of them, growing heavier, as more and more figures joined the tight circle of bodies around the two of them kneeling in the snow.

A low humming began—though it seemed to have no clear origin—and the electric buzz made the hairs on Macella's arms stand on end. The icy air had grown thick, making it difficult for her to draw breath.

Darkness.

Shadows.

Screams.

Her head on Aithan's chest. Silence. Cold. So cold her bones ached, and her teeth chattered.

Swirling smoke. Silence.

Inky black nothingness.

"Macella, are you okay?" Aithan pulled her against his chest. With his other arm, he lifted Aisling from the snow, careful not to touch her exposed skin. Around them, spirits flickered and disappeared as though they'd never been there at all. "What are you two doing out here? Aisling, what did you see? Never mind. Let's get you both inside."

It took a moment for Macella and Aisling to get their bearings, but soon they were back inside the castle in the relative warmth of the corridor. Aithan found a quiet alcove and made them sit down, commandeering a nearby lantern to provide some additional heat. Once he was sure they were in no immediate danger, he disappeared briefly, returning with two mugs of hot cider. They sipped in silence for several minutes, Aithan waiting patiently despite his obvious concern.

"I saw my mother," Macella said quietly, once she was sure she could speak without bursting into tears. "I spoke to her."

Aithan's amber eyes filled with sympathy. He hugged her to him, stroking her back, and planting a kiss in her curls. Macella leaned into his embrace, pressing her face to his chest and listening to the steady, reassuring rhythm of his heartbeat. He didn't ask any questions, just held her tightly. Macella knew he would let her tell the rest in her own time, if she wanted to, and until then he would hold space for her feelings, whatever they might be. It was exactly what she needed.

"What did you see, Aisling?" he asked, turning his attention to the silent mage without releasing Macella.

"I—" Aisling began, then broke off abruptly. "I don't know. Nothing of consequence. Nothing clear."

Macella lifted her head from Aithan's chest to look at her mage, but the younger woman refused to meet her gaze.

"You don't know, or you know but it was not clear?" Aithan pressed.

Aisling bit her lip.

"What don't you want to tell us?"

"She saw me die," Macella stated matter-of-factly, remembering the flashes she'd gleaned during the moments they'd been tangled in the snow. "She saw *us* die, Aithan. Me and you."

She didn't need the confirmation in Aisling's face to know she was right. Hadn't she suspected as much, deep down, perhaps from that very first prophecy? Was this not where their Fate had always been leading them?

Aisling's eyes were shiny with unshed tears when she finally met Macella's gaze. "It wasn't clear. And my Sight cannot always be interpreted literally."

Macella smiled at her friend, surprised by a sudden lightness in her shoulders. Maybe it was seeing her mother, or having a good cry, or being resigned to her own inevitable doom, but she suddenly felt better. She was certain everything would work out as it was meant to.

"You needn't weep for the dead, my friend. They are well." Macella stood, extending a hand to her husband and beckoning Aisling to join them. "Let us honor them by living well until we meet them again."

Aithan took her hand, pressing it to his lips before intertwining their fingers. Together, they returned to the party, where they celebrated life and death late into the night.

Aithan

Aithan did not let himself think about Aisling's vision.

He focused on his wife, on the celebration of her life, on the friends who had come together to make the day special for her. They danced and drank and told stories of their loved ones who had gone on to the Otherworlds. They laughed and laughed and lived until people began to fall asleep in their ale and the night threatened to become morning.

Finally, they parted ways and Aithan and Macella stumbled back to their chambers with Zahra in tow. He left the two women alone for a few minutes, finding his way to Macella's office. He sat down with a piece of paper and pen and began to write.

Ten minutes later, Aithan folded his letter neatly and slid it into an envelope. He sealed it and wrote Macella's name across the front in a steady, even hand. He'd been thinking about this letter for a long time and was surprised by how easy it was to write. Of course, he would never have the way with words that Macella did, but pouring out his heart to her felt natural. Everything about loving her had felt natural from the very beginning. Aithan knew it would feel that way to the bitter end.

It was amazing how unremarkable a day it'd been when his world changed entirely. When he'd wandered into that brothel, hungry, ennuied, and still stained with popobawa blood, he'd had no idea his life was about to change so drastically. He couldn't have known that the next two years would be the best of his long life. The warm season had hardly begun when he'd eagerly left the capital's chaos behind, ready to roam free and do what he did best—fight, fuck, and mind his own business. But Fate had other ideas, and it led him to the woman who would change everything.

In a few months, that adventurous day would be two years behind him. And yet it felt like so much more, simultaneously a lifetime and a single breath. After seventy years, nearly all spent in solitude, he was given the gift of twelve hundred days with the woman who'd forced him to finally live, rather than simply exist.

It wasn't enough.

It was more than enough.

If the warm season dawned and their two years ended in tragedy, Aithan would go to the Otherworlds carrying a heart full of gratitude. He would wait for Macella, would do whatever it took to spend the next life at her side. And no matter what happened, she would know how much he loved her, how loving her had saved his life.

Aithan put the letter in a drawer for safe keeping. He would leave it for her to find when the time came. If the time came.

Until then, he was going to spend every minute of these last days loving his wife.

As soon as he returned to the bedchamber, the sheriff produced a package, which Aithan had tucked away in his wardrobe that morning. Zahra held it out to Macella, her face split in a wide grin.

"What is this?" Macella asked, examining the parcel quizzically. "My nameday has been wonderful. You needn't have gotten me anything at all, let alone multiple gifts."

Zahra just grinned wider, bouncing on her toes and watching Macella with sparkling, mischievous eyes. "Blah blah blah! Always so humble and selfless. Be a little greedy for a change. Besides, it's not *just* for you. Open it!"

"So, you're saying that, for my nameday, you got *yourself* a gift?" Macella demanded indignantly.

Zahra slapped her palm against her face dramatically. "For the love of all the gods, Macella, open the damn present!"

Aithan smiled and moved to his second favorite spot in the bedchamber as the two women bickered good-naturedly. He settled comfortably into an armchair against the wall nearest the bed. Since Zahra had taken up residence in the keep, the chair had been quite useful whenever he was feeling voyeuristic.

Aithan looked up to find Macella watching him as she toyed with the wrappings on her gift. He sat back, letting his eyes drift slowly over his wife, lovingly taking in the familiar curves he would never grow tired of. With their sexy little sheriff hovering impatiently beside her, it was hard not to think about all the fun they would be getting into very, very soon. As soon as Macella opened her gift. He winked at her, then flicked his gaze to the parcel.

Macella shivered, reading the hunger in his eyes, and returned to the package with increased interest. Zahra hopped onto the bed, plopping down on her belly and resting her chin in both hands to watch Macella expectantly. Macella chuckled before taking the hint and carefully undoing the ribbons holding the parcel closed.

Her eyes widened as she lifted the item from the box, turning it in her hands to examine its assortment of straps and buckles. Zahra bounced on the bed, her smile full of characteristic devilry. When Macella discovered the carved wooden phallus attached to the harness, she let out a garbled noise of surprise, and Zahra collapsed into a fit of giggles.

Macella turned her astonished expression on Aithan, and he had to fight back his own laughter. He'd never seen her so wide-eyed and speechless. Her mouth opened and closed several times before she managed to speak.

"Is this...what *is* this?" Macella asked, then glared half-heartedly when Zahra cackled raucously. Undeterred by the stern look, Zahra rolled onto her back and kicked her little feet in the air. Macella rolled her eyes. "I mean, I think I know what it is, but why did you two get it for me?"

Zahra sat up before Aithan could answer, her mismatched eyes full of concern. "You don't like it?"

Macella brushed Zahra's cheek affectionately. "That is not what I am saying. I do not know what I think yet. I'm still processing. But I know I love that the two of you got something special for us."

(29) Aithan stood and joined the two women, gently taking the harness from Macella. "Let me help. It'll probably be best for you to undress first. Both of you."

His wife lifted an eyebrow and smirked at him—a look that never failed to awaken his cock. "Well, now I'm starting to understand what Zahra meant when she said this gift isn't just for me."

Aithan chuckled low in his throat. Zahra rolled out of the bed and out of her clothes as quickly as she did everything else, grinning maniacally the entire time, like the mad pixie demon she was. Aithan caught a glimpse of telltale shine on her thighs that indicated just how excited she was by what they'd planned for the night. His nostrils flared and his cock stiffened further at the growing scent of arousal in the air. It was going to be exquisite torture returning to his chair to watch things unfold.

Zahra helped Macella out of her clothes, her small hands lingering on his wife's ample ass and brushing over her breasts more than was strictly necessary. Macella's nipples strained against the fabric of her binder, making his mouth water. The little scraps of satin she called underwear laced up the sides and would be easy to remove even with the harness on, so Aithan decided she could wear them for now. He would enjoy the sight of the satin hugging her ass while she fucked Zahra. There was something about the way the perfect triangle of fabric clung and stretched, revealing just a tease of each luscious cheek. It made him ravenous. He wanted to take a bite every time he caught a glimpse.

Aithan crouched behind Macella and gave in to the urge, nipping at the tempting flesh and making her squeal adorably. From this vantage point, he couldn't help but breathe in the delicious smell of her pussy. He kissed the spot he'd bitten to soothe the sting, then forced himself to move his face away from the danger zone before he bent her over and devoured her, which was not what he and Zahra had planned.

There would be time for that later.

Carefully, he lifted Macella's foot, guiding her into the harness. He let his hands linger as he slid the straps up her legs, then buckled them around her waist. Her lips parted and pupils dilated as she watched him tighten various straps, making sure the phallus was secured against her mound. He'd known she was going to love it. And he was going to love exploring this new passion with her.

He held her gaze as he gave the wooden cock an experimental suck. It was intricately carved, complete with very convincing ridges and veins, and was sealed with a waxy substance that gave it a more lifelike feel. Aithan was impressed with the craftmanship, and with his ability to swallow a fair bit of it. It had been quite a while since he'd had a cock in his mouth, but it seemed it was like riding a horse. Muscle memory.

Aithan winked at his wife again as he slowly pulled back, releasing the phallus with a playful pop. Her whole body shuddered in response. She watched as he took a bottle of olive oil from the bottom of the parcel and poured a bit into his palm. She gasped when he stroked the phallus, spreading the oil from root to tip. Aithan could scent just how wet she was already, and the smell was intoxicating. He needed to take his seat before he forgot all about the plan.

Probably sensing his unraveling resolve, Zahra slid back on the bed and opened her slender legs, revealing her delicious, drenched pussy. She licked her lips, drawing their attention to her perfect cupid's bow mouth. Her thick, dark hair fell over one of her big, beautiful eyes, which were hooded with undisguised lust.

Aithan marveled at how damn lucky he was. Swiftly, he stood and bent to run his tongue up her dripping slit. She moaned huskily, arching her back and pushing out her pert little breasts. The sheriff was so different from his wife, but an absolutely amazing woman in her own right. Aithan loved her. More than that, he loved that Macella loved her and that she loved Macella back so fiercely. Aithan didn't know what their future held, but he knew that Zahra was welcome to spend as much of it with them as she and Macella wished.

"She's ready for you, hell goddess," he said, straightening and tugging Macella toward the bed. He ran his hand over her ass, before squeezing it and pressing his lips against her ear. "I'm going to watch you fuck our Zahra until she comes all over your cock. Can you do that, love?"

"I am damn sure willing to try," Macella replied, giving him a frenetic smile.

Aithan smacked her ass approvingly, then helped her onto the bed.

Macella crawled up the mattress to kneel between Zahra's thighs. Her skimpy satin panties juxtaposed against the leather straps and metal buckles in an indescribably alluring way that was so very Macella. She was a warrior and a writer, a paladin and a poet, strong and soft and simply complex.

His hell goddess.

Macella positioned herself over Zahra, kissing the other woman softly as she notched the toy against her entrance. Then she looked over her shoulder at Aithan, and he was grateful for his chair because the spark in her eyes made his knees weak. Her grin was a little bit wild and a little bit nervous and a whole lot sexy.

Aithan felt a thrill that was more than arousal. He loved this. He loved that he got to try new things and experience firsts with Macella. He loved watching her enjoy life. She did so much for others, had changed so many lives—his most of all. It elated him to share exciting moments like this with her, to make memories no one would ever take from them.

Aithan loved her so fucking much.

Watching his wife slide inside the lovely sheriff was almost enough to make him cum in his pants. She swiveled her wide hips, easing into Zahra's pussy with shallow thrusts. Zahra moaned throatily, gripping Macella's ass and arching to meet each stroke. Aithan heard his wife chuckle.

"Easy, Sheriff," she purred in a voice that made him grip the arms of the chair to keep from pouncing on her. "This cock is less forgiving than flesh. I don't want to hurt you."

Zahra lifted her hips, still obviously trying to coax Macella deeper. "Fuck that! Give me your unforgiving cock! I don't want to be able to walk straight tomorrow."

Macella laughed, nipping at the other woman's bottom lip. "You will take what I give you and you will like it."

Fucking hell. Aithan massaged his cock through his trousers, trying to soothe the ache that only intensified as he watched his wife take charge. She gripped Zahra's hip with one hand, pinning her in place, and kissed her roughly to drown out her protests. The sheriff moaned into Macella's mouth as she pulled back before thrusting hard, the muscles in her plump ass clenching enticingly as she did so. She pulled out slowly again, only to thrust a little deeper. Finally, after a few more strokes, Macella buried the phallus completely, her body flush against Zahra's trembling form.

They were so utterly beautiful together. Aithan couldn't look away. He'd had plenty of sex in his life, but he had never seen anything as erotic as his wife buried to the hilt in her beautiful friend. As unbearably aroused as he was, he thought it might be a pity to join in and interfere with the perfection—especially once both women began to pant and moan in unison.

Soon, Macella found a rhythm that made Zahra cry out in a familiar way that Aithan knew meant she was close to her orgasm. A moment later, she found her release, Macella fucking her through it, even as her body shook with her own mounting pleasure. Aithan wondered if she could orgasm from giving pleasure this way. He added it to his mental list of things to explore with their new toy.

When she was satisfied Zahra had had enough, Macella pulled out, pushing herself up onto her hands and knees. Her panties were askew, and Aithan could see her pussy glistening around the wet fabric. She looked over her shoulder at him and he forgot the noble thoughts he'd had about not getting involved tonight.

"Fuck me, Aithan. I'm so close," she said, and he was absolutely undone.

In a moment he was kneeling naked behind her, and in another he'd ripped her panties free and taken ahold of the straps across her hips. Then he was plunging inside of her, again and again, and she was warm and wet and tight and perfect, and Zahra was watching them with smoldering eyes, and then Macella's pussy was fluttering around him, and they were falling into the stars.

Afterward, they lay together in a tangle of limbs, each drifting in and out of a satisfied semi-doze. Aithan felt pleasantly wrung out, both from the day's celebration and the night's exertions. A new day was already dawning, and he should've been trying to get a few hours of sleep before the king's inevitable summons, but he found himself clinging to these quiet moments more and more lately.

"Where did you all even get that amazing thing?" Macella yawned, breaking the silence. "I think I would like to send a letter of thanks to the craftsperson."

Zahra chuckled sleepily. "There is a woman in Ellasburg who makes them. She gave Aisling one as payment for a healing tea. I found her and Lotta giggling over it one afternoon and knew we had to have one made. The woman wouldn't let me pay for this one when she found out it was a gift for the future queen, but I bet she'll be delighted to get a thank you note from you."

"Consider it done," Macella declared, snuggling closer and draping an arm across Aithan's chest. "She should advertise them as cocks fit for a queen."

"Cocks cut for the Crown," Zahra amended.

"Rods for rutting royals," Macella added.

"Jolly sticks for royal pricks," Zahra countered.

They were both still giggling as Aithan drifted off to sleep.

Chapter Nineteen

Macella

After Samhain, the cold season became a runaway carriage ride toward the throne. The days were steadily growing longer, and the worst of the freeze had passed. The warm season was coming, the final months of the year trickling away like sand in a glass. The twentieth month would bring the rite and Macella's coronation, so that, when the warm season and the new year dawned, King Khari could have her grand wedding and celebrate her centennial with all the pomp she desired, and guests would have clear travels to come pay their respects with gifts and oaths.

Of course, if Macella succeeded, the new year would begin a new era for the kingdom, free of Khari's tyrannical rule. Every moment not spent with her friends, or being a pin cushion for the Grand Mage, was occupied with preparations for her ascension to the throne. Planning a coronation and royal wedding was plenty time-consuming enough without the added pressure of orchestrating a coup. And no matter how much they planned and studied, their best chance of defeating Khari still hinged on attacking while she was weakened by the rite, which would require precise timing and a large helping of luck, especially since they couldn't expect the Royal Guard and the Chosen to sit idly by while they made their move.

With the assistance of the Grand Mage, however, the Wildfire Court felt more hopeful about their odds of success. They were all but sure Kiama would be able to keep Macella alive during the rite, though Macella was still determined to do whatever she must, no matter the cost. Each day, she was reminded that they weren't alone in the fight. Staff and nobles alike showed their allegiance to Macella in small ways, from hidden flame adornments to small gifts and encouraging words. With so many people behind them, Macella and Aithan might truly fulfill the prophecy once and for all.

A shield. A scribe. A sword. A pen. Against hell's fury. Against our end.

It felt like Macella barely blinked before the Blessed Rite was upon them. With just a few days remaining, she was informed that her throne and crown were complete, which was surprising considering she'd never given the artisans the directions they'd so anxiously awaited. The last she remembered was asking for more time to consider, and that had been during the harvest season.

"Lynn took care of it," Charlotte said with a shrug when Macella remarked on it. "You know nothing goes on around here without her knowledge. She told the artisans that you'd given her all of the information they needed to design the perfect crown and throne for you, which technically isn't a lie. Nobody is more attuned to your style than she is."

Charlotte was right, of course, and Macella was eternally grateful to the high tailor for taking the burden of yet another decision off her shoulders. She was sure that Lynn's designs would be much better than anything she would've come up with—not that she cared much what her royal regalia looked like, since she did not plan to ever make use of it. If she lived through the Blessed Rite, it was still unlikely that she'd be crowned or ever sit on the throne, considering her survival would mean she had murdered the king.

On the evening before she was to undergo the rite, Macella slipped into the throne room alone. Soon, she'd be having dinner with the Wildfire Court, and they would try and enjoy the evening without worrying over their plans for the following day. Then they'd all try and sleep as if it might not be their last night in this realm. The next time Macella stepped into this room, it would be for the Blessed Rite.

She breathed deeply, making herself move slowly across the grand space. Tomorrow, it would be full of her closest allies and worst enemies. They would all watch as she stood before this dais, the king, and the Chosen. They would all witness whatever happened next.

She didn't know how she'd expected to feel when she saw her throne, but the pang of sad longing still surprised her. She was glad she'd decided to view it alone, during a rare moment while the throne room was empty, because she wasn't prepared for the contradictory emotions it evoked.

Macella did not want to be queen. She did not want to spend her days confined to this place, carrying the weight of the kingdom on her shoulders. She did not want the power or the responsibility.

All of that was true, and yet her crown and throne called to her just the same.

She had been right to trust Lynn to capture her queenly persona perfectly. The throne's wrought iron frame was woven into intricate vines and swirls, while amber gems and crimson rubies glinted among the roses blossoming from the vines.

In the right light, the roses looked more like flames.

Her crown sat on the throne's crimson seat cushion, looking simple and elegant. It was exactly as Macella remembered from the dream she'd had on the day Khari declared they'd be wed, and this moment had become her destiny. Silver with onyx gemstones, the colors a near-perfect match to her hair. She remembered how, in her dream, her reflection's eyes had glowed onyx and her skin had been alight with hellfire. She'd looked fierce and regal and powerful.

The warrior queen.

Without even realizing it, Macella ascended the dais to brush her hand over the cool iron of her throne. The rose flames flickered as she circled it, examining the craftsmanship. When she reached the front again, she gingerly touched the crown's sharp points. It was truly beautiful, and the temptation to try it on was strong.

Finally, on the precipice of her supposed ascension to the throne, she truly considered the possibility for the first time. She could do a great deal of good as queen. All she'd accomplished so far would pale in comparison to what she could do with the full might of the Crown behind her. With that kind of power, monsters like Khari would never be able to stand in her way again. She could put an end to all the injustice and cruelty still plaguing the kingdom, and she could make the perpetrators pay. King Khari would be the first example made, then those who'd enabled her, and those who'd profited from the oppression she wrought. Macella could punish them all.

No.

Macella backed away from the throne, wiping her hands on her trousers, as if she could wipe away the blood of her imagined reign. The call of such power was dangerous. She wouldn't let it lure her in. Maybe she wouldn't be corrupted, as so many before her had been, or maybe all of her darker urges would find their way to the surface, and she'd become as bad as the one she sought to depose. She'd never know, because she would not be queen.

Macella of Shively was a warrior, like her father before her. Tomorrow, she would return to this room and endure the rite long enough to remove Khari's head. She would do what Hades has tasked her to do, would save the people she loved, and then she would be free to enjoy that love. She would help form the new world, but she would not lead it.

(30) "I cannot wait to set it upon your head. You will look divine."

Macella jumped, her head snapping up at the sound of the last voice she wanted to hear. King Khari stood at the rear of the dais, just inside the private entrance for the monarchy. She leaned against the wall wearing an enigmatic smile, her arms crossed and adder eyes watchful as ever. Macella knew the room had been empty when she'd entered.

Or had it? She hadn't attended to her sense of smell. Perhaps the king had been watching her the entire time.

"You startled me, your grace." Macella bowed politely, her fingers already itching for her daggers. "And you flatter me as always. I will be but a rose in the bouquet, a complement to the beauty of Queen Annika and Monarch Meztli."

King Khari made a dismissive sound, drawing nearer. "You cannot help but stand out, my northern rose. There is something unique about you that simply demands notice and veneration."

Macella shivered. Khari's voice held a mixture of want and warning that unsettled her. She wasn't sure if the king's desire to possess her outweighed her jealousy and distrust. Either way, she would never be safe as her queen.

"Thank you, your grace," Macella murmured, bowing again and backing toward the steps. "I suppose I should be going. I must prepare for the great honor before me. Enjoy your evening."

"Lady Macella." King Khari stopped her before she could back away, catching her hand and pressing a kiss to it. Macella tried not to recoil. "After tonight, I will expect more of your time. And we have a honeymoon to plan as well. I do hope you've had the opportunity and inclination to reconsider my offer of intimacy."

Macella swallowed hard, her cheeks growing hot. Once upon a time, she'd found the concept of sex with Khari disturbingly appealing, but not anymore. Now, the thought filled her with nothing but abhorrence.

"Of course, my king. Perhaps we can talk of it over dinner tomorrow evening," she lowered her gaze demurely, hoping she looked flirtatious rather than disgusted. "I have given it much thought."

Before she could pull her hand away, the king squeezed it tightly—almost painfully—forcing Macella to meet her cold ochre eyes. "I look forward to it. But before you go, there is one more thing, my lady."

The room grew cold, the walls suddenly closer than they'd been before. Claustrophobia clawed at her, and her throat threatened to close. The air was suffocating, as if Macella and the king had been buried together, entombed in the throne room for eternity. Macella's heart hammered in her chest, her free hand once more twitching toward her daggers.

"Do not cross me, Macella. You have seen but a glimpse of my true power. I can show you things that will make you long for the jorōgumo's web." King Khari pulled her close, and Macella could smell her pomegranate and vanilla scent, its metal and ash undertones as unpleasant as a bad aftertaste. "Either you will stand at my side, or you will kneel at my feet. Tell me you understand."

Macella felt herself trembling. The king's lips curled in a smirk, undoubtedly reading Macella's reaction as fear. King Khari liked that fear, she thrived on instilling it in others. She enjoyed seeing someone as strong and vibrant as Macella shaking with it while trapped in her viper's grip.

But she was so very wrong. It wasn't fear spreading like wildfire through Macella's veins.

It was rage.

"I understand perfectly, your grace. I look forward to our meeting here again tomorrow. We will show everyone how well your new bride understands her place."

Macella turned her back on King Khari and the throne and walked away.

⚜

(31) "I would thoroughly enjoy removing the hand she dared lay on you," Finley purred, staring thoughtfully at the ceiling as if envisioning the torment they'd inflict on the king. "I would start by severing each finger at the first joint, then the second and third. I think I'd make her eat the pieces before cutting the rest of her hand off at the wrist."

Zahra gave them an appreciative look. "You have an artist's soul, fancy fox. That was beautiful."

Macella laughed and shook her head. "We are not spending tonight talking about the king. We are having a quiet family evening."

"Are you sure you're thinking of the right family? Quiet is not really our style." Aisling plopped down on the rug with a fresh goblet of wine, her round cheeks already rosy. "Lucy left us far too much strong wine and good ale for a subdued evening."

"Okay, well we won't be quiet, but we will be cheerful, so no more talk of Khari," Macella insisted.

"Talking about dismembering her makes me very cheerful!" Finley argued, their hand sign for dismemberment performed with far more gusto than necessary.

Macella hit them with a pillow as she passed the chaise on her way to respond to a knock on the outer door. Zahra pounced on them before they could return the blow, and Macella left the sound of scuffling and laughter filling the room behind her.

She opened the door and had to crane her neck to look up at Valen and then had to dodge a wet kiss from Váli. The big Aegis shook her hand enthusiastically but refused her invitation to come in. Instead, he pressed something into her palm as he held her gaze with an uncharacteristically solemn expression.

"I will not keep you or intrude on such an auspicious night. I've only come because we spoke of you in the Aegis dining hall this evening, and the others tasked me with passing on our well wishes for the Blessed Rite. We will all be there with you, Lady Macella. Tomorrow, and to the end."

Then he was striding away, Váli padding along at his side. Macella looked down at her palm. In it lay a small wooden token that someone had painstakingly carved into the shape of a shield and engraved with a surprisingly intricate shape. A rose wrapped in flames.

Macella put the token in her pocket and returned to the parlor to find Finley and Jacan arguing over the details of yet another embarrassing story Finley had drudged up from their days training the young Aegis. Macella curled up beside Aithan on the sofa. He lifted an eyebrow questioningly, so she mentally filled him in on Valen's errand, lingering on the image of the burning rose. She could feel his surge of pride at the gesture, and it warmed her insides. She rested her head on his shoulder and turned her attention back to her noisy family.

"I'm sorry Finley is so cruel to you, Jacan!" Macella interrupted Finley's reenactment of a particularly amusing sparring session. "Would you feel better if I told you about the time Lotta peed her pants during worship?"

Lotta's mouth dropped open. "I was six years old!"

"You were nine," Macella countered, and Finley cackled with delight. "And I got in trouble for it, because I was supposed to have made you all go before the service began, but you wouldn't because Etienne told you the Grunch was hiding in the outhouse."

"Ella!" Lotta cried, covering her face with both hands while Aisling and Zahra laughed until they were blue in the face. "Let's hear more from Finley! I much prefer their Jacan stories."

"I think Jacan should get to tell his own stories," Jacan grumbled.

Lotta laughed and patted his cheek.

Macella saw him melt beneath her sister's touch, unable to maintain his grumpy expression. It made her heart sing. She was so grateful she'd been able to bring Lotta along on this journey. She was glad they'd had this time together. When Macella left Shively to strike out on her own, against everyone's advice, she'd thought she would never see her family again. It hadn't seemed like much of a loss, aside from Lotta, but she was happy she'd been able to build a new family that included her sister after all.

"If you keep picking on Jacan, I am going to start telling stories from my training days, when you were much younger and prone to unfortunate entanglements," Aithan warned.

"You wouldn't dare!" Finley exclaimed indignantly.

Aithan did dare, and over the next few hours, the Wildfire Court laughed themselves to tears. They progressed from embarrassing one another, to competing to share the most mortifying personal anecdotes they could muster, and then the funniest they could recall. By the hour of Soma, Macella's abdominal muscles ached, and she had a pleasant buzz from the wine and fellowship.

"We all need to rest. Jacan, will you stay with me tonight?" Lotta stood, yawning, and smiled at the young Aegis.

He lit up in response. "I will follow you anywhere, Lottie Bell," Jacan replied with his big, puppy dog grin.

They made their goodbyes, hugging everyone tightly before they left. Aisling and Lotta whispered together for an extra moment before Finley joined them and added something to their conversation that made them both dissolve into a fit of giggles. Then, Jacan took Lotta's hand, and the pair practically floated from the room, their friends all watching them go.

"Jacan is a lucky man," Aisling said. "And he deserves it too."

"He knows it well. Lotta will have a protector for life, no matter what path their relationship takes," Finley agreed. "I would like to spend tonight surrounded by such love as that."

Zahra poked them in their side and wiggled her eyebrows suggestively. "So, will you spend the night with your dashing young captain?"

To Macella's surprise, Finley shook their head and took Zahra's hand. "No, dearest. If Aithan and Macella can spare you, I'd like to spend tonight with you. And Aisling, if she and Nyx will indulge me. I think we should camp on your lanai and drink wine and tell all of our juiciest stories until we can no longer keep our eyes open."

Aisling's gray eyes sparkled as she gathered her skirts and climbed to her feet. "That sounds like the most fun ever. I think the Grand Mage will overlook me missing bed checks tonight."

"Yes!" Zahra agreed, grabbing a basket of bread from the table and tossing a few hunks of cheese and other vittles into it. "The lanai always makes me feel so at home. Kiss me good, Macella! We shall see one another again tomorrow, and then we will change the world!"

Macella kissed Zahra, then Aisling and Finley, before scooping Nyx up to plant a kiss on her head, which the cat tolerated with only mild annoyance. After more hugs and kisses all around, the rest of the Wildfire Court headed to Zahra's rooms for their sleepover, leaving Macella and Aithan alone. Her Aegis took her hand and led her to their bedchamber.

(32) They undressed and climbed into bed, Aithan pulling her against him immediately. Macella molded her body to his, burying her face in his chest and

breathing him in. His hands traced over her back and arms, across her hips and ass. They lay that way a long while, somewhere between arousal and exhaustion, enjoying each other's touch.

"Do you remember the first time you told me you loved me?" Macella asked, smiling against Aithan's chest as she recalled her less-than-enthusiastic reaction to his declaration. She'd been so afraid of attachments, and hadn't understood what true love was, or how it helped you fly rather than clipping your wings.

Aithan chuckled. "Do you suppose I have forgotten the first time I ever professed my love to another person? Mind you, this person had also just survived facing down a lamia twice, as well as being beaten and thrown in jail for her trouble."

"And you, like an absolute lunatic, looked at my swollen face, filthy clothes, and propensity for attracting trouble, and fell in love," Macella added.

"I started falling in love with you the minute you marched across that brothel with your chin up despite the taunts following you," Aithan corrected. "I was well into the middle of loving you by the time I told you about it. And I think I chose a much better time than you did for returning the sentiment."

Macella ran her hand through the soft, silver hair on his chest, sighing contentedly. "I didn't actually choose to tell you during the battle with Kiho. You just scared the hell out of me by almost dying, and all I could think about was how much I loved you, and you happened to overhear it."

"You were thinking very loudly right at me," Aithan protested, laughing when Macella smacked his chest playfully. "I could have died happy right then, but it was much better waking up to you and hearing the words from your lips."

Macella lifted her face and brushed her mouth against his. "I love you, Aithan of Auburndale."

Her Aegis smiled, his amber eyes crinkling at the corners in that way she loved so much because it meant she'd made him show genuine joy. That smile had appeared slowly at first, surprising her in their quiet moments between roaming the kingdom and fighting hellspawn. He'd been so used to solitude and ostracism that it hadn't come naturally, but she'd gradually gotten past his walls and found the deeply caring person beneath. Now, he was generous with his smiles, sharing them not just with her but with the rest of their family. Macella still cherished every single one.

"I love you, Macella of Shively," Aithan said, cupping her face in one of his big hands. "I will love you always and across every realm."

Macella kissed him again, before repeating a promise she intended to keep, no matter what happened during the Blessed Rite. "I am yours and you are mine, for all of this life and every other if the gods will it. And if they do not will it, I will still make it so."

They made love languidly, exploring each other's bodies with the comfort of familiarity and the awe inspired by knowing their time was fleeting. Afterward, Macella fell asleep in her husband's arms, secure in the knowledge that, no matter what came next, she would be okay. She had lived fully, loved deeply, and done her duty to the end.

The rest was up to Fate.

⋅⋅⋅⋅⋅⋅⋅⋅

Aithan

Aithan pulled the envelope from its hiding place in the back of a drawer in Macella's desk. The letter inside held words he hoped his wife would never have to read, but was glad to have prepared, nonetheless. He wanted her to have these written words to return to if ever he couldn't speak them himself.

Aithan closed his eyes and took a deep breath, then he crept silently back into their bedchamber. Macella slept soundly, tangled in the blankets as always.

Incredibly, nightmares had not troubled her this night. She slept as if it was not the eve of the most dangerous day of her life. After so many long seasons of dread and uncertainty, she seemed calmed by the knowledge that things were coming to a head at last.

Aithan slid back into bed beside her, carefully slipping the envelope beneath his pillow. If Macella returned to this bed without him, it wouldn't take long to find. As he pulled her into his arms and inhaled her exquisite scent, he knew that it did not matter whether he survived the day or if he awoke again in the Otherworlds. He'd already found his heaven.

CHAPTER TWENTY

Macella

Today, I face my Fate, and I know that I do not face it alone. I have you beside me and the family we've created standing behind me. I am completely filled with and surrounded by love, and it is all because of you, my Aegis. You gave me this family, this home, this life. Most importantly, you gave me your heart and protected mine in return.

I love you with all that I am, all that I have ever been, and all I will ever become. And if I am not back in your arms tonight, I will be waiting to embrace you when it is your time to leave the mortal realm. I love you, my Aithan, my protector, my husband, my Aegis. I love you always.

Forever yours,

Macella of Shively

Macella placed her note inside an envelope, her hands trembling slightly. She had promised to leave nothing unsaid, and she intended to keep that promise. Even if the Blessed Rite went terribly wrong today, she would make sure Aithan had a tangible profession of her love, something he could return to whenever he needed reminding of how truly amazing he was.

She carefully wrote his name on the envelope, before placing it in one of his drawers. Even as a few wayward tears rolled down her face, she smiled to herself. She'd chosen a cheeky hiding place, hoping it would bring a smile to his face as well. He'd find it when he next sought clean undergarments and be reminded of the silly, lustful woman he'd shared a few wonderful, fleeting years with. They'd been the best of her life and thinking of them being over so soon filled her chest with a pain so sharp it stole her breath.

She squeezed her eyes shut and forced her nerves to still, to be steel. She had followed Fate this far. She could not doubt her path now. The story of Macella of Shively and Aithan of Auburndale would not end here. The story of Kōsaten would not conclude with their defeat and the destruction of the realm.

Macella was the scribe of this story. It was time to finish it.

Macella waited at the Crown's private entrance to the throne room with her heart in her throat. Everything was in place. She was as prepared for this moment as she could possibly be. This was her Fate, her purpose, and her duty. She could do this.

She was also so anxious she thought she might faint.

Instead, she focused on taking deep, steadying breaths. She slid her hands into the hidden holsters of her jacket to touch her daggers. Their presence was familiar and comforting. She was grateful for the millionth time that Lynn made all of her clothes with weapon access in mind.

For today's ceremonies, the high tailor had combined the practical with the processional flawlessly, as usual. She'd styled Macella all in silver, crimson, and black to match her crown and throne. A fitted blouse, high-waisted pants, and boots were topped by the jacket Lotta had designed, its high collar, ornate buttons, and impressive train adding formality and flair to the look. The ensemble was elegant but easy to move in, which was crucial for the task before her.

Furthermore, it turned out that not just Lynn, but Aisling, had also helped Lotta with the design, and together they'd added an extra feature. Armed with Lotta's tireless research and some rare magical plants the people of Ellasburg had foraged, the young mage had done her most impressive spellwork yet. If all went to plan, Macella would never have to activate it, but it was reassuring to have, nonetheless.

"They're ready for you, my lady." The door opened and a servant bowed to her, touching his chest with his fist in a salute that was a bit premature, given she wasn't yet queen. As she passed through the doorway, she thought she heard the servant whisper something that sounded like a prayer on her behalf.

(33) This was it. Macella took one more deep breath before stepping into her Fate.

King Khari, Queen Annika, and Monarch Meztli stood at the center of the dais in front of their thrones. Grand Mage Kiama faced them, her back to the onlookers in the throne room. The Grand Vizier and Grand Treasurer stood below the dais, alongside Aithan and Captain Drudo. The Crown's entourages, including the Wildfire Court, formed a few neat rows at the front of the room, while the other Aegises and the Royal Guard lined the walls.

Macella knew that the great hall was already filling with guests, while the crowd outside in the bailey had been growing since early morning. After the rite, she'd be presented to the nobility, then she'd be paraded out on the wall-walk to smile down upon the commonfolk packed into the bailey. Or, at least, that was the official plan. In actuality, she didn't know if she'd ever leave this room.

The Chosen stood against the back wall of the dais. Macella felt their ominous presence as she passed, their arctic otherness brushing against her mind in an unsettling way. There was something indescribable about them, something so otherworldly it defied words. Though she'd seen them several times now, they remained more of an impression than actual beings. Tall and slender, completely cloaked in pristine white robes, and emitting a constant glow that was difficult to look at directly. Did they have faces beneath their hoods? Were their bodies corporeal? It was impossible to say, as the only parts of them anyone ever saw were their hands, which were long and slender and unnaturally smooth.

Their very presence was uncomfortable, especially to Aegises. Macella could sense the others shivering, reacting to the preternatural cold. Their discomfort would only intensify during the rite, when the Chosen revealed more of their uncanny light. They could completely debilitate the Aegises and blind the humans if they wished. Only Macella and Aithan could resist, their crossbreed natures providing a layer of protection.

The blasphemer must be stopped. Child of both worlds, you and the son of Lucifer must stop her. Only you can.

Macella moved down the steps to stand before the dais, facing the Crown. Monarch Meztli looked down at her with an inscrutable expression, while Queen Annika looked tired and bored. King Khari, however, looked every bit the Sovereign, decked out fully in garnet and gold and already glowing with power. Macella knew that the king often manipulated perception to make herself appear intimidating to those around her, but she thought that this display might be real. Khari had been blessed by the gods for a hundred years and had done all she could to hoard power during her reign. Yes, she shared that blessing with her spouses, but there was no reason to believe that she meted it out equally.

How powerful was the king, truly?

And, more importantly, was Macella strong enough to defeat her?

You're not alone, hell goddess, Aithan whispered in her mind. *Your family is behind you. We are stronger than any king.*

Macella straightened her shoulders and stood taller. She met King Khari's gaze, nodding her readiness to begin. The king looked at her coldly, though she sounded as besotted as ever when she leaned forward conspiratorially and murmured a saccharine welcome that Macella knew was for the benefit of the crowd. With her below the dais, the distance between them was too great for an intimate word.

Macella was glad. If the king had ventured too close, she'd have been tempted to bury a dagger in her chest before their plan could be properly enacted. Khari turned her attention back to her audience, turning her false charm on them instead.

"Today, Macella of Shively will undergo the Blessed Rite in preparation to become my queen," King Khari intoned solemnly. "I willingly share my Sovereign power with her, as I have with my beloveds, Queen Annika and Monarch Meztli. Let all present bear witness to the gods' divine blessing, which I generously bestow upon my spouses for the good of the kingdom. Grand Mage Kiama, you may begin."

"Let us begin by thanking the gods of light for their favor," the Grand Mage declared, before launching into a lengthy prayer.

Macella hardly heard a word of it. Her mind was reviewing the plan, scanning the room, counting guards, and measuring the distance between herself and the king. The gods of light would have to do without her prayers. She was here to serve a dark deity.

She had time to run through everything thrice before the invocation concluded. Reminding herself that she was being observed, she forced herself to watch the Grand Mage pour a large circle of earth on the dais around the Crown. Macella had to appear interested, must play her part until the end. It wouldn't do to raise suspicions this close to the critical moment.

The Grand Mage sprinkled water over the circle of earth, before anointing the foreheads of each monarch. When she descended the steps to anoint Macella, her eyes warned that things were about to intensify. Macella braced herself.

I'm right here. We all are. Aithan's voice in her mind held only calm certainty. *You can do this.*

"Lady Macella, King Khari of Kōsaten has chosen you to share her honorable burden as her wife and queen," Kiama proclaimed, stepping aside so that Macella could climb the steps of the dais. "We invite you into this sacred circle, that you may receive the gods' blessing."

Macella kept her head high and posture upright, though her heart seemed to be trying to escape her chest, and her instincts wanted her to get as far away from that circle of earth as possible. Her star charm, despite being practically made of ice these days, grew somehow colder, almost pulsating against her skin. She forced one foot in front of the other, focusing on the middle distance just above the king's head. She didn't dare meet those adder eyes again, for fear of betraying her true intentions.

Macella stepped into the circle.

Suddenly, the Chosen were there. One figure hovered behind the three monarchs, while the other two stood on opposite sides of the circle facing one another. Kiama returned to her place, now behind Macella, as the fourth point on the compass the Chosen created. The figures' cold glow intensified. Macella fought the urge to shiver.

An alabaster hand appeared from within the pristine white robes of the figure behind the Crown. It extended its long, marble fingers over the heads of the three monarchs, and they began to emit a cold light similar to that of the Chosen. Their hair and clothes lifted and rustled in an invisible breeze, or perhaps it was the world inverting. The air on the dais began to shimmer, thick with an electric buzzing on a frequency just outside the range of human hearing. Macella's curls felt alive on her head and her teeth ached. The hair on her arms and the back of her neck stood on end.

An amber hand emerged from the robes of another of the willowy figures. This time, those strange fingers reached toward Macella, and she knew this was the moment she'd been dreading. The Chosen would touch her with their light, preparing to bestow a fraction of the king's Sovereign power. And they would recognize her for what she was.

The third figure extended a hand that looked hewn from onyx stone. A frigid breeze swirled around Macella, raising gooseflesh on her arms. She glanced at the

Grand Mage, hoping for a sign. If they didn't act soon, her secret would be out and, worse, she'd find out the hard way if she could withstand the full focus of the Chosen's icy power.

Grand Mage Kiama was watching the alabaster figure and the light still growing brighter around the king and her spouses. Even so, she must've sensed Macella's attention, because she shook her head ever so slightly. Macella clenched her teeth against the cold.

The frigid white light emanating from the Chosen grew starker still, bathing the dais in their cold glow. Macella could sense the other Aegises reacting to it as it illuminated the rest of the throne room—teeth chattering and bodies shaking as the hellfire within them pushed against the dampening effects of the white light. Her own hellfire fought toward the surface as the two Chosen seemed to lean nearer to her. Their inhuman hands reached closer, and the glacial touch of their magic burned against her own. Then they spoke in unison, their eerie voices a harsh, echoing hiss.

"Abomination."

It was as if that word released the torrent she'd been holding back. Power surged through Macella's veins, and her eyes shifted into their hellform. Rebellious onyx flames burst from her skin.

And then all hell broke loose.

(34) The Chosen recoiled as if they'd been burned, drawing together like limbs on a single organism. They reminded her of a giant spider curling in on itself. Their sinister hissing continued, reverberating around the throne room as if coming from everywhere at once. They glided as one toward the glowing monarchs, and Macella knew that she was almost out of time. They would redistribute the Sovereign power, rendering Khari unstoppable. In another moment, this opportunity would slip through her grasp, and all her careful plans would fail.

Macella felt the shifting of her train, Aisling's spell activated by her hellfire. Swiftly, she detached the train from the jacket, finding it no longer fabric, but something solid and heavy. She slipped an arm through the straps and lifted her train-turned-shield toward the Chosen. Her daggers were ready, but she didn't reach for them. She only had one shot, and it had to count. She needed her sword.

Just as the Chosen reached their marble hands toward the monarchs, the Grand Mage made her move. A glass bead appeared in her palm, then shot into the air above them, where it began to expand, absorbing the monarchy's light. The Grand Mage lifted her hand and the orb returned to her palm, still growing steadily larger and brighter. Kiama's gray eyes went completely white, her skin taking on a silvery glow. She turned her sightless gaze toward Macella and spoke a single word in a voice thrumming with raw power.

"Now."

All around them, soldiers were drawing their swords and closing the visors of their helmets to shield their eyes from the Chosen's light. A chorus of voices shouted conflicting orders as onlookers ran for cover. The Grand Vizier and Grand Treasurer took refuge among those from the Crown's entourages who didn't manage to flee, huddling behind clusters of soldiers in the corners of the room.

Just as they'd planned, the Wildfire Court sprang into action, retrieving weapons they'd hidden in the secret passages, arming themselves and the other Aegises. Charlotte and Aisling herded civilians toward safety, Aisling keeping a protection spell around them both as they worked. Zahra moved through the fray swiftly, tossing Macella her sword in a fluid movement as she passed.

Macella caught it easily, her hellfire expanding to encompass the blade. The Chosen surged toward her with their blinding light, but Aithan was there, driving them back, his body and sword ablaze with crimson flames. His attack seemed to weaken the Chosen's effect on the other Aegises, who charged into the battle, holding off the Royal Guard.

Defending the warrior queen so that she could do her duty.

The Grand Mage followed Aithan as he pushed the Chosen back, keeping herself between them and Macella. Even as she moved with the battle, Kiama shook with the effort of trapping the Sovereign power within the orb, which was now the size of a scrying glass. It sparked and crackled in her upturned palm, the electricity reflecting uncannily in her white eyes. She extended her free hand toward Macella, enveloping her in a warm glow that chased away the Chosen's cold light. Even as it continued to visibly chill the other Aegises, their power could no longer touch Macella.

Macella ignored the tumult surrounding them, her eyes locked on King Khari. Monarch Meztli and Queen Annika retreated from the chaos, leaving Macella and the king alone in the circle of the spell. Macella exhaled, her grip tightening on her sword hilt. She could feel its inlaid obsidian jewels digging into her palm. She let the sensation ground her.

She only had this moment of vulnerability, this one chance to strike the king at her weakest. The icy light around them threatened to blind her, but Macella knew her aim was true. She lunged forward, burying her sword in the king's belly.

For a moment, time seemed to slow completely. Khari's face froze, contorted in pain and surprise. Macella pushed the sword deeper, her hands slick with sweat and blood. So much blood. So much blood she could practically taste it on her tongue.

So much blood she could *almost* smell it.

King Khari's face melted into a grin before she disappeared, leaving Macella alone in the circle of earth.

Thankfully, Macella's sword was buried in Khari's throne, and not some unfortunate person who'd wandered too close. She yanked it free, leaving a blackened hole in the ornate iron, then frantically scanned the room for the real king.

Monarch Meztli and Queen Annika huddled in a corner, behind a protective circle of guards. Macella knew they were in no danger, at least not from her and her allies. Their focus was on Khari and those who stood between her and the tip of a blade. They would do their best to minimize harm to the knights doing their duty to the Crown. Macella wasn't sure if the Chosen could even be hurt, but her friends would still try not to do so if they could help it. Their new world would not be built on bones and blood.

Despite their good intentions, her friends were still very much fighting for their lives. Zahra circled the perimeter, alternating between sending well-aimed arrows to distract the Chosen from their battle with Aithan and the Grand Mage, and leveling non-lethal shots at the guards. Finley moved through the crowd as if they were dancing, fluidly disarming one knight before sweeping another off his feet with their spear, then pivoting gracefully to block another's path to Aisling and Charlotte, who stood off to one side, the former casting a shielding spell while the latter called out orders and warnings to the fighters.

The other Aegises fought alongside them, instinctively protecting the Wildfire Court and following their command. Macella breathed a sigh of relief. She'd believed the Aegises would come to her aid today, but there had been no way of knowing for sure how they'd react when dropped in the middle of a coup. It was most likely Khari herself who'd secured Macella the Aegises' allegiance. When the king callously executed three of their kin, she'd made enemies of them all.

Valen wielded a pair of axes as gigantic as he was, but was impressively managing not to murder anyone, obviously following her family's lead. Váli was a humongous streak of white and gray at the big Aegis's side. As Macella watched, the wolf caught the arm of a knight who'd been about to attack Cressida. He shook his massive head, disarming the knight before flinging them aside like a rag doll. Then, at a whistle from Valen, Váli darted across the floor to knock the legs out from beneath a trio of soldiers who'd managed to corner Jacan. Finley appeared and kicked away one of the fallen soldiers' swords, then fell gracefully into a lunge, parrying and knocking the second soldier's sword from his grip. Jacan disarmed the third soldier before whirling away to another opponent.

It all happened so fast.

Macella caught a glimpse of gold, and then she spotted Khari cutting through the crowd. Even at this distance, the king's eyes were cold and flat, trained on her target. Macella followed Khari's predatory gaze, and her blood turned to ice.

Finley and Drudo faced off near the rear of the room, sword crossed against spear, their gazes locked. Even from this distance, it was clear that the captain of the Royal Guard was reluctant to do his duty to the Crown, and Finley was obviously loathe to do Drudo any harm. Neither noticed the approaching king. They only had eyes for one another.

Finally, Finley drew back, lowering their spear. Drudo hesitated, then turned to look toward the dais. He saw Macella watching, but before she could signal to him, he'd saluted her and turned back to Finley. The captain of the Royal Guard sheathed his sword and bowed, saying something to Finley that was lost in the chaos. And still, King Khari prowled toward them.

Macella was running before she'd realized it, throwing herself into the fray and carving a path toward her friends. Without the high ground of the dais, she couldn't see Finley and Drudo through the throng of bodies. She pushed forward anyway, fear coiling around her lungs and threatening to steal her breath. Macella forced herself to inhale, narrowly avoiding the slashes and thrusts of weapons as she barreled ahead.

Sir Griselda stepped into her path, a regretful expression on her face, even as she lifted her sword. Macella reluctantly raised her own. She liked the knight a great deal, but she couldn't let anyone stand between her and Finley. She shifted her weight, considering the best method of incapacitating the big woman without causing any true damage.

Suddenly, a gigantic mountain of white and gray fur collided with Sir Griselda, knocking her to the ground. Just as suddenly, Nyx materialized and rubbed against Macella's leg, before trotting off between the fighters. Váli woofed and bounded forward, following the cat, and clearing a path that happened to lead in the direction Macella was headed. Her heart hammered in her chest as she wove through the battle, occasionally blocking attacks or offering aid, but always following closely in the wolf's wake.

Macella would reach Finley before Khari did.

She would.

She must.

She did not.

CHAPTER TWENTY-ONE

Macella

She found Finley on the ground, Drudo kneeling next to them, his blood-soaked hands pressed against their side (35). Váli whined, sniffing Finley's face and pawing at the ground near their head. The king was gone, no doubt off to hurt someone else Macella loved. She couldn't think about that just yet. Not when Finley's fair skin was alarmingly pale and the fabric beneath Drudo's hands was growing damper and darker each moment.

"Finley!" she screamed, crouching beside Drudo and pressing her hand to Finley's forehead. She found it clammy and cold. "You're going to be fine. Keep your eyes open! We'll find a healer."

Finley smirked. They opened their mouth, obviously to say something sarcastic, but coughed a spray of blood instead. Macella's heart sank.

"Move!" she commanded, shoving Drudo's hands out of the way and pressing her own to the wound. It was warm and sticky and far, far too wet. "Keep them awake, Captain."

Macella didn't look away from the wound as she spoke. She concentrated on it, calling to the shadows slumbering beneath her skin. Waking them was different from conjuring her hellfire. Summoning her hellfire felt natural, whereas calling the shadows was like drawing from a deep, nearly empty well. They were not a part of her, just a temporary gift from Hades to help in this grand task he'd charged her with. And they came with a cost.

Macella didn't care. She ignored the nausea that washed over her as the shadows danced along her arms and over her hands. Slowly, they seeped into the wound, draining the warmth from Macella's body with them. She shivered, barely aware of Drudo's panicked voice begging Finley to keep their eyes open. Váli pressed himself against her side, his body warm and comforting.

Macella swallowed against bile, applying more pressure to the wound and reaching deeper into that fathomless well. It had gotten so very low, the metaphorical bucket scraping against rocky earth. Váli whined again, lying down and curling his big body around her. Macella gritted her teeth against the cold permeating her muscles.

More shadows ghosted over her skin and sank slowly into Finley's wound. She wasn't sure if it was wishful thinking, but the bleeding seemed to be slowing. Her own blood felt sluggish, as if the cold spreading through her body had clogged her veins. The nausea threatened to overwhelm her, but she pushed through it, thinking only of Finley.

Finley, who loved beautiful things but didn't turn away from ugliness. Finley, who was fearless in the face of danger, but secretly vulnerable beneath the allure and swagger. Finley, who had spent so much of their life caged but still singing, and who had finally begun to live fully and freely.

Finley, who'd shown her kindness from their very first meeting, though they'd been on opposite sides of a heated battle. Finley, who'd written her letters every week for two seasons, until they moved to the castle to join her entourage. Finley, who'd become her closest sibling and best friend.

She had to save them.

Shivers racked her frame, and still she pressed on, willing the wound to close, the bleeding to stop, the world to stop spinning if it had to. The shadows grew fainter, and her stomach roiled, but she pressed on. Still whining pitifully, Váli shoved his head under her arm, as if trying to cover her with his body. Macella leaned against him gratefully, appreciating the warmth and needing the support. She was starting to feel a little lightheaded.

I'm fine, dearest. Stop fretting over me and go finish this.

Macella's head snapped up, the fog and cold lifting when she saw Finley smirking at her, their eyes alert and their skin a healthier pallor. Macella threw her arms around them, drawing back quickly when they winced in pain.

"Get them to a healer," Macella ordered Drudo as she pulled away.

"I'm not leaving you," Finley snarled, gripping her hand tightly, their orange eyes blazing briefly emerald. "Not until this is done. Not ever."

Macella swallowed hard, eyes stinging with unshed tears. Some of the warmth returned to her body as her heart clenched. She cupped Finley's cheek in one hand, leaving behind a bloody streak when she pulled away and climbed to her feet.

"Fine," she relented. She turned back to Drudo. "But don't leave their side."

"Not until this is done." Drudo didn't look away from Finley as he replied. "Not ever."

He was still cradling their head as he'd been doing since Macella had taken charge of their wound. Finley's eyes were suspiciously shiny as they looked from Macella to the handsome captain. Drudo bent and pressed a heartbreakingly gentle kiss to their forehead.

Macella left them to it. She felt as if she might burst into shreds. How could the human body hold so much emotion at one time? The relief and joy and sheer love coursing through her should've been enough to overflow her, and yet there was room for so much more. There was fear, and plenty of it, crawling into all the cracks and crevices, insidiously worming into every corner of her mind. And there was exhaustion—a bone deep fatigue that had sank into the very core of her soul. There shouldn't have been room for anything else.

But there was more. So much more.

There was rage. There was so much rage that it chased the chill from her limbs, melting the ice the healing shadows had left behind. There was enough rage to consume her, enough rage to consume them all.

Nyx appeared, weaving through Macella's legs and slowing her progress across the floor. She huffed impatiently, but the cat didn't seem to care, staying in her path and forcing her to stop. Satisfied, Nyx ran off, disappearing into the fray.

Macella scanned the crowd, trying to force the lingering dizziness away. The shadows had taken a lot out of her, but she didn't have time to faint right now. She needed to find Khari. She needed to channel her rage and set fire to this tyrannical empire. It was time to burn this world down, so that a better one could rise.

It was time for the king to die.

"Lady Macella, wait!" Aisling's voice drew Macella up short. The mage moved toward her, flanked by Charlotte and Nyx, and still maintaining the protective shield around them. "Come here!"

Macella fought her way toward them through a battle that had grown thicker while she healed Finley's wounds. There were far more soldiers present than before. The king must have summoned reinforcements. She vaguely registered the roar of a large crowd—perhaps another battle?—somewhere far off, but it was hard to distinguish over the clang of metal and cries of the wounded.

"You've drained yourself," Aisling yelled over the clamor, her brow furrowed in concern. "You'll be no match for the king in this state. Eat this."

Macella obediently took the handful of herbs Aisling pulled from one of her many pockets and shoved them into her mouth. While she chewed the bitter mixture, Aisling murmured a spell that wrapped Macella in warm white smoke. Her head cleared and her stomach settled. The chill left her limbs, giving way to simmering hellfire.

(36) And rage. So. Much. Rage.

"Go! Find her and finish her." Charlotte threw her arms around Macella, pulling her into Aisling's warm bubble of protection. The embrace was just as warm, but her sister's voice was uncharacteristically cold when she spoke again. "Tear her fucking throat out for what she did to Finley."

Aisling nodded sharply in agreement, her pale face full of a fierceness that matched Lotta's words. Macella nodded once, her hellfire flaring as she set off on the hunt.

The throne room was a landscape of chaos.

On the dais, Queen Annika and Monarch Meztli still sheltered behind a wall of soldiers while Aithan and the Grand Mage focused on keeping the Chosen contained. Aithan evaded blasts of white light while driving the huge figures back with targeted slashes of his blazing sword. Though the Chosen were able to move short distances in a blink, they recoiled from the heat of hellfire. The Wildfire Court had been right in their assumption that the celestial beings were accustomed to their power neutralizing that of the Aegises. They had no defenses against undiluted hellfire. It might not be able to destroy them, but it could deter them.

The Grand Mage was using that weakness to full advantage. Macella watched as one of the Chosen attempted to peel off from the trio while its partners occupied Aithan by attacking from both sides. Kiama, still balancing the glowing orb of Sovereign power in one palm, extended her free hand toward Aithan. A streak of crimson flame sliced through the air between them, gathering in a swirling vortex around the Grand Mage's outstretched hand, before she flung it toward the escaping figure.

An inhuman shriek tore through the throne room, so piercing that it cut through the din of battle, drawing the attention of everyone in the room. Many fell to the floor, covering their ears against the shrill echoes. The Aegises fared better than the knights, keeping their feet and using the distraction to disarm and incapacitate the opponents around them. Macella saw more than one soldier wiping trails of blood from their ears as their weapons were knocked away.

The Chosen jerked backward in unison, as though they'd all been struck. They drew together once more, a wounded spider, colliding with the back wall with enough force to crack the stone. They were up again in a flash, but Aithan and Kiama were ready, facing the Chosen from opposite sides of the dais, a wall of crimson hellfire blazing between them, suspended between Aithan's sword and the Grand Mage's outstretched hand.

I don't know how long I can hold both the Chosen and the orb. The voice in Macella's mind was both familiar and strange. The Grand Mage had never spoken to her this way, and it felt foreign. Her mind was not like the Aegis minds Macella had grown used to, nor was it like the corrupted snippets of thought she'd glimpsed from Khari. *Find the king. Finish it quickly. The Sovereign power seeks her. You must stop her before she can reclaim it.*

Macella pulled her gaze away from the spectacle on the dais to scan the room once more. The Chosen's interruption had provided enough of a diversion to clear the floor a bit, and the battle had once more shifted in her favor, with most of the Royal Guard forced into surrender. Macella caught a glimpse of garnet and gold across the room, moving toward the front. She charged toward it, weaving between the recovering soldiers and conquering Aegises, intent on reaching the king before she could get near the Grand Mage and that glowing orb of power.

Another flash of garnet and gold to her right. Macella pivoted, spotting the king's blond head making a circuitous path around toward the back of the throne room. Macella stalked after her, narrowly dodging an axe blow, and leaping over the knight who took the brunt of the attack instead. She resisted the urge to check on the injured, unwilling to let her quarry out of her sight.

A garnet and gold shape slipped through the crowd to her left, streaking through the fighters toward the throne room's massive doors. Macella drew up short, pivoting again to follow her. Was the king trying to escape? To gather more reinforcements?

Macella! Here!

Macella spun toward her husband, only to see the king nearing the dais. How had she gotten there? Macella had been right behind her only a moment ago, about to thwart her escape. When Macella looked back at the exit, the king was nowhere to be found as the doors burst open for a fresh regiment of soldiers. The Aegises around the room took in the reinforcements with grim expressions, lifting their weapons and shifting into fighting stances once more. Aithan and

Grand Mage Kiama looked equally grim, their faces lined with the effort of holding the Chosen at bay, the wall of crimson flames between them flickering dangerously low.

The king before the dais laughed, her voice carrying across the throne room. She pointed an imperious finger at the new regiment, then at her weary opponents around the room. Finally, her ochre eyes landed on Macella.

"Kill them all," King Khari commanded. "But leave my bride to me."

The soldiers surged into the room. There were dozens of them. More than Macella's allies could manage for long. She ran for the dais, knowing that she must stop the king and end the battle before it was too late to keep her friends alive. King Khari grinned, beckoning her forward.

But just when the clash of soldiers and Aegises should've resumed behind her, there was a new commotion. That distant roaring that Macella had forgotten rose to a fever pitch.

The door behind the dais banged open, as did the servants' entrances and secret panels. Bodies flooded into the crowded space. Macella wouldn't have believed the day had many more surprises left, but her mouth fell open when she saw who'd arrived.

Lynn and her apprentices. Castle staff and people from Ellasburg. Brontë and her workers. Some armed with steel and others with whatever they could find, from garden tools to rolling pins. Commonfolk surrounded the soldiers, putting themselves in front of the Aegises and the Wildfire Court. Standing behind their warrior queen.

They looked at her with loyalty and hope and steadfast determination. Despite seeing her skin glowing with onyx flames, they showed no fear. Perhaps it was fitting that she was aflame, because her followers were as well. Flames flickered in their lapels, in the patterns of their skirts and pocket handkerchiefs, on their belts and boots. Macella had the fleeting thought that Finley had predicted this long ago.

"The thing about wildfire is, it is not easily contained or controlled. It spreads," they'd said. *"It's time Khari learned the consequences of playing with fire. Let's burn her empire to the fucking ground."*

The civilians pushed the soldiers back with the force of sheer numbers, pressing them toward the walls and thereby clearing a path down the center of the room to the dais and leaving nothing between Macella and the king but space and opportunity.

The knights looked between Macella and Khari uncertainly, weapons raised before them. Macella's followers awaited her command, ready to fight for her if she asked. They might not all be soldiers, but they had warriors' hearts.

(37) Macella grinned fiercely, looking from her people to the shocked king standing on the bottom step of the dais. It was indeed time to teach Khari the consequences of her actions. It was time for Macella to be who she was born to be. There would be no more hiding, no more pretending. Her secrets were out, and she was standing before them all as her true self. Now, she must walk in that truth.

Macella was their warrior queen. She was Aithan's hell goddess. She was the spark of revolution, carrying an everflame of rebellion within her that had been fed by so many others who'd paved the path to this moment. Macella was their champion, their avenging angel, their reckoning. She was an ember of the Wildfire Court, a family that grew larger and stronger each day.

Macella of Shively was the crossbreed daughter of a Hades-blessed Aegis and an ordinary human poet. She was an impossible child born of unbearable pain, destined to stand against the fury of hell at the end of the world. She had come into this realm already imbued with unknown power and carrying prophetic truth.

The stars had aligned, bringing her here, to this moment, with these people beside and behind her. She'd fought for peace among warmongers and maintained hope among the hopeless. Her Fate was never meant to be safe, but neither had it been meant to end in defeat. Macella had been baptized in blood and forged in flame.

It was time to burn.

Macella raised her sword and began to stalk toward the dais, black eyes fixed on the king. Some of the knights tried to move toward her, but her people met them with steel and determination.

The king's face darkened as she took in the scene. "Kill them all!" King Khari screamed, spittle flying, her pretty face contorted and monstrous with wrath. "Soldier or civilian, I don't care! Slaughter every last person standing with that traitorous crossbreed whore!"

"Stand down!" Queen Annika's voice was hard, lacking any trace of its customary false syrupy sweetness. She sounded like the woman Macella had only met a few months ago—the one who swore her child would never be a pawn. She pushed her way free of the soldiers protecting her and stood in front of her throne. "Sheathe your weapons and stand down, now!"

"*What?*" Khari hissed, her head whipping toward her young queen. Her expression shifted when she saw Annika staring at her coldly. The king smiled thinly. "My love, I know you must be terribly upset, but don't let these traitors take advantage of your soft heart."

Queen Annika laughed, the tinkling sound of it at odds with the resoluteness in her cobalt eyes. She dropped her voice, her words laced with venom. "Why? Because that's *your* job, *my love*?"

King Khari cocked her head as Queen Annika descended the dais, lessening, but not completely closing the distance between them. Macella could practically see the wheels turning in the king's mind. Calculating the risks and rewards of her possible responses.

"You're no good, Khari," the young queen said sadly, but firmly. "You're no good for Kōsaten, you're no good for me, and you're no good for my baby."

King Khari huffed out a laugh. "Is that what this is about? Darling, that's the pregnancy hormones talking. We'll discuss it later. Guards! Seize them!"

"Stand down!" Queen Annika ordered again. "We will not discuss this later. There is no later for you, Khari."

"You and you! Escort my wife to her chambers. She is unwell and obviously in need of rest," King Khari barked at a pair of nearby knights. "The rest of you, subdue the traitors for execution. I may share my throne, but I am the Sovereign, and my commands supersede all others."

The knights looked to Captain Drudo, who stood with Finley in the center of the fray, as they moved to follow the king's commands. Before the knights could go far, however, Monarch Meztli glided down the first few steps of the dais to stand beside Annika. The black of their pupils and irises faded until their eyes were completely white.

"Stand down," they said with quiet command.

Macella could feel the tension in the air lifting. All around them, the Royal Guard relaxed, lowering their weapons, and retreating a few steps.

King Khari's face darkened, rage etched into every feature. Her murderous gaze traveled slowly over her spouses. The temperature in the room dropped several degrees.

"Even you, Meztli?" she said finally, her voice low and icy.

"Especially me, Khari," Monarch Meztli replied coldly, lifting their chin.

King Khari took a deep breath, closing her eyes. A moment later, she nodded. The rage on her face melted away. She loosened her shoulders and stood taller. When she opened her eyes again, they were completely empty—soulless, emotionless voids. And when the king spoke, her words were just as vacant as her eyes.

"So be it," King Khari said.

And everything went black.

Chapter Twenty-Two

Aithan

Macella and Khari disappeared.

The minds around him reflected nothing but total darkness. Humans, mages, and Aegises alike had all been plunged into black nothingness. Aithan could see them, sightless eyes frantically scanning the room, bewildered and on edge. Some folks seemed primed to bolt and others ready to fight. He needed to intervene before panic began to spread.

"Hold steady!" Aithan roared, his tone that of the high commander, brooking no argument. "Make no move and none will be harmed. Your sight will return when your rightful Sovereign emerges from this conflict. Hold your places until Fate decides our course."

Perhaps they trusted him, or maybe they were tired, or they were just relieved to have someone tell them what to do in a terrifying moment, but they listened. Everyone lowered their weapons and settled into more relaxed postures. Aithan was glad for the easy victory, because he had very little mental capacity to spend on the people around him. He knew they were afraid, robbed of sight by Khari at such a pivotal moment, but he could do nothing more for them.

Because Aithan was well past being afraid. He was absolutely petrified. His vision was perfectly intact, the throne room just as clear as it'd been throughout the battle. He could see the people huddled against the walls, the fighters holding their positions, the two remaining monarchs standing near their thrones, and the Chosen shrinking from the barrier of hellfire he and the Grand Mage wielded. Aithan's mage-Aegis crossbreed blood and determined practice made it simple for him to see through this latest of Khari's illusions. He could see everything.

Except for his wife.

Macella and the king were gone, vanished into thin air.

"*We will wait for Fate to decide the Sovereign,*" the ghostly voices of the Chosen hissed, echoing eerily from every direction at once. "*We will await the will of the gods.*"

They were gone in a blinding flash of light, leaving Aithan alone on the dais with an empty-handed Grand Mage and two somber monarchs. Meztli and Annika seemed at least somewhat accustomed to Khari's antics. Rather than panic at the loss of sight, they carefully found each other's hands. The middle monarch gingerly felt around for the thrones behind them, then helped the young queen to sit on hers, before perching on its arm at her side.

Without the orb, the silvery glow faded from Kiama's skin, but her sightless white eyes still held an electric power. She surveyed the room, her brow furrowed, and full mouth pressed into a tight line. Aithan let his hellfire die, following her gaze back to the space where Macella should have been.

"Can you see her?" he asked, knowing the answer even as he wished for it to be different. "Can you help her?"

"No," Kiama replied. "This is more than one of Khari's typical illusions. They are somewhere just beyond our realm, and we cannot follow. It is in Lady Macella's hands now. We can only wait. And pray."

Aithan clenched his fists, glaring at the empty path through the center of the room. Usually, he was unerringly patient. But this was far from usual, and he was going to do more than wait and pray.

He was going to find his fucking wife.

"That is odd," the Grand Mage said, almost to herself, before he could move. "Perhaps she is nearer than we think."

Aithan opened his mouth to reply but was cut off by a clatter. He leapt in front of the Grand Mage, his sword at the ready. Before he'd completed the movement, he'd recognized the source of the sound and was already shifting toward it.

Macella's sword scraped across the floor, sliding into existence from thin air. One moment, the floor was empty, and the next, his wife's sword was skidding to a stop before the dais.

Aithan's throat felt tight, his heart racing. Where was Macella? What was happening to her? He'd promised to protect her, to stand at her side until the end, to die for her if he must. He could not break that promise.

"Breathe, Lord Protector," the Grand Mage commanded, placing a hand on his forearm. "The warrior queen needs you now. She needs to know she is not alone, no matter how dark it might seem. Find her. Find her and guide her back."

Aithan closed his eyes, breathing deeply, searching for cinnamon and citrus and sweet burning acacia, for streams and crackling fires and evening breezes. He listened for the voice that spoke in all of his best dreams and favorite memories. He reached out with his mind, searching for the thoughts that felt like home.

⚜

Macella

(38) The darkness was so total that it seemed she was alone in a depthless void. Macella held her sword before her, straining to hear the noise of the throne room, to hear anything at all beyond the oppressive silence of the darkness. She knew that she must still be surrounded by others, but she may as well have been buried deep in the bowels of the keep. She was completely alone.

Completely alone with King Khari.

"You are such a disappointment, Lady Macella."

She spun toward the sound, sword lifted, but there was still only blackness. Endless, empty blackness. She could feel the king's presence though, could feel her watching, waiting, prowling. The weight of Khari's gaze was like hundreds of tiny legs crawling over her skin—centipedes and spiders and thousands more insects swarming her skin, vomited from the mouth of the jorōgumo.

Macella bared her teeth, furious that the memory still haunted her. She hated that Khari could make her feel weak and vulnerable. Yet, as terrible as it'd been to be trapped in the king's visions, it was nothing compared to how helpless she'd felt when Khari hurt Finley. That was a helplessness Macella refused to ever feel again.

"I would say the feeling is mutual, Khari," she spat at the darkness. "But that would imply that I have even a modicum of respect for you, which I don't. The only time you've ever disappointed me was in the moment I realized you weren't impaled on my blade."

A flash of blinding pain stole her breath as something hard struck the back of her head. Macella stumbled but kept her feet, ignoring the wet trickle of blood on her neck. She whirled around, scanning the boundless blackness for her attacker.

"You ungrateful sow. After all I've done—lifting you from obscurity, lavishing you with gifts, elevating you and your mongrel whore to an honored position in my court. I offered to make you a queen, you wretched sack of gutter piss. You were going to stand beside the greatest king in Kōsaten's history, were going to be the muse of bards for centuries to come. You could've borne my children and become mother of a long line of kings."

Macella's skin grew hotter, her hellfire blazing brighter. "I was never going to be your queen. I would rather drink actual gutter piss. You disgust me."

Another blow, this time across her back, so hard that Macella felt something crack. She hissed in pain, whirling again to search for her assailant. The empty darkness mocked her.

"I have shared my power long enough, selflessly sacrificing of myself to unite the kingdom, and yet my spouses compete to betray me. I give and I give and am repaid with treachery on every side. Well, I have learned my lesson well.

Henceforth, I will rule alone, and with a fist of iron. I will make an example of you, warrior queen. The bards will sing of you still. They will sing of your folly and of the severity of your punishment. It will be epic. You will teach the realms what suffering is."

"The scribes will write of your folly in believing yourself worthy of the throne," Macella retorted. "Enough talk. Come out and speak with steel."

Khari's laughter boomed, seeming to come from everywhere at once. It was far too loud, and Macella had to resist the childish urge to plug her ears. Instead, she kept her sword raised, rotating slowly, eyes still searching for any sign of her adversary.

"Before you die, you will beg for my mercy. I will teach you the meaning of regret."

"I already know regret. I regret not killing you sooner," Macella sneered.

This time, the strike targeted her calves, forcing Macella to her knees. Before she could recover, a weight fell upon her shoulders, as if a dozen hands were pressing her down, holding her in place. She couldn't move as her sword was knocked from her hands. She never heard it hit the ground. It simply evaporated into the darkness.

"You could've had everything and now you will have nothing. I will destroy everything you love."

Suddenly, Lotta was there in the void, her face full of concern. She started toward Macella but halted abruptly when the king appeared in her path, catching her by the throat. Khari forced Macella's sister to her knees, wrapping both hands around her neck. Lotta clawed at the king's arms uselessly, her eyes bulging and face going purple as Khari squeezed harder and harder.

It wasn't real. There wasn't a hint of cinnamon or cherry blossoms in the air. There was only the smell of her own fear and Khari's stench of metal and death. Lotta wasn't there.

It wasn't real. Macella knew it wasn't real. And yet her heart raced, and her blood froze in her veins.

She knew it wasn't real this time, but it might be next time. Because if Macella didn't stop Khari here and now, her sister would die, alongside everyone else Macella cared about.

Charlotte's resistance grew weaker and weaker until she finally went limp in the king's grip. Khari let her fall to the floor, wiping her hands on her trousers as she stared down at the lifeless body disinterestedly. Charlotte's head was cocked at an odd angle, her wide, unfocused eyes gazing at Macella from behind cracked spectacles.

"Quiet already?" Khari taunted. "And here I was enjoying all of your brave little speeches."

"Fuck you," Macella spat, struggling against the pressure bearing down on her shoulders. It didn't do any good.

Khari laughed cruelly. "I'm afraid it's too late for bargaining now, pet. You missed your opportunity, which really is a pity. Imagine the sights I could've shown you, the sensations I could've lavished upon you. I hope your vicereine was a decent substitute."

Zahra appeared, only for the king to slit her throat with a hunting knife and toss her body on top of Charlotte's. Macella gritted her teeth against the urge to cry out, forcing herself to focus on the telltale lack of lavender and honeysuckle in the air.

Khari watched her reaction with a wicked gleam in her ochre eyes. She nudged Zahra's head with her foot, making sure Macella could see the sheriff's beautiful, lifeless face.

A screech cut through the air and a black owl whizzed past Macella's head, flying so close that its talons snagged in her curls, yanking a hunk of hair free. Tears of pain pricked at her eyes, but she refused to let them fall, even when the bird landed on Zahra's chest and began to peck at her mismatched eyes. Macella swallowed bile when it managed to pluck Zahra's green eye from the socket.

"This isn't real," Macella ground out through clenched teeth. "This is just an illusion."

Khari smiled and swaggered closer to Macella, purposely stepping on the dark hair fanning out around Zahra's head as she did so. She stopped just beyond arm's reach and crouched low so that she could look into Macella's face. The king's eyes were every bit as cold and dead as the illusions on the ground.

"It isn't real," she said, smiling her cruel smile. "Not yet, at least. But will you still feel that way after watching them die for hours?"

Aisling appeared on a platform to their left, a noose around her pale throat. Her arms were bound behind her, so that she could only kick her feet uselessly when a trap door opened and she dropped with a sickening crack. The broken neck didn't kill her immediately. Macella had to listen for several excruciating minutes as she choked and gasped and her face darkened from red to purple to nearly black. Her glossy red hair fell over her face but didn't obscure her bulging gray eyes, staring accusingly at Macella.

"How about after a few days?"

The darkness to her right became a dank, windowless cell. Inside, Finley wasted away in chains, their skin sallow and cheeks sunken. Their cracked, bleeding lips moved silently, but Macella could still hear their pleas for help echoing in her ears.

"Will it still feel fake in a few weeks?"

Jacan covered in bruises, face puffy and unrecognizable. With his lips swollen and fingers severed, he couldn't beg for help, but Macella could still hear his pained whimpers.

"After ten months?"

Meztli. Drudo. Lynn. Lucy. Burning. Beaten. Tortured. Murdered. Their bodies piling up in the blackness around her. Their cries for mercy ringing through the void. They begged her, they blamed her, they berated her, all asking why the warrior queen would not come to their aid.

"After so long you've lost all sense of time, and you hardly know if *you* are real anymore?"

Aithan strapped to a table, body mutilated in unthinkable ways, a laboratory rat for the king's experimentations. Reduced to nothing more than a tool to refine her Aegis offspring army. His beautiful amber eyes pleaded with her, but not for help or mercy. He only asked to be freed from his misery, to be granted death at last.

"And the whole time I am teaching you this valuable lesson, I will be learning. Learning what hurts you the most, discovering which of my masterpieces keeps you awake at night. And when you are completely broken, I will make your worst nightmares a reality. I will kill each one of the people you care for in the ways that you fear most. I will let you kiss them goodbye so that you know they are real, and then I will butcher them in Ellasburg's town square. You will watch me hurt them, and the people will watch you suffer, and they will know that I am their salvation."

White hot rage burned in Macella's veins. She screamed, her onyx flames blazing, and pushed against the weight holding her down. It took all of her strength but, in painstaking increments, she pressed herself up to one knee.

"No. There will be none of that." King Khari lifted her hand, palm up, producing a flash of white light and flicking it toward Macella. "You will kneel before your king, peasant."

(39) When the light hit her, it was as though Macella had been plunged into a frozen pond. First, there was the terrible pain of impact, her body breaking through the frozen surface. Then there was the obliterating cold of the water beneath. It took her breath and locked her muscles.

She hit the floor again hard, barely registering the agony of her body cracking against the wood, so overwhelmed was she with the shock to her system.

Her hellfire disappeared.

It seemed like a long time before Macella was able to fill her lungs again, and when she did, she exhaled a ragged scream. Everything hurt. Her body felt broken in a million places. She was so cold, colder than she'd ever been in her life. She tried to find the onyx flames beneath her skin, to ignite her hellfire and chase away the cold and fear with heat and rage.

It wasn't there.

Her hellfire was gone. Khari had taken it. And now she would take everything else.

The king's face was suddenly inches away, her teeth bared in an expression too full of menace to be rightly called a smile. "There it is. You're finally starting to realize how badly you've fucked up, aren't you? Poor little fool. Did you think your aberration gave you some chance of defeating me?"

The king grabbed her face roughly, forcing Macella's head up. She squeezed tightly enough that Macella knew she'd have finger-shaped bruises on her cheeks if she lived through this. For a terrible moment, Macella thought the king would kiss her. Instead, Khari slapped her hard enough that she tasted blood, then pushed her away roughly and stood.

"You're a monstrosity. A mongrel beast who would have tainted my line," King Khari declared coldly. "You've done me a favor by revealing your true nature before I could commit myself to a life with you."

Macella lifted her head to return Khari's haughty glare. She was cold and frightened and tired and in pain, but the king's disdain still grated on her nerves. How many times had someone looked down on her like this? How many times had people in power tried to convince her that she was less than they were—less worthy, less qualified, less capable? Time and again, despite repeatedly proving herself, pompous pricks tried to put her in what they deemed to be her place. And every damn time, she refused to go quietly.

"Tell yourself whatever you need to save your ego. You still got rejected by a mongrel peasant sack of gutter piss. All your coin and all your power and I'd still rather die than be your queen." Macella punctuated the declaration by spitting blood on the king's boots.

She couldn't help but scream as her arms were yanked over her head and her body dragged upward. Rope scraped harshly against her skin as her arms were bound above her, suspending her in the inky blackness. Only the tips of her toes reached the floor, preventing her from gaining any purchase or taking pressure off her tightly bound wrists. The ropes that wound around her ankles were even tighter, cutting into her flesh so much that they quickly became stained with blood.

"I am going to kill everyone you know," Khari swore. She stood before Macella, studying her with the methodical detachment of the truly deranged. Another Khari appeared at Macella's side, continuing the first king's thought.

"I am going to kill everyone who has ever laid eyes on you. I am going to kill everyone who dares speak your name. I am going to erase the very idea of you."

There were five kings now, or perhaps seven, and several of them were engaged in dispatching Macella's loved ones in increasingly horrifying ways. She turned from a Khari sticking pins under Lucy's fingernails, only to face another methodically branding Laird Parul's bloodied body with an iron poker. Macella tried to close her eyes, but they were forced open and stuck that way, not even allowing her to blink.

"I once told you I liked your fire and prayed it would never cool," Khari taunted her. "But you mistakenly believed that meant I couldn't tame it if I wished. And now I have the pleasure of disabusing you of that notion."

There was Valen, his massive body in chains, covered in thousands of cuts. His back had been split open, his exposed ribs broken and twisted upward into grotesque wings. As Macella watched, King Khari smeared a handful of salt into his wounds. Valen's screams were deafening in the blackness.

Kenji skinned alive. Cassian boiled in tar. Cressida left maimed and covered in honey for the creatures of the forest to consume. Loi drawn and quartered.

Dozens of kings. Hundreds of victims. Everyone she knew, murdered and mutilated all because of her. She couldn't save them. She couldn't look away.

Time became a terrible, liquid thing. She had no way of measuring it except by deaths and there were too many deaths. Too many to count. Too many to bear.

Macella couldn't breathe. She could hear herself wheezing for air but couldn't stop. Her arms ached and her feet had gone numb and there was a vise around her chest. She couldn't move, couldn't escape, couldn't beat Khari.

She was alone in this endless blackness, and she had failed her friends.

CHAPTER TWENTY-THREE

Aithan

Aithan stretched his mind, searching for a presence that was usually so easy to find. Touching Macella's mind had always been effortless and had grown more natural as they spent more time together. These days, it was like breathing. He didn't have to think about it. She was just always there.

Until now.

If she was anywhere in the castle, he should be able to feel her, but he couldn't. The Grand Mage was right that the magic Khari had used for this illusion was unique. Aithan knew they had to be in the throne room, but they simply weren't in this realm.

So, how was he going to reach her?

"I can't feel her," Aithan growled in frustration. He opened his eyes to find the space where his wife should be still infuriatingly empty. "Why can I not feel her?"

The Grand Mage shook her head. "Tranquilo, Lord Protector. Do not let fear cloud your connection. Tell me more about this gift you share. Does Lady Macella communicate telepathically with others often?"

"It started with her hearing hellspawn, even before she went through the trials, but even Hades's blessing doesn't explain it. Perhaps it's her crossbreed nature. Now, she can speak telepathically to any Aegis, and theoretically anything else Otherworldly." Aithan glanced around at his siblings scattered throughout the room. They'd stood with Macella today, as he'd known they ultimately would. She'd earned their loyalty, and Aithan couldn't have been prouder. "She and Finley use it for all manner of mischief. None outside our circle are aware of it."

"Perhaps it is time that changed," Grand Mage Kiama suggested, turning her attention back to the room. "It might be easier for her to find her way if there were more voices calling her home."

Aithan considered the idea. He didn't know that it was his place to reveal Macella's secret. However, everyone in the room had seen her hellfire and, thus, knew she was no typical human. Besides, Macella wanted to build a world where they didn't have to hide who they were. This could be a first step toward that goal, and more importantly, it could bring her back to him.

Aithan took a deep breath and descended the dais. "Everyone! Hear me a moment. I am Aithan of Auburndale, Protector of the Crown, and high commander of the Royal Guard. I am also husband to Lady Macella of Shively, who is in this moment engaged in a battle of unknown danger with King Khari. Depending on who invited you to this ceremony, you may have differing opinions about those points. I am not going to speak to you of Khari's virtues or vices. I will not speak to you of Khari at all."

Aithan paused, giving his thoughts a moment to coalesce, even as he agonized over every second that passed without seeing Macella safe. A great deal had happened in a short time, and they were still in the middle of an intense situation. If he chose his words correctly, he could not only help Macella in this battle, but he could help set the tone for the aftermath.

"I want to speak to you of Lady Macella of Shively, who I know doesn't need biographing here. You know of her deeds, and many of you are here in support of her reign. However, few of you were aware of her parentage, and I imagine you were surprised by her hellfire. We have guarded that secret carefully, because we do not live in a world where Aegiskind has been well-treated. Her parentage is considered a crime. Macella of Shively was born of a union between an Aegis and a human. She was hidden among humans and only learned of her true nature after she met and fell in love with an Aegis of her own. Lady Macella has been through the trials and blessed by Hades and charged with a mighty task by the god of the Underworld himself. That is the battle she fights here today.

"She fights for the love of Kōsaten, and to make it a better place for those like her and me and like all of you. Her foe has plunged this room into darkness, robbed you of your sight, and left you unprotected. She has taken Lady Macella and shrouded her in magic and has undoubtedly convinced her that she is fighting alone. But my lady is far from alone and she needs to know it. Fortunately for us, the gods gifted her with an enhancement of her natural empathy, a third eye awareness stronger than most. I need you to help me tap into that awareness."

Aithan paused again, swallowing an uncharacteristic stab of anxiety. He was good at leading soldiers, and he'd grown more comfortable conversing with friends and even making polite chatter when required, but he rarely spoke so publicly or at such lengths. It was foreign and uncomfortable, but for Macella, he would do much worse.

"Open your minds. Reach for your warrior queen and remind her what she's fighting for. Remind her that she's not fighting alone."

⁓⟊⟊⟊⟊⁓

Macella

Macella couldn't feel her hands or feet. Her eyes were painfully dry and hurt almost as much as her obviously broken ribs. She wished it hurt more.

Because perhaps if she was in enough physical pain, she would be distracted from the emotional devastation of this macabre hellscape. Her closest friends and most perfunctory associates continued to die in gruesome ways all around her, their corpses piling up grotesquely. Some began to rot and, despite knowing it wasn't real, she could almost smell the stench of decay. Macella understood how Khari had driven her family mad in a single week. Hell, she could see why Khari's father had slit his own throat after only a day. Time passed differently in the dark corners of the king's mind.

Macella was so cold. It was a bone deep chill, unlike anything she'd felt before, even when confronted with the Chosen. Without her hellfire, she couldn't seem to regulate her body temperature. She'd always been the type of person who ran hot, as Babette often said. Her siblings had fought over who got to sleep next to her during the cold months. Now, however, Macella felt as if she might never get warm again.

Self-doubt had begun to take hold of her, and each corpse Khari added to the pile strengthened its grip. She'd always been an outsider, and maybe she always would be. Maybe she wasn't Aegis enough after all. Nor was she human. Why had she believed she could change things?

She was so disappointed in herself. The guilt was much worse than the physical pain racking her body. How had she lost this battle so spectacularly? The only bright spot in her failure was that, when she dwelled on it long enough, she was inclined to cry a bit, which soothed her dry eyes. On the downside, no matter how much she hyperventilated, she couldn't seem to pass out, which would've been a relief at this point. The best she could do was disassociate and try to stare past the awful spectacle the king had conjured.

A cold splash of water hit Macella in the face, making her choke and sputter. It was a terrible shock to her system, but she couldn't help her relief when the moisture hit her eyes and tongue. She tried to swallow what water she could, but it was difficult to manage while coughing uncontrollably.

King Khari appeared before her, grabbing Macella's face roughly again. "I thought you might be asleep with your eyes open. Are you not enjoying the show, pet? You've gotten so quiet."

Macella thought of several snappy comebacks but didn't have the energy to deliver any of them. She glared at the king instead, but it wasn't very intimidating given she was still trying to recover from her coughing fit.

Khari surveyed her with malevolent glee. "I've been trying to figure out where you came from, since those filthy yokels in Shively obviously couldn't have spawned you, and it has just hit me." The king looked genuinely delighted, which couldn't mean anything good for Macella. "You do look like him, and you certainly inherited many of his skills. Matthias of the Highlands was a damn good liar."

Macella might've stopped breathing. She hated how her voice shook when she replied. "You know nothing of my father."

"No, *you* know nothing of your father." King Khari laughed. "I, on the other hand, watched the Chosen suck the life out of him."

Macella would've given anything at that moment for the freedom to blink. Her brain was almost at capacity already, and this might be the final straw. "The records say my father died under Queen Rhiannon."

Khari laughed again, the sound grating against Macella's frayed nerves. "And how does that math work, you dense donkey? I suppose you have extended youth because of your mongrel blood, but you're not a hundred years old. How could your father have died under my predecessor, child?"

Macella was stunned into silence. She'd learned so little about her father and remembered even less, thanks to Meng Po's soup of forgetfulness. When she'd seen Matthias's name listed on the roster for Queen Rhiannon's reign, she'd just been pleased to learn his birthplace. And with all that had transpired since then, she hadn't spared it much thought.

"The records say what I wish for them to say. No one cares about Aegises. Or, at least, no one did until you started writing your silly little stories for the papers," King Khari explained with a shrug. "Allowing crossbreeds to be born during her reign was Rhiannon's downfall. I'd ingratiated myself to her for years and even managed to become king consort, but it was the secret of Aithan of Auburndale's parentage that gave me the leverage I needed to take the throne. Of course, I couldn't have such a birth tainting my stellar reputation, so when I found out Matthias had reproduced, I altered the records. Since you and your lowborn mother had supposedly died, there wasn't much chance anyone would learn of your existence, but if they ever did tie crossbreed offspring to Matthias, his indiscretions would be on Rhiannon."

"When they questioned me, I swore that you and your mother had both died in childbirth. I assume they believed me, since they gave me to the Chosen for execution instead of torturing me for more information." Matthias had told her as much in the realm between the living and the dead. He'd never explicitly said which monarch had questioned him.

"I guess I should've spent more time on his interrogation, but I just wanted to be rid of him." Khari shook her head ruefully. "He was so convincing. I truly believed his grief over both of you. Just as I believed you could be worthy of my hand. Foolish of me. And to think I granted him such a quick death. I will not make the same mistake with you."

"And yet you plan to repeat Rhiannon's mistake?" Macella managed to find her voice again, though it was still weak. "Your crossbreed child is due into the world soon. Hiding their nature won't be as easy as altering old books."

"You really aren't as smart as I believed you were," King Khari clucked, looking genuinely disappointed. She turned and walked away as though bored with the conversation. "Your scribblings have made Aegises much more palatable to the masses, and anyway, I no longer care about adhering to rules. Henceforth, I *am* the rules. I shall shape the world as I choose, and you will help me begin by showing those who resist me what horrors await them. Let us get back to the show!"

And so, the torment began anew. Armed with her newfound knowledge of Macella's father, Khari altered the visions to feature Matthias in the montage of murder. Desperate as she was for any bit of her father, his addition made it so much harder to look away from the torment, no matter how depraved it became.

Her father had wiped her memory and sent her away to save her from this woman. He'd died protecting her secret. And she'd stupidly traipsed right into the king's clutches anyway.

Khari had taken everything from her. Her identity, her freedom, her father. She'd left nothing but guilt and loneliness.

I am right here, love, though you cannot see me, Aithan's mental voice cut through the thick fog around her mind. *You are not alone.*

Macella's panicked breaths slowed involuntarily. For a moment, she thought it must be another trick of the king, or wishful thinking. But it felt real.

We are all here, love. We are here with you. I am always going to be with you.

That was her husband. She knew that mind, that cadence of thought, that tone. He had found her. He was still there.

I am yours and you are mine, hell goddess. In this life and every other, if the gods will it. And if they do not will it, I will still make it so.

The blood rushing in her ears couldn't drown out her husband's reassuring thoughts. Their connection refused to be broken. Macella blinked, freeing her eyelids from Khari's hold. The sensation brought welcome tears to her dry eyes.

Macella, I can't see a thing, but I know you're still fighting. Show that bitch what happens when you play with fire. Finley's voice joined Aithan's in Macella's mind.

The ropes around her arms loosened slightly. Macella flexed fingers that prickled with what felt like a thousand needles. Her body slipped a little lower, her feet finding purchase on the ground beneath, taking some weight off of her arms. King Khari tilted her head, eyes narrowing at Macella.

I know you can do this, big sister. Jacan's thoughts were filled with such steadfast confidence that Macella felt a smile tugging at her lips. The silly boy truly believed she was some kind of hero.

The ropes on her wrists snapped. Macella's arms fell to her sides just in time for her to steady herself on her bound feet. King Khari gasped, her brow furrowing. The corpses of Macella's friends began to flicker out around her, as the blood flowed back into her arms and hands, warming her chilled limbs.

Fight her, warrior queen!

The unfamiliar voice was followed by another that was oddly similar. *Our faith is in you, Lady Macella!*

Cassian and Cressida? Macella massaged her wrists, the darkness around her seeming to lift just a bit. The horrible visions of her friends were gone, leaving only a line of Khari duplicates glowering at her, their adder eyes full of cold rage.

Avenge our fallen siblings, Lady Macella!

I believe in you, warrior queen.

For the daughters of Kali and son of Apophis!

You are the best of us, Lady Macella.

(40) The chorus of voices grew until all of the Aegises were there, speaking encouragement into her mind. All of them. Those that had come before and those that still dwelt in this realm. They were all with her.

Macella straightened. The ropes on her ankles melted away, disappearing into the emptiness around them. Her hellfire began to simmer beneath her skin once more. She grinned.

And burst into onyx flames.

Khari gasped, staggering backward in surprise. She recovered almost immediately, but Macella caught the slightest delay. One of the kings had moved just a beat before the others. Macella kept her eyes moving, scanning them all steadily, not yet wanting to reveal to King Khari that she'd been discovered.

Aithan, can you see my sword?

Yes. His response was immediate, though he still seemed far away. *But I cannot see you.*

You found me without your eyes. Give me my sword when I call for it. I love you.

Macella caught his wordless reply—a mental deluge of trust and love and fear and hope. The other Aegises were still there, too, reminding her of her duty to their murdered siblings, and their trust in her ability to save them all. And though she couldn't touch their minds, Macella still felt Zahra and Charlotte, Aisling and Nyx, the servants and citizens, and everyone else who'd come to her aid in this fateful hour.

Her family was with her. Her people were with her. She was not alone.

Never, Aithan assured her.

Macella exhaled, her heart slowing even as she charged toward the false Khari on the true king's immediate right. All of the duplicates scattered, preparing to attack and distract, while the real king crept around them, producing a wicked-looking knife from a sheath at her back. Macella let Khari get behind her, pretending to be focused on the false foes.

It was only a moment, but how it stretched. She had time to take in everything around her as she waited for the king to plunge that hunting blade into her back. For the first time, she noticed small flaws in the Khari copies. One had too long a nose, another's hair was the wrong shade of blond, and all were missing the spark of authentic life, just as empty as the black void they'd trapped her in. When she looked past the false kings, she could almost make out the shape of the true world just beyond the conjured darkness.

Macella smelled King Khari before she felt her closeness. Musky vanilla and pomegranate. Metal and ash. Power and death.

Now.

Macella extended her hand and a moment later she felt the grip of her sword hit her palm. She wrapped her fingers around it, spinning and dropping low as her hellfire extended to engulf the blade. For the second time that day, she buried her sword in the king's gut.

King Khari's knife clattered to the floor. She looked down at Macella with an expression of utter disbelief that was almost comical. She opened and closed her mouth, but no sound came out. Around them, the other Kharis began to flicker and disappear.

Macella rose slowly, pushing her sword deeper, then dragging it upward to widen the wound. Fire spread with her blade, catching the fabric of Khari's tunic, and it burned away to reveal the bubbling golden brown skin beneath. Macella felt a vicious satisfaction as the flesh around the wound blackened. Blood and viscera gushed over her hands, but she hardly felt it through the burn of hellfire and the buzz of adrenaline. She smelled it, though. Charred and sickly sweet with a coppery undertone. It smelled triumphant.

Macella stood to her full height, steadily slicing through bone and muscle and organs as she met the king's ochre gaze. King Khari gurgled, and the throne room began to reappear around them. Macella smiled and dragged her sword higher, her arms trembling with the effort. Khari clutched at the sword weakly, her breaths rattling as she tried to pull free.

Macella twisted the hilt. "I am not so easily tamed after all, but I suppose I am as skilled at deception as my father," she hissed, holding Khari's dying gaze, their faces inches apart for a final time. "I will not erase you from the histories, because you do not deserve to have your sins forgotten. I will tell your story far and wide, and our descendants will remember how greed and pride and cruelty died on the blade of a crossbreed peasant."

Macella jerked her sword free, finding savage glee in the parts of Khari's insides that came out with her blade. Around them, the throne room rematerialized in a sudden rush of sound and color. The gasps and cries of the crowd drowned out the sound of Khari collapsing to the floor, clutching futilely at her skewered torso.

Macella went to one knee, wincing from her broken ribs. She was exhausted, and every inch of her body seemed to have individual complaints, but she needed to witness Khari's death up close. She needed to watch the light leave her viper eyes. Macella leaned over her, straining to hear the king's final breaths over the commotion around them.

"You will still know suffering." The king's mouth curved into her cruelest smile, her bloody teeth turning it monstrous. "You will regret this day for as long as you live. And I will not die alone."

Aithan had nearly reached them, having broken into a sprint the moment Macella and the king reappeared. When Khari turned her dying gaze toward him, Macella knew immediately what she intended. But it was already too late to stop her.

As the life faded from Khari's eyes, a final flash of white light exploded from her palm. It hit Aithan in the center of his chest, blasting him backward. He hit the ground with a sickening thud.

And did not move again.

Chapter Twenty-Four

Macella

Once there was a woman who did not belong.

Her family wanted her to comply. Her community wanted her to conform.

Instead, she left them behind in search of a home of her own. A place where she could be herself and help others do the same.

It wasn't easy, but she found it. She fought and worked and she gave and gave. She carved a place for herself where there was none, and she filled it with love.

And though she could have, she was fortunate not to have to do it alone.

Always, her Aegis was there. The drumbeat beneath her song. Always steady, always strong. Just like the heartbeat she fell asleep to each night.

The heartbeat that had gone silent.

(41) Macella pressed her face to Aithan's chest, her fingers fisted tightly in his shirt. A ragged sob ripped from her throat, the sound a wordless screech of rage, denial, and despair. The cry echoed hollowly against his silent chest.

Absolutely, savagely, silent.

She might've been the face of their little rebellion, but Aithan of Auburndale had always been the heartbeat, steady and strong. He never wavered in his conviction that they would succeed, because he never wavered in his belief in her.

He'd followed that belief to his death, without hesitation.

"No," Macella whispered.

The others had gathered around them. She could feel their grief, triumph, relief and disbelief, all warring for dominance in the aftermath of the battle. But she could not hear their murmured words, or any of the other sounds coming from far away, outside of Aithan's silent chest. She'd been enveloped in that silence, had become utterly lost in it.

"No," she said again, louder this time. "No, no, no. I do not accept this."

She lifted her head, her eyes quickly finding the sorrowful gray eyes of her mage—the mage who had prophesized this moment on Macella's forty-second nameday. Aisling had seen them die, and Macella had been prepared to face her demise. But now her husband was gone, and she was left behind in this Aithanless realm.

Aisling was paler than ever, her plump cheeks wet with tears. Macella looked into those keen eyes, through them to that bit of familiarity she'd always sensed in Aisling, so similar to the minds of Otherworldly beings. She reached for that pulse, using it to find and touch the mage's mind.

Aisling's eyes went white, her posture rigid. The connection between them was electric, sharp, almost painful. Macella didn't understand it, didn't care to try. She'd looked to Aisling for answers and had somehow touched not just the mage's mind, but her Sight.

Macella did not pretend to know from whence Aisling's visions came or what consequences might come of tampering with another's Sight. She didn't care about any of that. She just needed to bring her husband back.

How do I save him? How do I get him back?

Aisling's lips moved, her voice a raspy whisper scratching against Macella's mind. The sensation was unsettling, like insects crawling over exposed organs, but Macella held onto the tenuous connection. She would endure any discomfort, make any sacrifice to save her Aegis, to fill the terrible silence in his chest with the steady beat of his heart.

Impossible children, unbearable pain, came the chilling falsetto. It was the voice of Aisling the oracle, the one that haunted Macella's dreams. She spoke the first line of their prophecy. Macella had recited and heard the prophecy many times, but never like this. Not while connected to Aisling's Sight, able to actually see as the mage did.

It was terrifying and marvelous and excruciating and profound. The Sight was indescribable. Even as she felt it, Macella knew that she wasn't fully perceiving all that Aisling received. It was as if she were standing beneath a waterfall with only a bucket. She gathered all the water she could carry, but it was all around her, rushing over and through and beneath her, this sea of Sight.

She saw her mother's face, her father's grief, Gabriela's devotion, Maia's resignation. A million memories that were and were not her own.

Suppressed so long, love blooms again, the voice of the oracle continued, the rasping whisper like a claw trailing down Macella's spine.

She saw Aithan, as she'd seen him all those seasons ago in that nameless brothel. She met his orange eyes in a looking glass and on some celestial plane the threads of this prophecy tightened around them.

Baptized in blood, forged in flame, the oracle voice hissed.

A screaming baby, still bloody, and coated in onyx flames. An auburn-haired woman murmured a spell, and the flames disappeared, but the damage was already done. All she could do was lay the child on her mother's chest as it rose and fell for the final time. The mother died smiling.

A small boy in a wooden cart, curled against a covered body. Emotionless orange eyes watching him weep from beneath a cloak. The scent of vanilla and blood lingering in the air.

Daggers and flames and a terrible voice demanding she start again. A young man staring stoically into the open fire below him, ignoring the burn of the whip against his back. Pain and steel and smoke.

Stars align, prophets proclaim, the oracle whispered against a backdrop of infinite vastness above a terrain awash in pinks and purples, a starless cosmic sea. Aithan reminding Macella who she was and making love to her on the mountain's edge beneath those endless stars.

Love leads wanderers to their truth.

Macella and Aithan, back-to-back, eyes in hellform, weapons raised, engulfed in crimson and onyx flames.

Unknown power now unloosed.

A flurry of images from their many adventures culminating in Aithan's sword in his outstretched hand, his other striking Khari, even as the veins on that arm brightened and bulged. Macella's shadows stopping the spread and later flitting over his wounds, healing them.

The answers she'd asked for began to take shape.

Darkness gathers, trouble brews. Predator or protector, one must choose, the oracle continued.

Macella had made her choice. The predatory King Khari had offered her everything, but all she'd wanted was her protector. Her shield. Her Aegis.

Fools fight for fortune, the peaceful court war. Not one prepared for that which is in store.

Macella rescuing Aithan from Duànzào, and then helping him to convince Kai, Diya, and Finley not to attempt to raise a hellspawn army against the Crown. The two of them navigating the royals' games until they ultimately arrived at this day, the day they were prophesized to save the realm.

A shield. A scribe. A sword. A pen. Against hell's fury. Against our end.

Macella and Aithan had stood against those fools, had prevented a war between realms. They'd given everything to stand against hell's fury, to thwart that end. Aithan had given everything.

Macella would too.

(42) She would either bring Aithan back to this realm, or she would join him in the Otherworlds.

Her star charm grew colder, impossibly colder than it had been throughout the day's ordeals. It grew so cold it burned against her flesh, branding her skin. Macella barely felt it.

Despite her exhaustion, it was nothing to call her shadows to her palms. It didn't feel at all taxing, as it had when she'd tried to save Awa back in Highview, and not nearly as difficult as it had been to summon the shadows that healed

Finley. No, calling her shadows for this felt as natural as breathing. As natural as a heartbeat.

Hades had known that it would take both Aithan and Macella to set things right, had known that it would take children of both worlds to restore the balance. He'd known it might kill them both but, in case only Macella survived, he'd given her the one thing he knew she'd want: Aithan.

Always Aithan. It had always been and always would be Aithan. Aithan's quiet, crinkle-eyed smile and mesmerizing amber gaze. Aithan's strong arms wrapped around her and his hands moving gently over her skin. Aithan's endless patience and unwavering faith in her. His devotion, adoration, and unquestionable loyalty.

Aithan of Auburndale, who had gone out of his way to prove to her he wasn't the monster she'd been taught he was, though he'd been more human than anyone she'd ever met, with his intuition and empathy. He'd risked everything when he agreed to let her travel with him and had been risking himself every day since. Right up to his end.

Aithan of Auburndale, who'd never made her feel like a burden or an oddity. He'd accepted her exactly as she was and loved her for it. He'd encouraged her to go after what she wanted, to be who she wanted to be. He'd been happy to stand behind her and watch her shine.

They'd found each other at the perfect moment and in the most unexpected place. They'd defied the odds and found joy in building a life together. Two crossbreed outsiders, neither looking for love, but both in need of it. Macella couldn't have written a love story more perfect than the one she'd lived.

Aithan of Auburndale was hers and she was his and that is how it would always be. And they would move through this life and the next just as they had promised. Together.

She pressed her hands to Aithan's silent heart. Distantly, Macella heard a tumult of voices. Jacan, Charlotte, Finley, Zahra. Her friends were calling to her. When she looked up, Macella saw that she and Aithan were completely cocooned in shadows. Shadows *she'd* summoned. Far more than the healing shadows she'd produced before, this was a sphere of darkness. The shapes of her friends moved just beyond the wall of shadow, hazy and indistinct.

Within the cocoon, there was only the stillness in Aithan's chest and the certainty of what she must do. Even Aisling and the oracle had left her, the link between their minds severed by the sphere of shadow, leaving Macella's nerve endings buzzing with energy.

"She'll *die*!" Finley was screaming, their voice uncharacteristically shrill. "She's too drained from saving me to attempt to heal him! He's dead and she will be, too, and it will be my fault!"

Finley's voice broke, and Macella felt a dull ache somewhere beyond the fathomless grief of Aithan's silent chest. She ignored it, refocusing her attention on the heart that lay still beneath her palms.

It didn't hurt at all. Even as she felt her limbs grow cold and her breathing grow labored. Her blood moved sluggishly through her veins, her heart slowing with each gulp of air she managed to drag into her reluctant lungs.

The metaphorical bucket scraped against gravel, but she willed more water to swell from the ground, from the bricks and stone. The well was not dry. Macella would wring every drop of healing energy from her bones. Whatever it took to save him.

A wolf howled somewhere in the distance. A moment later, a single shadow detached itself from the rest and padded toward her, yellow eyes glowing in its nebulous form. Macella hardly noticed it.

No, it didn't hurt at all. All Macella felt was boundless love. She shivered as she gazed into Aithan of Auburndale's beautiful face, watching his golden skin regain its vibrancy. There was a thump against her palms and his eyelids fluttered. Another thump. Another.

Aithan's eyes opened, his gaze meeting hers, love and devotion and concern reflected in their amber depths. He reached up to touch her face. His fingertips came away crimson, and Macella realized she'd been weeping blood.

"I love you," she managed to whisper through chattering teeth, before collapsing against his chest.

She heard his heartbeat, steady and strong. Then she let the cold and darkness take her and she knew nothing else.

Chapter Twenty-Five

Aithan

It had gone quiet in Aithan's mind. So very quiet.

(43) Once, a very long time ago, a small boy had lain beside his mother's corpse and his mind had gone utterly silent, just like this.

Then, the air had smelled of vanilla. Vanilla and blood.

The coppery tang of blood tinted the air now. And beneath it, something else. Something familiar and warm and lovely.

The quiet in his head grew louder, the silence desperately trying to crowd out the truth that threatened to destroy him.

Distantly, he knew that there were others around him, pressing close, whispering, screaming, crying. None of it mattered.

Because there was silence in his mind. Silence replacing a familiar, constant presence.

Nothing but silence and that lovely scent.

Cinnamon, citrus, and flame. Sweet and earthy like burning acacia wood. A combination that smelled like a burbling stream, a crackling fire, an evening breeze.

Slowly—so very slowly—Aithan sat up. He tried not to think about the curly head against his chest or the limp body he held cradled in his arms. He thought only of the terrible, cacophonous silence.

He tried to hold onto that silence for as long as possible. He needed it to keep the truth at bay.

Slowly—so very slowly—Aithan lowered his gaze to the still, silent face resting against his chest.

Someone began roaring then. The sound was pure primal rage and absolute agony.

Even when he realized that the sound was coming from him, he could not make it stop. Not as he stared into his wife's unmoving face. The truth was there, in her face. He couldn't deny it because his wife, his love, his life, his Macella—her face was never still.

Even in her sleep, she had the most expressive face he'd ever seen. Her emotions were so loud, so pronounced. Even if he couldn't hear minds, he could have easily read her thoughts on her face. He'd learned the meaning of every twitch of her full mouth, of every shift in those bright black eyes, and every quirk of her brow. And he'd never once seen her face so still and empty.

Macella was dead.

Slowly—so very slowly—Aithan climbed to his feet. It had never been so difficult to lift Macella. It was as if she were made of stone, or perhaps the strength had drained from his body when his wife left this realm. He held her tightly against him, her head resting limply against his chest, her wild, soft curls brushing against his chin.

Aithan lifted his head, searching. He found Finley, their face twisted in an expression of anguish so acute that any vestige of hope Aithan might have been holding on to shriveled immediately. He used the last of his restraint to touch their mind. A warning.

"Get back everyone, right now!" Finley commanded, grabbing a sobbing Zahra with one hand, and a deathly pale Aisling with the other. Jacan lifted a weeping Charlotte and hauled her away. Following the Aegises' lead, everyone else raced for the edges of the throne room.

Aithan exploded.

He erupted into crimson flames brighter, higher, hotter, and wilder than any he'd ever conjured. The flames engulfed them, him and his Macella, and yet they did not burn. No, his pain was within, burning away all that he had ever been. He could feel his very core withering to ash.

And still it wasn't enough. The pain was too huge to be contained. He could not bury the agony within himself. Not this time.

His crimson flames flared brighter. He could smell the acrid scent of burning wood—not acacia, but mahogany. Distantly, people shielded themselves while running, shouting, calling for buckets of water, blankets, anything to fight the spreading flames.

Macella, marching out of a brothel with her head high, unafraid and ready to embark upon an unknown adventure. Macella, materializing before him in Duànzào, onyx eyes alight with a fire that stole his breath, skin glowing with obsidian flames—a beautiful, terrible goddess of death. His hell goddess. Macella, wearing a pale blue dress, eyes glistening with tears, saying yes, she would marry him, yes, she would bind herself to him by all the laws of gods and man.

For all of this life and every other if the gods will it. And if they do not will it, I will still make it so.

Somehow, the air was filled not only with embers and ash, but objects. It seemed that anything not securely tethered was at the mercy of howling, violent gusts of wind. Part of him knew that there was no wind, only uncontrolled surges of telekinetic power. His power.

And still he burned, his crimson flames blazing brighter, higher, hotter. And still, Macella's face was unmoving. Her mind remained utterly, devastatingly, unbearably silent.

He hadn't been able to protect her in the end, when it mattered. She was supposed to shape the world anew. It had been his duty to shield her so that she could. He had failed.

The fire wasn't enough. This pain would consume him completely. He would burn and burn until the world was nothing but ash.

Macella

(44) Macella opened her eyes, squinting against the glare of the setting sun. The sky above her was awash in pinks and purples, stars blooming as darkness slowly devoured the sunlight. She felt hard earth beneath her but felt no discomfort. Her body was a weightless, impenetrable thing.

She felt something soft nudging at her hand and then a shift in the air as something sniffed her face. After a moment, a warm, furry body settled against her head with a scratchy purr. Macella turned her head toward the sound, her vision adjusting enough for her to make out a familiar face.

"Nyx?" she whispered.

The cat blinked her yellow eyes, stood, and stretched. Macella reached out a hand to scratch the creature's chin. Nyx leaned into her touch.

"You did well, crossbreed," came a low and sonorous voice that was both familiar and strange.

Macella sat up quickly, realizing two things simultaneously: she was on a cliff's edge overlooking the Highview desert and she was not alone. A shadowy figure stood with its back to her, staring at the endless expanse of land. Macella stood carefully, hands sliding instinctively toward her thigh holsters.

"Relax, daughter of mine," the figure said, still not turning to face her. **"You are safe. I only wished to speak to you. I do so enjoy our little talks."**

Macella shuddered, the strangely familiar voice somehow both repellent and alluring at once. Tentatively, she stepped toward the figure, Nyx winding around her ankles and purring steadily. "Where am I?"

"Underworld, obviously," the figure replied, his voice mocking and amused. **"Considering you are dead, and you belong to me, where else would you be? Foolish girl."**

Macella remembered then. The deafening silence in Aithan's chest. The searing cold in her limbs as she forced the healing shadows from her palms. Aithan's beautiful amber eyes opening. Then...nothing.

"Aithan of Auburndale lives," she whispered, heart racing. "You made sure I would be able to save him."

"Yes. The abomination son of Lucifer lives."

Macella stopped a few steps from the cliff's edge, waiting. Nyx walked ahead of her, stopping to sit at the other person's feet. Slowly, the shadowy figure turned. Macella gasped.

He was beautiful and terrible. Power rippled in the air around him, shadows coiling and slithering over his skin, forming into vast wings then melting into a mass of writhing limbs, then becoming obsidian flames. He was tall and leanly muscled with earthy brown skin—deep, dark earth ready to nurture new life or to reclaim the dead.

His black gaze was dangerous and sorrowful and ancient. His hair was as dark as his eyes, cut close on the sides but with night glossy curls crowning his head. He had sharp cheekbones and a cruel, voluptuous mouth framed by a neatly sculpted beard. The finely tailored suit he wore appeared to be sewn from ash and starlight. It clung to his chiseled form and yet flowed seamlessly into the shadows around him. The shadows never stopped moving, continuously shifting and reshaping themselves. A warm breeze wafted from him, bringing with it the smell of mint and asphodel. The touch of that air left her cold. It was like an exhale against skin, warm at first but leaving goosebumps in its wake.

(45) Macella dropped to a knee, bowing her head. "Lord Hades, King of the Underworld, God of Death."

"Yes, yes. Rise, crossbreed and let me look at you," Hades commanded, voice still laced with that mocking amusement.

Macella stood, lifting her face to meet the ancient god's terrible gaze. She couldn't help the trembling in her limbs as those infinite eyes took her in, but she would not let herself shrink away. She stood tall, shoulders squared before the scrutiny of the dark deity who had blessed her, had allowed her to save her love.

"Macella of Shively, born of Matthias and Lenora, magic and suffering. Macella, orphan abomination, blood of Hades. You have served me well."

Macella shuddered and inclined her head, accepting the praise. "Thank you, my Lord. You mean, then, that the balance is indeed restored?"

Hades smiled and Macella knew that if she gazed into that smile for too long, she would go mad. As if reading her thoughts, Hades smiled wider, revealing far too many sharp, white teeth. The shadows around him slithered like a mass of snakes.

"It is *almost* restored," Hades corrected, tilting his head. **"It is a rare thing to surprise a god, crossbreed. You, however, continue to do so."**

Macella didn't quite know how to answer that. She wasn't certain it was a good thing to confound the gods. Though Hades had yet to cause her harm, she was under no illusion that she was safe in his presence. Every time they'd met before, Macella had walked away changed, only to step into some new danger.

The thought gave Macella pause. This was her third encounter with the god of the Underworld, not counting the endless trials Meng Po had wiped from her memory. On their first meeting, he'd puppeteered her dead father. The second time they'd met, he'd spoken through Aisling. It had been horrible hearing his unfathomable voice from the lips of her loved ones.

"How is it that you are speaking to me this way?" Macella asked, struggling to frame her question respectfully. "I am honored, of course, but have never known of someone speaking directly to a god. You sound...different."

Hades waved a dismissive hand, the movement causing the shadows around him to swirl and rumble like thunder as they contorted into a throng of arms. One shadow hand drifted to Nyx's head and scratched behind her ears, while another scratched beneath her chin. Nyx sat up tall with her tail curled neatly around her body, closing her eyes and stretching her neck toward the shadowy hands.

"You are dead, little abomination, and in my realm. I do not need a vessel to commune with you here. In Underworld, I shape myself and everything around me as I please. I plucked this place from your mind so that you might find comfort in the familiarity. I believe you had

an incredibly enjoyable time on this mountain. And as for this form, I thought you might find it appealing. It is one of my favorites. I wanted you to enjoy our visit."

Macella had no idea how to respond to that. She and Aithan had spent the night before the public announcement of her betrothal on a cliff's edge in Highview. After she'd ridden Aithan's cock with reckless abandon, they'd joked that they had put on quite a show for the cosmos. But surely, no gods had actually been watching...especially not the god standing before her. Right?

She could feel Hades's amusement in the very air around her, his teasing tone reflected in the breeze ruffling the curls at the nape of her neck. Somewhere nearby, an owl screeched. Macella shivered, scowling when Hades smirked and another gust of minty air brushed over her neck.

"Why is the balance only *almost* restored?" she demanded, choosing to change the subject and ignore the god of the Underworld's taunts. "What is left to be righted? We gave everything."

Hades sighed and his shadows formed into a massive black ram before folding in on themselves and again becoming dark, undulating wings. Macella felt a heavy gust of chilly warm wind. The smell of mint and asphodel washed over her again.

"You did, indeed. And that is why I must send you back. You do not belong here, crossbreed. Not yet."

Macella's eyes widened as she realized what Hades was saying. She opened her mouth to speak, but the Lord of the Many Dead cut her off.

"The healing shadows have been spent, crossbreed. You will not be able to save your protector should he fall again. Nor will you evade me if you should perish. When next you die, you will be mine."

Macella looked into the death deity's eyes, knowing that those depthless black pits held galaxies and eons she couldn't begin to comprehend. She could fall into those eyes and never find her way out again. She could drown there, and become another of his liquid shadows, another fathomless secret buried in his depths.

A shiver crept along her spine, dread curling in her stomach. It was no wonder the gods no longer communed with humans so directly. People weren't meant to perceive their awful immensity.

Macella trembled but squared her shoulders again and gave him a defiant smile. She was no match for such creatures, nor could she ever hope to be. All she could be was herself, and that was enough.

"As I told you once before, my Lord, my mind is my own, my heart belongs to Aithan of Auburndale, and my life belongs to Fate. You can take whatever's left," she said.

Hades laughed, the sound like worms devouring decaying flesh. **"You have amused and surprised me since first we met. That is a rare thing, for which I am inclined to reward you. I shall send you back with a parting gift—a favor from one of my colleagues. The prophet's familiar will lead you safely back to the land of the living. Hurry before the son of Lucifer razes the keep."**

Nyx slunk to Macella's side, purring, and rubbing her silken body against Macella's legs before stretching luxuriantly and reaching up to paw at Macella's thigh. Macella picked the cat up, her attention still fixed on Hades.

"What kind of gift?" she asked as the stars began to dim above them.

Hades only smiled his terrifying smile, making her stomach flip and her skin crawl. She opened her mouth to speak again, but Hades lifted a hand and the shadows around him swelled, engulfing Macella and Nyx, the cliff, and all the stars. His black eyes and white teeth lingered as the rest of him melted away into the swirling darkness.

"Until we meet again, crossbreed."

Then the blackness swallowed her completely.

CHAPTER TWENTY-SIX

Macella

Macella dreamed of her father (46). Bright, vivid dreams that filled her with peace and wonder.

Matthias reading to her before she fell asleep. Matthias guiding her to breathe and focus on the coin he rolled across his knuckles to calm her from a bout of panic. Matthias holding her on his shoulders so she could peer into a bird's nest and scribble notes in one of her little journals. Matthias swooping her through the air so she could pretend to fly.

Matthias chasing her through a field of white and purple flowers while she squealed gleefully. When he caught her, she screamed with laughter, and he called her a screeching owl, which only made her laugh harder. Falling asleep in Matthias's arms while he told her stories about her mother, even though she insisted she wasn't sleepy and that owls stayed awake all night.

Matthias, teaching her how to control the mysterious flames that sometimes rose from her skin. Matthias, staring at her in wide-eyed wonderment when she responded to things he hadn't said aloud. Matthias with tears in his eyes, realizing that she, too, could see Lenora wandering through the field with her sad smile and crown of purple flowers in her hair.

So many moments of love and joy and laughter and tears. There were times when he went away to protect the kingdom, and she had to stay inside with her books and the stories she made up in her head. Other times, when the danger took him farther from their little home, she had to be very quiet in a covered cart, but then they had fun adventures camping deep in the woods or mountains far away from other people. It never bothered Macella that it was just the two of them—especially since she often had friends to talk to, like her mother or the boy who was killed by a jumbie before Matthias could dispatch the malevolent spirit and close the rift it came through.

One day, Matthias explained that she had to go away and live a different life, far away from people like him and the monsters he fought. He told her that she would be safe, that once she was away from him, she'd learn to be like other children. She'd forget about fire and ghosts and wouldn't hear voices in her head. He promised that even, though she wouldn't remember him, he would always be with her.

Macella fought and wailed and burst into flames, but it didn't matter. He'd given her something sweet to drink before telling her about her journey, and her eyelids had grown heavy before she'd even finished her tantrum. Matthias loaded up all her belongings and held her against his side as he took the reins of the horse and cart for their final adventure. Macella kept her eyes open as long as she could, determined to remember every detail about the father who was her entire world.

"You are such a fiery little thing," Matthias told her, his dark eyes sad and shining. "You're so much like your mother."

Macella yawned and burrowed closer to him. "I am like her and like you and like the birds and the stories. All mixed up to make a Macella."

"I love you, little firebird," Matthias whispered to her. "I love you so much, my girl."

Macella opened her eyes.

Round, yellow eyes gazed back at her.

Nyx nudged Macella's foot affectionately with her little head, lifting up on her hind legs to reach. It was then Macella noticed that her feet did not seem to be touching the ground. And she was surrounded by flames.

Aithan was holding her, engulfed in a torrent of crimson hellfire and swirling debris. Though she could hardly see the room around them, she knew that everyone must've taken cover. This level of destruction was clearly beyond the staff's ability to contain.

Hurry before the son of Lucifer razes the keep.

Hades had apparently sent her back just in time for there to still be a keep to return to. Macella exhaled, feeling as if she'd come back to her body from a great distance. It was a difficult adjustment, as though there was too much of her for her worldly vessel. She felt expansive, like smoke, and was unsurprised when shadows stretched from her skin, reaching outward. The shadows wrapped around Aithan to envelop them both. Macella caught a lingering whiff of mint and asphodel, before it was drowned out by her husband's sweet, smoky scent.

When the shadows met his hellfire, the flames calmed, receding toward his skin. The wind whipping around them ebbed, allowing some of the larger items in its throes to fall to the floor. Slowly—ever so slowly—Aithan bent his head toward her, as if afraid to look into her face.

"Macella?" he croaked.

Then his mouth was on hers and the storm fell silent. The shadows and flames faded, the air stilling completely, the remaining debris dropping to the floor all at once. A moment later, they were bombarded with bodies, their family piling into a mass of hugging arms and teary faces.

Around them, servants were extinguishing any lingering fires and mages tended to the injured. Though all weaponry had been sheathed and the tension in the room had abated, not many of the gathered crowd seemed inclined to leave. They simply watched the Wildfire Court's tearful reunion in respectful silence.

Finally, Macella and her family managed to pry themselves apart. She looked around at the expectant faces of the soldiers, Aegises, staff, and citizens all waiting for her next move. Even Lord Kasper, Lord Anwir, Monarch Meztli, and Queen Annika seemed to be allowing her to take the lead.

Grand Mage Kiama stepped forward, her expression solemn though her eyes sparkled. She held out Macella's crown. "We await your command, your grace."

Macella swallowed hard. She'd thought defeating Khari would be the hard part, but this would be even harder. Winning the battle was only the beginning. The real challenge would be bringing everyone together and convincing them to create something new.

Aithan squeezed her hand. She squeezed back. He'd not stopped touching her since she woke up in his arms. Macella never wanted him to stop.

"Lord Anwir, please invite the rest of our royal guests to join us on the wall-walk. Lord Kasper, if you would, send for the rest of the staff. Your graces, please walk with me," Macella gave the orders in the voice of the warrior queen. She might not feel like a true ruler, but she knew she'd earned the title that day and her people needed her to lead them. "Join us, everyone. I would be honored to have you at my side as we address our people."

The Royal Guard fell into step around them, though the Aegises had already flanked the Wildfire Court. Aithan held tightly to her hand, and Finley stayed closer behind her than strictly necessary. Monarch Meztli walked on her other side, supporting Queen Annika on their arm. While the procession was quiet, everyone still undoubtedly processing the day's tumultuous events, a festive air was growing beneath the aftershock. Everyone knew that they were on the precipice of something big, that they were all a part of it. A great victory had been won, and they were the victors.

Macella ruminated as she walked. Her customary way with words seemed inadequate for the occasion. What tone would be best received? What did the people need to hear?

As they stepped out into the brightness of the afternoon, Macella felt some of the weight lift from her shoulders. The air had lost its frigid bite and was refreshingly cool after the heat of battle and the confinement of Khari's illusion.

She breathed it in gratefully as she and the other monarchs stepped to the parapet.

The roar of noise from below grew louder. Nobles and staff streamed out onto the wall-walk, adding to the uproar. It sounded as if everyone in Pleasure Ridge Park had packed themselves inside the gates. Macella felt them all watching her. Waiting.

"I believe they wish to greet their new queen," Annika said with a wry smile. "Speak to them before they storm the castle."

Macella pushed down the fatigue trying to creep back into her limbs now that the adrenaline of battle had begun to fade. The people deserved the truth, and they should hear it from the person who'd destroyed the world they were used to.

She'd stood against hell's fury and her own end. Now she must stand by her decisions and with those she'd saved. They were her responsibility now.

Aithan reluctantly pried his hand from hers. He cupped her cheek, lifting her face so that she had to meet his eyes. The echo of the torment he'd just endured was there in their amber depths, but it was obscured beneath layers of love, gratitude, and overwhelming pride. His mind swelled with it, filling Macella with calm and conviction.

"Finish the story, my love," he told her gently. "They need their scribe, their champion, their warrior queen. This is where Fate has been leading us. This is what you were meant to do."

Macella swallowed down her fear and exhaustion. Aithan was right. This was the Fate that had called to her, drawing her away from Shively and to that brothel where she'd met her Aegis. It had led them to Aisling and her prophecy, to Smoketown and Duànzào and the truth of their parentage. Fate had brought them to Kōsaten Keep and made Aithan Protector of the Crown. And now Fate had made her queen.

She still did not wish to rule. Yes, it was in her nature to push against injustice, to challenge norms, and to fight for those who'd been wronged. But she didn't want to be the warrior queen, to stand in the public eye, to give her life to a crown. She had a wandering heart that did not want to be tamed.

Aithan leaned closer, lowering his voice so that only she could hear. "You may be their warrior queen, but you are *my* wife, my hell goddess. Go and speak to your people and then I will escort you to our chambers, where I will worship you properly."

Macella shivered, her core pulsing in response to the seductive promise in his voice. She took a deep breath, squaring her shoulders. Then she turned to the crowd.

"Aisling, can you provide amplification?" she asked, glancing at her mage.

The young woman looked pale and shaken, but she smiled. "I don't know how much I have left in me, your grace, but I'm happy to try."

"Allow me, your grace." Grand Mage Kiama stepped forward. She bowed at Macella, her pale gray eyes shining with emotion. In them, Macella thought she saw something familiar.

Hope.

"People of Kōsaten, allow me to present your newest leader, Queen Macella!" Kiama's amplified voice was drowned out by uproarious applause.

Macella waited for the cheers to die down, feeling a strange mixture of pride and nervousness. At first, she wasn't sure how to begin. And yet, when she opened her mouth, the words were there. She was the scribe. It only made sense to begin with a story.

"For thousands of years, Kōsaten was a desolate battleground. In this land of gods and monsters, humanity stood little chance of survival. When the first human mage, Khalid, was born, he devoted his life to making Kōsaten safe for human habitation. After much negotiation with the gods of both light and darkness, Khalid succeeded. The gods of light were weary of war, while the darker gods saw an opportunity for gain. In exchange for their power and favor, the death deities would receive the souls of all those mighty warriors recruited into the line of the Aegis. To keep those deities and their offspring in check, however, the gods of light created the Chosen—three beings of immense power and mystery. And all of these great beings—Aegis and Chosen alike—are bound to the Crown.

"While the Aegises protect us, Kōsaten's leaders also keep us safe. We owe the Crown our gratitude for centuries of peace. After Khalid's initial brokering, each successive monarch has undergone rigorous scrutiny from the gods of light. After all, Kōsaten's ruler is essentially the hand of the gods, implementing their will in our realm. Each new leader must be tried and deemed worthy before being bound to the Chosen, the Aegises, and all of Kōsaten.

"The balance of light and dark and countless lives—it is a heavy burden, carrying such immense responsibility. Only six have borne the weight of the crown since Kōsaten's inception: Khalid of Kōsaten, Orla of Bonnycastle, Maël of Beechmont, Omari of Audubon, Rhiannon of Wyandotte, and Khari of Butchertown. King Khari has endured the longest, ruling for nigh a century, sharing her power with her spouses Monarch Meztli, Queen Annika, and Queen Awa."

Macella paused, weighing her words. If the crowd hadn't already noticed Khari's absence, they were certainly wondering about it now. It was time for the part of the story they didn't already know.

"You're doing beautifully, Macella," Finley whispered behind her. "Just speak true."

Macella exhaled, looking out over the sea of upturned faces. What did they see when they looked at her? How would they react to learning what she truly was?

She lifted her chin. No more hiding. No more lies. She would no longer shrink for anyone. She would live loudly and give others permission to do the same.

(47) "King Khari's reign has come to an end. The king is dead."

Gasps. Murmurs. General outcry. Macella gave them a moment to process, using the time to refine her next words. After a minute or so she nodded, and the Grand Mage snapped her fingers. It sounded like a clap of thunder. The crowd quieted to a whisper.

"King Khari and some of the monarchs that preceded her took advantage of the gods' blessings. At some point, their dreams of peace became only dreams of power. While Kōsaten is no longer a battleground between light and dark, a quieter, more insidious violence has continued to thrive. In places like Shively, where I spent my formative years, good, hardworking people suffer every day, scraping to survive, while those within these walls grow fat off their labor."

When Macella paused this time, it was only the noble guests on the wall-walk who needed a moment to react and process. The commonfolk packed into the bailey already knew the truth of her words.

"Thanks to the greed and selfishness of Kōsaten's leaders, those born into the wrong families or communities have been condemned to lives of drudgery and destitution—like my sister Charlotte, who would've been forced to pair or perish, barely surviving, making babies, and trying to keep those babies alive. If people in these neglected communities happen to be born with the gift of sorcery, they'll be destined for death or madness, denied access to the training they need to be proper mages, as was nearly the fate of my mage Aisling. If people in these abandoned communities are extraordinarily unlucky, they'll be sold into Aegis service, subjected to the brutal conditions of Smoketown. On the slim chance they survive the training, transformations, and trials, they'll spend the rest of their very long lives protecting a society that shuns them, forbidden from having homes and families, committed to being unloved, as was the destiny for my siblings Finley and Jacan, and the other Aegises around me."

Macella looked to her family, buoyed by the confidence and pride on their faces. Finley winked and Zahra blew her a kiss. Even Meztli and Annika gave her nods of encouragement. Macella turned back to the crowd, who seemed to be hanging on her every word.

She'd told them the story of what had been. Now she needed to weave the tale of what could be. She took a deep breath and smiled.

"It doesn't have to be this way. People shouldn't have to work sunup to sundown to provide for themselves and loved ones they're too exhausted to enjoy. Both nobility and commonfolk can live well, while the kingdom prospers. We've proven that with the Ellasburg initiative."

Macella was forced to wait for the assembled masses to quiet down again, since the mention of Ellasburg was greeted with wild cheers and applause from its inhabitants throughout the crowd.

"We've opened a new mage academy in Shively, proving that our poorest communities contain magic just waiting to be nourished." Macella smiled inwardly as she carefully selected her next words. "We evaluated and...restructured the training process in Smoketown, proving that we can protect our kingdom without sacrificing children to cruelty. And we've been able to do these things because my husband, Protector of the Crown Aithan of Auburndale, was allowed to build a home and a family, proving that when everyone is given equitable opportunities, we all thrive."

A mixture of surprise and applause greeted the announcement, with lots of smiles and cheers balancing out the shocked or disapproving faces. Macella had expected the fairly positive response, given the rise in popular opinion Aegises had undergone. Though she'd obviously surprised and worried them, the general public sentiment seemed to still be in her favor.

She was about to put that to the test.

"I have already been able to do so much to serve Kōsaten, and with the help of all of you, I intend to help the Crown do much more. Together, we can build a kingdom in which we can all thrive, a kingdom founded on valuing differences rather than despising them, where we are free to use our unique gifts to enrich our communities. As the child of an Aegis and a human, I am living proof of that possibility."

With that, Macella burst into flames.

The responding roar of noise could probably be heard from Pleasure Ridge Park to Bardstown. It was a wonder everyone stayed put, though there were quite a few frightened faces, both on the wall-walk and below. Macella waited again, letting them take her in.

She knew exactly how she looked: eyes glowing obsidian, skin alight with onyx flames. She was fierce and regal and powerful. She was marked by Hades, chosen by Fate.

She was a poor, orphaned crossbreed, who'd scraped her way by while dreaming of more. She hadn't dreamed of fame nor fortune, but she *had* dreamed of the world she was painting with her words.

Macella hoped the people could see it. More than that, she hoped they could believe it. She knew it could be done, but she could not do it alone. She would not. She refused to be a dictator.

She lifted a hand and the assembly went silent.

"This will not be easy, nor will it be accomplished quickly, but it will be worth it. I hope you will stand with us as we build something new."

Macella let her flames recede. She'd said all there was to say. Now it was up to the people.

Beside her, Aithan placed his fist over his heart in salute. The rest of the Wildfire Court immediately followed suit. The other Aegises were next. Then the citizens and staff who'd come to her aid during the battle emulated the motion.

The clang of armor startled her as the Royal Guard echoed a salute from Captain Drudo. Grand Mage Kiama repeated the motion and, glancing surreptitiously between her and Queen Annika, Lord Anwir and Lord Kasper did too...with significantly less enthusiasm. Soon enough, the nobles on the wall-walk and commonfolk below began to salute as well.

Macella let herself bask in the moment. This was what they'd fought for, after all—this moment of hope and possibility and promise.

Was the hard part over? Not even close.

Was everyone truly on side? Surely not.

But this was a beginning. Macella was far from alone and that was enough.

Chapter Twenty-Seven

Macella

The days that followed were long. Macella spent a great deal of time speaking, and even more time listening, trying to help her people find common ground. She invited nobles, citizens, mages, Aegises, and soldiers alike to the great hall for long sessions where they shared their grievances, hopes, and ideas. It was often tense and sometimes downright dangerous, but they managed to avoid bloodshed and learn a great deal.

It might've been easier, had she been willing to shut herself up with the small council and make decisions as they'd been made for the last century or more, but that was not what she'd fought for. After the listening sessions, Macella assembled a new temporary council, one she hoped would serve as a model for what was to come. Her fellow monarchs (which still felt strange to say), the Grand Vizier, Grand Treasurer, and Grand Mage were all included, but they were no longer the only voices in the room. In fact, they had to have a larger table moved into the small council chamber to accommodate them all.

Aithan was there, not just as Royal Protector, but seated at the table beside Captain Drudo to advise on military matters and offer additional expertise. The Aegises selected Finley to serve as their representative, and Lynn agreed to represent the castle's staff. Ellasburg sent one of their leaders to sit alongside a respected community member from Pleasure Ridge Park proper. Lastly, Macella invited a noble guest from each region of the kingdom.

In the end, they came to an agreed-upon structure that gave Macella real hope. Not only would all of the kingdom's people have representation in governing matters, but the council mandated immediate changes that would counteract Kōsaten's most unjust conditions. It wasn't perfect, but it was a vast improvement for those who had long been disenfranchised.

The first major change focused on the Aegises. No longer would they be required to lead transient, lonely lives. Instead, each of the shields would be given a territory to patrol, where they'd have a home and the freedom to build families and put down roots as they wished. Furthermore, recruit training duties would rotate so that none were confined to Duànzào for long, unless they chose to serve for longer periods of their own volition.

Additionally, recruitment was paused until decisions could be made regarding fair and equitable methods for maintaining the ranks. Macella wasn't sure what would happen once Aegises began marrying and reproducing as freely as everyone else, but she knew they deserved their autonomy. Based on Macella's returned memories and further work with the Grand Mage, it quickly became clear that the Aegis ranks had been capped at thirteen, not out of necessity, but because someone along the way had calculated that as the number able to protect against hellspawn without being a danger to their oppressors.

In reality, sterilization had been incorporated into the transformation process through a series of elixirs so complex that even the mages themselves hadn't known their ministrations would ultimately render their subjects unable to conceive. Without their interventions, there would be many more Aegisborn and, likely, a much larger Aegis army. Undoubtedly, there were many, many dark gods who'd see value in bestowing their blessings if offered a larger selection of naturally gifted soldiers and more opportunities to try them.

Grand Mage Kiama and her team were already working on a solution to reverse the sterilization process for those who wished, and the results so far were promising. Of course, the first Aegisborn child to enter this new world would be Queen Annika's baby. A mage would still be necessary to facilitate such births, not because of any inherent incompatibility between humans and Aegises but because, as Macella's memories proved, Aegisborn children weren't able to control their hellfire until they were taught or after they'd been separated from Otherworldly influences. Grand Mage Kiama would be able to counteract the effects during the birthing process, ensuring Annika's survival. And she would share the knowledge with mages around the kingdom so that, if and when other Aegises sired children with humans, they could do so without fear.

Improving the lives of the rest of Kōsaten's citizens would take more time and effort and would require a governing body unlike any the kingdom had ever attempted. The temporary council established parameters for a new permanent council. It would include three representatives from each region, to be decided upon by regional leaders, with representatives from different cities, including the poorest and wealthiest of the region, and who would be permitted to serve for only a fixed term. After the council had a few years to find its footing, one member from each region would be replaced annually over staggered cycles. Gone were the days of folks taking up residence at court, losing touch with their constituents, and serving only their own interests.

The Protector of the Crown would hold a seat on the council, serving as a representative for Aegiskind, while continuing to offer military expertise. The captain of the Royal Guard would also maintain a permanent seat. Additionally, there would also be a spot for two members of staff—one from interior castle staff and one from among the fieldworkers of Ellasburg. The Grand Mage, Grand Vizier, and Grand Treasurer would still be appointed by the Crown, but their power on the council would be equal to that of the rest of its members.

The Crown itself would undergo the most significant change. It would now consist of one human, one Aegis, and one mage. Together, the three would rule under the advisement of the new council and their succession would be decided by fit rather than treachery. Each race would decide for themselves how they wished to select their ruling representative—a process Macella decided not to oversee, and which would probably take decades to settle on.

Macella didn't know exactly what transpired between the Grand Mage and the Chosen when she presented them with the council's wishes, but in the end, the gods of light gave the new structure their blessing, agreeing to enhance any human monarchs with gifts equal to those of their Aegis and mage counterparts. No one who sat the throne would be over the others, and none would be allowed to amass power and upset the balance as Khari had ever again.

Surprisingly, neither Monarch Meztli nor Queen Annika wished to remain on the throne. Though Annika told the council she'd never had a mind for politics and didn't want to be a part of their strange new government, Macella suspected the truth was that Annika had never wanted to be queen. She'd been raised to be a pawn and had married only to acquire wealth and status for her family. Now, she just wanted a place at court with her accustomed luxuries and the freedom to raise her child as she saw fit.

Meztli, on the other hand, expressed the utmost confidence in the new Crown. However, they were understandably weary with life in the capital and wanted to live the rest of their days more peacefully. They promised to help with the transition but would then return home to Park Duvalle.

Fortunately, the temporary council had no trouble choosing new monarchs to fill the seats for the present. Everyone agreed that those selected had proven themselves during the battle for the throne. And, after some reluctance and demurring, all three accepted the responsibility.

Thus, on a bright afternoon during the second month of the new year, Macella and Aithan walked arm-in-arm to the great hall for the coronation ceremony for Kōsaten's brand-new monarchs. Macella wore her crown at the council's insistence, even though she would be renouncing the throne shortly. It was a surprisingly bittersweet thought. She didn't want to be shackled to the keep, but she loved all the good she was able to do with the might of the Crown behind her.

"You'll still be able to do plenty of good. You are beloved by the Crown and her people. Your influence won't diminish one jot, no matter your title," Aithan said before leaning closer and lowering his voice. "And I'll kneel at your feet whenever you wish. We're keeping the crown for you to wear for me whenever you're feeling particularly regal."

Macella laughed and let him guide her into the great hall. The tables were laid for a grand feast and decorated in lavender, jade, and violet, in keeping with the preferred colors of the new monarchs, along with accents of both silver and gold. It felt festive and hopeful, the mood buoyed by the cheerfulness of the guests.

Though the room was filled mostly with nobles who had lingered after the cold season to participate in the governing conversations, a fair number of additional guests had arrived especially for the coronation. Macella saw Tomas and Babette sitting with Laird Parul, Lady Seondeok, and other nobles from the north. Zahra's father, Viceroy Shelby, was talking animatedly to Annika's father, the Lord of Edgewood, and Lord Kasper, who both looked less than enthusiastic about the day's event. Annika had mostly avoided her father since he'd arrived, but Lord Kasper seemed to be constantly murmuring in his ear. Macella wondered if anything would come of their scheming but wasn't too worried about it. She and her allies had faced much worse.

Thankfully, sour faces like theirs were few and far between. Macella and Aithan greeted scores of well-wishers as they made their way to the raised table for the guests of honor. When they stopped at the Aegis table, Váli crept out from beneath it for pets, and Macella laughed with delight at the sight of Nyx curled up on the wolf's back as if he was her portable bed. It seemed the cat had finally accepted their inevitable friendship, though it was clear which of them was the boss of the relationship.

The tables nearest the stage held royal entourages and temporary council members, and Macella was pleased to see the staff and commonfolk among them looking comfortable enough to eat, drink, and make merry. She was equally pleased to see Jacan and Lotta being openly affectionate, since she'd worried her parents' presence might cause her sister to revert to her meek ways. Apparently, she needn't have worried. Perhaps deposing a powerful king had made Babette's disapproval much less frightening.

The monarchy was to be seated on one side of the long table on stage so that they could see and be seen throughout the meal. Meztli and Annika were already settled at one end, so Macella and Aithan took their places at the other, leaving the seats in the center open for the Crown. They had only enough time for a servant to fill their goblets, before a herald announced the arrival of the new leaders of Kōsaten.

(48) "Esteemed guests and beloved friends, allow me to present your new rulers: Queen Kiama, Queen Zahra, and Monarch Finley!"

The room erupted in applause as Captain Drudo escorted Kiama into the great hall, followed by a swaggering Finley with Zahra on their arm. The new monarchs made an absurdly beautiful picture, decked out in their finery and with gleaming crowns atop their heads. When the Crown reached the stage, the guests rose as one to bow. Macella didn't try to hide the tears in her eyes as she looked around at the gathering.

They'd done this. With her Wildfire Court and many, many others, they had laid the foundation for something new and wonderful. She couldn't have been happier.

Or so she thought, until after each of the monarchs had addressed the crowd. That's when Finley turned and gestured for her to join them. She gave Aithan a questioning look as she rose, but he just grinned, indicating that once again, her husband and her sibling had been scheming behind her back. She suppressed an eye roll as she joined the Crown at the front of the stage.

"As you all know, Queen Macella has been instrumental in bringing us to where we are today, on the precipice of a new era for Kōsaten and all her people." Finley paused to allow for the raucous cheers that followed their words.

Macella smiled widely, still aglow with happiness despite having no idea what her sibling was up to.

Finley took her hand before continuing. "Our warrior queen also has a wandering heart and has expressed a desire to vacate the throne to serve the kingdom in a different capacity. We believe she deserves her freedom, but we also just aren't willing to let her go."

More cheers and hoots of agreement greeted Finley's proclamation. Zahra moved to Macella's other side to take her free hand.

"We, the Crown, have agreed that Queen Macella will retain her throne and quarters at court, serving with us during the cold season. During the rest of the year, she will be our wandering queen and will explore her kingdom as she sees fit under the protection of our finest shield, Aithan of Auburndale—who absolutely knew about this plan and is the person she should fuss at if she doesn't like it." Zahra grinned impishly, earning peals of laughter from the guests. "Say you'll accept, dearest."

Macella looked around at the joyous faces and knew she couldn't say no to a request that so perfectly married her need for freedom and her desire to create lasting change. When she nodded her acquiescence, the applause and cheers were almost deafening. She hugged each member of the Crown before retaking her seat beside a smug-looking Aithan.

"You knew the whole time, you sneak," she whispered in mock outrage. "If you think I'm wearing the crown for you tonight, you're in for a rude awakening."

Aithan chuckled. "Fine. I'll wear it. Whatever you wish, my queen."

The celebration went on for hours. Macella spoke to nearly everyone in the room, and they were overwhelmingly pleased with the Crown's decision to keep her involved. It turned out, the temporary council had proposed the compromise, and the three monarchs had delightedly endorsed the decision.

It seemed that all of the people Macella cared about would be better off under this new leadership. Valen was to be the new Protector of the Crown, so Váli and Nyx would be able to continue their friendship, while Aisling continued her mage training. Though Jacan would return to patrol as a shield, he was assigned to the region nearest the capital, and more importantly near Charlotte, who was glad to stay on as Royal Scribe, and continue her work with Lynn, as well as her teaching duties in Ellasburg.

It was comforting to know they would come together every cold season, despite the drastic changes to their lives. And during the fifteen months of the year that the Wildfire Court was apart, Macella knew they'd keep up constant correspondence. She could already imagine the stories Zahra and Finley would share. Already, Zahra was musing about the lovers she might take.

"Who should I get to warm my bed while you're wandering?" she demanded over dinner, making Macella snort laughter in a very unqueenly way. "I think I might see if I can climb that muscly mountain over there."

Macella followed Zahra's gaze to where the soon-to-be Protector of the Crown stood below the stage, chatting with Jacan, Lotta, and Aisling. She covered her mouth to hide her laughter when the big Aegis's head snapped toward them.

"Climb aboard, lass. I'll gladly give ya a ride on whatever muscle you fancy," he called in his booming voice, before remembering his manners and bowing. "Your grace."

Macella couldn't smother her laughter this time, especially when Zahra's olive skin darkened in a blush. The new queen glared at Macella, but her mismatched eyes still twinkled playfully. She gave Valen another sidelong glance.

"Damn your kind and your exceptional hearing," she grumbled. "But now I'm very intrigued."

Though the occasion was joyous, change always came with growing pains, and Macella knew there would be plenty for all of them. The life she'd built with the Wildfire Court had been comfortable, aside from the war planning, and it would be odd not seeing them every day. She was also a little sad about Meztli, but they assured her over dinner that it was for the best.

"I have spent more than enough time in this place, and my ancestral land is calling me home," they said, pressing her hand affectionately. "You must come and see me whenever your wanderings bring you near Park Duvalle. Thank you for freeing me, my friend."

***

(49) When they finally fell into bed that night, Macella was almost too happy to even be able to sleep. Instead, she lay awake thinking over all that had passed.

After the pain and anxiety they'd endured to reach this moment, she wanted to bask in it, to hold on tight and dwell in the hopefulness of it all.

Though there was still much to do and the road ahead of them was uncertain, Macella felt more at peace than she ever had. She'd set out to find a better life for herself but had instead shaped a better world. She had a family, a purpose, and a heart full of hope.

When the world failed her, Macella had written a new one. She'd refused to accept a narrative that erased her and had boldly demanded to be seen. She'd done it for others like her and for those not like her and for herself. And this was only the beginning.

It was the start of a new tale—the *Epic of the Aegis and the Wanderer.* Macella curled against her husband's side, thinking of their first night together, when he'd scoffed at her request to accompany him on his journey.

"Do you remember what you said when I asked you if I could travel with you?" she murmured.

Aithan winced at the memory. "I was an ass about it. I believe I said, 'What do you expect? You believe we will have glamorous adventures, and you will join me at court for fancy parties?' And then you taught me the first of several lessons about underestimating you."

Macella giggled. "You were a pretty quick study. I didn't have to dress you down too many times before you shaped up. Tell me what I said back."

Aithan adopted a haughty tone, lifting his chin in a mirror of her defiant habit. "I expect that it will be nice to have companionship on my wanderings, especially when that companion is a skilled protector. I expect that I will leave this place soon, like I have left so many before it. I expect I will keep going until Fate tells me to stop, because it is Fate that set me on this path and only Fate that can stop me. I expect that Fate led me to my first and last client tonight and that we were destined to meet, Aithan of Auburndale."

Macella laughed before scowling and lowering her voice to a raspy baritone. "I expect that I am going to come to regret this decision."

"I said that?" Aithan asked incredulously, though Macella knew he remembered the conversation exactly. "What a young, dumb fool I was."

Macella sighed contentedly. "You truly never regretted it? Not even after all the chaos I've caused?"

Aithan kissed the top of her head before burying his face in her curls and inhaling deeply. "Not once, not for a single moment. You have been my greatest adventure, hell goddess. I cannot wait to see what tales you shall write for us next."

He kissed her then, like it was the first time and the millionth time, and Macella felt expansive, too immense for her body to contain. The moment seemed to unfurl like a wisp of smoke, stretching into timelessness. When he pulled back, she stared into his beautiful, warm amber eyes and saw in them a future so glorious and full of promise that she knew she could never capture it in words.

"I will tell you again what I told the madame when we took our leave of that fortuitous brothel," Macella said, brushing her lips against his and feeling him stiffen against her, his arms tightening around her waist. "Fate led me here and to Aithan of Auburndale. I am not afraid of where it—or he—will lead me next."

As her husband made love to her like it was the first time and the millionth time, Macella said a prayer of thanks for the forces that had brought them together and the determination that had brought them so far since that fateful meeting. She knew that, no matter what came next for them or for Kōsaten, they would face it without fear and with joy in their hearts.

A shield. A scribe. A sword. A pen. Against hell's fury. Against our end.

There was nothing they could not stand against. Together.

> *Together, we can build a kingdom in which we can all thrive, a kingdom founded on valuing differences rather than despising them, where we are free to use our unique gifts to enrich our communities. Together, we will usher in a new age in Kōsaten's illustrious history—one in which all of its citizens know what it is to be seen and safe. Together, we will build something beautiful.*
> -Royal Bulletin, Warm Season, Year of the Phoenix

GLOSSARY OF PROPER NOUNS

Aegis (ē-jis): (from Merriam-Webster): In ancient Greek mythology, an aegis was something that offered physical protection, and it has been depicted in various ways, including as a magical protective cloak made from the skin of the goat that suckled Zeus as an infant and as a shield fashioned byHephaestusthat bore the severed head of theGorgonMedusa. The word first entered English in the 15th century as a noun referring to the shield or protective garment associated with Zeus or Athena. It later took on a more general sense of "protection" and, by the late 19th century, it had acquired the extended senses of "auspices" and "sponsorship."

Pronunciations include dictionary style followed by the author's attempt at phonetic spelling.

    Aisling [ash-liŋ; ash-ling]: (Irish) a dream or vision

    Aithan [ā-than; a-than]: (Greek) firm, strong

    Annika [an-ik-ə; an-ick-uh]: (Swedish) grace

Anwansi [än-vän-sē; on-von-see]: (Igbo) uncanny, magic

Anwir [an-wɪr; an-weer]: (Welsh) liar

Awa [ä-wə; ah-wuh]: (Arabic) beautiful angel, night

Bellona [bə-lō-nə; bell-o-nuh]: (Roman) to fight

Cassian [kas-sē-in; kas-see-in]: (Latin) hollow

Citali [sē-tä-lē; see-tall-ee]: (Aztec/Nahuatl) star

Cressida [kres-ə-də; kres-uh-duh]: (Greek) gold

Diya [dē-ə; dee-uh]: (Sanskrit, Arabic) light, glow

Duànzào [dü-in-zaʊ; doo-in-zow]: (Chinese) the forge

Drudo [drü-dō; droo-doh]: (Italian) strong, defender, loyal, faithful

Epanofório [ā-pän-ō-fòr-ē-ō; a-pon-o-for-ee-o]: (Greek) cloak

Finley [fin-lē; fin-lee]: (Irish, Celtic, Gaelic) a hero or battle warrior with fair skin

Gabriela [ga-brē-el-ə; gab-ree-el-uh]: (Hebrew) God is my strength

Griselda [grɪ-zel-də; griz-el-duh]: (German) gray battle

Hülya [hü-lē-ä; hoo-lee-ah]: (Turkish) a daydream that brings happiness

Igor [ē-gòr; ee-gore]: (Russian) warrior

Jacan [jak-in; jack-in]: (Hebrew) trouble

Kai [kī; kye]: (Hawaiian, Japanese) of the sea; keeper of the keys

Kamau [kə-maʊ; kuh-mow]: (Kenyan) quiet warrior

Kasper [kas-pər; kas-per]: (Polish) treasurer

Kenji [kin-jē; kin-jee]: (Japanese) vigorous, intelligent second son

Khalid [kä-lēd; kah-leed]: (Arabic) immortal, eternal

Khari [kä-rē; kar-ee]: (West African) kingly

Kiama [kē-ä-mə; kee-ah-muh]: (Kenyan) magic

Kōsaten [kō-sə-ten; ko-suh-ten]: (Japanese) intersection

Kiho [kē-hō; kee-ho]: (African, Japanese) fog; hope or beg or sail

Lenora [lə-nòr-ə; luh-nor-uh]: (English, Greek) light; compassion

Loi [lòi; loy]: (Chinese) thunder

Macella [mä-sel-ə; mah-sel-uh]: (French) she who is warlike

Maia [mī-ə; my-uh]: (Greek) mother; one who has unconditional love like a mother

Matthias [mə-tī-əs; muh-tie-us] (Hebrew) gift of God

Meztli [māz-lē; maze-lee] (Aztec/Nahuatl) moon

Orla [ȯr-lə; or-luh]: (Irish) golden princess

Omari [ō-mär-ē; o-mar-ee]: (Swahili, Egyptian) God the highest; highborn

Pooja [pū-jə; poo-juh]: (Hindi, Sanskrit) prayer or worship

Quirino [kwē-rē-nō; kwee-ree-no]: (Italian, Latin) spear

Rhiannon [rē-an-in; ree-an-in]: (Welsh) divine queen

Shamira [shə-mi-rə; shuh-mere-uh]: (Hebrew) guardian, protector

Theomund [tē-ō-mənd; tee-oh-muhn]: (Anglo-Saxon) wealthy defender

Tuwile [tū-wē-lā; too-wee-lay]: (Kenyan) death is invincible

Valen [vä-lən; vah-luhn]: (Latin) healthy, strong

Váli [vä-lē; vah-lee]: mighty warrior, brave

Vespera [ves-per-ə; ves-pair-uh]: (Latin) evening star

Zahra [zä-rə; zah-ruh]: (Arabic) bright, brilliant, radiant

 # KŌSATEN

CLOCK

TIME	HOUR OF	TIME	HOUR OF
2400	NÓTT (NORSE GODDESS OF NIGHT)	1200	HELIOS (GREEK GOD OF THE SUN)
0100	KHONSHU (EGYPTIAN GOD OF THE MOON)	1300	TAWA (HOPI GOD OF THE SUN)
0200	EREBUS (GREEK GOD OF DARKNESS)	1400	ARINNA (HITTITE SUN GODDESS)
0300	NYX (GREEK GODDESS OF NIGHT)	1500	XIHE (CHINESE SOLAR GODDESS)
0400	MÊN (PHRYGIAN LUNAR GOD)	1600	NUHA (ARABIC SUN GODDESS)
0500	ZORYA (SLAVIC GODDESS OF DAWN)	1700	LIZA (WEST AFRICAN SUN GOD)
0600	RA (EGYPTIAN SUN GOD)	1800	MAWU (DAHOMEY GODDESS OF SUN AND MOON)
0700	SOL (ROMAN SUN GOD)	1900	SHALIM (CANAANITE GOD OF DUSK)
0800	SURYA (HINDU SUN GOD)	2000	FATI (POLYNESIAN MOON GOD)
0900	INTI (INCAN SUN GOD)	2100	TÒLZE (MARI MOON GOD)
1000	LUGH (CELTIC GOD OF SUN AND LIGHT)	2200	SOMA (HINDU MOON GOD)
1100	MITHRA (IRANIAN GOD OF SUN AND LIGHT)	2300	IX CHEL (MAYAN MOON GODDESS)

AEGIS GUILDS

Very little is known of the training the Aegises endure. Once they cross the mountains of Smoketown into Duànzào, they are lost to us until they emerge anew. They are no longer members of the families they were born into, but instead, belong to one of the otherworldly Shield Guilds. You can determine an Aegis's guild by the hue of their hair. While all Aegises have hair of silver, the ends of their tresses vary, those colors denoting which hellish deity they faced during the trials. If they survive their encounter, they are thus marked and given magical gifts by these dark gods. While the nature of these gifts is unknown to average citizens, we do know which colors align with which dark deity: crimson for Lucifer, onyx for Hades, emerald for Apophis, cerulean for Kali, gold for Mictlantecuhtli, violet for Meng Po. Presumably, there are many other death deities our Aegises may encounter, but with such a low survival rate, we can never know their true number.

~ From The Epic of the Aegis and the Wanderer by S.S. (The Shield's Scribe)

APOPHIS (EGYPTIAN)
COLOR: EMERALD

Known Gifts:
- resistance to extreme temperatures
- shapeshifting

Apophis Aegises:
- Finley of Fairdale
- Kai of Clarksdale
- Jacan of Prestonia
- Kiho of Russell

HADES (GREEK)
COLOR: ONYX

Known Gifts:
- communion with the dead
- invisibility

Hades Aegises:
- Macella of Shively
- Matthias of the Highlands

KALI (HINDU)
COLOR: CERULEAN

Known Gifts:
- superior strength
- electrokinesis

Kali Aegises:
- Bellona of Glenview
- Diya of Park Hill
- Shamira of Beechmont

LUCIFER (JUDEO-CHRISTIAN)
COLOR: CRIMSON

Known Gifts:
- telepathy
- menticide (mind control)

Lucifer Aegises:
- Aithan of Auburndale
- Gabriela of Edgewood

MENG PO (CHINESE)
COLOR: VIOLET

Known Gifts:
- memory manipulation
- poison resistance and dispersion

Meng Po Aegises:
- Kenji of Butchertown
- Loi of Hillview
- Vespera of Valley Station

MICTLĀNTĒCUTLI (AZTEC)
COLOR: GOLD

Known Gifts:
- regenerative abilities
- bio energy absorption

Mictlāntēcutli Aegises:
- Cassian of Crescent Hill
- Cressida of Crescent Hill
- Valen of Valley Station

ABOUT THE AUTHOR

A.J. grew up voraciously reading her grandmother's Harlequin romance novels alongside Madeline L'Engle and R.L. Stine. She has remained an avid reader, whose book choices are as eclectic as her personality. As an anxious, Black, chaotic bisexual, A.J. Shirley writes spicy romance and romantasy that is unapologetically inclusive. A.J.'s books include romantasy series The Aegis Saga and contemporary omegaverse romance series Knotty Omegas.

Learn more and sign up for A.J.'s newsletter at https://ajshirleyauthor.com and follow A.J. on social media for updates.

instagram.com/ajshirleyauthor/

facebook.com/ajshirleyauthor/

ACKNOWLEDGEMENTS

I am so grateful to the friends, family, readers, and other authors who have helped me out, cheered me on, and encouraged me on this journey. I can't even begin to name you all (I'd miss someone and be mortified forever), but I love and appreciate you so much. To my amazing editor, Shannon Cave, thank you for making the Aegis Saga the best it could be.

And to my number one alpha reader and damn near coauthor, thank you (as always) for being the Jay to my Missy. I love you.